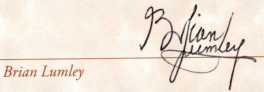

Brian Lumley

Bob Eggleton

NO SHARKS IN THE MED

AND OTHER STORIES

The Best Macabre Stories of Brian Lumley

NO SHARKS IN THE MED

AND OTHER STORIES

BRIAN LUMLEY

Subterranean Press 2012

First Edition

ISBN
978-1-59606-434-8

Subterranean Press
PO Box 190106
Burton, MI 48519

www.subterraneanpress.com

ACKNOWLEDGEMENTS

"Introduction" © Brian Lumley March 2011, and new to this collection. "Fruiting Bodies", *Weird Tales* No. 291, Summer 1988, Terminus Publishing Co. "The Sun, the Sea, and the Silent Scream", *The Magazine of Fantasy & Science Fiction*, Feb 1988, Mercury Press. "The Picnickers", *Final Shadows*, Ed. Charles L. Grant, 1991, Doubleday. "The Viaduct", *Superhorror*, Ed. Ramsey Campbell, 1976, W. H. Allen. "The Luststone", *Weird Tales*, Fall 1991, Terminus Publishing Co. "The Whisperer", *Frights*, Ed. Kirby McCauley, 1976, St. Martin's Press. "No Sharks in the Med", *Weird Tales* No. 295, Winter 1989/90, Terminus Publishing Co. "The Pit-Yakker", *Weird Tales* No. 294, Fall 1989, Terminus Publishing Co. "The Place of Waiting", *The Ghost Quartet*, Ed. Marvin Kaye, 2008, TOR Books. "The Man who Killed Kew Gardens", *Dark Homage*, 2004. "My Thing Friday", *Dark Delicacies*, Eds. Howison and Gelb, 2005, Carroll and Graf. "The Disapproval of Jeremy Cleave", *Weird Tales* No. 295, Winter 1989/90, Terminus Publishing Co.

— "For Barbara Ann" —

CONTENTS

INTRODUCTION

In 2007 Subterranean Press honoured me by publishing *The Taint and Other Stories* in a deluxe hardcover edition signed by both Bob Eggleton—who painted the fabulous wraparound jacket and also did the interior illustrations—and myself. That volume was followed a year later by a companion volume, *Haggopian and Other Stories*, in a format that duplicated the superb production values of *The Taint*. Both books contained tales considered (if only by myself, and I'm not the best judge of my own work) the best of my Cthulhu Mythos tales, chosen from my more than forty years of writing. The first book contained the novellas, and the second a great many shorter stories. This current volume has no Mythos stories; it simply does what it says on the jacket, collecting the best of my macabre tales, five of which saw their first outings in the "Unique Magazine," *Weird Tales*, while others found homes in many fine award-winning books and magazines.

Now I have to prevail upon Bill Schafer to present this new collection in a format uniform with the others—including the marvellous artwork of Mr. Eggleton, together with his and my own signatures—so that all three volumes will form a trilogy of my best work where they sit side by side on whichever bookshelves they may get to occupy.

I shall mention in passing just two of these stories:

"My Thing Friday" is quite obviously Science Fiction with a touch of Nasty; I include it here if only to illustrate a bit of versatility. And the final story, "The Disapproval of Jeremy Cleave," is more than a tad sick/humorous, which mainly demonstrates the fact that I don't take any genre too seriously. (If we can't have a laugh now and then—even a slightly shuddery sort of laugh—then what's the point?)

I'll say no more about this collection of stories, except to tell you that the greatest favour you could do me would be to enjoy them…

Brian Lumley
Devon, England, March 2011

FRUITING BODIES

My great-grandparents, and my grandparents after them, had been Easingham people; in all likelihood my parents would have been, too, but the old village had been falling into the sea for three hundred years and hadn't much looked like stopping, and so I was born in Durham City instead. My grandparents, both sets, had been among the last of the village people to move out, buying new homes out of a government-funded disaster grant. Since then, as a kid, I had been back to Easingham only once.

My father had taken me there one spring when the tides were high. I remember how there was still some black, crusty snow lying in odd corners of the fields, colored by soot and smoke, as all things were in those days in the Northeast. We'd gone to Easingham because the unusually high tides had been at it again, chewing away at the shale cliffs, reducing shoreline and derelict village both as the North Sea's breakers crashed again and again on the shuddering land.

And of course we had hoped (as had the two hundred or so other sightseers gathered there that day) to see a house or two go down in smoking ruin, into the sea and the foaming spray. We witnessed no such spectacle; after an hour, cold and wet from the salt moisture in the air, we piled back into the family car and returned to Durham. Easingham's main street, or what had once been the main street, was teetering on the brink as we left. But by nightfall that street was no more. We'd missed it: a further twenty feet of coastline, a bite one street deep and a few yards more than one street long, had been undermined, toppled, and gobbled up by the sea.

That had been that. Bit by bit, in the quarter century between then and now, the rest of Easingham had also succumbed. Now only a house or two remained—no more than a handful in all—and all falling into decay, while the closest lived-in buildings were those of a farm all of a mile inland from the cliffs. Oh, and of course there was one other inhabitant: old Garth Bentham, who'd been demolishing the old houses by hand and selling bricks and timbers from the village for years. But I'll get to him shortly.

So there I was last summer, back in the Northeast again, and when my business was done of course I dropped in and stayed overnight with the Old Folks at their Durham cottage. Once a year at least I made a point of seeing them, but last year in particular I noticed how time was creeping up on them. The "Old Folks"; well, now I saw that they really were old, and I determined that I must start to see a lot more of them.

Later, starting in on my long drive back down to London, I remembered that time when the Old Man had taken me to Easingham to see the houses tottering on the cliffs. And probably because the place was on my mind, I inadvertently turned off my route and in a little while found myself heading for the coast. I could have turned round right there and then—indeed, I intended to do so—but I'd got to wondering about Easingham and how little would be left of it now, and before I knew it...

Once I'd made up my mind, Middlesborough was soon behind me, then Guisborough, and in no time at all I was on the old road to the village. There had only ever been one way in and out, and this was it: a narrow road, its surface starting to crack now, with tall hedgerows broken here and there, letting you look through to where fields rolled down to the cliffs. A beautiful day, with sea gulls wheeling overhead, a salt tang coming in through the wound-down windows, and a blue sky coming down to merge with...with the blue-grey of the North Sea itself! For cresting a rise, suddenly I was there.

An old, leaning wooden signpost said EASINGH—, for the tail had been broken off or rotted away, and "the village" lay at the end of the road. But right there, blocking the way, a metal barrier was set in massive concrete posts and carried a sign bearing the following warning:

DANGER!
SEVERE CLIFF SUBSIDENCE.
NO VEHICLES BEYOND THIS POINT...

I turned off the car's motor, got out, leaned on the barrier. Before me the road went on—and disappeared only thirty yards ahead. And there stretched the new rim of the cliffs. Of the village, Easingham itself—forget it! On this side of the cliffs, reaching back on both sides of the road behind overgrown gardens, weedy paths, and driveways, here stood the empty shells of what had once been residences of the "posh" folks of Easingham. Now, even on a day as lovely as this one, they were morose in their desolation.

The windows of these derelicts, where there were windows, seemed to gaze gauntly down on approaching doom, like old men in twin rows of death-beds. Brambles and ivy were rank; the whole place seemed despairing as the cries of the gulls rising on the warm air; Easingham was a place no more.

Not that there had ever been a lot of it. Three streets lengthwise with a few shops; two more, shorter streets cutting through the three at right angles and going down to the cliffs and the vertiginous wooden steps that used to climb down to the beach, the bay, the old harbor, and fish market; and standing over the bay, a Methodist church on a jutting promontory, which in the old times had also served as a lighthouse. But now—

No streets, no promontory or church, no harbor, fish market, rickety steps. No Easingham.

"Gone, all of it," said a wheezy, tired old voice from directly behind me, causing me to start. "Gone forever, to the devil and the deep blue sea!"

I turned, formed words, said something barely coherent to the leathery old scarecrow of a man I found standing there.

"Eh? Eh?" he said. "Did I startle you? I have to say you startled me! First car I've seen in a three-month! After bricks, are you? Cheap bricks? Timber?"

"No, no," I told him, finding my voice. "I'm—well, sight-seeing, I sup-pose." I shrugged. "I just came to see how the old village was getting on. I didn't live here, but a long line of my people did. I just thought I'd like to see how much was left—while it *was* left! Except it seems I'm too late."

"Oh, aye, too late." He nodded. "Three or four years too late. That was when the last of the old fishing houses went down; four years ago. Sea took 'em. Takes six or seven feet of cliff every year. Aye, and if I lived long enough it would take me, too. But it won't 'cos I'm getting on a bit." And he grinned and nodded, as if to say: So that's that! "Well, well, sight-seeing! Not much to see, though, not now. Do you fancy a coffee?"

Before I could answer he put his fingers to his mouth and blew a pierc-ing whistle, then paused and waited, shook his head in puzzlement. "Ben," he explained. "My old dog. He's not been himself lately and I don't like him to stray too far. He was out all night, was Ben. Still, it's summer, and there may have been a bitch about..."

While he had talked I'd looked him over and decided that I liked him. He reminded me of my own grandfather, what little I could remember of him. Grandad had been a miner in one of the colliery villages farther north, retiring here to doze and dry up and die—only to find himself denied the choice. The sea's incursion had put paid to that when it finally made the place untenable. I fancied this old lad had been a miner, too. Certainly he bore the scars, the stigmata, of the miner: the dark, leathery skin with black specks bedded in; the bad, bowed legs; the shortness of breath, making for short sentences. A generally gritty appearance overall, though I'd no doubt he was clean as fresh scrubbed.

"Coffee would be fine," I told him, holding out my hand. "Greg's my name—Greg Lane."

He took my hand, shook it warmly, and nodded. "Garth Bentham," he said. And then he set off stiffly back up the crumbling road some two or three houses, turning right into an overgrown garden through a fancy wooden gate recently painted white. "I'd intended doing the whole place up," he said, as I followed close behind. "Did the gate, part of the fence, ran out of paint!"

Before letting us into the dim interior of the house, he paused and whistled again for Ben, then worriedly shook his head in something of concern. "After rats in the old timber yard again, I suppose. But God knows I wish he'd stay out of there!"

Then we were inside the tiny cloakroom, where the sun filtered through fly-specked windows and probed golden searchlights on a few fairly dilapidated furnishings and the brassy face of an old grandfather clock that clucked like a mechanical hen. Dust motes drifted like tiny planets in a cosmos of faery, eddying round my host where he guided me through a door and into his living room. Where the dust had settled on the occasional ledge, I noticed that it was tinged red, like rust.

"I cleaned the windows in here," Garth informed, "so's to see the sea. I like to know what it's up to!"

"Making sure it won't creep up on you." I nodded.

His eyes twinkled. "Nah, just joking," he said, tapping on the side of his blue-veined nose. "No, it'll be ten or even twenty years before all this goes, but I don't have that long. Five if I'm lucky. I'm sixty-eight, after all!"

Sixty-eight! Was that really to be as old as all that? But he was probably right: a lot of old-timers from the mines didn't even last *that* long, not entirely mobile and coherent, anyway. "Retiring at sixty-five doesn't leave a lot, does it?" I said. "Of time, I mean."

He went into his kitchen, called back: "Me, I've been here a ten-year. Didn't retire, quit! Stuff your pension, I told 'em. I'd rather have my lungs, what's left of 'em. So I came here, got this place for a song, take care of myself and my old dog, and no one to tip my hat to and no one to bother me. I get a letter once a fortnight from my sister in Dunbar, and one of these days the postman will find me stretched out in here and he'll think: 'Well, I needn't come out here anymore.'"

He wasn't bemoaning his fate, but I felt sorry for him anyway. I settled myself on a dusty settee, looked out of the window down across his garden of brambles to the sea's horizon. A great curved millpond—for the time being. "Didn't you have any savings?" I could have bitten my tongue off the moment I'd said it, for that was to imply he hadn't done very well for himself.

Cups rattled in the kitchen. "Savings? Lad, when I was a young 'un I had three things: my lamp, my helmet, and a pack of cards. If it wasn't pitch-'n-toss with weighted pennies on the beach banks, it was three-card brag in the back room of the pub. Oh, I was a game gambler, right enough, but a bad one. In my blood, like my Old Man before me. My mother never did see a penny; nor did my wife, I'm ashamed to say, before we moved out here—God bless her! Savings? That's a laugh. But out here there's no bookie's runner, and you'd be damned hard put to find a card school in Easingham these days! What the hell," he shrugged as he stuck his head back into the room, "it was a life..."

We sipped our coffee. After a while I said, "Have you been on your own very long? I mean...your wife?"

"Lily-Anne?" He glanced at me, blinked, and suddenly there was a peculiar expression on his face. "On my own, you say..." He straightened his shoulders, took a deep breath. "Well, I *am* on my own in a way, and in a way I'm not. I have Ben—or would have if he'd get done with what he's doing and come home—and Lily-Anne's not all that far away. In fact, sometimes I suspect she's sort of watching over me, keeping me company, so to speak. You know, when I'm feeling especially lonely."

"Oh?"

"Well." He shrugged again. "I mean she *is* here, now isn't she." It was a statement, not a question.

"Here?" I was starting to have my doubts about Garth Bentham.

"I had her buried here." He nodded, which explained what he'd said and produced a certain sensation of relief in me. "There was a Methodist church here once over, with its own burying ground. The church went a donkey's years ago, of course, but the old graveyard was still here when Lily-Anne died."

"Was?" Our conversation was getting one-sided.

"Well, it still is—but right on the edge, so to speak. It wasn't so bad then, though, and so I got permission to have a service done here, and down she went where I could go and see her. I still do go to see her, of course, now and then. But in another year or two...the sea..." He shrugged again. "Time and the tides, they wait for no man."

We finished our coffee. I was going to have to be on my way soon, and suddenly I didn't like the idea of leaving him. Already I could feel the loneliness creeping in. Perhaps he sensed my restlessness or something. Certainly I could see that he didn't want me to go just yet. In any case, he said:

"Maybe you'd like to walk down with me past the old timber yard, visit her grave. Oh, it's safe enough, you don't have to worry. We may even come across old Ben down there. He sometimes visits her, too."

"Ah, well I'm not too sure about that," I answered. "The time, you know?" But by the time we got down the path to the gate I was asking: "How far is the churchyard, anyway?" Who could tell, maybe I'd find some long-lost Lanes in there! "Are there any old markers left standing?"

Garth chuckled and took my elbow. "It makes a change to have some company," he said. "Come on, it's this way."

He led the way back to the barrier where it spanned the road, bent his back, and ducked groaning under it, then turned left up an overgrown communal path between gardens where the houses had been stepped down the declining gradient. The detached bungalow on our right—one of a pair still standing, while a third slumped on the raw edge of oblivion—had decayed almost to the point where it was collapsing inward. Brambles luxuriated everywhere in its garden, completely enclosing it. The roof sagged and a chimney threatened to topple, making the whole structure seem highly suspect and more than a little dangerous.

"Partly subsidence, because of the undercutting action of the sea," Garth explained, "but mainly the rot. There was a lot of wood in these places, but it's all being eaten away. I made myself a living, barely, out of the old bricks and timber in Easingham, but now I have to be careful. Doesn't do to sell stuff with the rot in it."

"The rot?"

He paused for breath, leaned a hand on one hip, nodded and frowned. "Dry rot," he said. "Or *Merulius lacrymans* as they call it in the books. It's been bad these last three years. Very bad! But when the last of these old houses are gone, and what's left of the timber yard, then it'll be gone, too."

"It?" We were getting back to single-word questions again. "The dry rot, you mean? I'm afraid I don't know very much about it."

"Places on the coast are prone to it," he told me. "Whitby, Scarborough, places like that. All the damp sea spray and the bad plumbing, the rains that come in and the inadequate drainage. That's how it starts. It's a fungus, needs a lot of moisture—to get started, anyway. You don't know much about it? Heck, I used to think I knew *quite* a bit about it, but now I'm not so sure!"

By then I'd remembered something. "A friend of mine in London did mention to me how he was having to have his flat treated for it," I said, a little lamely. "Expensive, apparently."

Garth nodded, straightened up. "Hard to kill," he said. "And when it's active, moves like the plague! It's active here, now! Too late for Easingham, and who gives a damn anyway? But you tell that friend of yours to sort out his exterior maintenance first: the guttering and the drainage. Get rid of the water spillage, then deal with the rot. If a place is dry and airy, it's OK. Damp and musty spells danger!"

I nodded. "Thanks, I will tell him."

"Want to see something?" said Garth. "I'll show you what old *Merulius* can do. See here, these old paving flags? See if you can lever one up a bit." I found a piece of rusting iron stave and dragged it out of the ground where it supported a rotting fence, then forced the sharp end into a crack between the overgrown flags. And while I worked to loosen the paving stone, old Garth stood watching and carried on talking.

"Actually, there's a story attached, if you care to hear it," he said. "Probably all coincidental or circumstantial, or some other big word like that—but queer the way it came about all the same."

He was losing me again. I paused in my leveling to look bemused (and maybe to wonder what on Earth I was doing here), then grunted, and sweated, gave one more heave, and flipped the flag over onto its back. Underneath was hard-packed sand. I looked at it, shrugged, looked at Garth.

He nodded in that way of his, grinned, said: "Look. Now tell me what you make of this!"

He got down on one knee, scooped a little of the sand away. Just under the surface his hands met some soft obstruction. Garth wrinkled his nose and grimaced, got his face down close to the earth, blew until his weakened lungs started him coughing. Then he sat back and rested. Where he'd scraped and blown the sand away, I made out what appeared to be a grey fibrous mass running at right angles right under the pathway. It was maybe six inches thick, looked like tightly packed cotton wool. It might easily have been glass fiber lagging for some pipe or other, and I said as much.

"But it isn't," Garth contradicted me. "It's a root, a feeler, a tentacle. It's old man cancer himself—timber cancer—on the move and looking for a new victim. Oh, you won't see him moving," that strange look was back on his face, "or at least you shouldn't—but he's at it anyway. He finished those houses there," he nodded at the derelicts stepping down toward the new cliffs, "and now he's gone into this one on the left here. Another couple of summers like this 'un and he'll be through the entire row to my place. Except maybe I'll burn him out first."

"You mean this stuff—this fiber—is dry rot?" I said. I stuck my hand into the stuff and tore a clump out. It made a soft tearing sound, like damp chipboard, except it was dry as old paper. "How do you mean, you'll 'burn him out'?"

"I mean like I say," said Garth. "I'll search out and dig up all these threads—mycelium, they're called—and set fire to 'em. They smoulder right through to a fine white ash. And God—it *stinks*! Then I'll look for the fruiting bodies, and—"

"The what?" His words had conjured up something vaguely obscene in my mind. "Fruiting bodies?"

"Lord, yes!" he said. "You want to see? Just follow me."

Leaving the path, he stepped over a low brick wall to struggle through the undergrowth of the garden on our left. Taking care not to get tangled up in the brambles, I followed him. The house seemed pretty much intact, but a bay window in the ground floor had been broken and all the glass tapped out of the frame. "My winter preparations," Garth explained. "I burn wood, see? So before winter comes, I get into a house like this one, rip out all the wooden fixings and break 'em down ready for burning. The wood just stays where I stack it, all prepared and waiting for the bad weather to come in. I knocked this window out last week, but I've not been inside yet. I could smell it, see?" He tapped his nose. "And I didn't much care for all those spores on my lungs."

He stepped up on a pile of bricks, got one leg over the sill, and stuck his head inside. Then, turning his head in all directions, he systematically sniffed the air. Finally he seemed satisfied and disappeared inside. I followed him. "Spores?" I said. "What sort of spores?"

He looked at me, wiped his hand along the window ledge, held it up so that I could see the red dust accumulated on his fingers and palm. "*These* spores," he said. "Dry-rot spores, of course! Haven't you been listening?"

"I *have* been listening, yes," I answered sharply. "But I ask you: spores, mycelium, fruiting bodies? I mean, I thought dry rot was just, well, rotting wood!"

"It's a fungus," he told me, a little impatiently. "Like a mushroom, and it spreads in much the same way. Except it's destructive, and once it gets started it's bloody hard to stop!"

"And you, an ex-coal miner," I stared at him in the gloom of the house we'd invaded, "you're an expert on it, right? How come, Garth?"

Again there was that troubled expression on his face, and in the dim interior of the house he didn't try too hard to mask it. Maybe it had something to do with that story he'd promised to tell me, but doubtless he'd be as circuitous about that as he seemed to be about everything else. "Because I've read it up in books, that's how," he finally broke into my thoughts. "To occupy my time. When it first started to spread out of the old timber yard, I looked it up. It's—" He gave a sort of grimace. "—it's *interesting*, that's all."

By now I was wishing I was on my way again. But by that I mustn't be misunderstood: I'm an able-bodied man and I wasn't afraid of anything—and certainly not of Garth himself, who was just a lonely, canny old-timer—but all of this really was getting to be a waste of my time. I had just made my mind up to go back out through the window when he caught my arm.

"Oh, *yes*!" he said. "This place is really ripe with it! Can't you smell it? Even with the window bust wide open like this, and the place nicely dried out in the summer heat, still it's stinking the place out. Now just you come over here and you'll see what you'll see."

Despite myself, I was interested. And indeed I could smell...something. A cloying mustiness? A mushroomy taint? But not the nutty smell of fresh field mushrooms. More a sort of vile stagnation. Something dead might smell like this, long after the actual corruption has ceased...

Our eyes had grown somewhat accustomed to the gloom. We looked about the room. "Careful how you go," said Garth. "See the spores there? Try not to stir them up too much. They're worse than snuff, believe me!" He was right: the red dust lay fairly thick on just about everything. By "everything" I mean a few old sticks of furniture, the worn carpet under our feet, the skirting-board, and various shelves and ledges. Whichever family had moved out of here, they hadn't left a deal of stuff behind them.

The skirting was of the heavy, old-fashioned variety: an inch and a half thick, nine inches deep, with a fancy moulding along the top edge; they hadn't spared the wood in those days. Garth peered suspiciously at the skirting-board, followed it away from the bay window, and paused every pace to scrape the toe of his boot down its face. And eventually when he did this—suddenly the board crumbled to dust under the pressure of his toe!

It was literally as dramatic as that: the white paint cracked away and the timber underneath fell into a heap of black, smoking dust. Another pace and Garth kicked again, with the same result. He quickly exposed a ten-foot length of naked wall, on which even the plaster was loose and flaky, and showed me where strands of the cotton-wool mycelium had come up between the brickwork and the plaster from below. "It sucks the cellulose right out of wood," he said. "Gets right into brickwork, too. Now look here," and he pointed at the old carpet under his feet. The threadbare weave showed a sort of raised floral blossom or stain, like a blotch or blister, spreading outward away from the wall.

Garth got down on his hands and knees. "Just look at this," he said. He tore up the carpet and carefully laid it back. Underneath, the floorboards were warped, dark stained, shriveled so as to leave wide gaps between them. And up through the gaps came those white, etiolated threads, spreading themselves along the underside of the carpet.

I wrinkled my nose in disgust. "It's like a disease," I said.

"It *is* a disease!" he corrected me. "It's a cancer, and houses die of it!" Then he inhaled noisily, pulled a face of his own, and said: "Here. Right here." He pointed at the warped, rotting floorboards. "The very heart of it. Give me a hand." He got his fingers down between a pair of boards and gave a tug, and it was at once apparent that he wouldn't be needing any help from me. What had once been a stout wooden floorboard a full inch thick was now brittle as dry bark. It cracked upward, flew apart, revealed the dark cavities between the floor joists. Garth tossed bits of crumbling wood aside, tore up more boards; and at last "the very heart of it" lay open to our inspection.

"There!" said Garth with a sort of grim satisfaction. He stood back and wiped his hands down his trousers. "Now *that* is what you call a fruiting body!"

It was roughly the size of a football, if not exactly that shape. Suspended between two joists in a cradle of fibers, and adhering to one of the joists as if partly flattened to it, the thing might have been a great, too-ripe tomato. It was bright yellow at its center, banded in various shades of yellow from the middle out. It looked freakishly weird, like a bad joke: this lump of...of *stuff*—never a mushroom—just nestling there between the joists.

Garth touched my arm and I jumped a foot. He said: "You want to know where all the moisture goes—out of this wood, I mean? Well, just touch it."

"Touch...that?"

"Heck, it can't bite you! It's just a fungus."

"All the same, I'd rather not," I told him.

He took up a piece of floorboard and prodded the thing—and it squelched. The splintered point of the wood sank into it like jelly. Its heart was mainly liquid, porous as a sponge. "Like a huge egg yolk, isn't it?" he said, his voice very quiet. He was plainly fascinated.

Suddenly I felt nauseous. The heat, the oppressive closeness of the room, the spore-laden air. I stepped dizzily backward and stumbled against an old armchair. The rot had been there, too, for the chair just fragmented into a dozen pieces that puffed red dust all over the place. My foot sank right down through the carpet and mushy boards into darkness and stench—and in another moment I'd panicked.

Somehow I tumbled myself back out through the window and ended up on my back in the brambles. Then Garth was standing over me, shaking his head and tut-tutting. "Told you not to stir up the dust," he said. "It chokes your air and stifles you. Worse than being down a pit. Are you all right?"

My heart stopped hammering and I was, of course, all right. I got up. "A touch of claustrophobia," I told him. "I suffer from it at times. Anyway, I think I've taken up enough of your time, Garth. I should be getting on my way."

"What?" he protested. "A lovely day like this and you want to be driving off somewhere? And besides, there were things I wanted to tell you, and others I'd ask you—and we haven't been down to Lily-Anne's grave." He looked disappointed. "Anyway, you shouldn't be driving if you're feeling all shaken up…"

He was right about that part of it, anyway: I did feel shaky, not to mention foolish! And perhaps more importantly, I was still very much aware of the old man's loneliness. What if it was my mother who'd died, and my father had been left on his own up in Durham? "Very well," I said, at the same time damning myself for a weak fool, "let's go and see Lily-Anne's grave."

"Good!" Garth slapped my back. "And no more diversions—we go straight there."

Following the paved path as before and climbing a gentle rise, we started walking. We angled a little inland from the unseen cliffs where the green, rolling fields came to an abrupt end and fell down into the sea; and as we went I gave a little thought to the chain of incidents in which I'd found myself involved through the last hour or so.

Now, I'd be a liar if I said that nothing had struck me as strange in Easingham, for quite a bit had. Not least the dry rot: its apparent profusion and migration through the place, and old Garth's peculiar knowledge and understanding of the stuff. His—affinity?—with it. "You said there was a story attached," I reminded him. "…To that horrible fungus, I mean."

He looked at me sideways, and I sensed he was on the point of telling me something. But at that moment we crested the rise and the view just took my breath away. We could see for miles up and down the coast: to the slow, white breakers rolling in on some beach way to the north, and southward to a distance-misted seaside town that might even be Whitby. And we paused to fill our lungs with good air blowing fresh off the sea.

"There," said Garth. "And how's this for freedom? Just me and old Ben and the gulls for miles and miles, and I'm not so sure but that this is the way I like it. Now wasn't it worth it to come up here? All this open space and the great curve of the horizon…" Then the look of satisfaction slipped from his face to be replaced by a more serious expression. "There's old Easingham's cemetery—what's left of it."

He pointed down toward the cliffs, where a badly weathered stone wall formed part of a square whose sides would have been maybe fifty yards long in the old days. But in those days there'd also been a stubby promontory and a church. Now only one wall, running parallel with the path, stood complete—beyond which two-thirds of the churchyard had been claimed by the sea. Its occupants, too, I supposed.

"See that half-timbered shack," said Garth, pointing, "at this end of the cemetery? That's what's left of Johnson's Mill. Johnson's sawmill, that is. That shack used to be Old Man Johnson's office. A long line of Johnsons ran a couple of farms that enclosed all the fields round here right down to the cliffs. Pasture, mostly, with lots of fine animals grazing right here. But as the fields got eaten away and the buildings themselves started to be threatened, that's when half the Johnsons moved out and the rest bought a big house in the village. They gave up farming and started the mill, working timber for the local building trade...

"Folks round here said it was a sin, all that noise of sawing and planing, right next door to a churchyard. But...it was Old Man Johnson's land after all. Well, the sawmill business kept going till a time some seven years ago, when a really bad blow took a huge bite right out of the bay one night. The seaward wall of the graveyard went, and half of the timber yard, too, and that closed old Johnson down. He sold what machinery he had left, plus a few stacks of good oak that hadn't suffered, and moved out lock, stock, and barrel. Just as well, for the very next spring his big house and two others close to the edge of the cliffs got taken. The sea gets 'em all in the end.

"Before then, though—at a time when just about everybody else was moving out of Easingham—Lily-Anne and me had moved in! As I told you, we got our bungalow for a song, and of course we picked ourselves a house standing well back from the brink. We were getting on a bit; another twenty years or so should see us out; after that the sea could do its worst. But...well, it didn't quite work out that way."

While he talked, Garth had led the way down across the open fields to the graveyard wall. The breeze was blustery here and fluttered his words back into my face:

"So you see, within just a couple of years of our settling here, the village was derelict, and all that remained of people was us and a handful of Johnsons still working the mill. Then Lily-Anne came down with something and died, and I had her put down in the ground here in Easingham—so's I'd be near her, you know?

"That's where the coincidences start to come in, for she went only a couple of months after the shipwreck. Now I don't suppose you'd remember that; it wasn't much, just an old Portuguese freighter that foundered in a storm. Lifeboats took the crew off, and she'd already unloaded her cargo somewhere up the coast, so the incident didn't create much of a to-do in the newspapers. But she'd carried a fair bit of hardwood ballast, that old ship, and balks of the stuff would keep drifting ashore: great long twelve-by-twelves of it. Of course, Old Man Johnson wasn't one to miss out on a bit of good timber like that, not when it was being washed up right on his doorstep, so to speak…

"Anyway, when Lily-Anne died I made the proper arrangements, and I went down to see old Johnson who told me he'd make me a coffin out of this Haitian hardwood."

"Haitian?" Maybe my voice showed something of my surprise.

"That's right," said Garth, more slowly. He looked at me wonderingly. "Anything wrong with that?"

I shrugged, shook my head. "Rather romantic, I thought," I said. "Timber from a tropical isle."

"I thought so, too," he agreed. And after a while he continued: "Well, despite having been in the sea, the stuff could still be cut into fine, heavy panels, and it still French-polished to a beautiful finish. So that was that: Lily-Anne got a lovely coffin. Except—"

"Yes?" I prompted him.

He pursed his lips. "Except I got to thinking—later, you know—as to how maybe the rot came here in that wood. God knows it's a damn funny variety of fungus after all. But then this Haiti—well, apparently it's a damned funny place. They call it 'the Voodoo Island,' you know?"

"Black magic?" I smiled. "I think we've advanced a bit beyond thinking such as that, Garth."

"Maybe and maybe not," he answered. "But voodoo or no voodoo, it's still a funny place, that Haiti. Far away and exotic…"

By now we'd found a gap in the old stone wall and climbed over the tumbled stones into the graveyard proper. From where we stood, another twenty paces would take us right to the raw edge of the cliff where it sheared dead straight through the overgrown, badly neglected plots and headstones. "So here it is," said Garth, pointing. "Lily-Anne's grave, secure for now in what little is left of Easingham's old cemetery." His voice fell a little, grew ragged: "But you know, the fact is I wish I'd never put her down here in the first place. And I'd give anything that I hadn't buried her in that coffin built of Old Man Johnson's ballast wood."

The plot was a neat oblong picked out in oval pebbles. It had been weeded round its border, and from its bottom edge to the foot of the simple headstone it was decked in flowers, some wild and others cut from Easingham's deserted gardens. It was deep in flowers, and the ones underneath were withered and had been compressed by those on top. Obviously Garth came here more often than just "now and then." It was the only plot in sight that had been paid any sort of attention, but in the circumstances that wasn't surprising.

"You're wondering why there are so many flowers, eh?" Garth sat down on a raised slab close by.

I shook my head, sat down beside him. "No, I know why. You must have thought the world of her."

"You don't know why," he answered. "I did think the world of her, but that's not why. It's not the only reason, anyway. I'll show you."

He got down on his knees beside the grave, began laying aside the flowers. Right down to the marble chips he went, then scooped an amount of the polished gravel to one side. He made a small mound of it. Whatever I had expected to see in the small excavation, it wasn't the cylindrical, fibrous surface—like the upper section of a lagged pipe—that came into view. I sucked in my breath sharply.

There were tears in Garth's eyes as he flattened the marble chips back into place. "The flowers are so I won't see it if it ever breaks the surface," he said. "See, I can't bear the thought of that filthy stuff in her coffin. I mean, what if it's like what you saw under the floorboards in that house back there?" He sat down again, and his hands trembled as he took out an old wallet and removed a photograph to give it to me. "That's Lily-Anne," he said. "But God!—I don't like the idea of that stuff fruiting on her…"

Aghast at the thoughts his words conjured, I looked at the photograph. A homely woman in her late fifties, seated in a chair beside a fence in a garden I recognized as Garth's. Except the garden had been well-tended then. One shoulder seemed slumped a little, and though she smiled, still I could sense the pain in her face. "Just a few weeks before she died," said Garth. "It was her lungs. Funny that I worked in the pit all those years, and it was her lungs gave out. And now she's here, and so's this stuff."

I had to say something. "But…where did it come from. I mean, how did it come, well, here? I don't know much about dry rot, no, but I would have thought it confined itself to houses."

"That's what I was telling you," he said, taking back the photograph. "The British variety does. But not this stuff. It's weird and different! That's why I think it might have come here with that ballast wood. As to how it got into the churchyard: that's easy. Come and see for yourself."

I followed him where he made his way between the weedy plots toward the leaning, half-timbered shack. "Is that the source? Johnson's timber yard?"

He nodded. "For sure. But look here."

I looked where he pointed. We were still in the graveyard, approaching the tumbledown end wall, beyond which stood the derelict shack. Running in a parallel series along the dry ground, from the mill and into the graveyard, deep cracks showed through the tangled brambles, briars, and grasses. One of these cracks, wider than the others, had actually split a heavy horizontal marble slab right down its length. Garth grunted. "That wasn't done last time I was here," he said.

"The sea's been at it again." I nodded. "Undermining the cliffs. Maybe we're not as safe here as you think."

He glanced at me. "Not the sea this time," he said, very definitely. "Something else entirely. See, there's been no rain for weeks. Everything's dry. And *it* gets thirsty same as we do. Give me a hand."

He stood beside the broken slab and got his fingers into the crack. It was obvious that he intended to open up the tomb. "Garth," I cautioned him. "Isn't this a little ghoulish? Do you really intend to desecrate this grave?"

"See the date?" he said. "1847. Heck, I don't think he'd mind, whoever he is. Desecration? Why, he might even thank us for a little sweet sunlight! What are you afraid of? There can only be dust and bones down there now."

Full of guilt, I looked all about while Garth struggled with the fractured slab. It was a safe bet that there wasn't a living soul for miles around, but I checked anyway. Opening graves isn't my sort of thing. But having discovered him for a stubborn old man, I knew that if I didn't help him he'd find a way to do it by himself anyway; and so I applied myself to the task. Between the two of us we wrestled one of the two halves to the edge of its base, finally toppled it over. A choking fungus reek at once rushed out to engulf us! Or maybe the smell was of something else and I'd simply smelled what I "expected" to.

Garth pulled a sour face. "*Ugh!*" was his only comment.

The air cleared and we looked into the tomb. In there, a coffin just a little over three feet long, and the broken sarcophagus around it filled with dust, cobwebs, and a few leaves. Garth glanced at me out of the corner of his eye. "So now you think I'm wrong, eh?"

"About what?" I answered. "It's just a child's coffin."

"Just a little 'un, aye." He nodded. "And his little coffin looks intact, doesn't it? *But is it?*" Before I could reply he reached down and rapped with his horny knuckles on the wooden lid.

And despite the fact that the sun was shining down on us, and for all that the sea gulls cried and the world seemed at peace, still my hair stood on end at what happened next. For the coffin lid collapsed like a puffball and fell into dusty debris, and—God help me—*something in the box gave a grunt and puffed itself up into view!*

I'm not a coward, but there are times when my limbs have a will of their own. Once when a drunk insulted my wife, I struck him without consciously knowing I'd done it. It was that fast, the reaction that instinctive. And the same now. I didn't pause to draw breath until I'd cleared the wall and was halfway up the field to the paved path; and even then I probably wouldn't have stopped, except I tripped and fell flat and knocked all the wind out of myself.

By the time I stopped shaking and sat up, Garth was puffing and panting up the slope toward me. "It's all right," he was gasping. "It was nothing. Just the rot. It had grown in there and crammed itself so tight, so confined, that when the coffin caved in…"

He was right and I knew it. I *had* known it even with my flesh crawling, my legs, heart, and lungs pumping. But even so: "There were…*bones* in it!" I said, contrary to common sense. "A skull."

He drew close, sank down beside me gulping at the air. "The little 'un's bones," he panted, "caught up in the fibers. I just wanted to show you the extent of the thing. Didn't want to scare you to death!"

"I know, I know." I patted his hand. "But when it moved—"

"It was just the effect of the box collapsing," he explained, logically. "Natural expansion. Set free, it unwound like a jack-in-the-box. And the noise it made—"

"—That was the sound of its scraping against the rotten timber, amplified by the sarcophagus." I nodded. "I know all that. It shocked me, that's all. In fact, two hours in your bloody Easingham have given me enough shocks to last a lifetime!"

"But you see what I mean about the rot?" We stood up, both of us still a little shaky.

"Oh, yes, I see what you mean. I don't understand your obsession, that's all. Why don't you just leave the damned stuff alone?"

He shrugged but made no answer, and so we made our way back toward his home. On our way the silence between us was broken only once. "There!" said Garth, looking back toward the brow of the hill. "You see him?"

I looked back, saw the dark outline of an Alsatian dog silhouetted against the rise. "Ben?" Even as I spoke the name, so the dog disappeared into the long grass beside the path.

"Ben!" Garth called, and blew his piercing whistle. But with no result. The old man worriedly shook his head. "Can't think what's come over him," he said. "Then again, I'm more his friend than his master. We've always pretty much looked after ourselves. At least I know that he hasn't run off..."

Then we were back at Garth's house, but I didn't go in. His offer of another coffee couldn't tempt me. It was time I was on my way again. "If ever you're back this way—" he said as I got into the car.

I nodded, leaned out of my window. "Garth, why the hell don't you get out of here? I mean, there's nothing here for you now. Why don't you take Ben and just clear out?"

He smiled, shook his head, then shook my hand. "Where'd we go?" he asked. "And anyway, Lily-Anne's still here. Sometimes in the night, when it's hot and I have trouble sleeping, I can feel she's very close to me. Anyway, I know you mean well."

That was that. I turned the car round and drove off, acknowledged his final wave by lifting my hand briefly, so that he'd see it.

Then, driving round a gentle bend and as the old man sideslipped out of my rearview mirror, I saw Ben. He was crossing the road in front of me. I applied my brakes, let him get out of the way. It could only be Ben, I supposed: a big Alsatian, shaggy, yellow eyed. And yet I caught only a glimpse; I was more interested in controlling the car, in being sure that he was safely out of the way.

It was only after he'd gone through the hedge and out of sight into a field that an afterimage of the dog surfaced in my mind: the way he'd seemed to limp—his belly hairs, so long as to hang down and trail on the ground, even though he wasn't slinking—a bright splash of yellow on his side, as if he'd brushed up against something freshly painted.

Perhaps understandably, peculiar images bothered me all the way back to London: yes, and for quite a long time after...

❖ ❖ ❖

Before I knew it a year had gone by, then eighteen months, and memories of those strange hours spent in Easingham were fast receding. Faded with them was that promise I had made myself to visit my parents more frequently. Then I got a letter to say my mother hadn't been feeling too well, and another right on its heels to say she was dead. She'd gone in her sleep, nice and easy. This last was from a neighbor of theirs: my father wasn't much up to writing right now, or much of anything else for that matter; the funeral would be on…at…etc, etc.

God!—how guilty I felt driving up there, and more guilty with every mile that flashed by under my car's wheels. And all I could do was choke the guilt and the tears back and drive and feel the dull, empty ache in my heart that I knew my father would be feeling in his. And of course that was when I remembered old Garth Bentham in Easingham, and my "advice" that he should get out of that place. It had been a cold sort of thing to say to him. Even cruel. But I hadn't known that then. I hadn't thought.

We laid Ma to rest and I stayed with the Old Man for a few days, but he really didn't want me around. I thought about saying: "Why don't you sell up, come and live with us in London." We had plenty of room. But then I thought of Garth again and kept my mouth shut. Dad would work it out for himself in the fullness of time.

It was late on a cold Wednesday afternoon when I started out for London again, and I kept thinking how lonely it must be in old Easingham. I found myself wondering if Garth ever took a belt or filled a pipe, if he could even afford to, and…I'd promised him that if I was ever back up this way I'd look him up, hadn't I? I stopped at an off-license, bought a bottle of half-decent whisky and some pipe and rolling baccy, and a carton of two hundred cigarettes and a few cigars. Whatever was his pleasure, I'd probably covered it. And if he didn't smoke, well I could always give the tobacco goods to someone who did.

My plan was to spend just an hour with Garth, then head for the motorway and drive to London in darkness. I don't mind driving in the dark, when the weather and visibility are good and the driving lanes all but empty, and the night music comes sharp and clear out of the radio to keep me awake.

But approaching Easingham down that neglected cul-de-sac of a road, I saw that I wasn't going to have any such easy time of it. A storm was gathering out to sea, piling up the thunderheads like beetling black brows all along the twilight horizon. I could see continuous flashes of lightning out there, and even before I reached my destination I could hear the high seas thundering against the cliffs. When I did get there—

Well, I held back from driving quite as far as the barrier, because only a little way beyond it my headlights had picked out black, empty space. Of the three houses that had stood closest to the cliffs only one was left, and that one slumped right on the rim. So I stopped directly opposite Garth's place, gave a honk on my horn, then switched off and got out of the car with my carrier-bag full of gifts. Making my way to the house, the rush and roar of the sea was perfectly audible, transferring itself physically through the earth to my feet. Indeed the bleak, unforgiving ocean seemed to be working itself up into a real fury.

Then, in a moment, the sky darkened over and the rain came on out of nowhere, bitter cold and squally, and I found myself running up the overgrown garden path to Garth's door. Which was when I began to feel really foolish. There was no sign of life behind the grimy windows, neither a glimmer of light showing, nor a puff of smoke from the chimney. Maybe Garth had taken my advice and got out of it after all.

Calling his name over the rattle of distant thunder, I knocked on the door. After a long minute there was still no answer. But this was no good; I was getting wet and angry with myself; I tried the doorknob, and the door swung open. I stepped inside, into deep gloom, and groped on the wall near the door for a light switch. I found it, but the light wasn't working. Of course it wasn't: there was no electricity! This was a ghost town, derelict, forgotten. And the last time I was here it had been in broad daylight.

But...Garth had made coffee for me. On a gas-ring? It must have been.

Standing there in the small cloakroom shaking rain off myself, my eyes were growing more accustomed to the gloom. The cloakroom seemed just as I remembered it: several pieces of tall, dark furniture, pine-paneled inner walls, the old grandfather clock standing in one corner. Except that this time...the clock wasn't clucking. The pendulum was still, a vertical bar of brassy fire where lightning suddenly brought the room to life. Then it was dark again—if anything even darker than before—and the windows rattled as thunder came down in a rolling, receding drumbeat.

"Garth!" I called again, my voice echoing through the old house. "It's me, Greg Lane. I said I'd drop in some time?..." No answer, just the *hiss* of the rain outside, the feel of my collar damp against my neck, and the thick, rising smell of...of what? And suddenly I remembered very clearly the details of my last visit here.

"Garth!" I tried one last time, and I stepped to the door of his living room and pushed it open. As I did so there came a lull in the beating rain. I heard the floorboards creak under my feet, but I also heard…a groan? My sensitivity at once rose by several degrees. Was that Garth? Was he hurt? *My God!* What had he said to me that time? "One of these days the postman will find me stretched out in here, and he'll think: 'Well, I needn't come out here anymore.'"

I had to have light. There'd be matches in the kitchen, maybe even a torch. In the absence of a mains supply, Garth would surely have to have a torch. Making my way shufflingly, very cautiously across the dark room toward the kitchen, I was conscious that the smell was more concentrated here. Was it just the smell of an old, derelict house, or was it something worse? Then, outside, lightning flashed again, and briefly the room was lit up in a white glare. Before the darkness fell once more, I saw someone slumped on the old settee where Garth had served me coffee…

"Garth?" The word came out half-strangled. I hadn't wanted to say it; it had just gurgled from my tongue. For though I'd seen only a silhouette, outlined by the split-second flash, it hadn't looked like Garth at all. It had been much more like someone else I'd once seen—in a photograph. That drooping right shoulder.

My skin prickled as I stepped on shivery feet through the open door into the kitchen. I forced myself to draw breath, to think clearly. *If* I'd seen anyone or anything at all back there (it could have been old boxes piled on the settee, or a roll of carpet leaning there), then it most probably had been Garth, which would explain that groan. It *was* him, of course it was. But in the storm, and remembering what I did of this place, my mind was playing morbid tricks with me. No, it was Garth, and he could well be in serious trouble. I got a grip of myself, quickly looked all around.

A little light came into the kitchen through a high back window. There was a two-ring gas cooker, a sink, and a drainer board with a drawer under the sink. I pulled open the drawer and felt about inside it. My nervous hand struck what was unmistakably a large box of matches, and—yes, the smooth heavy cylinder of a hand torch!

And all the time I was aware that someone was or might be slumped on a settee just a few swift paces away through the door to the living room. With my hand still inside the drawer, I pressed the stud of the torch and was rewarded when a weak beam probed out to turn my fingers pink. Well, it wasn't a powerful beam, but any sort of light had to be better than total darkness.

Armed with the torch, which felt about as good as a weapon in my hand, I forced myself to move back into the living room and directed my beam at the settee. But oh, Jesus—all that sat there was a monstrous grey mushroom! It was a great fibrous mass, growing out of and welded with mycelium strands to the settee, and in its center an obscene yellow fruiting body. But for God's sake, it had the shape and outline and *look* of an old woman, and it had Lily-Anne's deflated chest and slumped shoulder!

I don't know how long I held onto the torch, how I kept from screaming out loud, why I simply didn't fall unconscious. That's the sort of shock I experienced. But I did none of these things. Instead, on nerveless legs, I backed away, backed right into an old wardrobe or Welsh dresser. At least, I backed into what had once *been* a piece of furniture. But now it was something else.

Soft as sponge, the thing collapsed and sent me sprawling. Dust and (I imagined) dark red spores rose up everywhere, and I skidded on my back in shards of crumbling wood and matted webs of fiber. And lolling out of the darkness behind where the dresser had stood—bloating out like some loathsome puppet or dummy—a second fungoid figure leaned toward me. And this time it was a caricature of Ben!

He lolled there, held up on four fiber legs, muzzle snarling soundlessly, for all the world tensed to spring—and all he was was a harmless fungous thing. And yet this time I did scream. Or I think I did, but the thunder came to drown me out.

Then I was on my feet, and my feet were through the rotten floorboards, and I didn't care except I had to get out of there, out of that choking, stinking, collapsing—

I stumbled, *crumbled* my way into the tiny cloakroom, tripped and crashed into the clock where it stood in the corner. It was like a nightmare chain reaction that I'd started and couldn't stop; the old grandfather just crumpled up on itself, its metal parts clanging together as the wood disintegrated around them. And all the furniture following suit, and the very wall paneling smoking into ruin where I fell against it.

And there where that infected timber had been, there he stood—old Garth himself! He leaned half out of the wall like a great nodding manikin, his entire head a livid yellow blotch, his arm and hand making a noise like a huge puffball bursting underfoot where they separated from his side to point floppingly toward the open door. I needed no more urging.

"God! Yes! *I'm going!*" I told him, as I plunged out into the storm…

After that…nothing, not for some time. I came to in a hospital in Stokesley about noon the next day. Apparently I'd run out of road on the outskirts of some village or other, and they'd dragged me out of my car where it lay upside down in a ditch. I was banged up and so couldn't do much talking, which is probably as well.

But in the newspapers I read how what was left of Easingham had gone into the sea in the night. The churchyard, Haitian timber, terrible dry-rot fungus, the whole thing, sliding down into the sea and washed away forever on the tides.

And yet now I sometimes think:

Where did all that wood *go* that Garth had been selling for years? And what of all those spores I'd breathed and touched and rolled around in? And sometimes when I think things like that it makes me feel quite ill.

I suppose I shall just have to wait and see…

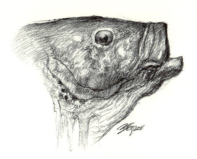

THE SUN, THE SEA,
AND THE SILENT SCREAM

This time of year, just as you're recovering from Christmas, they're wont to appear, all unsolicited, *plop* on your welcome mat. I had forgotten that fact, but yesterday I was reminded.

Julie was up first, creating great smells of coffee and frying bacon. And me still in bed, drowsy, thinking how great it was to be nearly back to normal. Three months she'd been out of *that* place, and fit enough now to be first up, running about after me for a change.

Her sweet voice called upstairs: "Post, darling!" And her slippers flip-flopping out into the porch. Then those long moments of silence—until it dawned on me what she was doing. I knew it instinctively, the way you do about someone you love. She was screaming—but silently. A scream that came drilling into all my bones to shiver into shards right there in the marrow. Me out of bed like a puppet on some madman's strings, jerked downstairs so as to break my neck, while the silent scream went on and on.

And Julie standing there with her head thrown back and her mouth agape, and the unending scream not coming out. Her eyes starting out with their pupils rolled down, staring at the thing in her white, shuddering hand—

A travel brochure, of course…

✤ ✤ ✤

Julie had done Greece fairly extensively with her first husband. That had been five or six years ago, when they'd hoped and tried for kids a lot. No kids had come; she couldn't have them; he'd gone off and found someone who could. No hard feelings. Maybe a few soft feelings.

So when we first started going back to Greece, I'd suggested places they'd explored together. Maybe I was looking for far-away expressions on her face in the sunsets, or a stray tear when a familiar *bousouki* tune drifted out on aromatic taverna exhalations. Somebody had taken a piece of my heart, too, once upon a time; maybe I wanted to know how much of Julie was really mine. As it happened, all of her was.

After we were married, we left the old trails behind and broke fresh ground. That is, we started to find new places to holiday. Twice yearly we'd pack a few things, head for the sunshine, the sea, and sometimes the sand. Sand wasn't always a part of the package, not in Greece. Not the golden or pure white varieties, anyway. But pebbles, marble chips, great brown and black slabs of volcanic rock sloping into the sea—what odds? The sun was always the same, and the sea...

The sea. Anyone who knows the Aegean, the Ionian, the Mediterranean in general, in between and around Turkey and Greece, knows what I mean when I describe those seas as indescribable. Blue, green, mother-of-pearl, turquoise in that narrow band where the sea meets the land: fantastic! Myself, I've always liked the colours *under* the sea the best. That's the big bonus I get, or got, out of the islands: the swimming, the amazing submarine world just beyond the glass of my face mask, the spearfishing.

And this time—last time, the very last time—we settled for Makelos. But don't go looking for it on any maps. You won't find it; much too small, and I'm assured that the British don't go there any more. As a holiday venue, it's been written off. I'd like to think I had something, everything, to do with that, which is why I'm writing this. But a warning: if you're stuck on Greece anyway, and willing to take your chances come what may, read no further. I'd hate to spoil it all for you.

So...what am I talking about? Political troubles, unfinished hotel apartments, polluted swimming pools? No, nothing like that. We didn't take that sort of holiday, anyway. We were strictly 'off-the-beaten-track' types. Hence Makelos.

We couldn't fly there direct; the island was mainly a flat-topped mountain climbing right out of the water, with a dirt landing strip on the plateau suitable only for Skyvans. So it was a packed jet to Athens, a night on the town, and in the mid-morning a flying Greek matchbox the rest of the way. Less than an hour out of Athens and into the Cyclades, descending through a handful of cotton-wool clouds, that was our first sight of our destination.

Less than three miles long, a mile wide—that was it. Makelos. There was a 'town', also called Makelos, at one end of the island where twin spurs formed something of a harbour; and the rest of the place around the central plateau was rock and scrub and tiny bays, olive groves galore, almonds and some walnuts, prickly pears and a few lonely lemons. Oh, and lots of wildflowers, so that the air seemed scented.

The year before, there'd been a few apartments available in Makelos town. But towns weren't our scene. This time, however, the island had something new to offer: a lone taverna catering for just three detached, cabin-style apartments, or 'villas', all nestling in a valley two miles down the coast from Makelos town itself. Only one or two taxis on the entire island (the coastal road was little more than a track), no fast-food stands, and no packed shingle beaches where the tideless sea would be one-third sun oil and two-thirds tourist pee!

We came down gentle as a feather, taxied up to a wind-blown shack that turned out to be the airport, deplaned and passed in front of the shack and out the back, and boarded our transport. There were other holiday makers; but we were too excited to pay them much attention; also a handful of dour-faced island Greeks—Makelosians, we guessed. Dour, yes. Maybe that should have told us something about their island.

Our passports had been stamped over the Athens stamp with a local variety as we passed through the airport shack, and the official doing the job turned out to be our driver. A busy man, he also introduced himself as the mayor of Makelos! The traction end of our 'transport' was a three-wheeler: literally a converted tractor, hauling a four-wheeled trolley with bucket seats bolted to its sides. On the way down from the plateau, I remember thinking we'd never make it; Julie kept her eyes closed for most of the trip; I gave everyone aboard As for nerve. And the driver-mayor sang a doleful Greek number all the way down.

The town was very old, with nowhere the whitewashed walls you become accustomed to in the islands. Instead, there was an air of desolation about the place. Throw in a few tumbleweeds, and you could shoot a Western there. But fishing boats bobbed in the harbour, leathery Greeks mended nets along the quayside; old men drank muddy coffee at wooden tables outside the tavernas, and bottles of Metaxa and ouzo were very much in evidence. Crumbling fortified walls of massive thickness proclaimed, however inarticulately, a one-time Crusader occupation.

Once we'd trundled to a halt in the town's square, the rest of the passengers were home and dry; Julie and I still had a mile and a half to go. Our taxi driver (transfer charges both ways, six pounds sterling: I'd wondered why it was so cheap!) collected our luggage from the tractor's trolley, stowed it away, waited for us while we dusted ourselves down and stretched our legs. Then we got into his 'taxi'.

I won't impugn anyone's reputation by remarking on the make of that old bus; come to think of it, I could possibly *make* someone's name, for anywhere else in the world this beauty would have been off the road in the late sixties! Inside—it was a shrine, of course. The Greek sort, with good-luck charms, pictures of the saints, photos of Mum and Dad, and icon-like miniatures in silver frames, hanging and jangling everywhere. And even enough room for the driver to see through his windscreen.

"Nichos," he introduced himself, grave-faced, trying to loosen my arm in its socket with his handshake where he reached back from the driver's seat. And to Julie, seated beside him up front: "Nick!" and he took her hand and bowed his head to kiss it. Fine, except we were already mobile and leaving the town, and holiday makers and villagers alike scattering like clucking hens in all directions in our heavy blue exhaust smoke.

Nichos was maybe fifty, hard to tell: bright brown eyes, hair greying, upward-turned moustache, skin brown as old leather. His nicotine-stained teeth and ouzo breath were pretty standard. "A fine old car," I opined, as he jarred us mercilessly on non-existent suspension down the patchy, pot-holed tarmacadam street.

"Eh?" He raised an eyebrow.

"The car," I answered. "She goes, er, well!"

"Very well, thank you. The car," he apparently agreed.

"Maybe he doesn't speak it too well, darling." Julie was straight-faced.

"Speaks it," Nichos agreed with a nod. Then, registering understanding: "Ah—*speak* it! I am speaking it, yes, and slowly. Very *slooowly*! Then is understanding. Good morning, good evening, welcome to my house—exactly! I am in Athens. Three years. Speaks it much, in Athens."

"Great!" I enthused, without malice. After all, I couldn't speak any Greek.

"You stay at Villas Dimitrios, yes?" He was just passing the time; of course we were staying there; he'd been paid to take us there, hadn't he? And yet at the same time, I'd picked up a note of genuine enquiry, even something of concern in his voice, as if our choice surprised or dismayed him.

"Is it a nice place?" Julie asked.

"Nice?" he repeated her. "Beautiful!" He blew a kiss. "Beautiful sea—for swim, *beautiful!*" Then he shrugged, said: "All Makelos same. But Dimitrios water—water for drink—him not so good. You drinking? OK—you drink Coke. You drink beer. Drinking water in bottle. Drinking wine—very cheap! Not drinking water. Is big hole in Dimitrios. Deep, er—well? Yes? Water in well bad. All around Dimitrios bad. Good for olives, lemons, no good for the people."

We just about made sense of everything he said, which wasn't quite as easy as I've made it sound here. As for the water situation: that was standard, too. We never drank the local water anyway. "So it's a beautiful place," I said. "Good."

Again he glanced at me over his shoulder, offered another shrug. "Er, beautiful, yes." He didn't seem very sure about it now. The Greeks are notoriously vague.

We were out of Makelos, heading south round the central plateau, kicking up the dust of a narrow road where it had been cut through steep, seaward-sloping strata of yellow-banded, dazzling white rock to run parallel with the sea on our left. We were maybe thirty or forty feet above sea level, and down there through bights in the shallow sea cliffs, we were allowed tantalizing glimpses of white pebble beaches scalloping an ocean flat as a mill-pond. The fishing would be good. Nothing like the south coast of England (no Dover sole basking on a muddy bottom here), but that made it more of a challenge. You had to be *good* to shoot fish here!

I took out a small paper parcel from my pocket and unwrapped it: a pair of gleaming trident spearheads purchased in Athens. With luck these heads should fit my spears. Nichos turned his head. "You like to fish? I catch plenty! *Big* fisherman!" Then that look was back on his face. "You fish in Dimitrios? No eat. You like the fishing—good! Chase him, the fish— shoot, maybe kill—but no eat. OK?"

I began to feel worried. Julie, too. She turned to stare at me. I leaned forward, said: "Nichos, what do you mean? Why shouldn't we eat what I catch?"

"My house!" he answered as we turned a bend through a stand of stunted trees. He grinned, pointed.

Above us, the compacted scree slope was green with shrubs and Mediterranean pines. There was a garden set back in ancient, gnarled olives,

41

behind which a row of white-framed windows reflected the late-morning sunlight. The house matched the slope rising around and beyond it, its ochre-tiled roof seeming to melt into the hillside. Higher up there were walled, terraced enclosures; higher still, where the mountain's spur met the sky, goats made gravity-defying silhouettes against the dazzle.

"I show you!" said Nichos, turning right onto a track that wound dizzily through a series of hairpins to the house. We hung on as he drove with practised ease almost to the front door, parking his taxi in the shade of an olive tree heavy with fruit. Then he was opening doors for us, calling out to his wife: "Katrin—hey, Katrin!"

We stayed an hour. We drank cold beer, ate a delicious sandwich of salami, sliced tomatoes, and goat's milk cheese. We admired the kids, the goats and chickens, the little house. It had been an effective way of changing the subject. And we didn't give Nichos's reticence (was that what it had been, or just poor communications?) another thought until he dropped us off at Villas Dimitrios.

The place was only another mile down the read, as the crow flies. But that coastal road knew how to wind. Still, we could probably have walked it while Katrin made us our sandwiches. And yet the island's natural contours kept it hidden from sight until the last moment.

We'd climbed up from the sea by then, maybe a hundred feet, and the road had petered out to little more than a track as we crested the final rise and Nichos applied his brakes. And there we sat in that oven of a car, looking down through its dusty, fly-specked windows on Villas Dimitrios. It was...idyllic!

Across the spur where we were parked, the ground dipped fairly steeply to a bay maybe a third of a mile point to point. The bay arms were rocky, formed of the tips of spurs sloping into the sea, but the beach between them was sand. *White* sand, Julie's favourite sort. Give her a book, a white beach, and a little shade, and I could swim all day. The taverna stood almost at the water's edge: a long, low house with a red-tiled roof, fronted by a wooden framework supporting heavy grapevines and masses of bougainvillaea. Hazy blue woodsmoke curled up from its chimney, and there was a garden to its rear. Behind the house, separate from it and each other and made private by screening groves of olives, three blobs of shimmering white stone were almost painful to look at. The chalets or 'villas'.

Nichos merely glanced at it; nothing new to him. He pointed across the tiny valley to its far side. Over there, the scree base went up brown and yellow to the foot of sheer cliffs, where beneath a jutting overhang the shadows were so dark as to be black. It had to be a cave. Something of a track had been worn into the scree, leading to the place under the cliff.

"In there," said Nichos with one of his customary shrugs, "the well. Water, him no good…" His face was very grave.

"The water was poisoned?" Julie prompted him.

"Eh?" he cocked his head, then gave a nod. "Now is poison!"

"I don't understand," I said. "What is it—" indicated the dark blot under the cliff "—over there?"

"The well," he said again. "Down inside the cave. But the water, he had, er—like the crabs, you know? You understand the crabs, in the sea?"

"Of course," Julie told him. "In England we eat them."

He shook his head, looked frustrated. "Here, too," he said. "But this thing not crab. Very small." He measured an inch between thumb and forefinger. "And no eat him. Very bad! People were…sick. They died. Men came from the government in Athens. They bring, er, chemicals? They put in well. Poison for the crabs." Again his shrug. "Now is OK—maybe. But I say, no drink the water."

Before we could respond, he got out of the car, unloaded our luggage onto the dusty track. I followed him. "You're not taking us down?"

"Going down OK," he shrugged, this time apologetically. "Come up again—difficult! Too—how you say?" He made an incline with his hand.

"Too steep?"

"Is right. My car very nice—also very old! I sorry." I picked up the cases; Julie joined us and took the travel bags. Nichos made no attempt to help; instead he gave a small, awkward bow, said: "You see my house? Got the problem, come speak. Good morning." Then he was into his car. He backed off, turned around, stopped, and leaned out his window. "Hey, mister, lady!"

We looked at him.

He pointed. "Follow road is long way. Go straight down, very easy. Er, how you say—short-cut? So, I go. See you in two weeks."

We watched his tyres kicking up dust and grit until he was out of sight. Then:

Taking a closer look at the terrain, I could see he was right. The track followed the ridge of the spur down to a sharp right turn, then down a hard-packed dirt ramp to the floor of the valley. It was steep, but a decent car should make it—even Nichos's taxi, I thought. But if we left the track here and climbed straight down the side of the spur, we'd cut two or three hundred yards off the distance. And actually, even the spur wasn't all that steep. We made it without any fuss, and I sat down only once when my feet shot out from under me.

As we got down onto the level, our host for the next fortnight came banging and clattering from the direction of the taverna, bumping over the rough scrub in a Greek three-wheeler with a cart at the back. Dimitrios wore a wide-brimmed hat against the sun, but still he was sweating just as badly as we were. He wiped his brow as he dumped our luggage into his open-ended cart. We hitched ourselves up at the rear and sat with our feet dangling. And he drove us to our chalet.

We were hot and sticky, all three of us, and maybe it wasn't so strange we didn't talk. Or perhaps he could see our discomfort and preferred that we get settled in before turning on the old Greek charm. Anyway, we said nothing as he opened the door for us, gave me the key, helped me carry our bags into the cool interior. I followed him back outside again while Julie got to the ritual unpacking.

"Hot," he said then. "Hot, the sun..." Greeks have this capacity for stating the obvious. Then, carrying it to extreme degrees, he waved an arm in the direction of the beach, the sea, and the taverna. "Beach. Sea. Taverna. For swimming. Eating. I have the food, drinks. I also selling the food for you the cooking..." The chalet came with its own self-catering kit.

"Fine," I smiled. "See you later."

He stared at me a moment, his eyes like dull lights in the dark shadow of his hat, then made a vague sort of motion halfway between a shrug and a nod. He got back aboard his vehicle and started her up, and as his clatter died away, I went back inside and had a look around.

Julie was filling a pair of drawers with spare clothing, at the same time building a teetering pyramid of reading material on a chair. Where books were concerned, she was voracious. She was like that about me, too. No complaints here.

Greek island accommodation varies from abominable to half decent. Or, if you're willing to shell out, you might be lucky enough to get good— but rarely better than that. The Villas Dimitrios chalets were...well, OK. But we'd paid for it, so it was what we expected.

I checked the plumbing first. Greek island plumbing is never better than basic. The bathroom was tastefully but totally tiled, even the ceiling! No bathtub, but a good shower and, at the other end of the small room, the toilet and washbasin. Enclosed in tiles, you could shower and let the water spray where-the-heck; if it didn't end up in the shower basin, it would end up on the floor, which sloped gently from all directions to one corner where there was a hole going—where? That's the other thing about Greek plumbing: I've never been able to figure out where everything goes.

But the bathroom did have its faults: like, there were no plugs for the washbasin and shower drainage, and no grilles in the plugholes. I suppose I'm quirky, but I like to see a grille in there, not just a black hole gurgling away to nowhere. It was the same in the little 'kitchen' (an alcove under an arch, really, with a sink and drainer unit, a two-ring gas stove, a cupboard containing the cylinder, and a wall-mounted rack for crockery and cutlery; all very nice and serviceable and equipped with a concealed overhead fan-extractor): no plug in the sink and no grille in the plughole.

I complained loudly to Julie about it.

"Don't put your toe down and you won't get stuck!" was her advice from the bedroom.

"Toe down?" I was already miles away, looking for the shaver socket.

"Down the shower plughole," she answered. And she came out of the bedroom wearing sandals and the bottom half of her bikini. I made slavering noises, and she turned coyly, tossed back her bra straps for me to fasten. "Do me up."

"You were quick off the mark," I told her.

"All packed away, too," she said with some satisfaction. "And the big white hunter's kit neatly laid out for him. And all performed free of charge—while he examines plugholes!" Then she picked up a towel and tube of lotion and headed for the door. "Last one in the sea's a pervert!"

Five minutes later I followed her. She'd picked a spot halfway between the chalet and the most northerly bay arm. Her red towel was like a splash of blood on the white sand two hundred yards north of the taverna. I carried my mask, snorkel, flippers, some strong string, and a tatty old blanket with torn corners; that was all. No spear gun. First I'd take a look-see, and the serious stuff could come later. Julie obviously felt the same as I did about it: no book, just a slim, pale white body on the red towel, green eyes three-quarters shuttered behind huge sunglasses. She was still wet from the sea, but that wouldn't last long. The sun was a furnace, steaming the water off her body.

On my way to her, I'd picked up some long, thin, thorny branches from the scrub; when I got there, I broke off the thorns and fixed up a sunshade. The old blanket's torn corners showed how often we'd done this before. Then I took my kit to the water's edge and dropped it, and ran gasping, pell-mell into the shallows until I toppled over! My way of getting into the sea quickly. Following which I outfitted myself and finned for the rocks where the spur dipped below the water.

As I've intimated, the Mediterranean around the Greek islands is short on fish. You'll find red mullet on the bottom, plenty of them, but you need half a dozen to make a decent meal. And grey mullet on top, which move like lightning and cause you to use up more energy than eating them provides; great sport, but you couldn't live on it. But there's at least one fish of note in the Med, and that's the grouper.

Groupers are territorial; a family will mark out its own patch, usually in deep water where there's plenty of cover, which is to say rock or weeds. And they love caves. Where there are plenty of rocks and caves, there'll also be groupers. Here, where the spur crumbled into the sea, this was ideal grouper ground. So I wasn't surprised to see this one—especially since I didn't have my gun! Isn't that always the way of it?

He was all of twenty-four inches long, maybe seven across his back, mottled red and brown to match his cave. When he saw me, he headed straight for home, and I made a mental note to mark the spot. Next time I came out here, I'd have my gun with me, armed with a single flap-nosed spear. The spear goes into the fish, the flap opens, and he's hooked, can't slip off. Tridents are fine for small fish, but not for this bloke. And don't talk to me about cruel; if I'm cruel, so is every fisherman in the world, and at least I eat what I catch. But it was then, while I was thinking these things, that I noticed something was wrong.

The fish had homed in on his cave all right, but as his initial reaction to my presence wore off, so his spurt of speed diminished. Now he seemed merely to drift toward the dark hole in the rock, lolling from side to side like some strange, crippled sub, actually missing his target to strike *against* the weedy stone! It was the first time I'd seen a fish collide with something underwater. This was one very sick grouper.

I went down to have a closer look. He was maybe ten feet down, just lolling against the rock face. His huge gill flaps pulsed open and closed, open and closed. I could have reached out and touched him. Then, as he rolled a little on one side, I saw—

46

I backed off, felt a little sick—felt sorry for him. And I wished I had my gun with me, if only to put him out of his misery. Under his great head, wedging his gill slits half open, a nest of fish lice or parasites of some sort were plainly visible. Not lampreys or remora or the like, for they were too small, only as big as my thumbs. Crustaceans, I thought—a good dozen of them—and they were hooked into him, leeching on the raw red flesh under his gills.

God, I have a *loathing* of this sort of thing! Once in Crete I'd come out of the sea with a suckerfish in my armpit. I hadn't noticed it until I was towelling myself dry and it fell off me. It was only three or four inches long but I'd reacted like I was covered with leeches! I had that same feeling now.

Skin crawling, I drifted up and away from the stricken fish, and for the first time got a good look at his eyes. They were dull, glazed, bubbly as the eyes of a fatally diseased goldfish. And they followed me. And then *he* followed me!

As I floated feet first for the surface, that damned grouper finned lethargically from the rocks and began drifting up after me. Several of his parasites had detached themselves from him and floated alongside him, gravitating like small satellites about his greater mass. I pictured one of them with its hooked feet fastened in my groin, or over one of my eyes. I mean, I knew they couldn't do that—their natural hosts are fish—but the thoughts made me feel vulnerable as hell.

I took off like Tarzan for the beach twenty-five yards away, climbed shivering out of the water in the shadow of the declining spur. As soon as I was out, the shudders left me. Along the beach my sunshade landmark was still there, flapping a little in a light breeze come up suddenly off the sea; but no red towel, no Julie. She could be swimming. Or maybe she'd felt thirsty and gone for a drink under the vines where the taverna fronted onto the sea.

Kit in hand, I padded along the sand at the dark rim of the ocean, past the old blanket tied with string to its frame of branches, all the way to the taverna. The area under the vines was maybe fifty feet along the front by thirty deep, a concrete base set out with a dozen small tables and chairs. Dimitrios was being a bit optimistic here, I thought. After all, it was the first season his place had been in the brochures. But…maybe next year there'd be more chalets, and the canny Greek owner was simply thinking well ahead.

I gave the place the once-over. Julie wasn't there, but at least I was able to get my first real look at our handful of fellow holiday makers.

A fat woman in a glaring yellow one-piece splashed in eighteen inches of water a few yards out. She kept calling to her husband, one George, to come on in. George sat half in, half out of the shade; he was a thin, middle-aged, balding man not much browner than myself, wearing specs about an inch thick that made his eyes look like marbles. "No, no, dear," he called back. "I'm fine watching you." He looked frail, timid, tired—and I thought: *Where the hell are marriages like this made?* They were like characters off a seaside postcard, except he didn't even seem to have the strength to ogle the girls—if there'd been any! His wife was twice his size.

George was drinking beer from a glass. A bottle, three-quarters empty and beaded with droplets of moisture, stood on his table. I fancied a drink but had no money on me. Then I saw that George was looking at me, and I felt that he'd caught me spying on him or something. "I was wondering," I said, covering up my rudeness, "if you'd seen my wife? She was on the beach there, and—"

"Gone back to your chalet," he said, sitting up a bit in his chair. "The girl with the red towel?" And suddenly he looked just a bit embarrassed. So he was an ogler after all. "Er, while you were in the sea…" He took off his specs and rubbed gingerly at a large red bump on the lid of his right eye. Then he put his glasses on again, blinked at me, held out the beer bottle. "Fancy a mouthful? To wash the sea out of your throat? I've had all I want."

I took the bottle, drained it, said: "Thanks! Bite?"

"Eh?" He cocked his head on one side.

"Your eye," I said. "Mosquito, was it? Horsefly or something?"

"Dunno." He shook his head. "We got here Wednesday, and by Thursday night this was coming up. Yesterday morning it was like this. Doesn't hurt so much as irritates. There's another back of my knee, not fully in bloom yet."

"Do you have stuff to dab on?"

He nodded in the direction of his wallowing wife and sighed, "She has *gallons* of it! Useless stuff! It will just have to take its own time."

"Look, I'll see you later," I said. "Right now I have to go and see what's up with Julie." I excused myself.

Leaving the place, I nodded to a trio of spinsterish types relaxing in summer frocks at one of the tables further back. They looked like sisters, and the one in the middle might just be a little retarded. She kept lolling first one way, then the other, while her companions propped her up. I caught a few snatches of disjointed, broad Yorkshire conversation:

"Doctor?…sunstroke, I reckon. Or maybe that melon?…taxi into town will fix her up…bit of shopping…pull her out of it…Kalamari?—*yechhh!* Don't know what decent grub is, these foreign folks…" They were so wrapped up in each other, or in complaint of the one in the middle, that they scarcely noticed me at all.

On the way back to our chalet, at the back of the house/taverna, I looked across low walls and a row of exotic potted plants to see an old Greek (male or female I couldn't determine, because of the almost obligatory floppy black hat tilted forward, and flowing black peasant clothes) sitting in a cane chair in one corner of the garden. He or she sat dozing in the shade of an olive tree, chin on chest, all oblivious of the world outside the tree's sun-dappled perimeter. A pure white goat, just a kid, was tethered to the tree; it nuzzled the oldster's dangling fingers like they were teats. Julie was daft for young animals, and I'd have to tell her about it. As for the figure in the cane chair: he/she had been there when Julie and I went down to the beach. Well, getting old in this climate had to be better than doing it in some climates I could mention…

I found Julie in bed, shivering for all she was worth! She was patchy red where the sun had caught her, cold to the touch but filmed with perspiration. I took one look, recognized the symptoms, said: "Oh-oh! Last night's moussaka, eh? You should have had the chicken!" Her tummy *always* fell prey to moussaka, be it good or bad. But she usually recovered quickly, too.

"Came on when I was on the beach," she said. "I left the blanket…"

"I saw it," I told her. "I'll go get it." I gave her a kiss.

"Just let me lie here and close my eyes for a minute or two, and I'll be OK," she mumbled. "An *hour* or two, anyway." And as I was going out the door: "Jim, this isn't Nichos's bad water, is it?"

I turned back. "Did you drink any?"

She shook her head.

"Got crabs?"

She was too poorly to laugh, so merely snorted.

I pocketed some money. "I'll get the blanket, buy some bottled drinks. You'll have something to sip. And then…will you be OK if I go fishing?"

She nodded. "Of course. You'll see; I'll be on my feet again tonight."

"Anyway, you should see the rest of them here," I told her. "Three old sisters, and one of 'em not all there—a little man and fat woman straight off a postcard! Oh, and I've a surprise for you."

"Oh?"

"When you're up," I smiled. I was talking about the white kid. Tonight or tomorrow morning I'd show it to her.

Feeling a bit let down—not by Julie but by circumstances in general, even by the atmosphere of this place, which was somehow odd—I collected the sunscreen blanket and poles, marched resolutely back to the taverna. Dimitrios was serving drinks to the spinsters. The 'sunstruck' one had recovered a little, sipped Coke through a straw. George and his burden were nowhere to be seen. I sat down at one of the tables, and in a little while Dimitrios came over. This time I studied him more closely.

He was youngish, maybe thirty, thirty-five, tall if a little stooped. He was more swarthy peasant Greek than classical or cosmopolitan; his natural darkness, coupled with the shadow of his hat (which he wore even here in the shade), hid his face from any really close inspection. The one very noticeable thing about that face, however, was this: it didn't smile. That's something you get to expect in the islands, the flash of teeth. Even badly stained ones. But not Dimitrios's teeth.

His hands were burned brown, lean, almost scrawny. Be that as it may, I felt sure they'd be strong hands. As for his eyes: they were the sort that make you look away. I tried to stare at his face a little while, then looked away. I wasn't afraid, just concerned. But I didn't know what about.

"Drink?" he said, making it sound like 'dring'. "Melon? The melon he is free. I give. I grow plenty. You like him? And water? I bring half-melon and water."

He turned to go, but I stopped him. "Er, no!" I remembered the conversation of the spinsters, about the melon. "No melon, no water, thank you." I tried to smile at him, found it difficult. "I'll have a cold beer. Do you have bottled water? You know, in the big plastic bottles? And Coke? Two of each, for the refrigerator. OK?"

He shrugged, went off. There was this lethargy about him, almost a malaise. No, I didn't much care for him at all...

"Swim!" the excited voice of one of the spinsters reached me. "Right along there, at the end of the beach. Like yesterday. Where there's no one to peep."

God! You'll be lucky, I thought.

"Shh!" one of her sisters hushed her, as if a crowd of rapacious men were listening to every word. "Don't tell the whole world, Betty!"

A Greek girl, Dimitrios's sister or wife, came out of the house carrying a plastic bag. She came to my table, smiled at me—a little nervously, I thought. "The water, the Coke," she said, making each definite article sound like 'thee'. *But at least she can speak my language,* I had to keep reminding myself. "Four hundred drachmas, please," she said. I nodded and paid up. About two pounds sterling. Cheap, considering it all had to be brought from the mainland. The bag and the bottles inside it were tingling cold in my hand.

I stood up—and the girl was still there, barring my way. The three sisters made off down the beach, and there was no one else about. The girl glanced over her shoulder toward the house. The hand she put on my arm was trembling and now I could see that it wasn't just nervousness. She was afraid.

"Mister," she said, the word very nearly sticking in her dry throat. She swallowed and tried again. "Mister, please. I—"

"Elli!" a low voice called. In the doorway to the house, dappled by splashes of sunlight through the vines, Dimitrios.

"Yes?" I answered her. "Is there—?"

"*Elli!*" he called again, an unspoken warning turning the word to a growl.

"Is all right," she whispered, her pretty face suddenly thin and pale. "Is—nothing!" And then she almost ran back to the house.

Weirder and weirder! But if they had some husband-and-wife thing going, it was no business of mine. I'm no Clint Eastwood—and they're a funny lot, the Greeks, in an argument.

On my way back to the chalet, I looked again into the garden. The figure in black, head slumped on chest, sat there as before; it hadn't moved an inch. The sun had, though, and was burning more fiercely down on the drowsing figure in black. The white kid had got loose from its tether and was on its hind legs, eating amazing scarlet flowers out of their tub. "You'll get hell, mate," I muttered, "when he/she wakes up!"

There were a lot of flies about. I swatted at a cloud of the ugly, buzzing little bastards as I hurried, dripping perspiration, back to the chalet.

Inside, I took a long drink myself, then poured ice-cold water into one glass, Coke into another. I put both glasses on a bedside table within easy reach of Julie, stored the rest of the stuff in the fridge. She was asleep: bad belly complicated by a mild attack of sunstroke. I should have insisted that Nichos bring us right to the door. He could have, I was sure. Maybe he and Dimitrios had a feud or something going. But…Julie was sleeping peacefully enough, and the sweat was off her brow.

Someone tut-tutted, and I was surprised to find it was I. Hey!—this was supposed to be a holiday, wasn't it?

I sighed, took up my kit—including the gun—went back into the sun. On impulse I'd picked up the key. I turned it in the lock, withdrew it, stooped, and slid it under the door. She could come out, but no one could go in. If she wasn't awake when I got back, I'd simply hook the key out again with a twig.

But right now it was time for some serious fishing!

There was a lot of uneasiness building up inside me, but I put it all out of my head (what was it anyway but a set of unsettling events and queer coincidence?) and marched straight down to the sea. The beach was empty here, not a soul in sight. No, wrong: at the far end, near the foot of the second spur, two of the sisters splashed in the shallows in faded bathing costumes twenty years out of date, while the third one sat on the sand watching them. They were all of two or three hundred yards away, however, so I wouldn't be accused of ogling them.

In a little while I was outfitted, in the water, heading straight out to where the sandy bottom sloped off a little more steeply. At about eight or nine feet, I saw an octopus in his house of shells—a big one, too, all coiled pink tentacles and cat eyes wary—but in a little while I moved on. Normally I'd have taken him, gutted him and beaten the grease out of him, then handed him in to the local taverna for goodwill. But on this occasion that would be Dimitrios. Sod Dimitrios!

At about twelve feet the bottom levelled out. In all directions I saw an even expanse of golden, gently rippled sand stretching away: beautiful but boring. And not a fish in sight! Then…the silvery flash of a belly turned side-on—no, two of them, three!—caught my eye. Not on the bottom but on the surface. Grey mullet, and of course they'd seen me before I saw them. I followed their darting shapes anyway, straight out to sea as before.

In a little while a reef of dark, fretted rocks came in view. It seemed fairly extensive, ran parallel to the beach. There was some weed but not enough to interfere with visibility. And the water still only twelve to fifteen feet deep. Things were looking up.

If a man knows the habits of his prey, he can catch him, and I knew my business. The grey mullet will usually run, but if you can surprise him, startle him, he'll take cover. If no cover's available, then he just keeps on running, and he'll very quickly outpace any man. But here in this pock-marked reef, there *was* cover. To the fish, it would seem that the holes in the rocks were a refuge, but in fact they'd be a trap. I went after them with a will, putting everything I'd got into the chase.

Coming up fast behind the fish, and making all the noise I could, I saw a central school of maybe a dozen small ones, patrolled by three or four full-grown outriders. The latter had to be two-pounders if they were an ounce. They panicked, scattered; the smaller fish shot off in all directions, and their big brothers went to ground! Exactly as I'd hoped they would. Two into one outcrop of honey-combed rock, and two into another.

I trod water on the surface, getting my breath, making sure the rubbers of my gun weren't tangled with the loose line from the spear, keeping my eyes glued to the silvery grey shapes finning nervously to and fro in the hollow rocks. I picked my target, turned on end, thrust my legs up, and let my own weight drive me to the bottom; and as my impetus slowed, so I lined up on one of the two holes. Right on cue, one of the fish appeared. He never knew what hit him.

I surfaced, freed my vibrating prize from the trident where two of the tines had taken him behind the gills, hung him from a gill ring on my belt. By now his partner had made off, but the other pair of fish was still there in the second hole. I quickly reloaded, made a repeat performance. My first hunt of the season, and already I had two fine fish! I couldn't wait to get back and show them to Julie.

I was fifty yards out. Easing the strain on muscles that were a whole year out of practice, I swam lazily back to the beach and came ashore close to the taverna. Way along the beach, two of the sisters were putting their dresses on over their ancient costumes, while the third sat on the sand with her head lolling. Other than these three, no one else was in sight.

I made for the chalet. As I went, the sun steamed the water off me and I began to itch; it was time I took a shower, and I might try a little protective after-sun lotion, too. Already my calves were turning red, and I supposed my back must be in the same condition. Ugly now, but in just a few days' time...

Passing the garden behind the house, this time I didn't look in. The elderly person under the tree would be gone by now, I was sure; but I did hear the lonely bleating of the kid.

Then I saw Dimitrios. He was up on the roof of the central chalet, and from where I padded silently between the olives, I could see him lifting a metal hatch on a square water tank. The roofs were also equipped with solar panels. So the sun heated the water, but...where did the water come from? Idiot question, even to oneself! From a well, obviously. But which well?

I passed under the cover of a clump of trees, and the Greek was lost to sight. When I came out again into the open, I saw him descending a ladder propped against the chalet's wall. He carried a large galvanized bucket—empty, to judge from its swing and bounce. He hadn't seen me, and for some hard-to-define reason, I didn't want him to. I ran the rest of the way to our chalet.

The door was open; Julie was up and about in shorts and a halter. She greeted me with a kiss, *oohed* and *aahed* at my catch. "Supper," I told her with something of pride. "No moussaka tonight. Fresh fish done over charcoal, with a little Greek salad and a filthy great bottle of retsina—or maybe two filthy great bottles!"

I cleaned the fish into the toilet, flushed their guts away. Then I washed them, tossed some ice into the sink unit, and put the fish in the ice. I didn't want them to stiffen up in the fridge, and they'd keep well enough in the sink for a couple of hours.

"Now you stink of fish," Julie told me without ceremony. "Your forearms are covered in scales. Take a shower and you'll feel great. I did."

"Are you OK?" I held her with my eyes.

"Fine now, yes," she said. "System flushed while you were out—you don't wish to know that—and now the old tum's settled down nicely, thank you. It was just the travel, the sun—"

"The moussaka?"

"That, too, probably." She sighed. "I just wish I didn't love it so!"

I stripped and stepped into the shower basin, fiddled with the knobs. "What'll you do while I shower?"

"Turn 'em both on full," she instructed. "Hot and cold both. Then the temperature's just right. Me? I'll go and sit in the shade by the sea, start a book."

"In the taverna?" Maybe there was something in the tone of my voice.

"Yes. Is that OK?"

"Fine," I told her, steeling myself and spinning the taps on. I didn't want to pass my apprehension on to her. "I'll see you there—*ahh!*—shortly." And after that, for the next ten minutes, it was hissing, stinging jets of water and blinding streams of medicated shampoo...

Towelling myself dry, I heard the clattering on the roof. Maintenance? Dimitrios and his galvanized bucket? I dressed quickly in lightweight flannels and a shirt, flip-flops on my feet, went out, and locked the door. Other places like this, we'd left the door open. Here I locked it. At the back of the chalet, Dimitrios was coming down his ladder. I came round the corner as he stepped down. If anything, he'd pulled his hat even lower over his eyes, so that his face was just a blot of shadow with two faint smudges of light for eyes. He was lethargic as ever, possibly even more so. We stood looking at each other.

"Trouble?" I eventually ventured.

Almost imperceptibly, he shook his head. "No troubles," he said, his voice a gurgle. "I just see all OK." He put his bucket down, wiped his hands on his trousers.

"And is it?" I took a step closer. "I mean, is it all OK?"

He nodded and at last grinned. Briefly a bar of whiteness opened in the shadow of his hat. "Now is OK," he said. And he picked up his bucket and moved off away from me.

Surly bastard! I thought. And: *What a dump! God, but we've slipped up this time, Julie, my love!*

I started toward the taverna, remembered I had no cigarettes with me, and returned to the chalet. Inside, in the cool and shade, I wondered what Dimitrios had been putting in the water tanks. Some chemical solution, maybe? To purify or purge the system? Well, I didn't want my system purified, not by Dimitrios. I flushed the toilet again. And I left the shower running full blast for all of five minutes before spinning the taps back to the off position. I would have done the same to the sink unit, but my fish were in there, the ice almost completely melted away. And emptying another tray of ice into the sink, I snapped my fingers: *Hah!* A blow for British eccentricity!

By the time I got to the taverna, Dimitrios had disappeared, probably inside the house. He'd left his bucket standing on the garden wall. Maybe it was simple curiosity, maybe something else; I don't know—but I looked into the bucket. Empty. I began to turn away, looked again. No, not empty, but almost. Only a residue remained. At the bottom of the bucket, a thin film of…jelly? That's what it looked like: grey jelly.

I began to dip a finger. Hesitated, thought: *What the hell! It's nothing harmful.* It couldn't be, or he wouldn't be putting it in the water tanks. Would he? I snorted at my mind's morbid fancies. Surly was one thing, but homicidal—?

I dipped, held my finger up to the sun where that great blazing orb slipped down toward the plateau's rim. Squinting, I saw…just a blob of goo. Except—black dots were moving in it, like microscopic tadpoles.

Urgh! I wiped the slime off my finger onto the rough concrete of the wall. Wrong bucket, obviously, for something had gone decidedly wrong in this one. Backing uncertainly away, I heard the doleful bleating of the white kid.

Across the garden, he was chewing on the frayed end of a rope hanging from the corner of a tarpaulin where it had been thrown roughly over the chair under the olive tree. The canvas had peaked in the middle, so that it seemed someone with a pointed head was still sitting there. I stared hard, felt a tic starting up at the corner of my eye. And suddenly I knew that I didn't want to be here. I didn't want it one little bit. And I wanted Julie to be here even less.

Coming round the house to the seating area under the vines, it became noisily apparent that I wasn't the only disenchanted person around here. An angry, booming female voice, English, seemed matched against a chattering wall of machine-gun-fire Greek. I stepped quickly in under the vines and saw Julie sitting in the shade at the ocean's edge, facing the sea. A book lay open on her table. She looked back over her shoulder, saw me, and even though she wasn't involved in the exchange, still relief flooded over her face.

I went to her, said, "What's up?" She looked past me, directing her gaze toward the rear of the seating area.

In the open door of the house, Dimitrios made a hunched silhouette, stiff as a petrified tree stump; his wife was a pale shadow behind him, in what must be the kitchen. Facing the Greek, George's wife stood with her fists on her hips, jaw jutting. "How *dare* you?" she cried, outraged at something or other. "What do you mean, you can't help? No phone? Are you actually telling me there's no telephone? Then how are we to contact civilization? I have to speak to someone in the town, find a doctor. My husband, George, *needs* a doctor! Can't you understand that? His lumps are moving. *Things are alive under his skin!*"

I heard all of this, but failed to take it in at once. George's lumps moving? Did she mean they were spreading? And still, Dimitrios stood there, while his wife squalled shrilly at him (at *him*, yes, not at George's wife as I'd first thought) and tried to squeeze by him. Whatever was going on here, someone had to do something, and it looked like I was the one.

"Sit tight," I told Julie, and I walked up behind the furious fat lady. "Something's wrong with George?" I said.

All eyes turned in my direction. I still couldn't see Dimitrios's face too clearly, but I sensed a sudden wariness in him. George's wife pounced on me. "Do you know George?" she said, grasping my arm. "Oh, of course! I saw you talking to him when I was in the sea."

I gently prized her sweaty, iron-band fingers from my arm. "His lumps?" I pressed. "Do you mean those swollen stings of his? Are they worse?"

"Stings?" I could see now that her hysteria had brought her close to the point of tears. "Is that what they are? Well, God only knows what stung him! Some of them are opening, and there's movement in the wounds! And George just lies there, without the will to do anything. He must be in agony, but he says he can't feel a thing. There's something terribly wrong…"

"Can I see him?"

"Are you a doctor?" She grabbed me again.

"No, but if I could see how bad it is—"

"—A waste of *time*!" she cut me off. "He needs a doctor now!"

"I take you to Makelos." Dimitrios had apparently snapped out of his rigor mortis mode, taken a jerky step toward us. "I take, find doctor, come back in taxi."

She turned to him. "Will you? Oh, *will* you, really? Thank you, oh, thank you! But…*how* will you take me?"

"Come," he said. They walked round the building to the rear, followed the wall until it ended, crossed the scrub to a clump of olives, and disappeared into the trees. I went with them part of the way, then watched them out of sight: Dimitrios stiff as a robot, never looking back, and Mrs George rumbling along massively behind him. A moment later there came the clattering and banging of an engine, and his three-wheeler bumped into view. It made for the packed-dirt incline to the road where it wound up the spur. Inside, Dimitrios at the wheel behind a flyspecked windscreen, almost squeezed into the corner of the tiny cab by the fat lady where she hunched beside him.

Julie had come up silently behind me. I gave a start when she said: "Do you think we should maybe go and see if this George is OK?"

I took a grip of myself, shrugged, said: "I was speaking to him just—oh, an hour and a half ago. He can't have got really bad in so short a time, can he? A few horsefly bites, he had. Nasty enough, but you'd hardly consider them as serious as all that. She's just got herself a bit hot and bothered, that's all."

Quite suddenly, shadows reached down to us from the high brown and purple walls of the plateau. The sun had commenced to sink behind the island's central hump. In a moment it was degrees cooler, so that I found myself shivering. In that same moment the cicadas stopped their frying-fat onslaught of sound, and a strange silence fell over the whole place. On impulse, quietly, I said: "We're out of here tomorrow."

That was probably a mistake. I hadn't wanted to get Julie going. She'd been in bed most of the time; she hadn't experienced the things I had, hadn't felt so much of the strangeness here. Or maybe she had, for now she said: "Good," and gave a little shudder of her own. "I was going to suggest just that. I'm sure we can find cheap lodging in Makelos. And this place is such—I don't know—such a dead and alive hole! I mean, it's beautiful—but it's also very ugly. There's just something morbid about it."

"Listen," I said, deciding to lighten the atmosphere if I could. "I'll tell you what we'll do. You go back to the taverna, and I'll go get the fish. We'll have the Greek girl cook them for us and dish them up with a little salad—and a bottle of retsina, as we'd planned. Maybe things will look better after a bite to eat, eh? Is your tummy up to it?"

She smiled faintly in the false dusk, leaned forward, and gave me a kiss. "You know," she said, "whenever you start worrying about me—and using that tone of voice—I always know that there's something you're worrying about yourself. But actually, you know, I do feel quite hungry!"

The shadows had already reached the taverna. Just shadows—in no way night, for it wasn't properly evening yet, though certainly the contrast was a sort of darkness—and beyond them the vast expanse of the sea was blue as ever, sparkling silver at its rim in the brilliant sunlight still striking there. The strangeness of the place seemed emphasized, enlarged…

I watched Julie turn right and disappear into the shade of the vines, and then I went for our fish.

The real nightmare began when I let myself into the chalet and went to the sink unit. Doubly shaded, the interior really was quite dark. I put on the light in the arched-over alcove that was the kitchen, and picked up the two fish, one in each hand—and dropped them, or rather tossed them back into the sink! The ice was all melted; the live-looking glisten of the scales had disappeared with the ice, and the mullets themselves had been—infected!

Attached to the gill flap of one of them, I'd seen a parasite exactly like the ones on the big grouper; the second fish had had one of the filthy things clamped half over a filmed eye. My hair actually prickled on my head; my scalp tingled; my lips drew back from my teeth in a silent snarl. The things were something like sheep ticks, in design if not in dimension, but they were pale, blind, spiky, and looked infinitely more loathsome. They were only—crustaceans? Insects? I couldn't be sure—but there was that about them which made them more horrific to me than any creature has a right to be.

Anyone who believes you can't go cold, break out in gooseflesh, on a hot, late afternoon in the Mediterranean is mistaken. I went so cold I was shaking, and I kept on shaking for long moments, until it dawned on me that just a few seconds ago, I'd actually handled these fish!

Christ!

I turned on the hot tap, thrust my hands forward to receive the cleansing stream, snatched them back again. God, no! I couldn't wash them, for Dimitrios had been up there putting something in the tank! Some kind of spawn. But that didn't make sense: hot water would surely kill the things. If there was any hot water...

The plumbing rattled, but no hot water came. Not only had Dimitrios interfered with the water, introduced something into it, but he'd also made sure that from now on we could use only the *cold* water!

I wiped my trembling hands thoroughly on sheets from a roll of paper towel, filled the kettle with water from a refrigerated bottle, quickly brought the water toward boiling. Before it became unbearable, I gritted my teeth, poured a little hot water first over one hand, then the other. It stung like hell, and the flesh of my hands went red at once, but I just hugged them and let them sting. Then, when the water was really boiling, I poured the rest of the contents of the kettle over the fish in the sink.

By that time the parasites had really dug themselves in. The one attached to the gill flap had worked its way under the gill, making it bulge; the other had dislodged its host's eye and was half-way into the skull. Worse, another had clawed its way up the plughole and was just now emerging into the light! The newcomer was white, whereas the others were now turning pink from the ingestion of fish juices.

But up from the plughole? This set me shuddering again; and again I wondered: *what's down there, down in the slop under the ground? Where does everything go?*

These fish had been clean when I caught them; I'd gutted them, and so I ought to know. But their scent had drawn these things up to the feast. Would the scent of human flesh attract them the same way?

As the boiling water hit them, the things popped like crabs tossed into a cooking pot. They seemed to hiss and scream, but it was just the rapid expansion and explosion of their tissues. And the stench that rose up from the sink was nauseating. God!—would I ever eat fish again?

And the thought kept repeating over and over in my head: what was down below?

I went to the shower recess, put on the light, looked in, and at once shrank back. The sunken bowl of the shower was crawling with them! Two, three dozen of them at least. And the toilet? And the cold-water system? And all the rest of the bloody plumbing? There'd be a cesspit down there, and these things were alive in it in their thousands! And the maniac Dimitrios had been putting their eggs in the water tanks!

But what about the spinsters? They had been here before us, probably for the past three or four days at least. And what about George? George and his lumps! And Julie: she wouldn't have ordered anything yet, would she! She wouldn't have *eaten* anything!

I left the door of the chalet slamming behind me, raced for the taverna.

The sun was well down now, with the bulk of the central mountain throwing all of the eastern coastline into shadow; halfway to the horizon, way out to sea, the sun's light was a line ruled across the ocean, beyond which silver-flecked blueness seemed to reach up to the sky. And moment by moment the ruled line of deeper blue flowed eastward as the unseen sun dipped even lower. On the other side of the island, the west coast, it would still be sweltering hot, but here it was noticeably cooler. Or maybe it was just my blood.

As I drew level with the garden at the back of the house, something came flopping over the wall at me. I hadn't been looking in that direction or I'd have seen her: Julie, panic-stricken, her face a white mask of horror. She'd seemed to fly over the wall—jumped or simply bundled herself over I couldn't say—and came hurtling into my arms. Nor had she seen me, and she fought with me a moment when I held her. Then we both caught our breath, or at least I did. Julie had a harder time of it. Even though I'd never heard her scream before, there was one building up in her, and I knew it.

I shook her, which served to shake me a little, too, then hugged her close. "What were you doing in the garden?" I asked, when she'd started to breathe again. I spoke in a whisper, and that was how she answered me, but drawing breath raggedly between each burst of words:

"The little goat...he was bleating...so pitifully...frightened! I heard him...went to see...got in through a gate on the other side." She paused and took a deep breath. "Oh *God*, Jim!"

I knew without asking. A picture of the slumped figure in the chair, under the olive tree, had flashed momentarily on my mind's eye. But I asked anyway: "The tarpaulin?"

She nodded, gulped. "Something had to be dead under there. I had no idea it would be a…a…a man!"

"English?" That was a stupid question, so I tried again: "I mean, did he look like a tourist, a holiday maker?"

She shook her head. "An old Greek, I think. But there are—*ugh!*— these things all over him. Like…like—"

"Like crabs?"

She drew back from me, her eyes wide, terror replaced by astonishment. "How did you know that?"

Quickly, I related all I knew. As I was finishing, her hand flew to her mouth. "Dimitrios? Putting their eggs in the tanks? But Jim, we've taken showers—both of us!"

"Calm down," I told her. "We had our showers *before* I saw him up there. And we haven't eaten here, or drunk any of the water."

"Eaten?" her eyes opened wider still. "But if I hadn't heard the kid bleating, I might have eaten!"

"What?"

She nodded. "I ordered wine and…some melon. I thought we'd have it before the fish. But the Greek girl dropped it, and—"

She was rapidly becoming incoherent. I grabbed her again, held her tightly. "Dropped it? You mean she dropped the food?"

"She dropped the melon, yes." She nodded jerkily. "The bottle of wine, too. She came out of the kitchen and just let everything drop. It all smashed on the floor. And she stood there wringing her hands for a moment. Then she ran off. She was crying: 'Oh Dimitrios, Dimitrios!'"

"I think he's crazy," I told her. "He has to be. And his wife—or sister, or whatever she is—she's scared to death of him. You say she ran off? Which way?"

"Toward the town, the way we came. I saw her climbing the spur."

I hazarded a guess: "He's pushed her to the edge, and she's slipped over. Come on, let's go and have a look at Dimitrios's kitchen."

We went to the front of the building, to the kitchen door. There on the floor by one of the tables, I saw a broken wine bottle, its dark red contents spilled. Also a half-melon, lying in several softly jagged chunks. And in the melon, crawling in its scattered seeds and pulpy red juices—

"Where are the others?" I said, wanting to speak first before Julie could cry out, trying to forestall her.

"Others?" she whispered. She hadn't really heard me, hadn't even been listening; she was concentrating on backing away from the half-dozen crawling things that moved blindly on the floor.

I stamped on them, crushed them in a frenzy of loathing, then scuffed the soles of my flip-flops on the dusty concrete floor as if I'd stepped in something nasty—which is one hell of an understatement. "The other people," I said. "The three sisters and...and George." I was talking more to myself than to Julie, and my voice was hoarse.

My fear transferred itself instantly. "Oh Jim, Jim!" she cried. She threw herself into my arms, shivering as if in a fever. And I felt utterly useless—no, defenceless—a sensation I'd occasionally known in deep water, without my gun, when the shadow of a rock might suddenly take on the aspect of a great, menacing fish.

Then there came one of the most dreadful sounds I've ever heard in my life: the banging and clattering of Dimitrios's three-wheeler on the road cut into the spur, echoing down to us from the rocks of the mountainside. "My spear gun," I said. "Come on, quickly!"

She followed at arm's length, half running, half dragged. "We're too vulnerable," I gasped as we reached the chalet. "Put clothes on, anything. Cover up your skin."

"What?" She was still dazed. "What?"

"*Cover yourself!*" I snapped. Then I regained control. "Look, he tried to give us these things. He gave them to George, and to the sisters for all I know. And he may try again. Do you want one of those things on your flesh, maybe laying its eggs in you?"

She emptied a drawer onto the floor, found slacks, and pulled them on; good shoes, too, to cover her feet. I did much the same: pulled on a long-sleeved pullover, rammed my feet into decent shoes. And all in a sort of frenzied blur, fingers all thumbs, heart thumping. And: "*Oh shit!*" she sobbed. Which wasn't really my Julie at all.

"Eh?" She was heading for the small room at the back.

"Toilet!" she said. "I have to."

"*No!*" I jumped across the space between, dragged her away from the door to the toilet-*cum*-shower unit. "It's crawling with them in there. They come up the plugholes." In my arms, I could feel that she was also crawling. Her flesh. Mine, too. "If you must go, go outside. But first let's get away from here." I picked up my gun and checked its single flap-nosed spear.

Leaving the chalet, I looked across at the ramp coming down from the rocky spur. The clatter of Dimitrios's three-wheeler was louder, it was there, headlight beams bobbing as the vehicle trundled lurchingly down the rough decline. "Where are we going?" Julie gasped, following me at a run across the scrub between clumps of olives. I headed for the other chalets.

"Safety in numbers," I answered. "Anyway, I want to know about George, and those three old spinsters."

"What good will they be, if they're old?" She was too logical by half.

"They're not that old." Mainly, I wanted to see if they were all right. Apart from the near-distant racket Dimitrios's vehicle was making, the whole valley was quiet as a tomb. Unnaturally quiet. It had to be a damned funny place in Greece where the cicadas keep their mouths shut.

Julie had noticed that too. "They're not singing," she said. And I knew what she meant.

"Rubbing," I answered. "They rub their legs together or something."

"Well," she panted, "whatever it is they do, they're not."

It was true evening now, and a half-moon had come up over the central mountain's southern extreme. Its light silvered our way through thorny shrubs and tall, spiked grasses, under the low grey branches of olives and across their tangled, groping roots.

We came to the first chalet. Its lights were out, but the door stood ajar. "I think this is where George is staying," I said. And calling ahead: "George, are you in?", I entered and switched on the light. He was in—in the big double bed, stretched out on his back. But he turned his head toward us as we entered. He blinked in the sudden, painful light. One of his eyes did, anyway. The other couldn't...

He stirred himself, tried to sit up. I think he was grinning. I can't be sure, because one of the things, a big one, was inside the corner of his mouth. They were hatching from fresh lumps down his neck and in the bend of his elbow. God knows what the rest of his body was like. He managed to prop himself up, hold out a hand to me—and I almost took it. And it was then that I began to understand something of the nature of these things. For there was one of them in his open palm, its barbed feet seeming poised, waiting.

I snatched back my hand, heard Julie's gasp. And there she was, backed up against the wall, screaming her silent scream. I grabbed her, hugged her, dragged her outside. For of course there was nothing we could do for George. And, afraid she would scream, and maybe start *me* going, I slapped her. And off we went again, reeling in the direction of the third and last chalet.

Down by the taverna, Dimitrios's three-wheeler had come to a halt, its engine stilled, its beams dim, reaching like pallid hands along the sand. But I didn't think it would be long before he was on the move again. And the nightmare was expanding, growing vaster with every beat of my thundering heart.

In the third chalet...it's hard to describe all I saw. Maybe there's no real need. The spinster I'd thought was maybe missing something was in much the same state as George; she, too, was in bed, with those god-awful things hatching in her. Her sisters...at first I thought they were both dead, and...But there, I've gone ahead of myself. That's how it always happens when I think about it, try to reconstruct it again in my own mind: it speeds up until I've outstripped myself. You have to understand that the whole thing was kaleidoscopic.

I went inside ahead of Julie, got a quick glimpse, an indistinct picture of the state of things fixed in my brain—then turned and kept Julie from coming in. "Watch for him." I forced the words around my bobbing Adam's apple and returned to take another look. I didn't want to, but I thought the more we knew about this monster, the better we'd know how to deal with him. Except that in a little while, I guessed there would be only one possible way to deal with him.

The sister in the bed moved and lolled her head a little; I was wary, suspicious of her, and left her strictly alone. The other two had been attacked. With an axe or a machete or something. One of them lay behind the door, the other on the floor on the near side of the bed. The one behind the door had been sliced twice, deeply, across the neck and chest and lay in a pool of her own blood, which was already congealing. Tick-things, coming from the bathroom, had got themselves stuck in the darkening pool, their barbed legs twitching when they tried to extricate themselves. The other sister...

Senses swimming, throat bobbing, I stepped closer to the bed with its grimacing, hag-ridden occupant, and I bent over the one on the floor. She was still alive, barely. Her green dress was a sodden red under the rib cage, torn open in a jagged flap to reveal her gaping wound. And Dimitrios had dropped several of his damned pets onto her, which were burrowing in the raw, dark flesh.

She saw me through eyes already filming over, whispered something. I got down on one knee beside her, wanted to hold her hand, stroke her hair, do something. But I couldn't. I didn't want those bloody things on me. "It's all right," I said. "It's all right." But we both knew it wasn't.

"The...the Greek," she said, her voice so small I could scarcely hear it.

"I know, I know," I told her.

"We wanted to...to take Flo into town. She was...was so *ill*! He said to wait here. We waited, and...and..." She gave a deep sigh. Her eyes rolled up, and her mouth fell open.

Something touched my shoulder where I knelt, and I leapt erect, flesh tingling. The one on the bed, Flo, had flopped an arm in my direction—deliberately! Her hand had touched me. Crawling slowly down her arm, a trio of the nightmare ticks or crabs had been making for me. They'd been homing in on me like a bee targeting a flower. But more slowly, thank God, far more slowly.

Horror froze me rigid; but in the next moment, Julie's sobbing cry—"Jim, he's coming!"—unfroze me at once.

I staggered outside. A dim, slender, dark and reeling shape was making its way along the rough track between the chalets. Something glinted dully in his hand. Terror galvanized me. "Head for the high ground," I said. I took Julie's hand, began to run.

"High ground?" she panted. "Why?" She was holding together pretty well. I thanked God I hadn't let her see inside the chalet.

"Because then we'll have the advantage. He'll have to come up at us. Maybe I can roll rocks down on him or something."

"You have your gun," she said.

"As a last resort," I told her, "yes. But this isn't a John Wayne Western, Julie. This is real! Shooting a man isn't the same as shooting a fish..." And we scrambled across the rough scrubland toward the goat track up the far spur. Maybe ten minutes later and halfway up that track, suddenly it dawned on both of us just where we were heading. Julie dug in her heels and dragged me to a halt.

"But the cave's up there!" she panted. "The well!"

I looked all about. The light was difficult, made everything seem vague and unreal. Dusk is the same the world over: it confuses shapes, distances, colours and textures. On our right, scree rising steeply all the way to the plateau: too dangerous by far. And on our left a steep, in places sheer, decline to the valley's floor. All you had to do was stumble once, and you wouldn't stop sliding and tumbling and bouncing till you hit the bottom. Up ahead the track was moon-silvered, to the place where the cliff over-hung, where the shadows were black and blacker than night. And behind...behind us came Dimitrios, his presence made clear by the sound his boots made shoving rocks and pebbles out of his way.

"Come on," I said, starting on up again.

"But where to?" Hysteria was in her whisper.

"That clump of rocks there." Ahead, on the right, weathered out of the scree, a row of long boulders like leaning graveyard slabs tilted at the moon. I got between two of them, pulled Julie off the track, and jammed her behind me. It was last-ditch stuff; there was no way out other than the way we'd come in. I loaded my gun, hauling on the propulsive rubbers until the spear was engaged. And then there was nothing else to do but wait.

"Now be quiet," I hissed, crouching down. "He may not see us, go straight on by."

Across the little valley, headlights blazed. Then came the echoing roar of revving engines. A moment more, and I could identify humped silhouettes making their way like beetles down the ridge of the far spur toward the indigo sea, then slicing the gloom with scythes of light as they turned onto the dirt ramp. Two cars and a motorcycle. Down on the valley's floor, they raced for the taverna.

Dimitrios came struggling out of the dusk, up out of the darkness, his breathing loud, laboured, gasping as he climbed in our tracks. His silhouette where he paused for breath was scarecrow-lean, and he'd lost his floppy, wide-brimmed hat. But I suspected a strength in him that wasn't entirely his own. From where she peered over my shoulder Julie had spotted him too. I heard her sharp intake of breath, breathed "*Shh!*" so faintly I wasn't even sure she'd hear me.

He came on, the thin moonlight turning his eyes yellow, and turning his machete silver. Level with the boulders he drew, and almost level with our hiding place, and paused again. He looked this way and that, cocked his head, and listened. Behind me, Julie was trembling. She trembled so hard I was sure it was coming right through me, through the rocks, too, and the earth, and right through the soles of his boots to Dimitrios.

He took another two paces up the track, came level with us. Now he stood out against the sea and the sky, where the first pale stars were beginning to switch themselves on. He stood there, looking up the slope toward the cave under the cliff, and small, dark silhouettes were falling from the large blot of his head. Not droplets of sweat, no, for they were far too big, and too brittle-sounding when they landed on the loose scree.

Again Julie snatched a breath, and Dimitrios's head slowly came round until he seemed to be staring right at us.

Down in the valley the cars and the motorcycle were on the move again, engines revving, headlight beams slashing here and there. There was some shouting. Lights began to blaze in the taverna, the chalets. Flashlights cut narrow searchlight swaths in the darkness.

Dimitrios seemed oblivious to all this; still looking in our direction, he scratched at himself under his right armpit. His actions rapidly became frantic, until with a soft, gurgling cry, he tore open his shirt. He let his machete fall clatteringly to the track and clawed wildly at himself with both hands! He was shedding tick-things as a dog sheds fleas. He tore open his trousers, dropped them, staggered as he stepped out of them. Agonized sulphur eyes burned yellow in his blot of a face as he tore at his thighs.

I saw all of this, every slightest action. And so did Julie. I felt her swell up behind me, scooping in air until she must surely burst—and then she let it out again. But silently, screaming like a maniac in the night—and nothing but air escaping her!

A rock slid away from under my foot, its scrape a deafening clatter to my petrified mind. The sound froze Dimitrios, too—but only for a moment. Then he stooped, regained his machete. He took a pace toward us, inclined his head. He couldn't see us yet, but he knew we were there. Then—*God*, I shall dream of this for the rest of my life!—

He reached down a hand and stripped a handful of living, crawling filth from his loins, and lobbed it in our direction as casually as tossing crumbs to starveling birds!

The next five seconds were madness.

I stumbled out from cover, lifted my gun, and triggered it. The spear struck him just below the rib cage, went deep into him. He cried out, reeled back, and yanked the gun from my hand. I'd forgotten to unfasten the nylon cord from the spear. Behind me, Julie was crumpling to the ground; I was aware of the latter, turned to grab her before she could sprawl. There were tick-things crawling about, and I mustn't let her fall on them.

I got her over my shoulder in a fireman's lift, went charging out onto the track, skipping and stamping my feet, roaring like a maddened bull. And I was mad: mad with shock, terror, loathing. I stamped and kicked and danced, never letting my feet stay in one place for more than a fraction of a second, afraid something would climb up onto me. And the wonder is I didn't carry both of us flying down the steep scree slope to the valley's floor.

Dimitrios was halfway down the track when I finally got myself under a semblance of control. Bouncing toward our end of the valley, a car came crunching and lurching across the scrub. I fancied it was Nichos's taxi. And sure enough, when the car stopped and its headlight beams were still, Nichos's voice came echoing up, full of concerned enquiry:

"Mister, lady—you OK?"

"Look out!" I shouted at the top of my voice, but only at the second attempt. "He's coming down! Dimitrios is coming down!"

And now I went more carefully, as in my mind the danger receded, and in my veins the adrenalin raced less rapidly. Julie moaned where she flopped loosely across my shoulder, and I knew she'd be all right.

The valley seemed alight with torches now, and not only the electric sort. Considering these people were Greeks, they seemed remarkably well organized. That was a thought I'd keep in mind, something else I would have to ask about. There was some shouting down there, too, and flaring torches began to converge on the area at the foot of the goat track.

Then there echoed up to me a weird, gurgled cry: a cry of fear, protestation—relief? A haunting, sobbing shriek—cut off at highest pitch by the dull boom of a shot fired, and a moment later by a blast that was the twin of the first. From twin barrels, no doubt.

When I got down, Julie was still out of it, for which I was glad. They'd poured gasoline over Dimitrios's body and set fire to it. Fires were burning everywhere: the chalets, taverna, gardens. Cleansing flames leaping. Figures moved in the smoke and against a yellow roaring background, searching, burning. And I sat in the back of Nichos's taxi, cradling Julie's head. Mercifully, she remained unconscious right through it.

Even with the windows rolled up, I could smell something of the smoke, and something that wasn't smoke…

In Makelos town, Julie began to stir. I asked for her to be sedated, kept down for the night. Then, when she was sleeping soundly and safely in a room at the mayor's house, I began asking questions. I was furious at the beginning, growing more furious as I started to get the answers.

I couldn't be sorry for the people of Makelos, though I did feel something for Elli, Dimitrios's wife. She'd run to Nichos, told him what was happening. And he'd alerted the townspeople. Elli had been a sort of prisoner at the taverna for the past ten days or so, after her husband had 'gone funny'. Then, when she'd started to notice things, he'd told her to keep quiet and carry on as normal, or she'd be the loser. And he meant she'd lose all the way. She reckoned he'd got the parasites off the goats, accidentally, and she was probably right, for the goats had been the first to die. Her explanation was likely because the goats used to go up there sometimes, to the cave under the mountain. And that was where the things bred, in that cave and in the well it contained, which now and then overflowed, and found its way to the sea.

But Elli, poor peasant that she was: on her way to alert Nichos, she'd seen her husband kill George's wife and push her over the cliffs into the sea. Then she'd hid herself off the road until he'd turned his three-wheeler round and started back toward the taverna.

As for the corpse under the tarpaulin: that was Dimitrios's grandfather, who along with his grandson had been a survivor of the first outbreak. He'd been lucky that time, not so lucky this time.

And the tick things? They were...a *disease*, but they could never be a plague. The men from Athens had taken some of them away with them that first time. But away from their well, away from the little shaded valley and from Makelos, they'd quickly died. This was their place, and they could exist nowhere else. Thank God!

Last time the chemicals hadn't killed them off, obviously, or maybe a handful of eggs had survived to hatch out when the poisons had dissolved away. For they *were* survivors, these creatures, the last of their species, and when they went, their secret would go with them. But a disease? I believe so, yes.

Like the common cold, or rabies, or any other disease, but far worse because they're visible, apparent. The common cold makes you sneeze, so that the disease is propagated, and hydrophobia makes its victims claw and bite, gets passed on in their saliva. The secret of the tick-things was much the same sort of thing: they made their hosts pass them on. It was the way their intelligent human hosts did it that made them so much more terrible.

In the last outbreak, only Greeks—Makelosians—had been involved; this time it was different. This time, too, the people would take care of the problem themselves: they'd pour hundreds of gallons of gasoline and fuel oil into the well, set the place on fire. And then they'd dynamite the cliff, bring it down to choke the well for ever, and they'd never, *ever*, let people go into that little valley again. That was their promise, but I'd made myself a couple of promises, too. I was angry and frightened, and I knew I was going to stay that way for a long time to come.

We were out of there first thing in the morning, on the first boat to the mainland. There were smart-looking men to meet us at the airport in Athens, Greek officials from some ministry or other. They had interpreters with them, and nothing was too much trouble. They, too, made promises, offers of compensation, anything our hearts desired. We nodded and smiled wearily, said yes to this, that, and the other, anything so that we could just get aboard that plane. It had been our shortest holiday ever: we'd been in Greece just forty-eight hours, and all we wanted now was to be out of it as quickly as possible. But when we were back home again—*that* was when we told our story!

It was played down, of course: the Common Market, international tensions, a thousand other economic and diplomatic reasons. Which is why I'm now telling it all over again. I don't want anybody to suffer what we went through, what we're still going through. And so if you happen to be mad on the Mediterranean islands…well, I'm sorry, but that's the way it was.

As for Julie and me: we've moved away from the sea, and come summer, we won't be going out in the sun too much or for too long. That helps a little. But every now and then, I'll wake up in the night, in a cold sweat, and find Julie doing her horrible thing: nightmaring about Dimitrios, hiding from him, holding her breath so that he won't hear her—

—And sometimes screaming her silent screams…

THE PICNICKERS

This story comes from a long time ago. I was a boy, so that shows how long ago it was. Part of it is from memory, and the rest is a reconstruction built up over the years through times when I've given it a lot of thought, filling in the gaps; for I wasn't privy to everything that happened that time, which is perhaps as well. But I do know that I'm prone to nightmares, and I believe that this is where they have their roots, so maybe getting it down on paper is my rite of exorcism. I hope so.

The summers were good and hot in those days, and no use anyone telling me that that's just an old man speaking, who only remembers the good things; they *were* better summers! I could, and did, go down to the beach at Harden every day. I'd get burned black by the time school came around again at the end of the holidays. The only black you'd get on that beach these days would be from the coal dust. In fact there isn't a beach any more, just a sloping moonscape of slag from the pits, scarred by deep gulleys where polluted water gurgles down to a scummy, foaming black sea.

But at that time...men used to crab on the rocks when the tide was out, and cast for cod right off the sandbar where the small waves broke. And the receding sea would leave blue pools where we could swim in safety. Well, there's probably still sand down there, but it's ten foot deep under the strewn black guts of the mines, and the only pools now are pools of slurry.

It was summer when the gypsies came, the days were long and hot, and the beach was still a great drift of aching white sand.

Gypsies. They've changed, too, over the years. Now they travel in packs, motorized, in vehicles that shouldn't even be on the roads: furtive and scruffy, long-haired thieves who nobody wants and who don't much try to be wanted. Or perhaps I'm prejudiced. Anyway, they're not the real thing any more. But in those days they were. Most of them, anyway...

Usually they'd come in packets of three or four families, small communities plodding the roads in their intricately painted, hand-carved horse-drawn caravans, some with canvas roofs and some wooden; all brass and black leather, varnished wood and lacquered chimney-stacks, wrinkled brown faces and shiny brown eyes; with clothes pegs and various gewgaws, hammered trinkets and rings that would turn your fingers green, strange songs sung for halfpennies and fortunes told from the lines in your hand. And occasionally a curse if someone was bad to them and theirs.

My uncle was the local doctor. He'd lost his wife in the Great War and never remarried. She'd been a nurse and died somewhere on a battlefield in France. After the war he'd travelled a lot in Europe and beyond, spent years on the move, not wanting to settle. And when she was out of his system (not that she ever was, not really; her photographs were all over the house) then he had come home again to England, to the north-east where he'd been born. In the summers my parents would go down from Edinburgh to see him, and leave me there with him for company through the holidays.

This summer in question would be one of the last—of that sort, anyway—for the next war was already looming; of course, we didn't know that then.

"Gypsies, Sandy!" he said that day, just home from the mine where there'd been an accident. He was smudged with coal dust, which turned his sweat black where it dripped off him, with a pale band across his eyes and a white dome to his balding head from the protection of a miner's helmet.

"Gypsies?" I said, all eager. "Where?"

"Over in Slater's copse. Seen 'em as I came over the viaduct. One caravan at least. Maybe there'll be more later."

That was it: I was supposed to run now, over the fields to the copse, to see the gypsies. That way I wouldn't ask questions about the accident in the mine. Uncle Zachary didn't much like to talk about his work, especially if the details were unpleasant or the resolution an unhappy one. But I wanted to know anyway. "Was it bad, down the mine?"

He nodded, the smile slipping from his grimy face as he saw that I'd seen through his ruse. "A bad one, aye," he said. "A man's lost his legs and probably his life. I did what I could." Following which he hadn't wanted to say any more. And so I went off to see the gypsies.

Before I actually left the house, though, I ran upstairs to my attic room. From there, through the binoculars Uncle Zachary had given me for my birthday, I could see a long, long way. And I could even see if he'd been telling the truth about the gypsies, or just pulling my leg as he sometimes did, a simple way of distracting my attention from the accident. I used to sit for hours up there, using those binoculars through my dormer window, scanning the land all about.

To the south lay the colliery: "Harden Pit", as the locals called it. Its chimneys were like long, thin guns aimed at the sky; its skeletal towers with their huge spoked wheels turning, lifting or lowering the cages; and at night its angry red coke ovens roaring, discharging their yellow and white-blazing tonnage to be hosed down into mounds of foul-steaming coke.

Harden Pit lay beyond the viaduct with its twin lines of tracks glinting in the sunlight, shimmering in a heat haze. From here, on the knoll where Uncle Zachary's house stood—especially from my attic window—I could actually look down on the viaduct a little, see the shining tracks receding toward the colliery. The massive brick structure that supported them had been built when the collieries first opened up, to provide transport for the black gold, one viaduct out of many spanning the becks and streams of the north-east where they ran to the sea. "Black gold", they'd called coal even then, when it cost only a few shillings per hundredweight!

This side of the viaduct and towards the sea cliffs, there stood Slater's Copse, a close-grown stand of oaks, rowans, hawthorns and hazelnuts. Old Slater was a farmer who had sold up to the coal industry, but he'd kept back small pockets of land for his and his family's enjoyment, and for the enjoyment of everyone else in the colliery communities. Long after this whole area was laid to waste, Slater's patches of green would still be here, shady oases in the grey and black desert.

And in the trees of Slater's Copse...Uncle Zachary hadn't been telling stories after all! I could glimpse the varnished wood, the young shire horse between his shafts, the curve of a spoked wheel behind a fence.

And so I left the house, ran down the shrub-grown slope of the knoll and along the front of the cemetery wall, then straight through the grave-yard itself and the gate on the far side, and so into the fields with their paths leading to the new coast road on the one side and the viaduct on the other. Forsaking the paths, I forged through long grasses laden with pollen, leaving a smoky trail in my wake as I made for Slater's Copse and the gypsies.

Now, you might wonder why I was so taken with gypsies and gypsy urchins. But the truth is that even old Zachary in his rambling house wasn't nearly so lonely as me. He had his work, calls to make every day, and his surgery in Essingham five nights a week. But I had no one. With my 'posh' Edinburgh accent, I didn't hit it off with the colliery boys. Them with their hard, swaggering ways, and their harsh north-eastern twang. They called themselves 'Geordies', though they weren't from Newcastle at all; and me, I was an outsider. Oh, I could look after myself. But why fight them when I could avoid them? And so the gypsies and I had something in common: we didn't belong here. I'd played with the gypsies before.

But not with this lot.

Approaching the copse, I saw a boy my own age and a woman, probably his mother, taking water from a spring. They heard me coming, even though the slight summer breeze off the sea favoured me, and looked up. I waved...but their faces were pale under their dark cloth hats, where their eyes were like blots on old parchment. They didn't seem like my kind of gypsies at all. Or maybe they'd had trouble recently, or were perhaps expecting trouble. There was only one caravan and so they were one family on its own.

Then, out of the trees at the edge of the copse, the head of the family appeared. He was tall and thin, wore the same wide-brimmed cloth hat, looked out at me from its shade with eyes like golden triangular lamps. It could only have been a sunbeam, catching him where he stood with the top half of his body shaded; paradoxically, at the same time the sun had seemed to fade a little in the sky. But it was strange and I stopped moving forward, and he stood motionless, just looking. Behind him stood a girl, a shadow in the trees; and in the dappled gloom her eyes, too, were like candle-lit turnip eyes in October.

"Hallo!" I called from only fifty feet away. But they made no answer, turned their backs on me and melted back into the copse. So much for 'playing' with the gypsies! With this bunch, anyway. But...I could always try again later. When they'd settled in down here.

I went to the viaduct instead.

The viaduct both fascinated and frightened me at one and the same time. Originally constructed solely to accommodate the railway, with the addition of a wooden walkway it also provided miners who lived in one village but worked in the other with a shortcut to their respective collieries. On this side, a mile to the north, stood Essingham; on the other, lying beyond the colliery itself and inland a half-mile or so toward the metalled so-called 'coast road', Harden. The viaduct fascinated me because of the trains, shuddering and rumbling over its three towering arches, and scared me because of its vertiginous walkway.

The walkway had been built on the ocean-facing side of the viaduct, level with the railway tracks but separated from them by the viaduct's wall. It was of wooden planks protected on the otherwise open side by a fence of staves five feet high. Upward-curving iron arms fixed in brackets underneath held the walkway aloft, alone sustaining it against gravity's unending exertions. But they always looked dreadfully thin and rusty to me, those metal supports, and the vertical distance between them and the valley's floor seemed a terribly great one. In fact it was about one hundred and fifty feet. Not a *terrific* height, really, but it only takes a fifth of that to kill or maim a man if he falls.

I had an ambition: to walk across it from one end to the other. So far my best attempt had taken me a quarterway across before being forced back. The trouble was the trains. The whistle of a distant train was always sufficient to send me flying, heart hammering, racing to get off the walkway before the train got onto the viaduct! But this time I didn't even make it that far. A miner, hurrying towards me from the other side, recognized me and called: "Here, lad! Are you the young 'un stayin' with Zach Gardner?"

"Yes, sir," I answered as he stamped closer. He was in his 'pit black', streaked with sweat, his boots clattering on the wooden boards.

"Here," he said again, groping in a grimy pocket. "A threepenny bit!" He pressed the coin into my hand. "Now *run*! God knows you can go faster than me! Tell your uncle he's to come at once to Joe Anderson's. The ambulance men won't move him. Joe won't let them! He's delirious but he's hangin' on. We diven't think for long, though."

"The accident man?"

"Aye, that's him. Joe's at home. He says he can feel his legs but not the rest of his body. It'd be reet funny, that, if it wasn't so tragic. Bloody cages! He'll not be the last they trap! Now scramble, lad, d'you hear?"

I scrambled, glad of any excuse to turn away yet again from the challenge of the walkway.

Nowadays…a simple telephone call. And in those days, too, we had the phone; some of us. But Zachary Gardner hated them. Likewise cars, though he did keep a motorcycle and sidecar for making his rounds. Across the fields and by the copse I sped, aware of faces in the trees but not wasting time looking at them, and through the graveyard and up the cobbled track to the flat crest of the knoll, to where my uncle stood in the doorway in his shirtsleeves, all scrubbed clean again. And I gasped out my message.

Without a word, nodding, he went to the lean-to and started up the bike, and I climbed slowly and dizzily to my attic room, panting my lungs out. I took up my binoculars and watched the shining ribbon of road to the west, until Uncle Zachary's bike and sidecar came spurting into view, the banging of its pistons unheard at this distance; and I continued to watch him until he disappeared out of sight toward Harden, where a lone spire stood up, half-hidden by a low hill. He came home again at dusk, very quiet, and we heard the next day how Joe Anderson had died that night.

The funeral was five days later at two in the afternoon; I watched for a while, but the bowed heads and the slim, sagging frame of the miner's widow distressed me and made me feel like a voyeur. So I watched the gypsies picnicking instead.

They were in the field next to the graveyard, but separated from it by a high stone wall. The field had lain fallow for several years and was deep in grasses, thick with clovers and wild flowers. And up in my attic room, I was the only one who knew the gypsies were there at all. They had arrived as the ceremony was finishing and the first handful of dirt went into the new grave. They sat on their coloured blanket in the bright sunlight, faces shaded by their huge hats, and I thought: *how odd*! For while they had picnic baskets with them, they didn't appear to be eating. Maybe they were saying some sort of gypsy grace first. Long, silent prayers for the provision of their food. Their bowed heads told me that must be it. Anyway, their inactivity was such that I quickly grew bored and turned my attention elsewhere...

The shock came (not to me, you understand, for I was only on the periphery of the thing, a child, to be seen and not heard) only three days later. The first shock of several, it came first to Harden village, but like a pebble dropped in a still pond its ripples began spreading almost at once.

It was this: the recently widowed Muriel Anderson had committed suicide, drowning herself in the beck under the viaduct. Unable to bear the emptiness, still stunned by her husband's absence, she had thought to follow him. But she'd retained sufficient of her senses to leave a note: a simple plea that they lay her coffin next to his, in a single grave. There were no children, no relatives; the funeral should be simple, with as few people as possible. The sooner she could be with Joe again the better, and she didn't want their reunion complicated by crowds of mourners. Well, things were easier in those days. Her grief quickly became the grief of the entire village, which almost as quickly dispersed, but her wishes were respected.

From my attic room I watched the gravediggers at work on Joe Anderson's plot, shifting soil which hadn't quite settled yet, widening the hole to accommodate two coffins. And later that afternoon I watched them climb out of the hole, and saw the way they scratched their heads. Then they separated and went off, one towards Harden on a bicycle, heading for the viaduct shortcut, and the other coming my way, towards the knoll, coming no doubt to speak with my Uncle Zachary. Idly, I looked for the gypsies then, but they weren't picnicking that day and I couldn't find them around their caravan. And so, having heard the gravedigger's cautious knock at the door of the house, and my uncle letting him in, I went downstairs to the latter's study.

As I reached the study door I heard voices: my uncle's soft tones and the harsher, local dialect of the gravedigger, but both used so low that the conversation was little more than a series of whispers. I've worked out what was said since then, as indeed I've worked most things out, and so am able to reconstruct it here:

"*Holes*, you say?" That was my uncle.

"Aye!" said the other, with conviction. "In the side of the box. Drilled there, like. Fower of them." (Fower meaning four.)

"Wormholes?"

"Bloody big worms, gaffer!" (Worms sounding like 'warms'.) "Big as half-crowns, man, those holes! And anyhow, he's only been doon a fortneet."

There was a pause before: "And Billy's gone for the undertaker, you say?"

"Gone for Mr Forster, aye. I told him, be as quick as you can."

"Well, John," (my uncle's sigh) "while we're waiting, I suppose I'd better come and see what it is that's so worried you..."

I ducked back then, into the shadows of the stairwell. It wasn't that I was a snoop, and I certainly didn't feel like one, but it was as well to be discreet. They left the house and I followed on, at a respectful distance, to the graveyard. And I sat on the wall at the entrance, dangling my long skinny legs and waiting for them, sunbathing in the early evening glow. By the time they were finished in there, Mr Forster had arrived in his big, shiny hearse.

"Come and see this," said my uncle quietly, his face quite pale, as Mr Forster and Billy got out of the car. Mr Forster was a thin man, which perhaps befitted his calling, but he was sweating anyway, and complaining that the car was like a furnace.

"That coffin," his words were stiff, indignant, "is of the finest oak. Holes? Ridiculous! I never heard anything like it! Damage, more like," and he glowered at Billy and John. "*Spade* damage!" They all trooped back into the graveyard, and I went to follow them. But my uncle spotted me and waved me back.

"You'll be all right where you are, Sandy my lad," he said. So I shrugged and went back to the house. But as I turned away I did hear him say to Mr Forster: "Sam, it's not spade damage. And these lads are quite right. Holes they said, and holes they are—four of them—all very neat and tidy, drilled right through the side of the box and the chips still lying there in the soil. Well, you screwed the lid down, and though I'll admit I don't like it, still I reckon we'd be wise to have it open again. Just to see what's what. Joe wouldn't mind, I'm sure, and there's only the handful of us to know about it. I reckon it was clever of these two lads to think to come for you and me."

"You because you're the doctor, and because you were closest," said Forster grudgingly, "and me because they've damaged my coffin!"

"No," John Lane spoke up, "because you built it—your cousin, anyhow—and it's got holes in it!"

And off they went, beyond my range of hearing. But not beyond viewing. I ran as quickly as I could.

Back in my attic room I was in time to see Mr Forster climb out of the hole and scratch his head as the others had done before him. Then he went back to his car and returned with a toolkit. Back down into the hole he went, my uncle with him. The two gravediggers stood at the side, looking down, hands stuffed in their trouser pockets. From the way they crowded close, jostling for a better position, I assumed that the men in the hole were opening the box. But then Billy and John seemed to stiffen a little. Their heads craned forward and down, and their hands slowly came out of their pockets.

They backed away from the open grave, well away until they came up against a row of leaning headstones, then stopped and looked at each other.

My uncle and Mr Forster came out of the grave, hurriedly and a little undignified, I thought. They, too, backed away; and both of them were brushing the dirt from their clothes, sort of crouched down into themselves.

In a little while they straightened up, and then my uncle gave himself a shake. He moved forward again, got down once more into the grave. He left Mr Forster standing there wringing his hands, in company with Billy and John. My binoculars were good ones and I could actually see the sweat shiny on Mr Forster's thin face. None of the three took a pace forward until my uncle stood up and beckoned for assistance.

Then the two gravediggers went to him and hauled him out. And silent, they all piled into Mr Forster's car which he started up and headed for the house. And of course I would have liked to know what this was all about, though I guessed I wouldn't be told. Which meant I'd have to eavesdrop again.

This time in the study the voices weren't so hushed; agitated, fearful, even outraged, but not hushed. There were four of them and they knew each other well, and it was broad daylight. If you see what I mean.

"Creatures? Creatures?" Mr Forster was saying as I crept to the door. "Something in the ground, you say?"

"Like rats, d'you mean?" (John, the senior gravedigger.)

"I really don't know," said my uncle, but there was that in his voice which told me that he had his suspicions. "No, not rats," he finally said; and now he sounded determined, firm, as if he'd come to a decision. "Now look, you two, you've done your job and done it well, but this thing mustn't go any further. There's a guinea for each of you—from me, my promise— but you can't say anything about what you've seen today. Do you hear?"

"Whatever you say, gaffer," said John, gratefully. "But what'll you do about arl this? I mean—"

"Leave it to me," my uncle cut him off. "And mum's the word, hear?"

I heard the scraping of chairs and ducked back out of sight. Uncle Zachary ushered the gravediggers out of the house and quickly returned to his study. "Sam," he said, his voice coming to me very clear now, for he'd left the door ajar, "I don't think it's rats. I'm sure it isn't. Neither is it worms of any sort, nor anything else of that nature."

"Well, it's certainly nothing to do with me!" the other was still indignant, but more shocked than outraged, I thought.

"It's something to do with all of us, Sam," said my uncle. "I mean, how long do you think your business will last if this gets out, eh? No, it has nothing to do with you or the quality of workmanship," he continued, very quickly. "There's nothing personal in it at all. Oh, people will still die here, of course they will—but you can bet your boots they'll not want to be *buried* here!"

"But what on earth *is* it?" Forster's indignation or shock had evaporated; his voice was now very quiet and awed.

"I was in Bulgaria once," said my uncle. "I was staying at a small village, very tranquil if a little backward, on the border. Which is to say, the Danube. There was a flood and the riverbank got washed away, and part of the local graveyard with it. Something like this came to light, and the local people went very quiet and sullen. At the place I was staying, they told me there must be an 'Obour' in the village. What's more, they knew how to find it."

"An Obour?" said Forster. "Some kind of animal?"

My uncle's voice contained a shudder when he answered: "The worst possible sort of animal, yes." Then his chair scraped and he began pacing, and for a moment I lost track of his low-uttered words. But obviously Mr Forster heard them clearly enough.

"*What?* Man, that's madness! And you a doctor!"

My uncle was ever slow to take offence. But I suspected that by now he'd be simmering. "They went looking for the Obour with lanterns in the dark—woke up everyone in the village, in the dead of night, to see what they looked like by lantern light. For the eyes of the Obour are yellow—and triangular!"

"Madness!" Forster gasped again.

And now my uncle *was* angry. "Oh, and do you have a better suggestion? So you tell me, Sam Forster, what *you* think can tunnel through packed earth and do…that?"

"But I—"

"Look at this book," my uncle snapped. And I heard him go to a bookshelf, then his footsteps crossing the room to his guest.

After a while: "Russian?"

"Romanian—but don't concern yourself with the text, look at the pictures!"

Again a pause before: "But…this is too…"

"Yes, I know it is," said my uncle, before Forster could find the words he sought. "And I certainly hope I'm wrong, and that it is something ordinary. But tell me, can *anything* of this sort be ordinary?"

"What will we do?" Forster was quieter now. "The police?"

"What?" (my uncle's snort.) "Sergeant Bert Coggins and his three flat-foot constables? A more down-to-earth lot you couldn't ask for! Good Lord, no! The point is, if this really is something of the sort I've mentioned, it mustn't be frightened off. I mean, we don't know how long it's been here, and we certainly can't allow it to go somewhere else. No, it must be dealt with here and now."

"How?"

"I've an idea. It may be feasible, and it may not. But it certainly couldn't be considered outside the law, and it has to be worth a try. We have to work fast, though, for Muriel Anderson goes down the day after tomorrow, and it will have to be ready by then. Come on, let's go and speak to your cousin."

Mr Forster's cousin, Jack Boulter, made his coffins for him; so I later discovered.

"Wait," said Forster, as I once more began backing away from the door. "Did they find this…this *creature*, these Bulgarian peasants of yours?"

"Oh, yes," my uncle answered. "They tied him in a net and drowned him in the river. And they burned his house down to the ground."

When they left the house and drove away I went into the study. On my uncle's desk lay the book he'd shown to Mr Forster. It was open, lying face down. Curiosity isn't confined to cats: small girls and boys also suffer from it. Or if they don't, then there's something wrong with them.

I turned the book over and looked at the pictures. They were wood-cuts, going from top to bottom of the two pages in long, narrow panels two to a page. Four pictures in all, with accompanying legends printed underneath. The book was old, the ink faded and the pictures poorly impressed; the text, of course, was completely alien to me.

The first picture showed a man, naked, with his arms raised to form a cross. He had what looked to be a thick rope coiled about his waist. His eyes were three-cornered, with radiating lines simulating a shining effect. The second picture showed the man with the rope uncoiled, dangling down loosely from his waist and looped around his feet. The end of the rope seemed frayed and there was some detail, but obscured by age and poor reproduction. I studied this picture carefully but was unable to understand it; the rope appeared to be fastened to the man's body just above his left hip. The third picture showed the man in an attitude of prayer, hands steepled before him, with the rope dangling as before, but crossing over at knee height into the fourth frame. There it coiled upward and was connected to the loosely clad body of a skeletally thin woman, whose flesh was mostly sloughed away to show the bones sticking through.

Now, if I tell my reader that these pictures made little or no sense to me, I know that he will be at pains to understand my ignorance. Well, let me say that it was not ignorance but innocence. I was a boy. None of these things which I have described made any great impression on me *at that time*. They were all incidents—mainly unconnected in my mind, or only loosely connected—occurring during the days I spent at my uncle's house; and as such they were very small pieces in the much larger jigsaw of my world, which was far more occupied with beaches, rock pools, crabs and eels, bathing in the sea, the simple but satisfying meals my uncle prepared for us, etc. It is only in the years passed in between, and in certain dreams I have dreamed, that I have made the connections. In short, I was not investigative but merely curious.

Curious enough, at least, to scribble on a scrap of my uncle's notepaper the following words:

"Uncle Zachary,
     Is the man in these pictures a gypsy?"

For the one connection I *had* made was the thing about the eyes. And I inserted the note into the book and closed it, and left it where I had found it—and then promptly forgot all about it, for there were other, more important things to do.

It would be, I think, a little before seven in the evening when I left the house. There would be another two hours of daylight, then an hour when the dusk turned to darkness, but I would need only a third of that total time to complete my projected walk. For it was my intention to cross the fields to the viaduct, then to cross the viaduct itself (!) and so proceed into Harden. I would return by the coast road, and back down the half-metalled dene path to the knoll and so home.

I took my binoculars with me, and as I passed midway between Slater's Copse and the viaduct, trained them upon the trees and the gleams of varnished woodwork and black, tarred roof hidden in them. I could see no movement about the caravan, but even as I stared so a figure rose up into view and came into focus. It was the head of the family, and he was looking back at me. He must have been sitting in the grass by the fence, or perhaps upon a tree stump, and had stood up as I focused my glasses. But it was curious that he should be looking at me as I was looking at him.

His face was in the shade of his hat, but I remember thinking: *I wonder what is going on behind those queer, three-cornered eyes of his?* And the thought also crossed my mind: *I wonder what he must think of me, spying on him so rudely like this!*

I immediately turned and ran, not out of any sort of fear but more from shame, and soon came to the viaduct. Out onto its walkway I proceeded, but at a slow walk now, not looking down through the stave fence on my left but straight ahead, and yet still aware that the side of the valley was now descending steeply underfoot, and that my physical height above solid ground was increasing with each pace I took. Almost to the middle I went, before thinking to hear in the still, warm evening air the haunting, as yet distant whistle of a train. A train! And I pictured the clattering, shuddering, rumbling agitation it would impart to the viaduct and its walkway!

I turned, made to fly back the way I had come…and there was the gypsy. He stood motionless, at the far end of the walkway, a tall, thin figure with his face in the shade of his hat, looking in my direction—looking, I knew, at me. Well, I wasn't going back *that* way! And now there *was* something of fear in my flight, but mainly I suspect fear of the approaching train. Whichever, the gypsy had supplied all the inspiration I needed to see the job through to the end, to answer the viaduct's challenge. And again I ran.

I reached the far side well in advance of the train, and looked back to see if the gypsy was still there. But he wasn't. Then, safe where the walkway met the rising slope once more, I waited until the train had passed, and thrilled to the thought that I had actually done it, crossed the viaduct's walkway! It would never frighten me again. As to the gypsy: I didn't give him another thought. It wasn't him I'd been afraid of but the viaduct, obviously…

❖ ❖ ❖

The next morning I was up early, knocked awake by my uncle's banging at my door. "Sandy?" he called. "Are you up? I'm off into Harden, to see Mr Boulter the joiner. Can you see to your own breakfast?"

83

"Yes," I called back, "and I'll make some sandwiches to take to the beach."

"Good! Then I'll see you when I see you. Mind how you go. You know where the key is." And off he went.

I spent the entire day on the beach. I swam in the tidal pools, caught small crabs for the fishermen to use as bait, fell asleep on the white sand and woke up itchy, with my sunburn already peeling. But it was only one more layer of skin to join many gone the same way, and I wasn't much concerned. It was late afternoon by then, my sandwiches eaten long ago and the sun beginning to slip; I felt small pangs of hunger starting up, changed out of my bathing costume and headed for home again.

My uncle had left a note for me pinned to the door of his study where it stood ajar:

Sandy,

I'm going back to the village, to Mr Boulter's yard and then to the Vicarage. I'll be in about 9.00 p.m.—maybe. See you then, or if you're tired just tumble straight into bed.

—Zach

P.S. There are fresh sandwiches in the kitchen!

I went to the kitchen and returned munching on a beef sandwich, then ventured into the study. My uncle had drawn the curtains (something I had never before known him to do during daylight hours) and had left his reading lamp on. Upon his desk stood a funny contraption that caught my eye immediately. It was a small frame of rough, half-inch timber off-cuts, nailed together to form an oblong shape maybe eight inches long, five wide and three deep—like a box without top or bottom. It was fitted where the top would go with four small bolts at the corners; these held in position twin cutter blades (from some woodworking machine, I imagined), each seven inches long, which were slotted into grooves that ran down the corners from top edge to bottom edge. Small magnets were set central of the ends of the box, level with the top, and connected up to wires which passed through an entirely separate piece of electrical apparatus and then to a square three-pin plug. An extension cable lay on the study floor beside the desk, but it had been disconnected from the mains supply. My last observation was this: that a three-quarter-inch hole had been drilled through the wooden frame on one side.

Well, I looked at the whole set-up from various angles but could make neither head nor tail of it. It did strike me, however, that if a cigar were to be inserted through the hole in the side of the box, and the bolts on that side released, that the cigar's end would be neatly severed! But my uncle didn't smoke...

I experimented anyway, and when I drew back two of the tiny bolts toward the magnets, the cutter on that side at once slid down its grooves like a toy guillotine, thumping onto the top of the desk! For a moment I was alarmed that I had damaged the desk's finish...until I saw that it was already badly scored by a good many scratches and gouges, where apparently my uncle had amused himself doing much the same thing; except that he had probably drawn the bolts mechanically, by means of the electrical apparatus.

Anyway, I knew I shouldn't be in his study fooling about, and so I put the contraption back the way I had found it and returned to the kitchen for the rest of the sandwiches. I took them upstairs and ate them, then listened to my wireless until about 9.00 p.m.—and still Uncle Zachary wasn't home. So I washed and got into my pyjamas, which was when he chose to return—with Harden's vicar (the Reverend Fawcett) and Mr Forster, and Forster's cousin, the joiner Jack Boulter, all in tow. As they entered the house I hurried to show myself on the landing.

"Sandy," my uncle called up to me, looking a little flustered. "Look, I'm sorry, nephew, but I've been very, very busy today. It's not fair, I know, but—"

"It's all right," I said. "I had a smashing day! And I'm tired." Which was the truth. "I'm going to read for a while before I sleep."

"Good lad!" he called up, obviously relieved that I didn't consider myself neglected. "See you tomorrow." And he ushered his guests into his study and so out of sight. But again he left the door ajar, and I left mine open, so that I could hear something of their voices in the otherwise still night; not everything they said, but some of it. I wasn't especially interested; I tried to read for a few minutes, until I felt drowsy, then turned off my light. And now their voices seemed to float up to me a little more clearly, and before I slept snatches of their conversation impressed themselves upon my mind, so that I've remembered them:

"I really can't say I like it very much," (the vicar's piping voice, which invariably sounded like he was in the pulpit). "But...I suppose we must know what this thing is."

"'Who',' (my uncle, correcting him). "Who it is, Paul. And not only know it but destroy it!"

"But...a person?"

"A sort of person, yes. An almost-human being."

Then Mr Forster's voice, saying: "What bothers me is that the dead are supposed to be laid to rest! How would Mrs Anderson feel if she knew that her coffin..." (fading out).

"But don't you see?" (My uncle's voice again, raised a little, perhaps in excitement or frustration.) "She is the instrument of Joe's revenge!"

"Dreadful word!" (the vicar.) "Most *dreadful!* Revenge, indeed! You seem to forget, Zachary, that God made all creatures, great, small, and—"

"And monstrous? No, Paul, these things have little or nothing to do with God. Now listen, I've no lack of respect for your calling, but tell me: if you were to die tomorrow—God forbid—then where would *you* want burying, eh?"

Then the conversation faded a little, or perhaps I was falling asleep. But I do remember Jack Boulter's voice saying: "Me, Ah'll wark at it arl neet, if necessary. An' divven worry, it'll look no different from any other coffin. Just be sure you get them wires set up, that's arl, before two o'clock."

And my uncle answering him: "It will be done, Jack, no fear about that..."

The rest won't take long to tell.

I was up late, brought blindingly awake by the sun, already high in the sky, striking slantingly in through my window. Brushing the sleep from my eyes, I went and looked out. Down in the cemetery the gravediggers John and Billy were already at work, tidying the edges of the great hole and decorating it with flowers, but also filling in a small trench only inches deep, that led out of the graveyard and into the bracken at the foot of the knoll. John was mainly responsible for the latter, and I focused my glasses on him. There was something furtive about him: the way he kept looking this way and that, as if to be sure he wasn't observed, and whistling cheerily to himself as he filled in the small trench and disguised his work with chippings. It seemed to me that he was burying a cable of some sort.

I aimed my glasses at Slater's Copse next, but the curtains were drawn in the caravan's window and it seemed the gypsies weren't up and about yet. Well, no doubt they'd come picnicking later.

I washed and dressed, went downstairs and breakfasted on a cereal with milk, then sought out my uncle—or would have, except that for the first time in my life I found his study door locked. I could hear voices from inside, however, and so I knocked.

"That'll be Sandy," came my uncle's voice, and a moment later the key turned in the lock. But instead of letting me in, he merely held the door open a crack. I could see Jack Boulter in there, working busily at some sort of apparatus on my uncle's desk—a device with a switch, and a small coloured light-bulb—but that was all.

"Sandy, Sandy!" my uncle sighed, throwing up his hands in despair.

"I know," I smiled, "you're busy. It's all right, Uncle, for I only came down to tell you I'll be staying up in my room."

That caused him to smile the first smile I'd seen on his face for some time. "Well, there's a bit of Irish for you," he said. But then he quickly sobered. "I'm sorry, nephew," he told me, "but what I'm about really is most important." He opened the door a little more. "You see how busy we are?"

I looked in and Jack Boulter nodded at me, then continued to screw down his apparatus onto my uncle's desk. Wires led from it through the curtains and out of the window, where they were trapped and prevented from slipping or being disturbed by the lowered sash. I looked at my uncle to see if there was any explanation.

"The, er—the wiring!" he finally blurted. "We're testing the wiring in the house, that's all. We shouldn't want the old place to burn down through faulty wiring, now should we?"

"No, indeed not," I answered, and went back upstairs.

I read, listened to the wireless, observed the land all about through my binoculars. In fact I had intended to go to the beach again, but there was something in the air: a hidden excitement, a muted air of expectancy, a sort of quiet tension. And so I stayed in my room, just waiting for something to happen. Which eventually it did.

And it was summoned by the bells, Harden's old church bells, pealing out their slow, doleful toll for Muriel Anderson.

But those bells changed everything. I can hear them even now, see and *feel* the changes that occurred. Before, there had been couples out walking: just odd pairs here and there, on the old dene lane, in the fields and on the paths. And yet by the time those bells were only half-way done the people had gone, disappeared, don't ask me where. Down in the graveyard, John and Billy had been putting the finishing touches to their handiwork, preparing the place, as it were, for this latest increase in the Great Majority; but now they speeded up, ran to the tiled lean-to in one tree-shaded corner of the graveyard and changed into clothes a little more fitting, before hurrying to the gate and waiting there for Mr Forster's hearse. For the bells had told everyone that the ceremony at Harden church was over, and that the smallest possible cortège was now on its way. One and a half miles at fifteen miles per hour, which meant a journey of just six minutes.

Who else had been advised by the bells, I wondered?

I aimed my binoculars at Slater's Copse, and…they were there, all four, pale figures in the trees, their shaded faces turned toward the near-distant spire across the valley, half-hidden by the low hill. And as they left the cover of the trees and headed for the field adjacent to the cemetery, I saw that indeed they had their picnic baskets with them: a large one which the man and woman carried between them, and a smaller one shared by their children. As usual.

The hearse arrived, containing only the coffin and its occupant, a great many wreaths and garlands, and of course the Reverend Fawcett and Mr Forster, who with John and Billy formed the team of pallbearers. Precise and practised, they carried Muriel Anderson to her grave where the only additional mourner was Jack Boulter, who had gone down from the house to join them. He got down into the flower-decked hole (to assist in the lowering of the coffin, of course) and after the casket had gone down in its loops of silken rope finally climbed out again, assisted by John and Billy. There followed the final service, and the first handful of soil went into the grave.

Through all of this activity my attention had been riveted in the grave-yard; now that things were proceeding towards an end, however, I once again turned my glasses on the picnickers. And there they sat cross-legged on their blanket in the long grass outside the cemetery wall, with their picnic baskets between them. But *motionless* as always, with their heads bowed in a sort of grace. They sat there—as they had sat for Joe Anderson, and Mrs Jones the greengrocer-lady, and old George Carter the retired miner, whose soot-clogged lungs had finally collapsed on him—offering up their silent prayers or doing whatever they did.

Meanwhile, in the graveyard:

At last the ceremony was over, and John and Billy set to with their spades while the Reverend Fawcett, Jack Boulter and Mr Forster climbed the knoll to the house, where my uncle met them at the door. I heard him greet them, and the Vicar's high-pitched, measured answer:

"Zach, Sam here tells me you have a certain book with pictures? I should like to see it, if you don't mind. And then of course there's the matter of a roster. For now that we've initiated this thing I suppose we must see it through, and certainly I can see a good many long, lonely nights stretching ahead."

"Come in, come in," my uncle answered. "The book? It's in my study. By all means come through."

I *heard* this conversation, as I say, but nothing registered—not for a minute or two, anyway. Until—

There came a gasping and a frantic clattering as my uncle, with the Reverend Fawcett hot on his heels, came flying up the stairs to the landing, then up the short stairs to my room. They burst in, quite literally hurling the door wide, and my uncle was upon me in three great strides.

"Sandy," he gasped then, "what's all this about gypsies?" I put my glasses aside and looked at him, and saw that he was holding the sheet of notepaper with my scribbled query. He gripped my shoulder. "Why do you ask if the man in these pictures is a gypsy?"

Finally I knew what he was talking about. "Why, because of their eyes!" I answered. "Their three-cornered eyes." And as I picked up my binoculars and again trained them on the picnickers, I added: "But you can't see their faces from up here, because of their great hats..."

My uncle glanced out of the window and his jaw dropped. "Good Lord!" he whispered, eyes bulging in his suddenly white face. He almost snatched the glasses from me, and his huge hands shook as he put them to his eyes. After a moment he said, "My God, my God!" Simply that; and then he thrust the glasses at the Reverend Fawcett.

The Reverend was no less affected; he said, "Dear Jesus! Oh my dear sweet Jesus! In broad daylight! Good heavens, Zach—*in broad daylight!*"

Then my uncle straightened up, towered huge, and his voice was steady again as he said: "Their shirts—look at their shirts!"

The vicar looked, and grimly nodded. "Their shirts, yes."

From the foot of the stairs came Jack Boulter's sudden query: "Zach, Reverend, are you up there? Zach, why man ar'm sorry, but there must be a fault. Damn the thing, but ar'm getna red light!"

"Fault?" cried my uncle, charging for the door and the stairs, with the vicar right behind him. "There's no fault, Jack! Press the button, man— *press the button!*"

Left alone again and not a little astonished, I looked at the gypsies in the field. Their shirts? But they had simply pulled them out of their trousers, so that they fell like small, personal tents to the grass where they sat. Which I imagined must keep them quite cool in the heat of the afternoon. And anyway, they always wore their shirts like that, when they picnicked.

But what was this? To complement the sudden uproar in the house, now there came this additional confusion outside! What could have startled the gypsies like this? What on earth was wrong with them? I threw open the window and leaned out, and without knowing why found my tongue cleaving to the roof of my mouth as once more, for the last time, I trained my glasses on the picnickers. And how to explain what I saw then? I saw it, but only briefly, in the moments before my uncle was there behind me, clapping his hand over my eyes, snatching the window and curtains shut, prising the glasses from my half-frozen fingers. Saw *and* heard it!

The gypsies straining to their feet and trying to run, overturning their picnic baskets in their sudden frenzy, seeming anchored to the ground by fat white ropes which lengthened behind them as they stumbled outward from their blanket. The agony of their dance there in the long grass, and the way they dragged on their ropes to haul them out of the ground, like strangely hopping blackbirds teasing worms; their terrified faces and shrieking mouths as their hats went flying; their shirts and dresses billowing, and their unbelievable screams. All four of them, screaming as one, but shrill as a keening wind, hissing like steam from a nest of kettles, or lobsters dropped live into boiling water, and yet cold and alien as the sweat on a dead fish!

And then the man's rope, incredibly long and taut as a bowstring, suddenly coming free of the ground—and likewise, one after another, the ropes of his family—and all of them *living things* that writhed like snakes and sprayed crimson from their raw red ends!

But all glimpsed so briefly, before my uncle intervened, and so little of it registering upon a mind which really couldn't accept it—not then. I had been aware, though, of the villagers where they advanced inexorably across the field, armed with the picks and shovels of their trade (what? Ask John and Billy to keep mum about such as this? Even for a guinea?). And of the gypsies spinning like dervishes, coiling up those awful appendages about their waists, then wheeling more slowly and gradually crumpling exhausted to the earth; and of their picnic baskets scattered on the grass, all tumbled and…empty.

I've since discovered that in certain foreign parts 'Obour' means 'night demon', or 'ghost', or 'vampire'. While in others it means simply 'ghoul'. As for the gypsies: I know their caravan was burned out that same night, and that their bones were discovered in the ashes. It hardly worried me then and it doesn't now, and I'm glad that you don't see nearly so many of them around these days; but of course I'm prejudiced.

As they say in the north-east, a burden shared is a burden halved. But really, my dreams have been a terrible burden, and I can't see why I should continue to bear it alone.

This then has been my rite of exorcism. At least I hope so...

THE VIADUCT

Horror can come in many different shapes, sizes, and colours and often, like death, which is sometimes its companion, unexpectedly. Some years ago horror came to two boys in the coalmining area of England's north-east coast.

Pals since they first started school seven years earlier, their names were John and David. John was a big lad and thought himself very brave; David was six months younger, smaller, and he wished he could be more like John.

It was a Saturday in the late spring, warm but not oppressive, and since there was no school the boys were out adventuring on the beach. They had spent most of the morning playing at being starving castaways, turning over rocks in the life-or-death search for crabs and eels—and jumping back startled, hearts racing, whenever their probing revealed too frantic a wriggling in the swirling water, or perhaps a great crab carefully sidling away, one pincer lifted in silent warning—and now they were heading home again for lunch.

But lunch was still almost two hours away, and it would take them less than an hour to get home. In that simple fact were sown the seeds of horror, in that and in one other fact—that between the beach and their respective homes there stood the viaduct...

Almost as a reflex action, when the boys left the beach they headed in the direction of the viaduct. To do this they turned inland, through the trees and bushes of the narrow dene that came right down to the sand, and followed the path of the river. The river was still fairly deep from the spring thaw and the rains of April, and as they walked, ran and hopped they threw stones into the water, seeing who could make the biggest splash.

In no time at all, it seemed, they came to the place where the massive, ominous shadow of the viaduct fell across the dene and the river flowing through it, and there they stared up in awe at the giant arched structure of brick and concrete that bore upon its back one hundred yards of the twin tracks that formed the coastal railway. Shuddering mightily whenever a train roared overhead, the man-made bridge was a never-ending source of amazement and wonder to them...And a challenge, too.

It was as they were standing on the bank of the slow-moving river, perhaps fifty feet wide at this point, that they spotted on the opposite bank the local village idiot, 'Wiley Smiley'. Now of course, that was not this unfortunate youth's real name: he was Miles Bellamy, victim of cruel genetic fates since the ill-omened day of his birth some nineteen years earlier. But everyone called him Wiley Smiley.

He was fishing, in a river that had supported nothing bigger than a minnow for many years, with a length of string and a bent pin. He looked up and grinned vacuously as John threw a stone into the water to attract his attention. The stone went quite close to the mark, splashing water over the unkempt youth where he stood a little way out from the far bank, balanced none too securely on slippery rocks. His vacant grin immediately slipped from his face; he became angry, gesturing awkwardly and mouthing incoherently.

"He'll come after us," said David to his brash companion, his voice just a trifle alarmed.

"No he won't, stupid," John casually answered, picking up a second, larger stone. "He can't get across, can he." It was a statement, not a question, and it was a fact. Here the river was deeper, overflowing from a large pool directly beneath the viaduct in which, in the months ahead, children and adults alike would swim during the hot weekends of summer.

John threw his second missile, deliberately aiming it at the water as close to the enraged idiot as he could without actually hitting him, shouting: "Yah! Wiley Smiley! Trying to catch a whale, are you?"

Wiley Smiley began to shriek hysterically as the stone splashed down immediately in front of him and a fountain of water geysered over his trousers. Threatening though they now were, his angry caperings upon the rocks looked very funny to the boys (particularly since his rage was impotent), and John began to laugh loud and jeeringly. David, not a cruel boy by nature, found his friend's laughter so infectious that in a few seconds he joined in, adding his own voice to the hilarity.

Then John stooped yet again, straightening up this time with two stones, one of which he offered to his slightly younger companion. Carried completely away now, David accepted the stone and together they hurled their missiles, dancing and laughing until tears rolled down their cheeks as Wiley Smiley received a further dousing. By that time the rocks upon which their victim stood were thoroughly wet and slippery, so that suddenly he lost his balance and sat down backwards into the shallow water.

Climbing clumsily, soggily to his feet, he was greeted by howls of laughter from across the river, which drove him to further excesses of rage. His was a passion which might only find outlet in direct retaliation, revenge. He took a few paces forward, until the water swirled about his knees, then stooped and plunged his arms into the river. There were stones galore beneath the water, and the face of the tormented youth was twisted with hate and fury now as he straightened up and brandished two which were large and jagged.

Where his understanding was painfully slow, Wiley Smiley's strength was prodigious. Had his first stone hit John on the head it might easily have killed him. As it was, the boy ducked at the last moment and the missile flew harmlessly above him. David, too, had to jump to avoid being hurt by a flying rock, and no sooner had the idiot loosed both his stones than he stooped down again to grope in the water for more.

Wiley Smiley's aim was too good for the boys, and his continuing rage was beginning to make them feel uncomfortable, so they beat a hasty retreat up the steeply wooded slope of the dene and made for the walkway that was fastened and ran parallel to the nearside wall of the viaduct. Soon they had climbed out of sight of the poor soul below, but they could still hear his meaningless squawking and shrieking.

A few minutes more of puffing and panting, climbing steeply through trees and saplings, brought them up above the wood and to the edge of a grassy slope. Another hundred yards and they could go over a fence and on to the viaduct. Though no word had passed between them on the subject, it was inevitable that they should end up on the viaduct, one of the most fascinating places in their entire world...

The massive structure had been built when first the collieries of the north-east opened up, long before plans were drawn up for the major coast road, and now it linked twin colliery villages that lay opposite each other across the narrow river valley it spanned. Originally constructed solely to accommodate the railway, and used to that end to this very day, with the addition of a walkway, it also provided miners who lived in one village but worked in the other with a short cut to their respective coalmines.

While the viaduct itself was of sturdy brick, designed to withstand decade after decade of the heavy traffic that rumbled and clattered across its triple-arched back, the walkway was a comparatively fragile affair. That is not to say that it was not safe, but there were certain dangers and notices had been posted at its approaches to warn users of the presence of at least an element of risk.

Supported upon curving metal arms—iron bars about one and a half inches in diameter which, springing from the brick and mortar of the viaduct wall, were set perhaps twenty inches apart—the walkway itself was of wooden planks protected by a fence five feet high. There were, however, small gaps where rotten planks had been removed and never replaced, but the miners who used the viaduct were careful and knew the walkway's dangers intimately. All in all the walkway served a purpose and was reasonably safe; one might jump from it, certainly, but only a very careless person or an outright fool would fall. Still, it was no place for anyone suffering from vertigo…

Now, as they climbed the fence to stand gazing up at those ribs of iron with their burden of planking and railings, the two boys felt a strange, headlong rushing emotion within them. For this day, of course, was *the* day!

It had been coming for almost a year, since the time when John had stood right where he stood now to boast: "One day I'll swing hand over hand along those rungs, all the way across. Just like Tarzan." Yes, they had sensed this day's approach, almost as they might sense Christmas or the beginning of long, idyllic summer holidays…or a visit to the dentist. Something far away, which would eventually arrive, but not yet.

Except that now it had arrived.

"One hundred and sixty rungs," John breathed, his voice a little fluttery, feeling his palms beginning to itch. "Yesterday, in the playground, we both did twenty more than that on the climbing-frame."

"The climbing-frame," answered David, with a naïve insight and vision far ahead of his age, "is only seven feet high. The viaduct is about a hundred and fifty."

John stared at his friend for a second and his eyes narrowed. Suddenly he sneered. "I might have known it—you're scared, aren't you?"

"No," David shook his head, lying, "but it'll soon be lunch-time, and—"

"You *are* scared!" John repeated. "Like a little kid. We've been practising for months for this, every day of school on the climbing-frame, and now we're ready. You know we can do it." His tone grew more gentle, urging: "Look, it's not as if we can't stop if we want to, is it? There's holes in the fence, and those big gaps in the planks."

"The first gap," David answered, noticing how very far away and faint his own voice sounded, "is almost a third of the way across…"

"That's right," John agreed, nodding his head eagerly. "We've counted the rungs, haven't we? Just fifty of them to that first wide gap. If we're too tired to go on when we get there, we can just climb up through the gap on to the walkway."

David, whose face had been turned towards the ground, looked up. He looked straight into his friend's eyes, not at the viaduct, in whose shade they stood. He shivered, but not because he was cold.

John stared right back at him, steadily, encouragingly, knowing that his smaller friend looked for his approval, his reassurance. And he was right, for despite the fact that their ages were very close, David held him up as some sort of hero. No daredevil, David, but he desperately wished he could be. And now…here was his chance.

He simply nodded—then laughed out loud as John gave a wild whoop and shook his young fists at the viaduct. "Today we'll beat you!" he yelled, then turned and clambered furiously up the last few yards of steep grassy slope to where the first rung might easily be reached with an upward spring. David followed him after a moment's pause, but not before he heard the first arch of the viaduct throw back the challenge in a faintly ringing, sardonic echo of John's cry: "Beat you…beat you…beat you…"

As he caught up with his ebullient friend, David finally allowed his eyes to glance upward at those skeletal ribs of iron above him. They looked solid, were solid, he knew—but the air beneath them was very thin indeed. John turned to him, his face flushed with excitement. "You first," he said.

"Me?" David blanched. "But—"

"You'll be up on to the walkway first if we get tired," John pointed out. "Besides, I go faster than you—and you wouldn't want to be left behind, would you?"

David shook his head. "No," he slowly answered, "I wouldn't want to be left behind." Then his voice took on an anxious note: "But you won't hurry me, will you?"

"'Course not," John answered. "We'll just take it nice and easy, like we do at school."

Without another word, but with his ears ringing strangely and his breath already coming faster, David jumped up and caught hold of the first rung. He swung forward, first one hand to the rung in front, then the other, and so on. He heard John grunt as he too jumped and caught the first rung, and then he gave all his concentration to what he was doing.

Hand over hand, rung by rung, they made their way out over the abyss. Below them the ground fell sharply away, each swing of their arms adding almost two feet to their height, seeming to add tangibly to their weight. Now they were silent, except for an occasional grunt, saving both breath and strength as they worked their way along the underside of the walkway. There were only the breezes that whispered in their ears and the infrequent toot of a motor's horn on the distant road.

As the bricks of the wall moved slowly by, so the distance between rungs seemed to increase, and already David's arms felt tired. He knew that John, too, must be feeling it, for while his friend was bigger and a little stronger, he was also heavier. And sure enough, at a distance of only twenty-five, maybe thirty rungs out towards the centre, John breathlessly called for a rest.

David pulled himself up and hung his arms and his rib-cage over the rung he was on—just as they had practised in the playground—getting comfortable before carefully turning his head to look back. He was shocked to see that John's face was paler than he'd ever known it, and that his eyes were staring. When John saw David's doubt, however, he managed a weak grin.

"It's OK," he said. "I was—I was just a bit worried about you, that's all. Thought your arms might be getting a bit tired. Have you—have you looked down yet?"

"No," David answered, his voice mouse-like. *No*, he said again, this time to himself, *and I'm not going to!* He carefully turned his head back to look ahead, where the diminishing line of rungs seemed to stretch out almost infinitely to the far side of the viaduct.

John had been worried about him. Yes, of course he had; that was why his face had looked so funny, so—shrunken. John thought he was frightened, was worried about his self-control, his ability to carry on. Well, David told himself, he had every right to worry; but all the same he felt ashamed that his weakness was so obvious. Even in a position like that, perched so perilously, David's mind was far more concerned with the other boy's opinion of him than with thoughts of possible disaster. And it never once dawned on him, not for a moment, that John might really only be worried about himself...

Almost as if to confirm beyond a doubt the fact that John had little faith in his strength, his courage—as David hung there, breathing deeply, preparing himself for the next stage of the venture—his friend's voice, displaying an unmistakable quaver, came to him again from behind: "Just another twenty rungs, that's all, then you'll be able to climb up on to the walkway."

Yes, David thought, *I'll be able to climb up. But then I'll know that I'll never be like you—that you'll always be better than me—because you'll carry on all the way across!* He set his teeth and dismissed the thought. It wasn't going to be like that, he told himself, not this time. After all, it was no different up here from in the playground. You were only higher, that was all. The trick was in not looking down—

As if obeying some unheard command, seemingly with a morbid curiosity of their own, David's eyes slowly began to turn downward, defying him. Their motion was only arrested when David's attention suddenly centred upon a spider-like dot that emerged suddenly from the cover of the trees, scampering frantically up the opposite slope of the valley. He recognized the figure immediately from the faded blue shirt and black trousers that it wore. It was Wiley Smiley.

As David lowered himself carefully into the hanging position beneath his rung and swung forward, he said: "Across the valley, there—that's Wiley Smiley. I wonder why he's in such a hurry." There had been something terribly urgent about the idiot's quick movements, as if some rare incentive powered them.

"I see him," said John, sounding more composed now. "Hah! He's just an old nutter. My dad says he'll do something one of these days and have to be taken away."

"Do something?" David queried, pausing briefly between swings. An uneasiness completely divorced from the perilous game they were playing rose churningly in his stomach and mind. "What kind of thing?"

"Dunno," John grunted. "But anyway, don't—*uh!*—talk."

It was good advice: don't talk, conserve wind, strength, take it easy. And yet David suddenly found himself moving faster, dangerously fast, and his fingers were none too sure as they moved from one rung to the next. More than once he was hanging by one hand while the other groped blindly for support.

It was very, very important now to close the distance between himself and the sanctuary of the gap in the planking. True, he had made up his mind just a few moments ago to carry on beyond that gap—as far as he could go before admitting defeat, submitting—but all such resolutions were gone now as quickly as they came. His one thought was of climbing up to safety.

It had something to do with Wiley Smiley and the eager, *determined* way he had been scampering up the far slope. Towards the viaduct. Something to do with that, yes, and with what John had said about Wiley Smiley being taken away one day...for *doing* something. David's mind dared not voice its fears too specifically, not even to itself...

Now, except for the occasional grunt—that and the private pounding of blood in their ears—the two boys were silent, and only a minute or so later David saw the gap in the planking. He had been searching for it, sweeping the rough wood of the planks stretching away overhead anxiously until he saw the wide, straight crack that quickly enlarged as he swung closer. Two planks were missing here, he knew, just sufficient to allow a boy to squirm through the gap without too much trouble.

His breath coming in sobbing, glad gasps, David was just a few rungs away from safety when he felt the first tremors vibrating through the great structure of the viaduct. It was like the trembling of a palsied giant. "What's that?" he cried out loud, terrified, clinging desperately to the rung above his head.

"It's a—*uh!*—train!" John gasped, his own voice now very hoarse and plainly frightened. "We'll have to—*uh!*—wait until it's gone over."

Quickly, before the approaching train's vibrations could shake them loose, the boys hauled themselves up into positions of relative safety and comfort, perching on their rungs beneath the planks of the walkway. There they waited and shivered in the shadow of the viaduct, while the shuddering rumble of the train drew ever closer, until, in a protracted clattering of wheels on rails, the monster rushed by unseen overhead. The trembling quickly subsided and the train's distant whistle proclaimed its derision; it was finished with them.

Without a word, holding back a sob that threatened to develop into full-scale hysteria, David lowered himself once more into the full-length hanging position; behind him, breathing harshly and with just the hint of a whimper escaping from his lips, John did the same. Two, three more forward swings and the gap was directly overhead. David looked up, straight up to the clear sky.

"Hurry!" said John, his voice the tiniest whisper. "My hands are starting to feel funny…"

David pulled himself up and balanced across his rung, tremulously took away one hand and grasped the edge of the wooden planking. Pushing down on the hand that grasped the rung and hauling himself up, finally he kneeled on the rung and his head emerged through the gap in the planks. He looked along the walkway…

There, not three feet away, legs widespread and eyes burning with a fanatical hatred, crouched Wiley Smiley. David saw him, saw the pointed stick he held, felt a thrill of purest horror course through him. Then, in the next instant, the idiot lunged forward and his mouth opened in a demented parody of a laugh. David saw the lightning movement of the sharpened stick and tried to avoid its thrust. He felt the point strike his forehead just above his left eye and fell back, off balance, arms flailing. Briefly his left hand made contact with the planking again, then lost it, and he fell with a shriek… across the rung that lay directly beneath him. It was not a long fall, but fear and panic had already winded David; he simply closed his eyes and sobbed, hanging on for dear life, motionless. But only for a handful of seconds.

Warm blood trickled from David's forehead, falling on his hands where he gripped the rung. Something was prodding the back of his neck, jabbing viciously. The pain brought him back from the abyss and he opened his eyes to risk one sharp, fearful glance upwards. Wiley Smiley was kneeling at the edge of the gap, his stick already moving downward for another jab. Again David moved his head to avoid the thrust of the stick, and once more the point scraped his forehead.

Behind him David could hear John moaning and screaming alternately: "Oh, Mum! Dad! It's Wiley Smiley! It's him, him, *him*! He'll kill us., kill us…" Galvanized into action, David lowered himself for the third time into the hanging position and swung forward, away from the inflamed idiot's deadly stick. Two rungs, three, then he carefully turned about-face and hauled himself up to rest. He looked at John through the blood that dripped slowly into one eye, blurring his vision.

David blinked to clear his eye of blood, then said: "John, you'll have to turn round and go back, get help. He's got me here. I can't go forward any further, I don't think, and I can't come back. I'm stuck. But it's only fifty rungs back to the start. You can do it easy, and if you get tired you can always rest. I'll wait here until you fetch help."

"Can't, can't, *can't*," John babbled, trembling wildly where he lay half across his rung. Tears ran down the older boy's cheeks and fell into space like salty rain. He was deathly white, eyes staring, frozen. Suddenly yellow urine flooded from the leg of his short trousers in a long burst. When he saw this, David, too, wet himself, feeling the burning of his water against his legs but not caring. He felt very tiny, very weak now, and he knew that fear and shock were combining to exhaust him.

Then, as a silhouette glimpsed briefly in a flash of lightning, David saw in his mind's eye a means of salvation. "John," he urgently called out to the other boy. "Do you remember near the middle of the viaduct? There are two gaps close together in the walkway, maybe only a dozen or so rungs apart." Almost imperceptibly, John nodded, never once moving his frozen eyes from David's face. "Well," the younger boy continued, barely managing to keep the hysteria out of his own voice, "if we can swing to—"

Suddenly David's words were cut off by a burst of insane laughter from above, followed immediately by a loud, staccato thumping on the boards as Wiley Smiley leapt crazily up and down.

"No, no, *no*—" John finally cried out in answer to David's proposal. His paralysis broken, he began to sob unashamedly. Then, shaking his head violently, he said: "I can't move—can't move!" His voice became the merest whisper. "Oh, God—Mum—Dad! I'll fall, I'll fall!"

"You won't fall, you git—*coward*!" David shouted. Then his jaw fell open in a gasp. John, a coward! But the other boy didn't even seem to have heard him. Now he was trembling as wildly as before and his eyes were squeezed tight shut.

"Listen," David said. "If you don't come...then I'll leave you. You wouldn't want to be left on your own, would you?" It was an echo as of something said a million years ago.

John stopped sobbing and opened his eyes. They opened very wide, unbelieving. "Leave me?"

"Listen," David said again. "The next gap is only about twenty rungs away, and the one after that is only another eight or nine more. Wiley Smiley can't get after both of us at once, can he?"

"You go," said John, his voice taking on fresh hope and his eyes blinking rapidly. "You go and maybe he'll follow you. Then I'll climb up and—and chase him off..."

"You won't be able to chase him off," said David scornfully, "not just you on your own. You're not big enough."

"Then I'll...I'll run and fetch help."

"What if he doesn't follow me?" David asked. "If we both go, he's bound to follow us."

"David," John said, after a moment or two. "David, I'm...frightened."

"You'll have to be quick across the gap," David said, ignoring John's last statement. "He's got that stick—and of course he'll be listening to us."

"I'm frightened," John whispered again.

David nodded. "OK, you stay where you are, if that's what you want—but I'm going on."

"Don't leave me, don't leave me!" John cried out, his shriek accompanied by a peal of mad and bubbling laughter from the unseen idiot above. "Don't go!"

"I have to, or we're both finished," David answered. He slid down into the hanging position and turned about-face, noting as he did so that John was making to follow him, albeit in a dangerous, panicky fashion. "Wait to see if Wiley Smiley follows me!" he called back over his shoulder.

"No. I'm coming, I'm coming!"

From far down below in the valley David heard a horrified shout, then another. They had been spotted. Wiley Smiley heard the shouting too, and his distraction was sufficient to allow John to pass by beneath him unhindered. From above, the two boys now heard the idiot's worried mutterings and gruntings, and the hesitant sound of his feet as he slowly kept pace with them along the walkway. He could see them through the narrow cracks between the planks, but the cracks weren't wide enough for him to use his stick.

David's arms and hands were terribly numb and aching by the time he reached the second gap, but seeing the gloating, twisted features of Wiley Smiley leering down at him he ducked his head and swung on to where he was once more protected by the planks above him. John had stopped short of the second gap, hauling himself up into the safer, resting position.

Above them Wiley Smiley was mewling viciously like a wild animal, howling as if in torment. He rushed crazily back and forth from gap to gap, jabbing uselessly at the empty air between the vacant rungs. The boys could see the bloodied point of the stick striking down first through one open space, then the other. David achingly waited until he saw the stick appear at the gap in front of him and then, when it retreated and he heard Wiley Smiley's footsteps hurrying overhead, swung swiftly across to the other side. There he turned about to face John, and with what felt like his last ounce of strength pulled himself up to rest.

Now, for the first time, David dared to look down. Below, running up the riverbank and waving frantically, were the ant-like figures of three men. They must have been out for a Saturday morning stroll when they'd spotted the two boys hanging beneath the viaduct's walkway. One of them stopped running and put his hands up to his mouth. His shout floated up to the boys on the clear air: "Hang on, lads, hang on!"

"Help!" David and John cried out together, as loud as they could. "Help—Help!"

"We're coming, lads," came the answering shout. The men hurriedly began to climb the wooded slope on their side of the river and disappeared into the trees.

"They'll be here soon," David said, wondering if it would be soon enough. His whole body ached and he felt desperately weak and sick.

"Hear that, Wiley Smiley?" John cried hysterically, staring up at the boards above him. "They'll be here soon—and then you'll be taken away and locked up!" There was no answer. A slight wind had come up off the sea and was carrying a salty tang to them where they lay across their rungs.

"They'll take you away and lock you up," John cried again, the ghost of a sob in his voice; but once more the only answer was the slight moaning of the wind. John looked across at David, maybe twenty-five feet away, and said: "I think...I think he's gone." Then he gave a wild shout. "He's gone. *He's gone!*"

"I didn't hear him go," said David, dubiously.

John was very much more his old self now. "Oh, he's gone, all right. He saw those men coming and cleared off. David, I'm going up!"

"You'd better wait," David cried out as his friend slid down to hang at arm's length from his rung. John ignored the advice; he swung forward hand over hand until he was under the far gap in the planking. With a grunt of exertion, he forced the tired muscles of his arms to pull his body up. He got his rib-cage over the rung, flung a hand up and took hold of the naked plank to one side of the gap, then—

In that same instant David sensed rather than heard the furtive movement overhead. "John!" he yelled. "He's still there—*Wiley Smiley's still there!*"

But John had already seen Wiley Smiley; the idiot had made his presence all too plain, and already his victim was screaming. The boy fell back fully into David's view, the hand he had thrown up to grip the edge of the plank returning automatically to the rung, his arms taking the full weight of his falling body, somehow sustaining him. There was a long gash in his cheek from which blood freely flowed.

"Move forward!" David yelled, terror pulling his lips back in a snarling mask. "Forward, where he can't get at you…"

John heard him and must have seen in some dim, frightened recess of his mind the common sense of David's advice. Panting hoarsely—partly in dreadful fear, partly from hideous emotional exhaustion—he swung one hand forward and caught at the next rung. And at that precise moment, in the split second while John hung suspended between the two rungs with his face turned partly upward, Wiley Smiley struck again.

David was witness to it all. He heard the maniac's rising, gibbering shriek of triumph as the sharp point of the stick lanced unerringly down, and John's answering cry of purest agony as his left eye flopped bloodily out on to his cheek, lying there on a white thread of nerve and gristle. He saw John clap *both hands* to his monstrously altered face, and watched in starkest horror as his friend seemed to stand for a moment, defying gravity, on the thin air. Then John was gone, dwindling away down a draughty funnel of air, while rising came the piping, diminishing scream that would haunt David until his dying day, a scream that was cut short after what seemed an impossibly long time.

John had fallen. At first David couldn't accept it, but then it began to sink in. His friend had fallen. He moaned and shut his eyes tightly, lying half across and clinging to his rung so fiercely that he could no longer feel his bloodless fingers at all. John had fallen…

Then—perhaps it was only a minute or so later, perhaps an hour, David didn't know—there broke in on his perceptions the sound of clumping, hurrying feet on the boards above, and a renewed, even more frenzied attack of gibbering and shrieking from Wiley Smiley. David forced his eyes open as the footsteps came to a halt directly overhead. He heard a gruff voice: "Jim, you keep that bloody—*Thing*—away, will you? He's already killed one boy today. Frank, give us a hand here."

A face, inverted, appeared through the hole in the planks not three feet away from David's own face. The mouth opened and the same voice, but no longer gruff, said: "It's OK now, son. Everything's OK. Can you move?"

In answer, David could only shake his head negatively. Overtaxed muscles, violated nerves had finally given in. He was frozen on his perch; he would stay where he was now until he was either taken off physically or until he fainted.

Dimly the boy heard the voice again, and others raised in an urgent hubbub, but he was too far gone to make out any words that were said. He was barely aware that the face had been withdrawn. A few seconds later there came a banging and tearing from immediately above him; a small shower of tiny pieces of wood, dust, and homogenous debris fell upon his head and shoulders. Then daylight flooded down to illuminate more brightly the shaded area beneath the walkway. Another board was torn away, and another.

The inverted face again appeared, this time at the freshly made opening, and an exploratory hand reached down. Using its kindly voice, the face said: "OK, son, we'll have you out of there in a jiffy. I—*uh!*—can't quite seem to reach you, but it's only a matter of a few inches. Do you think you can—"

The voice was cut off by a further outburst of incoherent shrieking and jabbering from Wiley Smiley. The face and hand withdrew momentarily and David heard the voice yet again. This time it was angry. "Look, see if you can keep that damned idiot back, will you? And keep him quiet, for God's sake!"

The hand came back, large and strong, reaching down. David still clung with all his remaining strength to the rung, and though he knew what was expected of him—what he must do to win himself the prize of continued life—all sense of feeling had quite gone from his limbs and even shifting his position was a very doubtful business.

"Boy," said the voice, as the hand crept inches closer and the inverted face stared into his. "If you could just reach up your hand, I—"

"I'll—I'll try to do it," David whispered.

"Good, good," his would-be rescuer calmly, quietly answered. "That's it, lad, just a few inches. Keep your balance now."

David's hand crept up from the rung and his head, neck, and shoulder slowly turned to allow it free passage. Up it tremblingly went, reaching to meet the hand stretching down from above. The boy and the man each peered into the other's straining face, and an instant later their fingertips touched—

There came a mad shriek, a frantic pounding of feet and cries of horror and wild consternation from above. The inverted face went white in a moment and disappeared, apparently dragged backwards. The hand disappeared, too. And that was the very moment that David had chosen to free himself of the rung and give himself into the protection of his rescuer...

He flailed his arms in a vain attempt to regain his balance. Numb, cramped, cold with that singular icy chill experienced only at death's positive approach, his limbs would not obey. He rolled forward over the bar and his legs were no longer strong enough to hold him. He didn't even feel the toes of his shoes as they struck the rung—the last of him to have contact with the viaduct—before his fall began. And if the boy thought anything at all during that fall, well those thoughts will never be known. Later he could not remember.

Oh, there was to be a later, but David could hardly have believed it while he was falling. And yet he was not unconscious. There were vague impressions: of the sky, the looming arch of the viaduct flying past, trees below, the sea on the horizon, then the sky again, all slowly turning. There was a composite whistling, of air displaced and air ejected from lungs contracted in a high-pitched scream. And then, it seemed a long time later, there was the impact...

But David did not strike the ground...he struck the pool. The deep swimming hole. The blessed, merciful river!

He had curled into a ball—the foetal position, almost—and this doubtless saved him. His tightly curled body entered the water with very little injury, however much of a splash it caused. Deep as the water was, nevertheless David struck the bottom with force, the pain and shock awakening whatever faculties remained functional in the motor areas of his brain. Aided by his resultant struggling, however weak, the ballooning air in his clothes bore him surely to the surface. The river carried him a few yards downstream to where the banks formed a bottle-neck for the pool.

Through all the pain David felt his knees scrape pebbles, felt his hands on the mud of the bank, and where will-power presumably was lacking, instinct took over. Somehow he crawled from the pool, and somehow he hung on grimly to consciousness. Away from the water, still he kept on crawling, as from the horror of his experience. Unseeing, he moved towards the towering unconquered colossus of the viaduct. He was quite blind as of yet; there was only a red, impenetrable haze before his bloodied eyes; he heard nothing but a sick roaring in his head. Finally his shoulder struck the bole of a tree that stood in the shelter of the looming brick giant, and there he stopped crawling, propped against the tree.

Slowly, very slowly, the roaring went out of his ears, the red haze before his eyes was replaced by lightning flashes and kaleidoscopic shapes and colours. Normal sound suddenly returned with a great pain in his ears. A rush of wind rustled the leaves of the trees, snatching away and then giving back a distant shouting which seemed to have its source overhead. Encased in his shell of pain, David did not immediately relate the shouting to his miraculous escape. Sight returned a few moments later and he began to cry rackingly with relief; he had thought himself permanently blind. And perhaps even now he had not been completely wrong, for his eyes had plainly been knocked out of order. Something was—must be—desperately wrong with them.

David tried to shake his head to clear it, but the action brought only fresh, blinding pain. When the nausea subsided he blinked his eyes, clearing them of blood and peering bewilderedly about at his surroundings. It was as he had suspected: the colours were all wrong. No, he blinked again, some of them seemed perfectly normal.

For instance: the bark of the tree against which he leaned was brown enough, and its dangling leaves were a fresh green. The sky above was blue, reflected in the river, and the bricks of the viaduct were a dull orange. Why then was the grass beneath him a lush red streaked with yellow and grey? Why was this unnatural grass wet and sticky, and—

—*And why were these tatters of dimly familiar clothing flung about in exploded, scarlet disorder?*

When his reeling brain at last delivered the answer, David opened his mouth to scream. Fainting before he could do so, he fell face down into the sticky embrace of his late friend.

THE LUSTSTONE

ONE

The ice was only a memory now, a racial memory whose legends had come down the years, whose evidence was graven in the land in hollow glacial tracts. Of the latter: time would weather the valley eventually, soften its contours however slowly. But the memories would stay, and each winter the snows would replenish them.

That was why the men of the tribes would paint themselves yellow in imitation of the sun-god, and stretch themselves in a line across the land east to west and facing north, and beat back the snow and ice with their clubs. And *frighten* it back with their screams and their leapings. With their magic they defeated winter and conjured spring, summer, and autumn, and thus were the seasons perpetuated.

The tribes, too, were perpetuated; each spring the tribal wizards—the witch-doctors—would perform those fertility rites deemed necessary to life, by means of which the grass was made to grow, the beasts to mate, and Man the weapon-maker to increase and prosper upon the face of the earth. It was the time of the sabretooth and the mammoth, and it was the springtime of Man, the thinking animal whose destiny is the stars. And even in those far dim primal times there were visionaries.

Chylos of the mighty Southern Tribe was one such: Chylos the Chief, the great wizard and seer whose word was law in the mid-South. And in that spring some ten thousand years ago, Chylos lay on his bed in

109

the grandest cave of all the caves of the Southern Tribe, and dreamed his dream.

He dreamed of invaders!

Of men not greatly unlike the men of the tribes, but fiercer far and with huge appetites for ale, war, and women. Aye, and there were gross-bearded ones, too, whose dragon-prowed ships were as snakes of the sea, whose horned helmets and savage cries gave them the appearance of demons! But Chylos knew that he dreamed only of the far future and so was not made greatly fearful.

And he dreamed that in that distant future there were others who came from the east with fire and thunder, and in his dreams Chylos heard the agonized screams of the descendants of his tribe, men, women, and children; and saw visions of black war, red rape, and rivers of crimson blood. A complex dream it was, and alien these invaders: with long knives and axes which were not of stone, and again wearing horned helmets upon their heads to make them more fearsome yet. From the sea they came, building mounds and forts where they garrisoned their soldiers behind great earthworks.

And some of them carried strange banners, covered with unknown runes and wore kilts of leather and rode in horse-drawn chairs with flashing spokes in their wheels; and their armies were disciplined thousands, moving and fighting with one mind…

Such were Chylos's dreams, which brought him starting awake; and so often had he dreamed them that he knew they must be more than mere nightmares. Until one morning, rising from his bed of hides, he saw that it was spring again and knew what must be done. Such visions as he had dreamed must come to pass, he felt it in his old bones, but not for many years. Not for years beyond his numbering. Very well: the gods themselves had sent Chylos their warning, and now he must act. For he was old and the earth would claim him long before the first invaders came, and so he must unite the tribes now and bring them together. And they must grow strong and their men become great warriors.

And there must be that which would remain long after Chylos himself was gone: a reminder, a monument, a *Power* to fuel the loins of the men and make the tribes strong. A driving force to make his people lusty, to ensure their survival. There must be children—many children! And their children in their turn must number thousands, and theirs must number… such a number as Chylos could not envisage. Then when the invaders came the tribes would be ready, unconquerable, indestructible.

So Chylos took up his staff and went out into the central plain of the valley, where he found a great stone worn round by the coming and going of the ice; a stone half as tall again as a man above the earth, and as much or more of its mass still buried in the ground. And upon this mighty stone he carved his runes of fertility, powerful symbols that spelled LUST. And he carved designs which were the parts of men and women: the rampant pods and rods of seed, and the ripe breasts and bellies of dawning life. There was nothing of love in what he drew, only of lust and the need to procreate; for man was much more the animal in those dim forgotten days and love as such one of his weaknesses. But when Chylos's work was done, still he saw that it was not enough.

For what was the stone but a stone? Only a stone carved with cryptic runes and symbols of sexuality, and nothing more. It had no power. Who would remember it in a hundred seasons, let alone years? Who would know what it meant?

He called all the leaders of the tribes together, and because there was a recent peace in the land they came. And Chylos spoke to those headmen and wizards, telling them of his dreams and visions, which were seen as great omens. Together the leaders of the tribes decided what must be done; twenty days later they sent all of their young men and women to Chylos the Seer, and their own wizards went with them.

Meanwhile a pit had been dug away from the foot of the great stone, and wedged timbers held back that boulder from tumbling into the pit. And of all the young men and women of the tribes, Chylos and the Elders chose the lustiest lad and a broad-hipped lass with the breasts of a goddess; and they were proud to be chosen, though for what they knew not.

But when they saw each other, these two, they drew back snarling; for their markings were those of tribes previously opposed in war! And such had been their enmity that even now when all the people were joined, still they kept themselves apart each tribe from the other. Now that the pair had been chosen to be together—and because of their markings, origins, and tribal taboos, the greatest of which forbade intercourse between them—they spoke thus:

"What is the meaning of this?" cried the young man, his voice harsh, affronted. "Why am I put with this woman? She is not of my tribe. She is of a tribe whose very name offends me! I am not at war with her, but neither may I know her."

And she said: "Do my own Elders make mock of me? Why am I insulted so? What have I done to deserve this? Take this thing which calls itself a man away from me!"

But Chylos and the Elders held up their hands, saying: "Be at peace, be at ease with one another. All will be made plain in due time. We bestow upon you a great honour. Do not dishonour your tribes." And the chosen ones were subdued, however grudgingly.

And the Elders whispered among each other and said: "We chose them and the gods were our witnesses and unopposed. They are more than fit for the task. Joining them like this may also more nearly fuse their tribes, and bring about a lasting peace. It must be right." And they were all agreed.

Then came the feasting, of meats dipped in certain spices and herbs known only to the wizards and flavoured with the crushed horn of mammoth; and the drinking of potent ales, all liberally sprinkled with the potions of the wizards. And when the celebrant horde was feasted and properly drunk, then came the oiled and perfumed and grotesquely-clad dancers, whose dance was the slow-twining dance of the grossly endowed gods of fertility. And as the dance progressed so drummers took up the beat, until the pulses of the milling thousands pounded and their bodies jerked with the jerking of the male and female dancers.

Finally the dance ended, but still the drummers kept to their madly throbbing beat; while in the crowd lesser dances had commenced, not so practised but no less intense and even more lusty. And as the celebrants paired off and fell upon each other, thick pelts were tossed into the pit where the great stone balanced, and petals of spring flowers gathered with the dew upon them, making a bower in the shadow of the boulder; and this was where the chosen couple were made to lie down, while all about the young people of the tribes spent themselves in the ritual spring orgy.

But the pair in the pit—though they had been stripped naked, and while they were drunk as the rest—nevertheless held back and drew apart, and scowled at each other through slitted eyes. Chylos stood at the rim and screamed at them: "Make love! Let the earth soak up your juices!" He prodded the young man with a spear and commanded him: "Take her! The gods demand it! What? And would you have the trees die, and all the animals, and the ice come down again to destroy us all? *Do you defy the gods?*"

At that the young man would obey, for he feared the gods, but she would not have him. "Let him in!" Chylos screamed at her. "Would you

be barren and have your breasts wither, and grow old before your time?"
And so she wrapped her legs about the young man. But he was uncertain,
and she had not accepted him; still, it seemed to Chylos that they were
joined. And as the orgy climbed to its climax he cried out his triumph
and signalled to a pair of well-muscled youths where they stood back
behind the boulder. And coming forward they took up hammers and
with mighty blows knocked away the chocks holding back the great stone
from the pit.

The boulder tilted—three hundred tons of rock keeling over—and in
the same moment Chylos clutched his heart, cried out and stumbled forward, and toppled into the pit!—and the rune-inscribed boulder with all
its designs and great weight slammed down into the hole with a shock that
shook the earth. But such was the power of the orgy that held them all in
sway, that only those who coupled in the immediate vicinity of the stone
knew that it had moved at all!

Now, with the drumming at a standstill, the couples parted, fell back,
lay mainly exhausted. A vast field, as of battle, with steam rising as a morning mist. And the two whose task it had been to topple the boulder going
amongst them, seeking still-willing, however aching flesh in which to
relieve their own pent passions.

Thus was the deed done, the rite performed, the magic worked, the luststone come into being. Or thus it was intended. And old Chylos never knowing
that, alas, his work was for nothing, for his propitiates had failed to couple…

Three winters after that the snows were heavy, meat was scarce, and
the tribes warred. Then for a decade the gods and their seasonal rites were
put aside, following which that great ritual orgy soon became a legend and
eventually a myth. Fifty years later the luststone and its carvings were
moss-covered, forgotten; another fifty saw the stone a shrine. One hundred more years passed and the domed, mossy top of the boulder was
hidden in a grove of oaks: a place of the gods, taboo.

The plain grew to a forest, and the stone was buried beneath a growing
mound of fertile soil; the trees were felled to build mammoth-pens, and
the grass grew deep, thick, and luxurious. More years saw the trees grow
up again into a mighty oak forest; and these were the years of the hunter,
the declining years of the mammoth. Now the people were farmers, of a
sort, who protected limited crops and beasts against Nature's perils. There

were years of the long-toothed cats and years of the wolf. And now and then there were wars between the tribes.

And time was the moon that waxed and waned, and the hills growing old and rounded, and forests spanning the entire land; and the tribes flourished and fought and did little else under the green canopy of these mighty forests...

Through all of this the stone slept, buried shallow in the earth, keeping its secret; but lovers in the forest knew where to lie when the moon was up. And men robbed by the years or by their own excesses could find a wonder there, when forgotten strength returned, however fleetingly, to fill them once more with fire.

As for old Chylos's dream: it came to pass, but his remedy was worthless. Buried beneath the sod for three thousand years the luststone lay, and felt the tramping feet of the nomad-warrior Celts on the march. Five thousand more years saw the Romans come to Britain, then the Anglo-Saxons, the Vikings, and still the luststone lay there.

There were greater wars than ever Chylos had dreamed, more of rape and murder than he ever could have imagined. War in the sea, on the land and in the air.

And at last there was peace again, of a sort. And finally—

Finally...

TWO

Garry Clemens was a human calculator at a betting shop in North London; he could figure the numbers, combinations and value of a winning ticket to within a doesn't matter a damn faster than the girls could feed the figures into their machines. All the punters knew him; generally they'd accept without qualms his arbitration on vastly complicated accumulators and the like. With these sort of qualifications Garry could hold down a job any place they played the horses—which was handy because he liked to move around a lot and betting on the races was his hobby. One of his hobbies, anyway.

Another was rape.

Every time Garry took a heavy loss, then he raped. That way (according to his figuring) he won every time. If he couldn't take it out on the horse that let him down, then he'd take it out on some girl instead. But he'd suffered a spate of losses recently, and that had led to some trouble. He hated those nights when he'd go back to his flat and lie down on his bed and have nothing good to think about for that day. Only bad things, like the two hundred he'd lost on that nag that should have come in at fifteen to one, or the filly that got pipped at the post and cost him a cool grand. Which was why he'd finally figured out a way to ease his pain.

Starting now he'd take a girl for every day of the week, and that way when he took a loss—no matter which day it fell on—he'd always have something good to think about that night when he went to bed. If it was a Wednesday, why, he'd simply think about the Wednesday girl, et cetera...

But he'd gone through a bad patch and so the rapes had had to come thick and fast, one and sometimes two a week. His Monday girl was a red-head he'd gagged and tied to a tree in the centre of a copse in a built-up area. He'd spent a lot of time with her, smoked cigarettes in between and talked dirty and nasty to her, raped her three times. Differently each time. Tuesday was a sixteen-year-old kid down at the bottom of the railway embankment. No gag or rope or anything; she'd been so shit-scared that after he was through she didn't even start yelling for an hour. Wednesday (Garry's favourite) it had been a heavily pregnant coloured woman he'd dragged into a burned-out shop right in town! He'd made that one do everything. In the papers the next day he'd read how she lost her baby. But that hadn't bothered him too much.

Thursday had been when it started to get sticky. Garry had dragged this hooker into a street of derelict houses but hadn't even got started when along came this copper! He'd put his knife in the tart's throat—so that she wouldn't yell—and then got to Hell out of there. And he'd reckoned himself lucky to get clean away. But on the other hand, it meant he had to go out the next night, too. He didn't like the tension to build up too much.

But Friday had been a near-disaster, too. There was a house-party not far from where he lived, and Garry had been invited. He'd declined, but he was there anyway—in the garden of the house opposite, whose people weren't at home. And when this really stacked piece had left the party on her own about midnight, Garry had jumped her. But just when he'd knocked her cold and was getting her out of her clothes, then the owners of the house turned up and saw him in the garden. He'd had to cut and run like the wind then, and even now it made his guts churn when he thought about it.

So he'd kept it quiet for a couple of weeks before starting again, and then he'd finally found his Thursday girl. A really shy thing getting off a late-night tube, who he'd carried into a parking lot and had for a couple of hours straight. And she hadn't said a word, just panted a lot and been sick. It turned out she was dumb—and Garry chuckled when he read that. No wonder she'd been so quiet. Maybe he should look for a blind one next time...

A week later, Friday, he'd gone out again, but it was a failure; he couldn't find anyone. And so the very next night he'd taken his Saturday girl—a middle-aged baglady! So what the Hell!—a rape is a rape is a rape, right? He gave her a bottle of some good stuff first, which put her away nicely, then gave her a Hell of a lot of bad stuff in as many ways as he knew how. She probably didn't even feel it, wouldn't even remember it, so afterwards he'd banged her face on the pavement a couple of times so that when she woke up at least she'd know *something* had happened! Except she hadn't woken up. Well, at least that way she wouldn't be talking about it. And by now he knew they'd have his semen type on record, and that they'd also have *him* if he just once slipped up. But he didn't intend to.

Sunday's girl was a lady taxi driver with a figure that was a real stopper! Garry hired her to take him out of town, directed her to a big house in the country and stopped her at the bottom of the drive. Then he hit her on the head, ripped her radio out, drove into a wood and had her in the back of the cab. He'd really made a meal of it, especially after she woke up; but as he was finishing she got a bit too active and raked his face—which was something he didn't much like. He had a nice face, Garry, and was very fond of it. So almost before he'd known that he was doing it, he'd gutted the whore!

But the next day in the papers the police were talking about skin under her fingernails, and now he knew they had his blood-group but definitely, too. *And* his face was marked; not badly, but enough. So it had been time to take a holiday.

Luckily he'd just had a big win on the gee-gees; he phoned the bookie's and said he wasn't up to it—couldn't see the numbers too clearly—he was taking time off. With an eye-patch and a bandage to cover the damage, he'd headed North and finally holed up in Chichester.

But all of that had been twelve days ago, and he was fine now, and he still had to find his girl-Friday. And today *was* Friday, so...Garry reckoned he'd rested up long enough.

This morning he'd read about a Friday night dance at a place called Athelsford, a hick village just a bus-ride away. Well, and he had nothing against country bumpkins, did he? So Athelsford it would have to be...

It was the middle of the long hot summer of '76. The weather forecasters were all agreed for once that this one would drag on and on, and reserves of water all over the country were already beginning to suffer. This was that summer when there would be shock reports of the Thames flowing backwards, when rainmakers would be called in from the USA to dance and caper, and when a certain Government Ministry would beg householders to put bricks in their WC cisterns and thus consume less of precious water.

The southern beaches were choked morning to night with kids on their school holidays, sun-blackened treasure hunters with knotted hankies on their heads and metal detectors in their hands, and frustrated fishermen with their crates of beer, boxes of sandwiches, and plastic bags of smelly bait. The pubs were filled all through opening hours with customers trying to drown their thirsts or themselves, and the resorts had never had it so good. The nights were balmy for lovers from Land's End to John o' Groat's, and nowhere balmier than in the country lanes of the Southern Counties.

Athelsford Estate in Hampshire, one of the few suburban housing projects of the Sixties to realize a measure of success (in that its houses were good, its people relatively happy, and—after the last bulldozer had clanked away—its countryside comparatively unspoiled) suffered or enjoyed the heatwave no more or less than anywhere else. It was just another small centre of life and twentieth-century civilization, and apart from the fact that Athelsford was 'rather select' there was little as yet to distinguish it from a hundred other estates and small villages in the country triangle of Salisbury, Reading, and Brighton.

Tonight being Friday night, there was to be dancing at The Barn. As its name implied, the place had been a half-brick, half-timber barn; but the Athelsfordians being an enterprising lot, three of their more affluent members had bought the great vault of a place, done it up with internal balconies, tables, and chairs, built a modest car park to one side—an extension of the village pub's car park—and now it was a dance hall, occasionally used for weddings and other private functions. On Wednesday nights the younger folk had it for their discotheques (mainly teenage affairs, in return for which they kept it in good repair), but on Friday nights the Barn became the focal point of the entire estate. The Barn and The Old Stage.

The Old Stage was the village pub, its sign a coach with rearing horses confronted by a highwayman in tricorn hat. Joe McGovern, a widower, owned and ran the pub, and many of his customers jokingly associated him with the highwayman on his sign. But while Joe was and always would be a canny Scot, he was also a fair man and down to earth. So were his prices. Ten years ago when the estate was new, the steady custom of the people had saved The Old Stage and kept it a free house. Now Joe's trade was flourishing, and he had plenty to be thankful for.

So, too, Joe's somewhat surly son Gavin. Things to be thankful for, and others he could well do without. Gavin was, for example, extremely thankful for The Barn, whose bar he ran on Wednesday and Friday nights, using stock from The Old Stage. The profits very nicely supplemented the wage he earned as a county council labourer working on the new road. The wage he *had* earned, anyway, before he'd quit. That had only been this morning but already he sort of missed the work, and he was sure he was going to miss the money. But...oh, he'd find other work. There was always work for good strong hands. He had that to be thankful for, too: his health and strength.

But he was *not* thankful for his kid sister, Eileen: her 'scrapes and narrow escapes' (as he saw her small handful of as yet entirely innocent friendships with the local lads), and her natural, almost astonishing beauty, which drew them like butterflies to bright flowers. It was that, in large part, which made him surly; for he knew that in fact she wasn't just a 'kid' sister any more, and that sooner or later she...

Oh, Gavin loved his sister, all right—indeed he had transferred to her all of his affection and protection when their mother died three years ago—but having lost his mother he wasn't going to lose Eileen, too, not if he could help it.

Gavin was twenty-two, Eileen seventeen. He was over six feet tall, narrow-hipped, wide in the shoulders: a tapering wedge of muscle with a bullet-head to top it off. Most of the village lads looked at Eileen, then looked at Gavin, and didn't look at Eileen again. But those of them who looked at her twice reckoned she was worth it.

She was blonde as her brother was dark, as sweet and slim as he was huge and surly; five-seven, with long shapely legs and a waist like a wisp, and blue eyes with lights in them that danced when she smiled; the very image of her mother. And that was Gavin's problem—for he'd loved his mother a great deal, too.

It was 5:30 p.m. and brother and sister were busy in workclothes, loading stock from the back door of The Old Stage onto a trolley and carting it across the parking lot to The Barn. Joe McGovern ticked off the items on a stock list as they worked. But when Gavin and Eileen were alone in The Barn, stacking the last of the bottles onto the shelves behind the bar, suddenly he said to her: "Will you be here tonight?"

She looked at her brother. There was nothing surly about Gavin now. There never was when he spoke to her; indeed his voice held a note of concern, of agitation, of some inner struggle which he himself couldn't quite put his finger on. And she knew what he was thinking and that it would be the same tonight as always. Someone would dance with her, and then dance with her again—and then no more. Because Gavin would have had 'a quiet word with him'.

"Of course I'll be here, Gavin," she sighed. "You know I will. I wouldn't miss it. I love to dance and chat with the girls—*and* with the boys—when I get the chance! Why does it bother you so?"

"I've told you often enough why it bothers me," he answered gruffly, breathing heavily through his nose. "It's all those blokes. They've only one thing on their minds. They're the same with all the girls. But you're not just any girl—you're my sister."

"Yes," she answered, a trifle bitterly, "and don't they just know it! You're always there, in the background, watching, somehow threatening. It's like having two fathers—only one of them's a tyrant! Do you know, I can't remember the last time a boy wanted to walk me home?"

"But...you *are* home!" he answered, not wanting to fight, wishing now that he'd kept his peace. If only she was capable of understanding the ways of the world. "You live right next door."

"Then simply *walk* me!" she blurted it out. "Oh, anywhere! Gavin, can't you understand? It's *nice* to be courted, to have someone who wants to hold your hand!"

"That's how it starts," he grunted, turning away. "They want to hold your hand. But who's to say how it finishes, eh?"

"Well not much fear of that!" she sighed again. "Not that I'm that sort of girl anyway," and she looked at him archly. "But even if I was, with you around—straining at the leash like...like a great hulking watchdog—nothing's very much likely to even get started, now is it?" And before he could answer, but less harshly now: "Now come on," she said, "tell me what's brought all this on? You've been really nice to me this last couple of weeks. The hot weather may have soured some people but you've been really sweet—like a Big Brother should be—until out of the blue, like this. I really don't understand what gets into you, Gavin."

It was his turn to sigh. "Aren't you forgetting something?" he said. "The assault—probably with sexual motivation—just last week, Saturday night, in Lovers' Lane?"

Perhaps Eileen really ought not to pooh-pooh that, but she believed she understood it well enough. "An assault," she said. "Motive: 'probably' sexual—the most excitement Athelsford has known in…oh, as long as *I* can remember! And the 'victim': Linda Anstey. Oh, my, *what* a surprise! *Hah!* Why, Linda's always been that way! Every kid in the school had fooled around with her at one time or another. From playing kids' games to…well, everything. It's the way she is and everyone knows it. All right, perhaps I'm being unfair to her: she might have asked for trouble and she might not, but it seems hardly surprising to me that if it was going to happen to someone, Linda would be the one!"

"But it *did* happen," Gavin insisted. "That kind of bloke does exist—plenty of them." He stacked the last half-dozen cans and made for the exit; and changing the subject (as he was wont to do when an argument was going badly for him, or when he believed he'd proved his point sufficiently) said: "Me, I'm for a pint before I get myself ready for tonight. Fancy an iced lemonade, kid?" He paused, turned back towards her, and grinned, but she suspected it was forced. If only she could gauge what went on in his mind.

But: "Oh, all right!" she finally matched his grin, "if you're buying." She caught up with him and grabbed him, standing on tip-toe to give him a kiss. "But Gavin—promise me that from now on you won't worry about me so much, OK?"

He hugged her briefly, and reluctantly submitted: "Yeah, all right."

But as she led the way out of The Barn and across the car park, with the hot afternoon sun shining in her hair and her sweet, innocent body moving like that inside her coveralls, he looked after her and worried all the harder; worried the way an older brother *should* worry, he thought, and yet somehow far more intensely. And the worst of it was that he *knew* he was being unreasonable and obsessive! But (and Gavin at once felt his heart hardening)…oh, he recognized well enough the way the village Jack-the-Lads looked at Eileen, and knew how much they'd like to get their itchy little paws on her—the grubby-minded, horny…

...But there Gavin's ireful thoughts abruptly evaporated, the scowl left his face, and he frowned as a vivid picture suddenly flashed onto the screen of his mind. It was something he'd seen just this morning, across the fields where they were laying the new road; something quite obscene which hadn't made much of an impression on him at the time, but which now...and astonished, he paused again. For he couldn't for the life of him see how he'd connected up a thing like that with Eileen! And it just as suddenly dawned on him that the reason he knew how the boys felt about his sister was because he sometimes felt that way too. Oh, not about *her*—no, of course not—but about...a boulder? Well, certainly it had been a boulder that did it to him this morning, anyway.

And: *Gavin, son,* he told himself, *sometimes I think you're maybe just a tiny wee bit sick*! And then he laughed, if only to himself.

But somehow the pictures in his mind just wouldn't go away, and as he went to his upstairs room in The Old Stage and slowly changed into his evening gear, so he allowed himself to go over again the peculiar occurrences of the morning...

THREE

That Friday morning, yes, and it had been hot as a furnace. And every member of the road gang without exception looking forward to the coming weekend, to cool beers in cool houses with all the windows thrown open; so that as the heat-shimmering day had drawn towards noon they'd wearied of the job and put a lot less muscle into it.

Also, and to make things worse, this afternoon they'd be a man short; for this was Gavin McGovern's last morning and he hadn't been replaced yet. And even when he was...well, it would take a long time to find someone else who could throw a bulldozer around like he could. The thing was like a toy in his hands. But...seeing as how he lived in Athelsford and had always considered himself something of a traitor anyway, working on the link road, he'd finally decided to seek employment elsewhere.

Foreman John Sykes wasn't an Athelsfordian, but he made it his business to know something about the people working under him—especially if they were local to the land where he was driving his road. He'd got to know Big Gavin pretty well, he reckoned, and in a way envied him. He certainly wouldn't mind it if *his* Old Man owned a country pub! But on the other hand he could sympathize with McGovern, too. He knew how torn he must feel.

This was the one part of his job that Sykes hated: when the people up top said the road goes here, and the people down here said oh no it doesn't, not in *our* back garden! Puffed up, awkward, defiant little bastards! But at the same time Sykes could sympathize with them also, even though they were making his job as unpleasant as they possibly could. And that was yet another reason why the work hadn't gone too well this morning.

Today it had been a sit-in, when a good dozen of the locals had appeared from the wood at the end of Lovers' Lane, bringing lightweight fold-down garden chairs with them to erect across the road. And there they'd sat with their placards and sandwiches on the new stretch of tarmac, heckling the road gang as they toiled and sweated into their dark-stained vests and tried to build a bloody road which wasn't wanted. And which didn't seem to want to be built! They'd stayed from maybe quarter-past nine to a minute short of eleven, then got up and like a gaggle of lemmings waddled back to the village again. Their 'good deed' for the day—*Goddam*!

Christ, what a day! For right after that…*big* trouble, mechanical trouble! Or rather an obstruction which had caused mechanical trouble. Not the more or less passive, placard-waving obstruction of people—which was bad enough—but a rather more physical, much more tangible obstruction. Namely, a bloody great boulder!

The first they'd known of it was when the bulldozer hit it while lifting turf and muck in a wide swath two feet deep. Until then there had been only the usual stony debris—small, rounded pebbles and the occasional blunt slab of scarred rock, nothing out of the ordinary for these parts—and Sykes hadn't been expecting anything quite this big. The surveyors had been across here, hammering in their long iron spikes and testing the ground, but they'd somehow missed this thing. Black granite by its looks, it had stopped the dozer dead in its tracks and given Gavin McGovern a fair old shaking! But at least the blade had cleared the sod and clay off the top of the thing. Like the dome of a veined, bald, old head it had looked, sticking up there in the middle of the projected strip.

"See if you can dig the blade under it," Sykes had bawled up at Gavin through clouds of blue exhaust fumes and the clatter of the engine. "Try to lever the bastard up, or split it. We have to get down a good forty or fifty inches just here."

Taking it personally—and with something less than an hour to go, eager to get finished now—Gavin had dragged his sleeve across his brown, perspiration-shiny brow and grimaced. Then, tilting his helmet back on his head, he'd slammed the blade of his machine deep into the earth half a dozen times until he could feel it biting against the unseen curve of the boulder. Then he'd gunned the motor, let out the clutch, shoved, and lifted all in one fluid movement. Or at least in a movement that should have been fluid. For instead of finding purchase the blade had ridden up, splitting turf and topsoil as it slid over the fairly smooth surface of the stone; the dozer had lurched forward, slewing round when the blade finally snagged on a rougher part of the surface; the offside caterpillar had parted in a shriek of hot, tortured metal.

Then Gavin had shut her off, jumped down, and stared disbelievingly at his grazed and bleeding forearm where it had scraped across the iron frame of the cab. "Damn—*damn!*" he'd shouted then, hurling his safety helmet at the freshly turned earth and kicking the dozer's broken track.

"Easy, Gavin," Sykes had gone up to him. "It's not your fault, and it's not the machine's. It's mine, if anybody's. I had no idea there was anything this big here. And by the look of it this is only the tip of the iceberg."

But Gavin wasn't listening; he'd gone down on one knee and was examining part of the boulder's surface where the blade had done a job of clearing it off. He was frowning, peering hard, breaking away small scabs of loose dirt and tracing lines or grooves with his strong, blunt fingers. The runic symbols were faint but the carved picture was more clearly visible. There were other pictures, too, with only their edges showing as yet, mainly hidden under the curve of the boulder. The ganger got down beside Gavin and assisted him, and slowly the carvings took on clearer definition.

Sykes was frowning, too, now. What the Hell? A floral design of some sort? Very old, no doubt about it. Archaic? Prehistoric?

Unable as yet to make anything decisive of the pictures on the stone, they cleared away more dirt. But then Sykes stared harder, slowly shook his head, and began to grin. The grin spread until it almost split his face ear to ear. Perhaps not prehistoric after all. More like the work of some dirty-minded local kid. And not a bad artist, at that!

The lines of the main picture were primitive but clinically correct, however exaggerated. And its subject was completely unmistakable. Gavin McGovern continued to stare at it, and his bottom jaw had fallen open.

Finally, glancing at Sykes out of the corner of his eye, he grunted: "Old, do you think?"

Sykes started to answer, then shut his mouth and stood up. He thought fast, scuffed some of the dirt back with his booted foot, bent to lean a large, flat flake of stone against the picture, mainly covering it from view. Sweat trickled down his back and made it itch under his wringing shirt. Made it itch like the devil, and the rest of his body with it. The boulder seemed hot as Hell, reflecting the blazing midday sunlight.

And "Old?" the ganger finally answered. "You mean, like ancient? Naw, I shouldn't think so...Hey, and Gavin, son—if I were you, I wouldn't go mentioning this to anyone. You know what I mean?"

Gavin looked up, still frowning. "No," he shook his head, "what do you mean?"

"What?" said Sykes. "You mean to say you can't see it? Why, only let this get out and there'll be people coming from all over the place to see it! Another bloody Stonehenge, it'll be! And what price your Athelsford then, eh? Flooded, the place would be, with all sorts of human debris come to see the famous dirty caveman pictures! You want that, do you?"

No, that was the last thing Gavin wanted. "I see what you mean," he said, slowly. "Also, it would slow you down, right? They'd stop you running your road through here."

"That, too, possibly," Sykes answered. "For a time, anyway. But just think about it. What would you rather have: a new road pure and simple— or a thousand yobs a day tramping through Athelsford and up Lovers' Lane to ogle this little lot, eh?"

That was something Gavin didn't have to think about for very long. It would do business at The Old Stage a power of good, true, but then there was Eileen. Pretty soon they'd be coming to ogle her, too. "So what's next?" he said.

"You leave that to me," Sykes told him. "And just take my word for it that this time tomorrow this little beauty will be so much rubble, OK?"

Gavin nodded; he knew that the ganger was hot stuff with a drill and a couple of pounds of explosive. "If you say so," he spat into the dust and dirt. "Anyway, I don't much care for the looks of the damned thing!" He scratched furiously at his forearm where his graze was already starting to scab over. "It's not right, this dirty old thing. Sort of makes me hot and...itchy!"

"Itchy, yeah," Sykes agreed. And he wondered what sort of mood his wife, Jennie, would be in tonight. If this hot summer sun had worked on her the way it was beginning to work on him, well tonight could get to be pretty interesting. Which would make a welcome change!

Deep, dark, and much disturbed now, old Chylos had felt unaccustomed tremors vibrating through his fossilized bones. The stamping of a thousand warriors on the march, roaring their songs of red death? Aye, perhaps. And:

"*Invaders!*" Chylos breathed the word, without speaking, and indeed without breathing.

"*No,*" Hengit of the Far Forest tribe contradicted him. "*The mammoths are stampeding, the earth is sinking, trees are being felled. Any of these things, but no invaders. Is that all you dream about, old man? Why can't you simply lie still and sleep like the dead thing you are?*"

"*And even if there were invaders,*" the revenant of a female voice now joined in, Alaze of the Shrub Hill folk, "*would you really expect a man of the Far Forest tribe to come to arms? They are notorious cowards! Better you call on me, Chylos, a woman to rise up against these invaders—if there really were invaders, which there are not.*"

Chylos listened hard—to the earth, the sky, the distant sea—but no longer heard the thundering of booted feet, nor warcries going up into the air, nor ships with muffled oars creeping and creaking in the mist. And so he sighed and said: "*Perhaps you are right—but nevertheless we should be ready! I, at least, am ready!*"

And: "*Old fool!*" Hengit whispered of Chylos into the dirt and the dark.

And: "*Coward!*" Alaze was scathing of Hengit where all three lay broken, under the luststone...

7:15 p.m.

The road gang had knocked off more than two hours ago and the light was only just beginning to fade a little. An hour and a half to go yet to the summer's balmy darkness, when the young people would wander hand in hand, and occasionally pause mouth to mouth, in Lovers' Lane. Or perhaps not until later, for tonight there was to be dancing at The Barn. And for now...all should be peace and quiet out here in the fields, where the luststone raised its veined dome of a head through the broken soil. All *should* be quiet—but was not.

"Levver!" shouted King above the roar of the bikes, his voice full of scorn. "What a bleedin' player you turned out to be! What the 'ell do you call this, then?"

"The end o' the bleedin' road," one of the other bikers shouted. "That's where!"

"Is it ever!" cried someone else.

Leather grinned sheepishly and pushed his Nazi-style crash-helmet to the back of his head. "So I come the wrong way, di'n I? 'Ell's teef, the sign said bleedin' Affelsford, dinnit?"

"Yers," King shouted. "Also NO ENTRY an' WORKS IN PRO-bleedin'-GRESS! 'Ere, switch off, you lot, I can't 'ear meself fink!"

As the engines of the six machines clattered to a halt, King got off his bike and stretched, stamping his feet. His real name was Kevin; but as leader of a chapter of Hell's Angels, who needed a name like that? A crude crown was traced in lead studs on the back of his leather jacket and a golden sovereign glittered where it dangled from his left earlobe. No more than twenty-five or -six years of age, King kept his head clean-shaven under a silver helmet painted with black eye-sockets and fretted nostrils to resemble a skull. He was hard as they come, was King, and the rest of them knew it.

"That's the place I cased over there," said Leather, pointing. He had jumped up onto the dome of a huge boulder, the luststone, to spy out the land. "See the steeple there? That's Affelsford—and Comrades, does it have *some* crumpet!"

"Well, jolly dee!" said King. "Wot we supposed to do, then? Ride across the bleedin' fields? Come on, Levver my son—you was the one rode out here and onced it over. 'Ow do we bleedin' *get* there?" The rest of the Angels sniggered.

Leather grinned. "We goes up the motorway a few 'undred yards an' spins off at the next turnin', that's all. I jus' made a simple mistake, di'n I."

"Yers," said King, relieving himself loudly against the luststone. "Well, let's not make no more, eh? I gets choked off pissin' about an' wastin' valuable time."

By now the others had dismounted and stood ringed around the dome of the boulder. They stretched their legs and lit 'funny' cigarettes. "That's right," said King, "light up. Let's have a break before we go in."

"Best not leave it too late," said Leather. "Once the mood is on me I likes to get it off…"

126

"One copper, you said," King reminded him, drawing deeply on a poorly constructed smoke. "Only one bluebottle in the whole place?"

"S'right," said Leather. "An' 'e's at the other end of town. We can wreck the place, 'ave our fun wiv the girlies, be out again before 'e knows we was ever in!"

"'Ere," said one of the others. "These birds is the real fing, eh, Levver?"

Leather grinned crookedly and nodded. "Built for it," he answered. "Gawd, it's ripe, is Affelsford."

The gang guffawed, then quietened as a dumpy figure approached from the construction shack. It was one of Sykes's men, doing night-watchman to bolster his wages. "What's all this?" he grunted, coming up to them.

"Unmarried muvvers' convention," said King. "Wot's it look like?" The others laughed, willing to make a joke of it and let it be; but Leather jumped down from the boulder and stepped forward. He was eager to get things started, tingling—even itchy—with his need for violence.

"Wot's it ter you, baldy?" he snarled, pushing the little man in the chest and sending him staggering.

Baldy Dawson was one of Sykes's drivers and didn't have a lot of muscle. He did have common sense, however, and could see that things might easily get out of hand. "Before you start any rough stuff," he answered, backing away, "I better tell you I took your bike numbers and phoned 'em through to the office in Portsmouth." He had done no such thing, but it was a good bluff. "Any trouble—my boss'll know who did it."

Leather grabbed him by the front of his sweat-damp shirt. "You little—"

"Let it be," said King. "'E's only doin' 'is job. Besides, 'e 'as an 'ead jus' like mine!" He laughed.

"Wot?" Leather was astonished.

"Why spoil fings?" King took the other's arm. "Now listen, Levver me lad—all you've done so far is bog everyfing up, right? So let's bugger off into bleedin' Affelsford an' 'ave ourselves some fun! You want to see some blood—OK, me too—but for Chrissakes, let's get somefing for our money, right?"

They got back on their bikes and roared off, leaving Baldy Dawson in a slowly settling cloud of dust and exhaust fumes. "Young bastards!" He scratched his naked dome. "Trouble for someone before the night's out, I'll wager."

Then, crisis averted, he returned to the shack and his well-thumbed copy of *Playboy*...

FOUR

"*This time,*" said Chylos, with some urgency, "*I cannot be mistaken.*"

The two buried with him groaned—but before they could comment:

"*Are you deaf, blind—have you no feelings?*" he scorned. "*No, it's simply that you do not have my magic!*"

"*It's your 'magic' that put us here!*" finally Hengit answered his charges. "*Chylos, we don't need your magic!*"

"*But the tribes do,*" said Chylos. "*Now more than ever!*"

"*Tribes?*" this time it was Alaze who spoke. "*The tribes were scattered, gone, blown to the four winds many lifetimes agone. What tribes do you speak of, old man?*"

"*The children of the tribes, then!*" he blustered. "*Their children's children! What does it matter? They are the same people! They are of our blood! And I have dreamed a dream…*"

"*That again?*" said Hengit. "*That dream of yours, all these thousands of years old?*"

"*Not the old dream,*" Chylos denied, "*but a new one! Just now, lying here, I dreamed it! Oh, it was not unlike the old one, but it was vivid, fresh, new! And I cannot be mistaken.*"

And now the two lying there with him were silent, for they too had felt, sensed, something. And finally: "*What did you see…in this dream?*" Alaze was at least curious.

"*I saw them as before,*" said Chylos, "*with flashing spokes in the wheels of their battle-chairs; except the wheels were not set side by side but fore and aft! And helmets upon their heads, some with horns! They wore shirts of leather picked our in fearsome designs, monstrous runes; sharp knives in their belts, aye, and flails—and blood in their eyes! Invaders—I cannot be mistaken!*"

And Hengit and Alaze shuddered a little in their stony bones, for Chylos had inspired them with the truth of his vision and chilled them with the knowledge of his prophecy finally come true. But…what could they do about it, lying here in the cold earth? It was as if the old wizard read their minds.

"*You are not bound to lie here,*" he told them. "*What are you now but will? And my will remains strong! So let's be up and about our work. I, Chylos, have willed it—so let it be!*"

"*Our work? What work?*" the two cried together. "*We cannot fight!*"

"*You could if you willed it,*" said Chylos, "*and if you have not forgotten how. But I didn't mention fighting. No, we must warn them. The children of*" the children of the tribes. *Warn them, inspire them, cause them to lust after the blood of these invaders!*" And before they could question him further:

"*Up, up, we've work to do!*" Chylos cried. "*Up with you and out into the night, to seek them out. The children of the children of the tribes…!*"

From the look of things, it was all set to be a full house at The Barn. Athelsfordians in their Friday-night best were gravitating first to The Old Stage for a warm-up drink or two, then crossing the parking lot to The Barn to secure good tables up on the balconies or around the dance floor. Another hour or two and the place would be in full swing. Normally Gavin McGovern would be pleased with the way things were shaping up, for what with tips and all it would mean a big bonus for him. And his father at the pub wouldn't complain, for what was lost on the swings would be regained on the roundabouts. And yet…

There seemed a funny mood on the people tonight, a sort of scratchiness about them, an abrasiveness quite out of keeping. When the disco numbers were playing the girls danced with a sexual aggressiveness Gavin hadn't noticed before, and the men of the village seemed almost to be eyeing each other up like tomcats spoiling for a fight. Pulling pints for all he was worth, Gavin hadn't so far had much of a chance to examine or analyse the thing; it was just that in the back of his mind some small dark niggling voice seemed to be urgently whispering: "*Look out! Be on your guard! Tonight's the night! And when it happens you won't believe it!*" But… it could simply be his imagination, of course.

Or (and Gavin growled his frustration and self-annoyance as he felt that old obsession rising up again) it could simply be that Eileen had found herself a new dancing partner, and that since the newcomer had walked into the place they'd scarcely been off the floor. A fact which in itself was enough to set him imagining all sorts of things, and uppermost the sensuality of women and sexual competitiveness, readiness, and willingness of young men. And where Gavin's sister was concerned, much too willing!

But Eileen had seen Gavin watching her, and as the dance tune ended she came over to the bar with her young man in tow. This was a ploy she'd used before: a direct attack is often the best form of defence. Gavin remembered his promise, however, and in fact the man she was with seemed a very decent sort at first glance: clean and bright, smartly dressed, seriously intentioned. Now Gavin would see if his patter matched up to his looks.

"Gavin," said Eileen, smiling warningly, "I'd like you to meet Gordon Cleary—Gordon's a surveyor from Portsmouth."

"How do you do, Gordon," Gavin dried his hands, reached across the bar to shake with the other, discovered the handshake firm, dry, and no-nonsense. But before they could strike up any sort of conversation the dance floor had emptied and the bar began to crowd up. "I'm sorry," Gavin shrugged ruefully. "Business. But at least you were here first and I can get you your drinks." He looked at his sister.

"Mine's easy," she said, smiling. "A lemonade, please." And Gavin was pleased to note that Cleary made no objection, didn't try to force strong drink on her.

"Oh, a shandy for me," he said, "and go light on the beer, please, Gavin, for I'll be driving later. And one for yourself, if you're ready."

The drinks were served and Gavin turned to the next party of customers in line at the bar. There were four of them: Tod Baxter and Angela Meers, village sweethearts, and Allan Harper and his wife, Val. Harper was a PTI at the local school; he ordered a confusing mixture of drinks, no two alike; Gavin, caught on the hop, had a little trouble with his mental arithmetic. "Er, that's two pounds—er—" He frowned in concentration.

"Three pounds and forty-seven pence, on the button!" said Gordon Cleary from the side. Gavin looked at him and saw his eyes flickering over the price list pinned up behind the bar.

"Pretty fast!" he commented, and carried on serving. But to himself he said: *except I hope it's only with numbers...*

Gavin wasn't on his own behind the bar; at the other end, working just as hard, Bill Salmons popped corks and pulled furious pints. Salmons was ex-Army, a parachutist who'd bust himself up jumping. You wouldn't know it, though, for he was strong as a horse. As the disc jockey got his strobes going again and the music started up, and as the couples gradually gravitated back towards the dance floor, Gavin crossed quickly to Salmons and said: "I'm going to get some of this sweat off. Two minutes?"

Salmons nodded, said; "Hell of a night, isn't it? Too damned *hot!*"

Gavin reached under the bar for a clean towel and headed for the gents' toilet. Out of the corner of his eye he saw that Eileen and Gordon Cleary were back on the floor again. Well, if all the bloke wanted was to dance...that was OK.

In the washroom Gavin took off his shirt, splashed himself with cold water, and towelled it off, dressed himself again. A pointless exercise: he was just as hot and damp as before! As he finished off Allan Harper came in, also complaining of the heat.

They passed a few words; Harper was straightening his tie in a mirror when there came the sound of shattering glass from the dance hall, causing Gavin to start. "What—?" he said.

"Just some clown dropped his drink, I expect," said Harper. "Or fainted for lack of air! It's about time we got some decent air-conditioning in this—"

And he paused as there sounded a second crash—which this time was loud enough to suggest a table going over. The music stopped abruptly and some girl gave a high-pitched shriek.

We warned you! said several dark little voices in the back of Gavin's mind. "What the Hell—?" he started down the corridor from the toilets with Harper hot on his heels.

Entering the hall proper the two skidded to a halt. On the other side of the room a village youth lay sprawled among the debris of a wrecked table, blood spurting from his nose. Over him stood a Hell's Angel, swinging a bike chain threateningly. In the background a young girl sobbed, backing away, her dress torn down the front. Gavin would have started forward but Harper caught his arm. "Look!" he said.

At a second glance the place seemed to be crawling with Angels. There was one at the entrance, blocking access; two more were on the floor, dragging Angela Meers and Tod Baxter apart. They had yanked the straps of Angela's dress down, exposing her breasts. A fifth Angel had clambered into the disco control box, was flinging records all over the place as he sought his favourites. And the sixth was at the bar.

Now it was Gavin's turn to gasp, "Look!"

The one at the bar, King, had trapped Val Harper on her bar stool. He had his arms round her, his hands gripping the bar top. He rubbed himself grindingly against her with lewdly suggestive sensuality.

For a moment longer the two men stood frozen on the perimeter of this scene, nailed down by a numbness which, as it passed, brought rage in its wake. The Angel with the chain, Leather, had come across the floor and swaggered by them into the corridor, urinating in a semicircle as he went, saying: "Evenin' gents. This the bog, then?"

What the Hell's happening? thought Harper, lunging towards the bar. There must be something wrong with the strobe lights: they blinded him as he ran, flashing rainbow colours in a mad kaleidoscope that flooded the entire room. The Angel at the bar was trying to get his hand down the front of Val's dress, his rutting movements exaggerated by the crazy strobes. Struggling desperately, Val screamed.

Somewhere at the back of his shocked mind, Harper noted that the Angels still wore their helmets. He also noted, in the flutter of the crazy strobes, that the helmets seemed to have grown horns! *Jesus, it's like a bloody Viking invasion!* he thought, going to Val's rescue...

It had looked like a piece of cake to King and his Angels. A gift. The kid selling tickets hadn't even challenged them. Too busy wetting his pants, King supposed. And from what he had seen of The Barn's clientele: pushovers! As soon as he'd spotted Val Harper at the bar, he'd known what he wanted. A toffy-nosed bird like her in a crummy place like this? She could only be here for one thing. And not a man in the place to deny him whatever he wanted to do or take.

Which is why it came as a total surprise to King when Allan Harper spun him around and butted him square in the face. Blood flew as the astonished Angel slammed back against the bar; his spine cracked against the bar's rim, knocking all the wind out of him; in another moment Bill Salmons's arm went round his neck in a stranglehold. There was no time for chivalry: Harper the PTI finished it with a left to King's middle and a right to his already bloody face. The final blow landed on King's chin, knocking him cold. As Bill Salmons released him he flopped forward, his death's-head helmet flying free as he landed face-down on the floor.

Gavin McGovern had meanwhile reached into the disc-jockey's booth, grabbed his victim by the scruff of the neck, and hurled him out of the booth and across the dance floor. Couples hastily got out of the way as the Angel slid on his back across the polished floor. Skidding to a halt, he brought out a straight-edged razor in a silvery flash of steel. Gavin was on him in a moment; he lashed out with a foot that caught the Angel in the throat, knocking him flat on his back again. The razor spun harmlessly away across the floor as its owner writhed and clawed at his throat.

Seeing their Angel at Arms on the floor like that, the pair who tormented Angela Meers now turned their attention to Gavin McGovern. They had already knocked Tod Baxter down, kicking him where he huddled. But they hadn't got in a good shot and as Gavin loomed large so

Tod got to his feet behind them. Also, Allan Harper was dodging his way through the now strangely silent crowd where he came from the bar.

The Angel at the door, having seen something of the melee and wanting to get his share while there was still some going, also came lunging in through the wild strobe patterns. But this one reckoned without the now fully roused passions of the young warriors of the Athelsford tribe. Three of the estate's larger youths jumped him, and he went down under a hail of blows. And by then Allan Harper, Gavin McGovern and Tod Baxter had fallen on the other two. For long moments there were only the crazily flashing strobes, the dull thudding of fists into flesh, and a series of fading grunts and groans.

Five Angels were down; and the sixth, coming out of the toilets, saw only a sea of angered faces all turned in his direction. Faces hard and full of fury—*and* bloodied, crumpled shapes here and there, cluttering the dance floor. Pale now and disbelieving, Leather ran towards the exit, found himself surrounded in a moment. And now in the absolute silence there was bloodlust written on those faces that ringed him in.

They rolled over him like a wave, and his Nazi helmet flew off and skidded to a rocking halt...at the feet of Police Constable Charlie Bennett, Athelsford's custodian of the law, where he stood framed in the door of the tiny foyer.

Then the normal lights came up and someone cut the strobes, and as the weirdly breathless place slowly came back to life, so PC Bennett was able to take charge. And for the moment no one, not even Gavin, noticed that Eileen McGovern and her new friend were nowhere to be seen...

FIVE

Chylos was jubilant. *"It's done!"* he cried in his grave. *"The invaders defeated, beaten back!"*

And: *"You were right, old man,"* finally Hengit grudgingly answered. *"They were invaders, and our warnings and urgings came just in time. But this tribe of yours—pah! Like flowers, they were, weak and waiting to be crushed— until we inspired them."*

And now Chylos was very angry indeed. *"You two!"* he snapped like a bowstring. *"If you had heeded me at the rites, these many generations flown, then were there no requirement for our efforts this night! But...perhaps I may still undo your mischief, even now, and finally rest easy."*

"That can't be, old man, and you know it," this time Alaze spoke up. *"Would that we could put right that of which you accuse us; for if our blood still runs in these tribes, then it were only right and proper. But we cannot put it right. No, not even with all your magic. For what are we now but worm-fretted bones and dust? There's no magic can give us back our flesh..."*

"There is," Chylos chuckled then. *"Oh, there is! The magic of this stone. No, not your flesh but your will. No, not your limbs but your lust. Neither your youth nor your beauty nor even your hot blood, but your spirit! Which is all you will need to do what must be done. For if the tribes may not be imbrued with your seed, strengthened by your blood—then it must be with your spirit. I may not do it for I was old even in those days, but it is still possible for you. If I will it—and if you will it.*

"Now listen, and I shall tell you what must be done..."

Eileen McGovern and 'Gordon Cleary' stood outside The Barn in the deepening dusk and watched the Black Maria come and take away the battered Angels. As the police van made off down the estate's main street Eileen leaned towards the entrance to the disco, but her companion seemed concerned for her and caught her arm. "Better let it cool down in there," he said. "There's bound to be a lot of hot blood still on the boil."

"Maybe you're right," Eileen looked up at him. "Certainly you were right to bundle us out of there when it started! So what do you suggest? We could go and cool off in The Old Stage. My father owns it."

He shrugged, smiled, seemed suddenly shy, a little awkward. "I'd rather hoped we could walk together," he said. "The heat of the day is off now—it's cool enough out here. Also, I'll have to be going in an hour or so. I'd hoped to be able to, well, talk to you in private. Pubs and dance halls are fine for meeting people, but they're dreadfully noisy places, too."

It was her turn to shrug. It would be worth it if only to defy Gavin. And afterwards she'd make him see how there was no harm in her friendships. "All right," she said, taking Cleary's arm. "Where shall we walk?"

He looked at her and sighed his defeat. "Eileen, I don't know this place at all. I wouldn't know one street or lane from the next. So I suppose I'm at your mercy!"

"Well," she laughed. "I do know a pretty private place." And she led him away from The Barn and into an avenue of trees. "It's not far away, and it's *the* most private place of all." She smiled as once more she glanced up at him in the flooding moonlight. "That's why it's called Lovers' Lane…"

Half an hour later in The Barn, it finally dawned on Gavin McGovern that his sister was absent. He'd last seen her with that Gordon Cleary bloke. And what had Cleary said: something about having to drive later? Maybe he'd taken Eileen with him. They must have left during the ruckus with the Angels. Well, at least Gavin could be thankful for that!

But at eleven o'clock when The Barn closed and he had the job of checking and then shifting the stock, still she wasn't back. Or if she was she'd gone straight home to The Old Stage and so to bed. Just before twelve midnight Gavin was finished with his work. He gratefully put out the lights and locked up The Barn, then crossed to The Old Stage where his father was still checking the night's take and balancing the stock ledger.

First things first, Gavin quietly climbed the stairs and peeped into Eileen's room; the bed was still made up, undisturbed from this morning; she wasn't back. Feeling his heart speeding up a little, Gavin went back downstairs and reported her absence to his father.

Burly Joe McGovern seemed scarcely concerned. "What?" he said, squinting up from his books. "Eileen? Out with a young man? For a drive? So what's your concern? Come on now, Gavin! I mean, she's hardly a child!"

Gavin clenched his jaws stubbornly as his father returned to his work, went through into the large private kitchen and dining room and flopped into a chair. Very well, then he would wait up for her himself. And if he heard that bloke's car bringing her back home, well he'd have a few words to say to him, too.

It was a quarter after twelve when Gavin settled himself down to wait upon Eileen's return; but his day had been long and hard, and something in the hot summer air had sapped his usually abundant energy. The evening's excitement, maybe. By the time his father went up to bed Gavin was fast asleep and locked in troubled dreams…

Quite some time earlier:

…In the warm summer nights, Lovers' Lane wasn't meant for fast-walking. It was only a mile and a half long, but almost three-quarters of an hour had gone by since Eileen and her new young man had left The Barn and started along its winding ways. Lovers' Lane: no, it wasn't the sort of walk you took at the trot. It was a holding-hands, swinging-arms-together, soft-talking walk; a kissing walk, in those places where the hedges were silvered by moonlight and lips softened by it. And it seemed strange to Eileen that her escort hadn't tried to kiss her, not once along the way...

But he had been full of talk: not about himself but mainly the night—how much he loved the darkness, its soft velvet, which he claimed he could feel against his skin, the *aliveness* of night—and about the moon: the secrets it knew but couldn't tell. Not terribly scary stuff but...strange stuff. Maybe too strange. And so, whenever she had the chance, Eileen had tried to change the subject, to talk about herself. But oddly, he hadn't seemed especially interested in her.

"Oh, there'll be plenty of time to talk about personalities later," he'd told her, and she'd noticed how his voice was no longer soft but...somehow coarse? And she'd shivered and thought: *time later? Well of course there will be...won't there?*

And suddenly she'd been aware of the empty fields and copses opening on all sides, time fleeting by, the fact that she was out here, in Lovers' Lane, with...a total stranger? What was this urgency in him, she wondered? She could feel it now in the way his hand held hers almost in a vice, the coarse, jerky tension of his breathing, the way his eyes scanned the moonlit darkness ahead and to left and right, looking for...what?

"Well," she finally said, trying to lighten her tone as much as she possibly could, digging her heels in a little and drawing him to a halt, "that's it—all of it—Lovers' Lane. From here on it goes nowhere, just open fields all the way to where they're digging the new road. And anyway it's time we were getting back. You said you only had an hour."

He held her hand more tightly yet, and his eyes were silver in the night. He took something out of his pocket and she heard a click, and the something gleamed a little in his dark hand. "Ah, but that was then and this is now," Garry Clemens told her, and she snatched her breath and her mouth fell open as she saw his awful smile. And then, while her mouth was still open, suddenly he *did* kiss her—and it was a brutal kiss and very terrible. And now Eileen knew.

As if reading her mind, he throatily said: "But if you're good and do *exactly* as you're told—then you'll live through it." And as she filled her lungs to scream, he quickly lifted his knife to her throat, and in his now choking voice whispered, "But if you're *not* good then I'll hurt you very, very much and you won't live through it. And one way or the other it will make no difference: I shall have you anyway, for you're my girl-Friday!"

"Gordon, I—" she finally breathed, her eyes wide in the dark, heart hammering, breasts rising and falling unevenly beneath her thin summer dress. And trying again: "Tell me this is just some sort of game, that you're only trying to frighten me and don't mean any…of…it." But she knew only too well that he did.

Her voice had been gradually rising, growing shrill, so that now he warningly hissed: "Be *quiet*!" And he backed her up to a stile in the fence, pressing with his knife until she was aware of it delving the soft skin of her throat. Then, very casually, he cut her thin summer dress down the front to her waist and flicked back the two halves with the point of his knife. Her free hand fluttered like a trapped bird, to match the palpitations of her heart, but she didn't dare do anything with it. And holding that sharp blade to her left breast, he said:

"Now we're going across this stile and behind the hedge, and then I'll tell you all you're to do and how best to please me. And that's important, for if you *don't* please me—well, then it will be good night, Eileen, Eileen!"

"Oh, God! *Oh, God!*" she whispered, as he forced her over the fence and behind the tall hedge. And:

"Here!" he said. "Here!"

And from the darkness just to one side of him, another voice, not Eileen's, answered, *"Yes, here! Here!"* But it was *such* a voice…

"What…?" Garry Clemens gulped, his hot blood suddenly ice. "Who…?" He released Eileen's hand and whirled, scything with his knife—scything nothing!—only the dark, which now seemed to close in on him. But:

"Here," said that husky, hungry, lusting voice again, and now Clemens saw that indeed there was a figure in the dark. A naked female figure, voluptuous and inviting. And, *"Here!"* she murmured yet again, her voice a promise of pleasures undreamed, drawing him down with her to the soft grass.

Out of the corner of his eye, dimly in his confused mind, the rapist saw a figure—fleeting, tripping, and staggering upright, fleeing—which he knew was Eileen McGovern where she fled wildly across the field. But he let her go. For he'd found a new and more wonderful, more exciting girl-Friday now. "Who…who *are* you?" he husked as he tore at his clothes—astonished that she tore at them, too.

And: "*Alaze*," she told him, simply. "*Alaze…*"

Eileen—running, crashing through a low thicket, flying under the moon—wanted to scream but had no wind for it. And in the end was too frightened to scream anyway. For she knew that someone ran with her, alongside her; a lithe, naked someone, who for the moment held off from whatever was his purpose.

But for how long?

The rattle of a crate deposited on the doorstep of The Old Stage woke Gavin McGovern up from unremembered dreams, but dreams which nevertheless left him red-eyed and rumbling inside like a volcano. Angry dreams! He woke to a new day, and in a way to a new world. He went to the door and it was dawn; the sun was balanced on the eastern horizon, reaching for the sky; Dave Gorman, the local milkman, was delivering.

"Wait," Gavin told him, and ran upstairs. A moment later and he was down again. "Eileen's not back," he said. "She was at the dance last night, went off with some bloke, an outsider. He hasn't brought her back. Tell them."

Gorman looked at him, almost said: *tell who?* But not quite. He knew who to tell. The Athelsford tribe.

Gavin spied the postman, George Lee, coming along the road on his early morning rounds. He gave him the same message: his sister, Eileen, a girl of the tribe, had been abducted. She was out there somewhere now, stolen away, perhaps hurt. And by the time Gavin had thrown water in his face and roused his father, the message was already being spread abroad. People were coming out of their doors, moving into the countryside around, starting to search. The tribe looked after its own…

And beneath the luststone:

Alaze was back, but Hengit had not returned. It was past dawn and Chylos could feel the sun warming their mighty headstone, and he wondered what had passed in the night: was his work now done and could he rest?

"*How went it?*" the old wizard inquired immediately, as Alaze settled back into her bones.

"*It went…well. To a point,*" she eventually answered.

"*A point? What point?*" He was alarmed. "*What went wrong? Did you not follow my instructions?*"

"Yes," she sighed, *"but—"*

"But?" And now it was Chylos's turn to sigh. *"Out with it."*

"I found one who was lusty. Indeed he was with a maid, which but for my intervention he would take against her will! Ah, but when he saw me he lusted after her no longer! And I heeded your instructions and put on my previous female form for him. According to those same instructions, I would teach him the true passions and furies and ecstasies of the flesh; so that afterwards and when he was with women of the tribe, he would be untiring, a satyr, and they would always bring forth from his potent seed. But because I was their inspiration, my spirit would be in all of them! This was why I put on flesh; and it was a great magic, a gigantic effort of will. Except...it had been a long, long time, Chylos. And in the heat of the moment I relaxed my will; no, he relaxed it for me, such was his passion. And...he saw me as I was, as I am..."

"Ah!" said Chylos, understanding what she told him. *"And afterwards? Did you not try again? Were there no others?"*

"There might have been others, aye—but as I journeyed out from this stone, the greater the distance the less obedient my will. Until I could no longer call flesh unto myself. And now, weary, I am returned."

Chylos sagged down into the alveolate, crumbling relics of himself. *"Then Hengit is my last hope,"* he said.

At which moment Hengit returned—but hangdog, as Chylos at once observed. And: *"Tell me the worst,"* the old man groaned.

But Hengit was unrepentant. *"I did as you instructed,"* he commenced his story, *"went forth, found a woman, put on flesh. And she was of the tribe, I'm sure. Alas, she was a child in the ways of men, a virgin, an innocent. You had said: let her be lusty, willing—but she was not. Indeed, she was afraid."*

Chylos could scarce believe it. *"But—were there no others?"*

"Possibly," Hengit answered. *"But this was a girl of the tribe, lost and afraid and vulnerable. I stood close by and watched over her, until the dawn..."*

"Then that is the very end of it," Chylos sighed, beaten at last. And his words were truer than even he might suspect.

But still, for the moment, the luststone exerted its immemorial influence...

❖ ❖ ❖

Of all the people of Athelsford who were out searching in the fields and woods that morning, it was Gavin McGovern who found the rapist

Clemens huddled beneath the hedgerow. He heard his sobbing, climbed the stile, and found him there. And in the long grass close by, he also found his knife still damp with dew. And looking at Clemens the way he was, Gavin fully believed that he had lost Eileen forever.

He cried hot, unashamed tears then, looked up at the blue skies she would never see again, and blamed himself. *My fault—my fault! If I'd not been the way I was, she wouldn't have needed to defy me!*

But then he looked again at Clemens, and his surging blood surged more yet. And as Clemens had lusted after Eileen, so now Gavin lusted after him—after his life!

He dragged him out from hiding, bunched his white hair in a hamlike hand, and stretched his neck taut across his knee. Then—three things, occurring almost simultaneously.

One: a terrific explosion from across the fields, where John Sykes had kept his word and reduced the luststone to so much rubble. Two: the bloodlust went out of Gavin like a light switched off, so that he gasped, released his victim, and thrust him away. And three, he heard the voice of his father, echoing from the near-distance and carrying far and wide in the brightening air:

"Gavin, we've found her! She's unharmed! She's all right!"

PC Bennett, coming across the field, his uniformed legs damp from the dewy grass, saw the knife in Gavin's hand and said, "I'll take that, son." And having taken it he also went to take charge of the gibbering, worthless, soul-shrivelled maniac thing that was Garry Clemens.

And so in a way old Chylos was right, for in the end nothing had come of all his works. But in several other ways he was quite wrong...

THE WHISPERER

The first time Miles Benton saw the little fellow was on the train. Benton was commuting to his office job in the city and he sat alone in a second-class compartment. The 'little fellow'—a very *ugly* little man, from what Benton could see of him out of the corner of his eye, with a lopsided hump and dark or dirty features, like a gnomish gypsy—entered the compartment and took a seat in the far corner. He was dressed in a floppy black wide-brimmed hat that fell half over his face and a black overcoat longer than himself that trailed to the floor.

Benton was immediately aware of the smell, a rank stench which quite literally would have done credit to the lowliest farmyard, and correctly deduced its source. Despite the dry acrid smell of stale tobacco from the ashtrays and the lingering odour of grimy stations, the compartment had seemed positively perfumed prior to the advent of the hunchback. The day was quite chill outside, but Benton nevertheless stood up and opened the window, pulling it down until the draft forced back the fumes from his fellow passenger. He was then obliged to put away his flapping newspaper and sit back, his collar upturned against the sudden cold blast, mentally cursing the smelly little chap for fouling 'his' compartment.

A further five minutes saw Benton's mind made up to change compartments. That way he would be removed from the source of the odorous irritation, and he would no longer need to suffer this intolerable blast of icy air. But no sooner was his course of action determined than the ticket collector arrived, sliding open the door and sticking his well-known and friendly face inside the compartment.

"Mornin', sir," he said briskly to Benton, merely glancing at the other traveller. "Tickets, please."

Benton got out his ticket and passed it to be examined. He noticed with satisfaction as he did so that the ticket collector wrinkled his nose and sniffed suspiciously at the air, eyeing the hunchback curiously. Benton retrieved his ticket and the collector turned to the little man in the far corner. "Yer ticket...*sir*...if yer don't mind." He looked the little chap up and down disapprovingly.

The hunchback looked up from under his black floppy hat and grinned. His eyes were jet and bright as a bird's. He winked and indicated that the ticket collector should bend down, expressing an obvious desire to say something in confidence. He made no effort to produce a ticket.

The ticket collector frowned in annoyance, but nevertheless bent his ear to the little man's face. He listened for a moment or two to a chuckling, throaty whisper. It actually appeared to Benton that the hunchback was *chortling* as he whispered his obscene secret into the other's ear, and the traveller could almost hear him saying: "Feelthy postcards! Vairy dairty pictures!"

The look on the face of the ticket collector changed immediately; his expression went stony hard.

"Aye, aye!" Benton said to himself. "The little blighter's got no ticket! He's for it now."

But no, the ticket collector said nothing to the obnoxious midget, but straightened and turned to Benton. "Sorry, sir," he said, "but this compartment's private. I'll 'ave ter arsk yer ter leave."

"But," Benton gasped incredulously, "I've been travelling in this compartment for years. It's never been a, well, a 'private' compartment before!"

"No, sir, p'raps not," said the ticket collector undismayed. "But it is now. There's a compartment next door; jus' a couple of gents in there; I'm sure it'll do jus' as well." He held the door open for Benton, daring him to argue the point further. "Sir?"

"Ah, well," Benton thought, resignedly, "I was wanting to move." Nevertheless, he looked down aggressively as he passed the hunchback, staring hard at the top of the floppy hat. The little man seemed to know. He looked up and grinned, cocking his head on one side and grinning.

Benton stepped quickly out into the corridor and took a deep breath. "Damn!" he swore out loud.

"Yer pardon, sir?" inquired the ticket collector, already swaying off down the corridor.

"Nothing!" Benton snapped in reply, letting himself into the smoky, crowded compartment to which he had been directed.

The very next morning Benton plucked up his courage (he had never been a *very* brave man), stopped the ticket collector, and asked him what it had all been about. Who had the little chap been. What privileges did he have that an entire compartment had been reserved especially for him, the grim little gargoyle?

To which the ticket collector replied: "Eh? An 'unchback? Are yer sure it was *this* train, sir? Why, we haint 'ad no private or reserved compartments on this 'ere train since it became a commuter special! And as fer an 'unchback—well!'"

"But surely you remember asking me to leave my compartment—*this* compartment?" Benton insisted.

"'Ere, yer pullin' me leg, haint yer, sir?" laughed the ticket collector good-naturedly. He slammed shut the compartment door behind him and smilingly strode away without waiting for an answer, leaving Benton alone with his jumbled and whirling thoughts.

"Well, I never!" the commuter muttered worriedly to himself. He scratched his head and then, philosophically, began to quote a mental line or two from a ditty his mother had used to say to him when he was a child:

> *The other day upon the stair*
> *I saw a man who wasn't there...*

Benton had almost forgotten about the little man with the hump and sewer-like smell by the time their paths crossed again. It happened one day some three months later, with spring just coming on, when, in acknowledgement of the bright sunshine, Benton decided to forego his usual sandwich lunch at the office for a noonday pint at the Bull & Bush.

The entire pub, except for one corner of the bar, appeared to be quite crowded, but it was not until Benton had elbowed his way to the corner in question that he saw why it was unoccupied; or rather, why it had only one occupant. The *smell* hit him at precisely the same time as he saw, sitting on a bar stool with his oddly humped back to the regular patrons, the little man in black with his floppy broad-brimmed hat.

That the other customers were aware of the cesspool stench was obvious—Benton watched in fascination the wrinkling all about him of at least a dozen pairs of nostrils—and yet not a man complained. And more amazing yet, no one even attempted to encroach upon the little fellow's territory in the bar corner. No one, that is, except Benton…

Holding his breath, Benton stepped forward and rapped sharply with his knuckles on the bar just to the left of where the hunchback sat. "Beer, barman. A pint of best, please."

The barman smiled chubbily and stepped forward, reaching out for a beer pump and slipping a glass beneath the tap. But even as he did so the hunchback made a small gesture with his head, indicating that he wanted to say something…

Benton had seen all this before, and all the many sounds of the pub— the chattering of people, the clink of coins, and the clatter of glasses— seemed to fade to silence about him as he focussed his full concentration upon the barman and the little man in the floppy hat. In slow motion, it seemed, the barman bent his head down toward the hunchback, and again Benton heard strangely chuckled whispers as the odious dwarf passed his secret instructions.

Curiously, fearfully, in something very akin to dread, Benton watched the portly barman's face undergo its change, heard the *hissss* of the beer pump, saw the full glass come out from beneath the bar…to plump down in front of the hunchback! Hard-eyed, the barman stuck his hand out in front of Benton's nose. "That's half a dollar to you, sir."

"But…" Benton gasped, incredulously opening and closing his mouth. He already had a coin in his hand, with which he had intended to pay for his drink, but now he pulled his hand back.

"Half a dollar, sir," the barman repeated ominously, snatching the coin from Benton's retreating fingers, "and would you mind moving down the bar, please? It's a bit crowded this end."

In utter disbelief Benton jerked his eyes from the barman's face to his now empty hand, and from his hand to the seated hunchback; and as he did so the little man turned his head towards him and grinned. Benton was aware only of the bright, bird-like eyes beneath the wide brim of the hat— not of the darkness surrounding them. One of those eyes closed suddenly in a wink, and then the little man turned back to his beer.

"But," Benton again croaked his protest at the publican, "that's *my* beer he's got!" He reached out and caught the barman's rolled-up sleeve, following him down the bar until forced by the press of patrons to let go. The barman finally turned.

"Beer, sir?" The smile was back on his chubby face. "Certainly—half a dollar to you, sir."

Abruptly the bar sounds crashed in again upon Benton's awareness as he turned to elbow his way frantically, almost hysterically, through the crowded room to the door. Out of the corner of his eye he noticed that the little man, too, had left. A crush of thirsty people had already moved into the space he had occupied in the bar corner.

Outside in the fresh air Benton glared wild-eyed up and down the busy street; and yet he was half afraid of seeing the figure his eyes sought. The little man, however, had apparently disappeared into thin air.

"God damn him!" Benton cried in sudden rage, and a passing policeman looked at him very curiously indeed.

He was annoyed to notice that the policeman followed him all the way back to the office.

At noon the next day Benton was out of the office as if at the crack of a starting pistol. He almost ran the four blocks to the Bull & Bush, pausing only to straighten his tie and tilt his bowler a trifle more aggressively in the mirror of a shop window. The place was quite crowded, as before, but he made his way determinedly to the bar, having first checked that the air was quite clean—ergo, that the little man with the hump was quite definitely *not* there.

He immediately caught the barman's eye. "Bartender, a beer, please. And—" He lowered his voice. "—a word, if you don't mind."

The publican leaned over the bar confidentially, and Benton lowered his tone still further to whisper: "Er, who *is* he—the, er, the little chap? Is he, perhaps, the boss of the place? Quite a little, er, *eccentric*, isn't he?"

"Eh?" said the barman, looking puzzledly about. "Who d'you mean, sir?"

The genuinely puzzled expression on the portly man's face ought to have told Benton all he needed to know, but Benton simply could not accept that, not a second time. "I mean the hunchback," he raised his voice in desperation. "The little chap in the floppy black hat who sat in the comer of the bar only yesterday—who stank to high heaven and drank *my* beer! Surely you remember him?"

The barman slowly shook his head and frowned, then called out to a group of standing men: "Joe, here a minute." A stocky chap in a cloth cap and tweed jacket detached himself from the general hubbub and moved to the bar. "Joe," said the barman, "you were in here yesterday lunch; did you see a—well, a—how was it, sir?" He turned back to Benton.

"A little chap with a floppy black hat and a hump," Benton patiently, worriedly repeated himself. "He was sitting in the bar corner. Had a pong like a dead rat."

Joe thought about it for a second, then said: "Yer sure yer got the right pub, guv'? I mean, we gets no tramps or weirdos in 'ere. 'Arry won't 'ave 'em, will yer, 'Arry?" He directed his question at the barman.

"No, he's right, sir. I get upset with weirdos. Won't have them."

"But...this *is* the Bull & Bush, isn't it?" Benton almost stammered, gazing wildly about, finding unaccustomed difficulty in speaking.

"That's right, sir," answered Harry the barman, frowning heavily now and watching Benton sideways.

"But—"

"Sorry, chief," the stocky Joe said with an air of finality. "Yer've got the wrong place. Must 'ave been some other pub." Both the speaker and the barman turned away a trifle awkwardly, Benton thought, and he could feel their eyes upon him as he moved dazedly away from the bar towards the door. Again lines remembered of old repeated themselves in his head:

> *He wasn't there again today—*
> *Oh how I wish he'd go away!*

"Here, sir!" cried the barman, suddenly, remembering. "Do you want a beer or not, then?"

"*No!*" Benton snarled. Then, on impulse: "Give it to—to *him!*—when next he comes in..."

✧ ✧ ✧

Over the next month or so certain changes took place in Benton, changes which would have seemed quite startling to anyone knowing him of old. To begin with, he had apparently broken two habits of very long standing. One: instead of remaining in his compartment aboard the morning train and reading his newspaper—as had been his wont for close on nine years—he was now given to spending the first half hour of his journey peering into the many compartments while wandering up and down the long corridor, all the while wearing an odd, part puzzled, part apologetic expression. Two: he rarely took his lunch at the office any more, but went out walking in the city instead, stopping for a drink and a sandwich at any handy local pub. (But never the Bull & Bush, though he always ensured that his strolling took him close by the latter house; and had anyone been particularly interested, then Benton might have been noticed to keep a very wary eye on the pub, almost as if he had it under observation.)

But then, as summer came on and no new manifestations of Benton's—problem—came to light, he began to forget all about it, to relegate it to that category of mental phenomena known as 'daydreams', even though he had known no such phenomena before. And as the summer waxed, so the nagging worry at the back of his mind waned, until finally he convinced himself that his daydreams were gone for good.

But he was wrong...

And if those two previous visitations had been dreams, then the third could only be classified as—nightmare!

July saw the approach of the holiday period, and Benton had long had places booked for himself and his wife at a sumptuously expensive and rather exclusive coastal resort, far from the small Midlands town he called home. They went there every year. This annual 'spree' allowed Benton to indulge his normally repressed escapism, when for a whole fortnight he could pretend that he was other than a mere clerk among people who usually accepted his fantasies as fact, thereby reinforcing them for Benton.

He could hardly wait for it to come round, that last Friday evening before the holidays, and when it did he rode home in the commuter special in a state of high excitement. Tomorrow would see him off to the sea and the sun; the cases were packed, the tickets arranged. A good night's rest now—and then, in the morning...

He was whistling as he let himself in through his front door, but the tone of his whistle soon went off key as he stepped into the hall. Dismayed, he paused and sniffed, his nose wrinkling. Out loud, he said: "Huh! The drains must be off again." But there was something rather special about that poisonous smell, something ominously familiar; and all of a sudden, without fully realising why, Benton felt the short hairs at the back of his neck begin to rise. An icy chill struck at him from nowhere.

He passed quickly from the hall into the living room, where the air seemed even more offensive, and there he paused again as it came to him in a flash of fearful memory just *what* the awful stench of ordure was, and *where* and *when* he had known it before.

The room seemed suddenly to whirl about him as he saw, thrown carelessly across the back of his own easy chair, a monstrously familiar hat— a floppy hat, black and wide-brimmed!

The hat grew beneath his hypnotized gaze, expanding until it threatened to fill the whole house, his whole mind, but then he tore his eyes away and broke the spell. From the upstairs bedroom came a low, muted sound: a moan of pain—or pleasure? And as an incredibly obscene and now well-remembered chuckling whisper finally invaded Benton's horrified ears, he threw off shock's invisible shackles to fling himself breakneck up the stairs.

"Ellen!" he cried, throwing open the bedroom door just as a second moan sounded—*and then he staggered, clutching at the wall for support, as the scene beyond the door struck him an almost physical blow!*

The hunchback lay sprawled naked upon Benton's bed, his malformed back blue-veined and grimy. The matted hair of his head fell forward onto Ellen's white breasts and his filthy hands moved like crabs over her arched body. Her eyes were closed, her mouth open and panting; her whole attitude was one of complete abandon. Her slender hands clawed spastically at the hunchback's writhing, scurvy thighs…

Benton screamed hoarsely, clutching wildly at his hair, his eyes threatening to pop from his head, and for an instant time stood still. Then he lunged forward and grabbed at the man, a great power bursting inside him, the strength of both God and the devil in his crooked fingers—but in that same instant the hunchback slipped from the far side of the bed and out of reach. At an almost impossible speed the little man dressed and, as Benton lurched drunkenly about the room, he flitted like a grey bat back across the bed. As he went his face passed close to Ellen's, and Benton was aware once again of that filthy whispered chuckle as the hunchback sprang to the floor and fled the room.

Mad with steadily mounting rage, Benton hardly noticed the sudden slitting of his wife's eyes, the film that came down over them like a silky shutter. But as he lunged after the hunchback Ellen reached out a naked leg, deliberately tripping him and sending him flying out onto the landing.

By the time he regained his feet, to lean panting against the landing rail, the little man was at the hall door, his hat once more drooping about grotesque shoulders. He looked up with eyes like malignant jewels in the shadow of that hat, and the last thing that the tormented householder saw as the hunchback closed the door softly behind him was that abhorrent, omniscient wink!

When he reached the garden gate some twoscore seconds later, Benton was not surprised to note the little man's complete disappearance...

Often, during the space of the next fortnight, Benton tried to think back on the scene which followed immediately upon the hunchback's departure from his house, but he was never able to resolve it to his satisfaction. He remembered the blind accusations he had thrown, the venomous bile of his words, his wife's patent amazement which had only served to enrage him all the more, the shock on Ellen's reddening face as he had slapped her mercilessly from room to room. He remembered her denial and the words she had screamed after locking herself in the bathroom: "Madman, madman!" she had screamed. And then she had left, taking her already packed suitcase with her.

He had waited until Monday—mainly in a vacant state of shock—before going out to a local ironmonger's shop to buy himself a sharp, long-bladed Italian knife...

It was now the fourteenth day, and still Benton walked the streets. He was grimy, unshaven, hungry, but his resolution was firm. Somewhere, *somewhere*, he would find the little man in the outsize overcoat and black floppy hat, and when he did he would stick his knife to its hilt in the hunchback's slimy belly and he would cut out the vile little swine's brains through his loathsomely winking eyes! In his mind's eye, even as walked the night streets, Benton could *see* those eyes gleaming like jewels, quick and bright and liquid, and faintly in his nostrils there seemed to linger the morbid stench of the hybrid creature that wore those eyes in its face.

And always his mother's ditty rang in his head:

> *The other day upon the stair*
> *I saw a man who wasn't there.*
> *He wasn't there again today—*
> *Oh, how I wish...*

But no, Benton did *not* wish the little man away; on the contrary, he desperately wanted to find him!

Fourteen days, fourteen days of madness and delirium; but through all the madness a burning purpose had shone out like a beacon. Who, what, why? Benton knew not, and he no longer wanted to know. But somewhere, *somewhere*...

Starting the first Tuesday after that evening of waking nightmare, each morning he had caught the commuter special as of old, to prowl its snakelike corridor and peer in poisonously through the compartment windows; every lunchtime he had waited in a shop doorway across the street from the Bull & Bush until closing time, and in between times he had walked the streets in all the villages between home and the city. Because somewhere, *somewhere*!

"Home." He tasted the word bitterly. "Home"—hah! That was a laugh! And all this after eleven years of reasonably harmonious married life. He thought again, suddenly, of Ellen, then of the hunchback, then of the two of them together...and in the next instant his mind was lit by a bright flash of inspiration.

Fourteen days—*fourteen days including today*—and this was Saturday night! Where would he be now if this whole nightmare had never happened? Why, he would be on the train with his wife, going home from their holiday!

Could it possibly be that—

Benton checked his watch, his hands shaking uncontrollably. Ten to nine; the nine o'clock train would be pulling into the station in only ten more minutes!

He looked wildly about him, reality crashing down again as he found himself in the back alleys of his home town. Slowly the wild light went out of his eyes, to be replaced by a strangely warped smile as he realised that he stood in an alley only a few blocks away from the railway station...

They didn't see him as they left the station, Ellen in high heels and a chic outfit, the hunchback as usual in his ridiculous overcoat and floppy black hat. But Benton saw them. They were (it still seemed completely unbelievable) arm in arm, Ellen radiant as a young bride, the little man reeking and filthy; and as Benton heard again that obscene chuckle he choked and reeled with rage in the darkness of his shop doorway.

Instantly the little man paused and peered into the shadows where Benton crouched. Benton cursed himself and shrank back; although the street was almost deserted, he had not wanted his presence known just yet.

But his presence *was* known!

The hunchback lifted up Ellen's hand to his lips in grotesque chivalry and kissed it. He whispered something loathsomely, and then, as Ellen made off without a word down the street, he turned again to peer with firefly eyes into Benton's doorway. The hiding man waited no longer. He leapt out into view, his knife bright and upraised, and the hunchback turned without ceremony to scurry down the cobbled street, his coat fluttering behind him like the wings of a great crippled moth.

Benton ran too, and quickly the gap between them closed as he drove his legs in a vengeful fury. Faster and faster his breath rasped as he drew closer to the fugitive hunchback, his hand lifting the knife for the fatal stroke.

Then the little man darted round a corner into an alleyway. No more than a second later Benton, too, rushed wildly into the darkness of the same alley. He skidded to a halt, his shoes sliding on the cobbles. He stilled his panting forcibly.

Silence...

The little devil had vanished again! He—

No, *there* he was—cringing like a cornered rat in the shadow of the wall.

Benton lunged, his knife making a crescent of light as it sped toward the hunchback's breast, but like quicksilver the target shifted as the little man ducked under his pursuer's arm to race out again into the street, leaving the echo of his hideous chuckle behind him.

That whispered chuckle drove Benton to new heights of raging bloodlust and, heedless now of all but the chase, he raced hot on the hunchback's trail. He failed to see the taxi's lights as he ran into the street, failed to hear its blaring horn—indeed, he was only dimly aware of the scream of brakes and tortured tyres—so that the darkness of oblivion as it rushed in upon him came as a complete surprise...

The darkness did not last. Quickly Benton swam up out of unconsciousness to find himself crumpled in the gutter. There was blood on his face, a roaring in his ears. The street swam round and round.

"Oh, God!" he groaned, but the words came out broken, like his body, and faint. Then the street found its level and steadied. An awful dull ache spread upwards from Benton's waist until it reached his neck. He tried to move, but couldn't. He heard running footsteps and managed to turn his head, lifting it out of the gutter in an agony of effort. Blood dripped from a torn ear. He moved an arm just a fraction, fingers twitching.

"God mister what were you doing what were you *doing?*" the taxi driver gabbled. "Oh Jesus Jesus you're hurt you're hurt. It wasn't my fault it wasn't me!"

"Never, uh...mind." Benton gasped, pain threatening to pull him under again as the ache in his lower body exploded into fresh agony. "Just...get me, uh, into...your car and...hospital or...doctor."

"Sure, yes!" the man cried, quickly kneeling.

If Benton's nose had not been clogged with mucus and drying blood he would have known of the hunchback's presence even before he heard the terrible chuckling from the pavement. As it was, the sound made him jerk his damaged head round into a fresh wave of incredible pain. He turned his eyes upwards. Twin points of light stared down at him from the darkness beneath the floppy hat.

"Uh...I suppose, uh, you're satisfied...now?" he painfully inquired, his hand groping uselessly, longingly for the knife which now lay half-way across the street.

And then he froze. Tortured and racked though his body was—desperate as his pain and injuries were—Benton's entire being *froze* as, in answer to his choked question, *the hunchback slowly, negatively shook his shadowed head!*

Dumbfounded, amazed, and horrified, Benton could only gape, even his agony forgotten as he helplessly watched from the gutter a repeat performance of those well-known gestures, those scenes remembered of old and now indelibly imprinted upon his mind: the filthy whispering in the taxi driver's ear; the winking of bright, bird eyes; the mazed look spreading like pale mud on the frightened man's face. Again the street began to revolve about Benton as the taxi driver walked as if in a dream back to his taxi.

Benton tried to scream but managed only a shuddering cough. Spastically his hand found the hunchback's grimy ankle and he gripped it tight. The little man stood like an anchor, and once more the street steadied about them as Benton fought his mangled body in a futile attempt to push it to its feet. He could not. There was something wrong with his back, something broken. He coughed, then groaned and relaxed his grip, turning his eyes upwards again to meet the steady gaze of the hunchback.

"Please..." he said. But his words were drowned out by the sudden sound of a revving engine, by the shriek of skidding tyres savagely reversing; and the last thing Benton saw, other than the black bulk of the taxi looming and the red rear lights, was the shuttering of one of those evil eyes in a grim farewell wink...

✣ ✣ ✣

Some few minutes later the police arrived at the seen of the most inexplicable killing it had ever been their lot to have to attend. They had been attracted by the crazed shrieking of a white-haired, utterly lunatic taxi driver.

NO SHARKS IN THE MED

Customs was non-existent; people bring duty frees *out* of Greece, not in. As for passport control: a pair of tanned, hairy, bored-looking characters in stained, too-tight uniforms and peaked caps were in charge. One to take your passport, find the page to be franked, scan photograph and bearer both with a blank gaze that took in absolutely nothing unless you happened to be female and stacked (in which case it took in everything and more), then pass the passport on. Geoff Hammond thought: *I wonder if that's why they call them passports?* The second one took the little black book from the first and hammered down on it with his stamp, impressing several pages but no one else, then handed the important document back to its owner—but grudgingly, as if he didn't believe you could be trusted with it.

This second one, the one with the rubber stamp, had a brother. They could be, probably were, twins. Five-eightish, late twenties, lots of shoulders and no hips; raven hair shiny with grease, so tightly curled it looked permed; brown eyes utterly vacant of expression. The only difference was the uniform: the fact that the brother on the home-and-dry side of the barrier didn't have one. Leaning on the barrier, he twirled cheap, yellow-framed, dark-lensed glasses like glinting propellers, observed almost speculatively the incoming holidaymakers. He wore shorts, frayed where they hugged his thick thighs, barely long enough to be decent. *Hung like a bull!* Geoff thought. It was almost embarrassing. Dressed for the benefit of the single girls, obviously. He'd be hoping they were taking notes for later. His chances might improve if he were two inches taller and had a face. But he didn't; the face was as vacant as the eyes.

Then Geoff saw what it was that was wrong with those eyes: beyond the barrier, the specimen in the bulging shorts was wall-eyed. Likewise his twin punching the passports. Their right eyes had white pupils that stared like dead fish. The one in the booth wore lightly-tinted glasses, so that you didn't notice until he looked up and stared directly at you. Which in Geoff's case he hadn't; but he was certainly looking at Gwen. Then he glanced at Geoff, patiently waiting, and said: "Together, you?" His voice was a shade too loud, making it almost an accusation.

Different names on the passports, obviously! But Geoff wasn't going to stand here and explain how they were just married and Gwen hadn't had time to make the required alterations. That really *would* be embarrassing! In fact (and come to think of it), it might not even be legal. Maybe she should have changed it right away, or got something done with it, anyway, in London. The honeymoon holiday they'd chosen was one of those get-it-while-it's-going deals, a last-minute half-price seat-filler, a gift horse; and they'd been pushed for time. But what the Hell—this was 1987, wasn't it?

"Yes," Geoff finally answered. "Together."

"Ah!" the other nodded, grinned, appraised Gwen again with a raised eyebrow, before stamping her passport and handing it over.

Wall-eyed bastard! Geoff thought.

When they passed through the gate in the barrier, the other wall-eyed bastard had disappeared...

Stepping through the automatic glass doors from the shade of the airport building into the sunlight of the coach terminus was like opening the door of a furnace; it was a replay of the moment when the plane's air-conditioned passengers trooped out across the tarmac to board the buses waiting to convey them to passport control. You came out into the sun fairly crisp, but by the time you'd trundled your luggage to the kerbside and lifted it off the trolley your armpits were already sticky. One o'clock, and the temperature must have been hovering around eighty-five for hours. It not only beat down on you but, trapped in the concrete, beat up as well. Hammerblows of heat.

A mini-skirted courier, English as a rose and harassed as Hell—her white blouse soggy while her blue and white hat still sat jaunty on her head—came fluttering, clutching her millboard with its bulldog clip and thin sheaf of notes. "Mr Hammond and Miss—" she glanced at her notes, "—Pinter?"

"Mr and Mrs Hammond," Geoff answered. He lowered his voice and continued confidentially: "We're all proper, legitimate, and true. Only our identities have been altered in order to protect our passports."

"Um?" she said.

Too deep for her, Geoff thought, sighing inwardly.

"Yes," said Gwen, sweetly. "We're the Hammonds."

"Oh!" the girl looked a little confused. "It's just that—"

"I haven't changed my passport yet," said Gwen, smiling.

"Ah!" Understanding finally dawned. The courier smiled nervously at Geoff, turned again to Gwen. "Is it too late for congratulations?"

"Four days," Gwen answered.

"Well, congratulations anyway."

Geoff was eager to be out of the sun. "Which is our coach?" he wanted to know. "Is it—could it possibly be—airconditioned?" There were several coaches parked in an untidy cluster a little farther up the kerb.

Again the courier's confusion, also something of embarrassment showing in her bright blue eyes. "You're going to—Achladi?"

Geoff sighed again, this time audibly. It was her business to know where they were going. It wasn't a very good start.

"Yes," she cut in quickly, before he or Gwen could comment. "Achladi— but not by coach! You see, your plane was an hour late; the coach for Achladi couldn't be held up for just one couple; but it's OK—you'll have the privacy of your own taxi, and of course Skymed will foot the bill."

She went off to whistle up a taxi and Geoff and Gwen glanced at each other, shrugged, sat down on their cases. But in a moment the courier was back, and behind her a taxi came rolling, nosing into the kerb. Its driver jumped out, whirled about opening doors, the boot, stashing cases while Geoff and Gwen got into the back of the car. Then, throwing his straw hat down beside him as he climbed into the driving seat and slammed his door, the young Greek looked back at his passengers and smiled. A single gold tooth flashed in a bar of white. But the smile was quite dead, like the grin of a shark before he bites, and the voice when it came was phlegmy, like pebbles colliding in mud. "Achladi, yes?"

"Ye—" Geoff began, paused, and finished: "—es! Er, Achladi, right!" Their driver was the wall-eyed passport-stamper's wall-eyed brother.

"I Spiros," he declared, turning the taxi out of the airport. "And you?"

Something warned Geoff against any sort of familiarity with this one. In all this heat, the warning was like a breath of cold air on the back of his neck. "I'm Mr Hammond," he answered, stiffly. "This is my wife." Gwen turned her head a little and frowned at him.

"I'm—" she began.

"My *wife*!" Geoff said again. She looked surprised but kept her peace.

Spiros was watching the road where it narrowed and wound. Already out of the airport, he skirted the island's main town and raced for foothills rising to a spine of half-clad mountains. Achladi was maybe half an hour away, on the other side of the central range. The road soon became a track, a thick layer of dust over pot-holed tarmac and cobbles; in short, a typical Greek road. They slowed down a little through a village where white-walled houses lined the way, with lemon groves set back between and behind the dwellings, and were left with bright flashes of bougainvillea-framed balconies burning like after-images on their retinas. Then Spiros gave it the gun again.

Behind them, all was dust kicked up by the spinning wheels and the suction of the car's passing. Geoff glanced out of the fly-specked rear window. The cloud of brown dust, chasing after them, seemed ominous in the way it obscured the so-recent past. And turning front again, Geoff saw that Spiros kept his strange eye mainly on the road ahead, and the good one on his rearview. But watching what? The dust? No, he was looking at...

At Gwen! The interior mirror was angled directly into her cleavage.

They had been married only a very short time. The day when he'd take pride in the jealousy of other men—in their coveting his wife—was still years in the future. Even then, look but don't touch would be the order of the day. Right now it was watch where you're looking, and possession was ninety-nine point nine percent of the law. As for the other point one percent: well, there was nothing much you could do about what the lecherous bastards were thinking!

Geoff took Gwen's elbow, pulled her close and whispered: "Have you noticed how tight he takes the bends? He does it so we'll bounce about a bit. He's watching how your tits jiggle!"

She'd been delighting in the scenery, hadn't even noticed Spiros, his eyes or anything. For a beautiful girl of twenty-three, she was remarkably naïve, and it wasn't just an act. It was one of the things Geoff loved best about her. Only eighteen months her senior, Geoff hardly considered himself a man of the world; but he did know a rat when he smelled one. In Spiros's case he could smell several sorts.

"He...*what*—?" Gwen said out loud, glancing down at herself. One button too many had come open in her blouse, showing the edges of her cups. Green eyes widening, she looked up and spotted Spiros's rearview. He grinned at her through the mirror and licked his lips, but without deliberation. He was naïve, too, in his way. In his different sort of way.

"Sit over here," said Geoff out loud, as she did up the offending button *and* the one above it. "The view is much better on this side." He half-stood, let her slide along the seat behind him. Both of Spiros's eyes were now back on the road...

Ten minutes later they were up into a pass through gorgeous pine-clad slopes so steep they came close to sheer. Here and there scree slides showed through the greenery, or a thrusting outcrop of rock. "Mountains," Spiros grunted, without looking back.

"You have an eye for detail," Geoff answered.

Gwen gave his arm a gentle nip, and he knew she was thinking *sarcasm is the lowest form of wit—and it doesn't become you!* Nor cruelty, apparently. Geoff had meant nothing special by his 'eye' remark, but Spiros was sensitive. He groped in the glove compartment for his yellow-rimmed sunshades, put them on. And drove in a stony silence for what looked like being the rest of the journey.

Through the mountains they sped, and the west coast of the island opened up like a gigantic travel brochure. The mountains seemed to go right down to the sea, rocks merging with that incredible, aching blue. And they could see the village down there, Achladi, like something out of a dazzling dream perched on both sides of a spur that gentled into the ocean.

"Beautiful!" Gwen breathed.

"Yes," Spiros nodded. "Beautiful, thee village." Like many Greeks speaking English, his definite articles all sounded like *thee*. "For fish, for thee swims, thee sun—is beautiful."

After that it was all downhill; winding, at times precipitous, but the view was never less than stunning. For Geoff, it brought back memories of Cyprus. Good ones, most of them, but one bad one that always made him catch his breath, clench his fists. The reason he hadn't been too keen on coming back to the Med in the first place. He closed his eyes in an attempt to force the memory out of mind, but that only made it worse, the picture springing up that much clearer.

He was a kid again, just five years old, late in the summer of '67. His father was a Staff-Sergeant Medic, his mother with the QARANCs; both of them were stationed at Dhekelia, a Sovereign Base Area garrison just up the coast from Larnaca where they had a married quarter. They'd met and married in Berlin, spent three years there, then got posted out to Cyprus together. With two years done in Cyprus, Geoff's father had a year to go to complete his twenty-two. After that last year in the sun…there was a place waiting for him in the ambulance pool of one of London's big hospitals. Geoff's mother had hoped to get on the nursing staff of the same hospital. But before any of that…

Geoff had started school in Dhekelia, but on those rare weekends when both of his parents were free of duty, they'd all go off to the beach together. And that had been his favourite thing in all the world: the beach with its golden sand and crystal-clear, safe, shallow water. But sometimes, seeking privacy, they'd take a picnic basket and drive east along the coast until the road became a track, then find a way down the cliffs and swim from the rocks up around Cape Greco. That's where it had happened.

"Geoff!" Gwen tugged at his arm, breaking the spell. He was grateful to be dragged back to reality. "Were you sleeping?"

"Daydreaming," he answered.

"Me, too!" she said. "I think I must be. I mean, just *look* at it!"

They were winding down a steep ribbon of road cut into the mountains flank, and Achladi was directly below them. A coach coming up squeezed by, its windows full of brown, browned-off faces. Holidaymakers going off to the airport, going home. Their holidays were over but Geoff's and Gwen's was just beginning, and the village they had come to *was* truly beautiful. Especially beautiful because it was unspoiled. This was only Achladi's second season; before they'd built the airport you could only get here by boat. Very few had bothered.

Geoff's vision of Cyprus and his bad time quickly receded; while he didn't consider himself a romantic like Gwen, still he recognized Achladi's magic. And now he supposed he'd have to admit that they'd made the right choice.

White-walled gardens; red tiles, green-framed windows, some flat roofs and some with a gentle pitch; bougainvillea cascading over white, arched balconies; a tiny white church on the point of the spur where broken rocks finally tumbled into the sea; massive ancient olive trees in walled plots at every street junction, and grapevines on trellises giving a little shade and dappling every garden and patio. That, at a glance, was Achladi. A high sea wall kept the sea at bay, not that it could ever be a real threat, for the entire front of the village fell within the harbour's crab's-claw moles. Steps went down here and there from the sea wall to the rocks; a half-dozen towels were spread wherever there was a flat or gently-inclined surface to take them, and the sea bobbed with a half-dozen heads, snorkels and face-masks. Deep water here, but a quarter-mile to the south, beyond the harbour wall, a shingle beach stretched like the webbing between the toes of some great beast for maybe a hundred yards to where a second claw-like spur came down from the mountains. As for the rest of this western coastline: as far as the eye could see both north and south, it looked like sky, cliff and sea to Geoff. Cape Greco all over again. But before he could go back to that:

"Is Villa Eleni, yes?" Spiros's gurgling voice intruded. "Him have no road. No can drive. I carry thee bags."

The road went right down the ridge of the spur to the little church. Half-way, it was crossed at right-angles by a second motor road which contained and serviced a handful of shops. The rest of the place was made up of streets too narrow or too perpendicular for cars. A few ancient scooters put-putted and sputtered about, donkeys clip-clopped here and there, but that was all. Spiros turned his vehicle about at the main junction (the *only* real road junction) and parked in the shade of a giant olive tree. He went to get the luggage. There were two large cases, two small ones. Geoff would have shared the load equally but found himself brushed aside; Spiros took the elephant's share and left him with the small-fry. He wouldn't have minded, but it was obviously the Greek's chance to show off his strength.

Leading the way up a steep cobbled ramp of a street, Spiros's muscular buttocks kept threatening to burst through the thin stuff of his cut-down jeans. And because the holidaymakers followed on a little way behind, Geoff was aware of Gwen's eyes on Spiros's tanned, gleaming thews. There wasn't much of anywhere else to look. "Him Tarzan, you Jane," he commented, but his grin was a shade too dry.

"Who you?" she answered, her nose going up in the air. "Cheetah?"

"*Uph, uph!*" said Geoff.

"Anyway," she relented. "Your bottom's nicer. More compact."

He saved his breath, made no further comment. Even the light cases seemed heavy. If he was Cheetah, that must make Spiros Kong! The Greek glanced back once, grinned in his fashion, and kept going. Breathing heavily, Geoff and Gwen made an effort to catch up, failed miserably. Then, toward the top of the way Spiros turned right into an arched alcove, climbed three stone steps, put down his cases and paused at a varnished pine door. He pulled on a string to free the latch, shoved the door open and took up his cases again. As the English couple came round the corner he was stepping inside. "Thee Villa Eleni," he said, as they followed him in.

Beyond the door was a high-walled courtyard of black and white pebbles laid out in octopus and dolphin designs. A split-level patio fronted the 'villa', a square box of a house whose one redeeming feature had to be a retractable sun-awning shading the windows and most of the patio. It also made an admirable refuge from the dazzling white of everything.

There were whitewashed concrete steps climbing the side of the building to the upper floor, with a landing that opened onto a wooden-railed balcony with its own striped awning. Beach towels and an outsize lady's bathing costume were hanging over the rail, drying, and all the windows were open. Someone was home, maybe. Or maybe sitting in a shady taverna sipping on iced drinks. Downstairs, a key with a label had been left in the keyhole of a louvred, fly-screened door. Geoff read the label, which said simply: "Mr Hammond." The booking had been made in his name.

"This is us," he said to Gwen, turning the key.

They went in, Spiros following with the large cases. Inside, the cool air was a blessing. Now they would like to explore the place on their own, but the Greek was there to do it for them. And he knew his way around. He put the cases down, opened his arms to indicate the central room. "For sit, talk, thee resting." He pointed to a tiled area in one corner, with a refrigerator, sink-unit and two-ring electric cooker. "For thee toast, coffee—thee fish and chips, eh?" He shoved open the door of a tiny room tiled top to bottom, containing a shower, wash-basin and WC. "And this one," he said, without further explanation. Then five strides back across the floor took him to another room, low-ceilinged, pine-beamed, with a Lindean double bed built in under louvred windows. He cocked his head on one side. "And thee bed—just one..."

"That's all we'll need," Geoff answered, his annoyance building.

"Yes," Gwen said. "Well, thank you, er, Spiros—you're very kind. And we'll be fine now."

Spiros scratched his chin, went back into the main room and sprawled in an easy chair. "Outside is hot," he said. "Here she is cool—*chrio*, you know?"

Geoff went to him. "It's *very* hot," he agreed, "and we're sticky. Now we want to shower, put our things away, look around. Thanks for your help. You can go now."

Spiros stood up and his face went slack, his expression more blank than before. His wall-eye looked strange through its tinted lens. "Go now?" he repeated.

Geoff sighed. "Yes, go!"

The corner of Spiros's mouth twitched, drew back a little to show his gold tooth. "I fetch from airport, carry cases."

"Ah!" said Geoff, getting out his wallet. "What do I owe you?" He'd bought drachmas at the bank in London.

Spiros sniffed, looked scornful, half turned away. "One thousand," he finally answered, bluntly.

"That's about four pounds and fifty pence," Gwen said from the bedroom doorway. "Sounds reasonable."

"Except it was supposed to be on Skymed," Geoff scowled. He paid up anyway and saw Spiros to the door. The Greek departed, sauntered indifferently across the patio to pause in the arched doorway and look back across the courtyard. Gwen had come to stand beside Geoff in the double doorway under the awning.

The Greek looked straight at her and licked his fleshy lips. The vacant grin was back on his face. "I see you," he said, nodding with a sort of slow deliberation.

As he closed the door behind him, Gwen muttered, "Not if I see you first! *Ugh!*"

"I am with you," Geoff agreed. "*Not* my favourite local character!"

"Spiros," she said. "Well, and it suits him to a tee. It's about as close as you can get to spider! And that one *is* about as close as you can get!"

They showered, fell exhausted on the bed—but not so exhausted that they could just lie there without making love.

Later—with suitcases emptied and small valuables stashed out of sight, and spare clothes all hung up or tucked away—dressed in light, loose gear, sandals, sunglasses, it was time to explore the village. "And afterwards," Gwen insisted, "we're swimming!" She'd packed their towels and swimwear in a plastic beach bag. She loved to swim, and Geoff might have, too, except…

But as they left their rooms and stepped out across the patio, the varnished door in the courtyard wall opened to admit their upstairs neighbours, and for the next hour all thoughts of exploration and a dip in the sea were swept aside. The elderly couple who now introduced themselves gushed, there was no other way to describe it. He was George and she was Petula.

"My *dear*," said George, taking Gwen's hand and kissing it, "such a *stunning* young lady, and how sad that I've only two days left in which to enjoy you!" He was maybe sixty-four or five, ex-handsome but sagging a bit now, tall if a little bent, and brown as a native. With a small grey moustache and faded blue eyes, he looked as if he'd—no, in all probability he *had*—piloted Spitfires in World War II! Alas, he wore the most blindingly colourful shorts and shirt that Gwen had ever seen.

Petula was very large, about as tall as George but two of him in girth. She was just as brown, though, (and so presumably didn't mind exposing it all), seemed equally if not more energetic, and was never at a loss for words. They were a strange, paradoxical pair: very upper-crust, but at the same time very much down to earth. If Petula tended to speak with plums in her mouth, certainly they were of a very tangy variety.

"He'll flatter you to death, my dear," she told Gwen, ushering the newcomers up the steps at the side of the house and onto the high balcony. "But you must *never* take your eyes off his hands! Stage magicians have nothing on George. Forty years ago he magicked himself into my bedroom, and he's been there ever since!"

"She seduced me!" said George, bustling indoors.

"I did not!" Petula was petulant. "What? Why he's quite simply a wolf in…in a Joseph suit!"

"A Joseph suit?" George repeated her. He came back out onto the balcony with brandy-sours in a frosted jug, a clattering tray of ice-cubes, slices of sugared lemon and an eggcup of salt for the sours. He put the lot down on a plastic table, said: "Ah!—glasses!" and ducked back inside again.

"Yes," his wife called after him, pointing at his Bermudas and Hawaiian shirt. "Your clothes of many colours!"

It was all good fun and Geoff and Gwen enjoyed it. They sat round the table on plastic chairs, and George and Petula entertained them. It made for a very nice welcome to Achladi indeed.

"Of course," said George after a while, when they'd settled down a little, "we first came here eight years ago, when there were no flights, just boats. Now that people are flying in—" he shrugged, "—two more seasons and there'll be belly-dancers and hotdog stands! But for now it's…just perfect. Will you look at that view?"

The view from the balcony was very fetching. "From up here we can see the entire village," said Gwen. "You must point out the best shops, the bank or exchange or whatever, all the places we'll need to know about."

George and Petula looked at each other, smiled knowingly.

"Oh?" said Gwen.

Geoff checked their expressions, nodded, made a guess: "There are no places we need to know about."

"Well, three, actually," said Petula. "Four if you count Dimi's—the taverna. Oh, there are other places to eat, but Dimi's is *the* place. Except I feel I've spoilt it for you now. I mean, that really is something you should have discovered for yourself. It's half the fun, finding the best place to eat!"

"What about the other three places we should know about?" Gwen inquired. "Will knowing those spoil it for us, too? Knowing them in advance, I mean?"

"Good Lord, no!" George shook his head. "Vital knowledge, young lady!"

"The baker's," said Petula. "For fresh rolls—daily." She pointed it out, blue smoke rising from a cluster of chimneypots. "Also the booze shop, for booze—"

"—Also daily," said George, pointing. "Right there on that corner— where the bottles glint. D'you know, they have an *ancient* Metaxa so cheap you wouldn't—"

"*And*," Petula continued, "the path down to the beach. Which is… over there."

"But tell us," said George, changing the subject, "are you married, you two? Or is that too personal?"

"Oh, of *course* they're married!" Petula told him. "But very recently, because they still sit so close together. Touching. You see?"

"Ah!" said George. "Then we shan't have another elopement."

"You know, my dear, you really are an old idiot," said Petula, sighing. "I mean, elopements are for lovers to be together. And these two already *are* together!"

Geoff and Gwen raised their eyebrows. "An elopement?" Gwen said. "Here? When did this happen?"

"Right here, yes," said Petula. "Ten days ago. On our first night we had a young man downstairs, Gordon. On his own. He was supposed to be here with his fiancée but she's jilted him. He went out with us, had a few too many in Dimi's and told us all about it. A Swedish girl—very lovely, blonde creature—was also on her own. She helped steer him back here and, I suppose, tucked him in. She had her own place, mind you, and didn't stay."

"But the next night she did!" George enthused.

"And then they ran off," said Petula, brightly. "Eloped! As simple as that. We saw them once, on the beach, the next morning. Following which—"

"—Gone!" said George.

"Maybe their holidays were over and they just went home," said Gwen, reasonably.

"No," George shook his head. "Gordon had come out on our plane, his holiday was just starting. She'd been here about a week and a half, was due to fly out the day after they made off together."

"They paid for their holidays and then deserted them?" Geoff frowned. "Doesn't make any sense."

"Does anything, when you're in love?" Petula sighed.

"The way I see it," said George, "they fell in love with each other, and with Greece, and went off to explore all the options."

"Love?" Gwen was doubtful. "On the rebound?"

"If she'd been a mousey little thing, I'd quite agree," said Petula. "But no, she really was a beautiful girl."

"And him a nice lad," said George. "A bit sparse but clean, good-looking."

"Indeed, they were much like you two," his wife added. "I mean, not *like* you, but like you."

"Cheers," said Geoff, wryly. "I mean, I know I'm not Mr Universe, but—"

"Tight in the bottom!" said Petula. "That's what the girls like these days. You'll do all right."

"See," said Gwen, nudging him. "Told you so!"

But Geoff was still frowning. "Didn't anyone look for them? What if they'd been involved in an accident or something?"

"No," said Petula. "They were seen boarding a ferry in the main town. Indeed, one of the local taxi drivers took them there. Spiros."

Gwen and Geoff's turn to look at each other. "A strange fish, that one," said Geoff.

George shrugged. "Oh, I don't know. You know him, do you? It's that eye of his which makes him seem a bit sinister..."

Maybe he's right, Geoff thought.

Shortly after that, their drinks finished, they went off to start their explorations...

The village was a maze of cobbled, white-washed alleys. Even as tiny as it was you could get lost in it, but never for longer than the length of a street. Going downhill, no matter the direction, you'd come to the sea. Uphill you'd come to the main road, or if you didn't, then turn the next corner and *continue* uphill, and then you would. The most well-trodden alley, with the shiniest cobbles, was the one that led to the hard-packed path, which in turn led to the beach. Pass the 'booze shop' on the corner twice, and you'd know where it was always. The window was plastered with labels, some familiar and others entirely conjectural; inside, steel shelving went floor to ceiling, stacked with every conceivable brand; even the more exotic and (back home) wildly expensive stuffs were on view, often in ridiculously cheap, three-litre, duty-free bottles with their own chrome taps and display stands.

"Courvoisier!" said Gwen, appreciatively.

"Grand Marnier, surely!" Geoff protested. "What, five pints of Grand Marnier? At that price? Can you believe it? But that's to take home. What about while we're here?"

"Coconut liqueur," she said. "Or better still, mint chocolate—to compliment our midnight coffees."

They found several small tavernas, too, with people seated outdoors at tiny tables under the vines. Chicken portions and slabs of lamb sputtering on spits; small fishes sizzling over charcoal; *moussaka* steaming in long trays...

Dimi's was down on the harbour, where a wide, low wall kept you safe from falling in the sea. They had a Greek salad which they divided two ways, tiny cubes of lamb roasted on wooden slivers, a half-bottle of local white wine costing pennies. As they ate and sipped the wine, so they began to relax; the hot sunlight was tempered by an almost imperceptible breeze off the sea.

Geoff said: "Do you really feel energetic? Damned if I do."

She didn't feel full of boundless energy, no, but she wasn't going down without a fight. "If it was up to you," she said, "we'd just sit here and watch the fishing nets dry, right?"

"Nothing wrong with taking it easy," he answered. "We're on holiday, remember?"

"Your idea of taking it easy means being bone idle!" she answered. "*I* say we're going for a dip, then back to the villa for siesta and you know, and—"

"Can we have the you know before the siesta?" He kept a straight face.

"—And then we'll be all settled in, recovered from the journey, ready for tonight. Insatiable!"

"OK," he shrugged. "Anything you say. But we swim from the beach, not from the rocks."

Gwen looked at him suspiciously. "That was almost too easy."

Now he grinned. "It was the thought of, well, you know, that did it," he told her...

Lying on the beach, panting from their exertions in the sea, with the sun lifting the moisture off their still-pale bodies, Gwen said: "I don't understand."

"Hmm?"

"You swim very well. I've always thought so. So what is this fear of the water you complain about?"

"First," Geoff answered, "I don't swim very well. Oh, for a hundred yards I'll swim like a dolphin—any more than that and I do it like a brick! I can't float. If I stop swimming I sink."

"So don't stop."

"When you get tired, you stop."

"What was it that made you frightened of the water?"

He told her:

"I was a kid in Cyprus. A little kid. My father had taught me how to swim. I used to watch him diving off the rocks, oh, maybe twenty or thirty feet high, into the sea. I thought I could do it, too. So one day when my folks weren't watching, I tried. I must have hit my head on something on the way down. Or maybe I simply struck the water all wrong. When they spotted me floating in the sea, I was just about done for. My father dragged me out. He was a medic—the kiss of life and all that. So now I'm not much for swimming, and I'm absolutely *nothing* for diving! I will swim—for a splash, in shallow water, like today—but that's my limit. And I'll only go in from a beach. I can't stand cliffs, height. It's as simple as that. You married a coward. So there."

"No I didn't," she said. "I married someone with a great bottom. Why didn't you tell me all this before?"

"You didn't ask me. I don't like to talk about it because I don't much care to remember it. I was just a kid, and yet I knew I was going to die. And I knew it wouldn't be nice. I still haven't got it out of my system, not completely. And so the less said about it the better."

A beach ball landed close by, bounced, rolled to a standstill against Gwen's thigh. They looked up. A brown, burly figure came striding. They recognized the frayed, bulging shorts. Spiros.

"Hallo," he said, going down into a crouch close by, forearms resting on his knees. "Thee beach. Thee ball. I swim, play. You swim?" (This to Geoff.) "You come swim, throwing thee ball?"

Geoff sat up. There were half-a-dozen other couples on the beach; why couldn't this jerk pick on them? Geoff thought to himself: *I'm about to get sand kicked in my face!* "No," he said out loud, shaking his head. "I don't swim much."

"No swim? You frighting thee big fish? Thee sharks?"

"Sharks?" Now Gwen sat up. From behind their dark lenses she could feel Spiros's eyes crawling over her.

Geoff shook his head. "There are no sharks in the Med," he said.

"Him right," Spiros laughed high-pitched, like a woman, without his customary gurgling. A weird sound. "No sharks. I make thee jokes!" He stopped laughing and looked straight at Gwen. She couldn't decide if he was looking at her face or her breasts. Those damned sunglasses of his! "You come swim, lady, with Spiros? Play in thee water?"

"My...*God!*" Gwen sputtered, glowering at him. She pulled her dress on over her still-damp, very skimpy swimming costume, packed her towel away, picked up her sandals. When she was annoyed, she really *was* annoyed.

Geoff stood up as she made off, turned to Spiros. "Now listen—" he began.

"Ah, you go now! Is OK. I see you." He took his ball, raced with it down the beach, hurled it out over the sea. Before it splashed down he was diving, low and flat, striking the water like a knife. Unlike Geoff, he swam very well indeed...

When Geoff caught up with his wife she was stiff with anger. Mainly angry with herself. "That was *so* rude of me!" she exploded.

"No it wasn't," he said. "I feel exactly the same about it."

"But he's so damned...persistent! I mean, he knows we're together, man and wife...'thee bed—just one.' How *dare* he intrude?"

Geoff tried to make light of it. "You're imagining it," he said.

"And you? Doesn't he get on your nerves?"

"Maybe I'm imagining it too. Look, he's Greek—and not an especially attractive specimen. Look at it from his point of view. All of a sudden there's a gaggle of dolly-birds on the beach, dressed in stuff his sister wouldn't wear for undies! So he tries to get closer—for a better view, as it were—so that he can get a wall-eyeful. He's no different to other blokes. Not quite as smooth, that's all."

"Smooth!" she almost spat the word out. "He's about as smooth as a badger's—"

"—Bottom," said Geoff. "Yes, I know. If I'd known you were such a bum-fancier I mightn't have married you."

And at last she laughed, but shakily.

They stopped at the booze shop and bought brandy and a large bottle of Coca-Cola. And mint chocolate liqueur, of course, for their midnight coffees...

That night Gwen put on a blue and white dress, very Greek if cut a little low in the front, and silver sandals. Tucking a handkerchief into the breast pocket of his white jacket, Geoff thought: *she's beautiful!* With her heart-shaped face and the way her hair framed it, cut in a page-boy style that suited its shiny black sheen—and her green, green eyes—he'd always thought she looked French. But tonight she was definitely Greek. And he was so glad that she was English, and his.

Dimi's was doing a roaring trade. George and Petula had a table in the corner, overlooking the sea. They had spread themselves out in order to occupy all four seats, but when Geoff and Gwen appeared they waved, called them over. "We thought you'd drop in," George said, as they sat down. And to Gwen: "You look charming, my dear."

"Now I feel I'm really on my holidays," Gwen smiled.

"Honeymoon, surely," said Petula.

"*Shh!*" Geoff cautioned her. "In England they throw confetti. Over here it's plates!"

"Your secret is safe with us," said George.

"Holiday, honeymoon, whatever," said Gwen. "Compliments from handsome gentlemen; the stars reflected in the sea; a full moon rising and bouzouki music floating in the air. And—"

"—The mouth-watering smells of good Greek grub!" Geoff cut in. "Have you ordered?" He looked at George and Petula.

"A moment ago," Petula told him. "If you go into the kitchen there, Dimi will show you his menu—live, as it were. Tell him you're with us and he'll make an effort to serve us together. Starter, main course, a pudding—the lot."

"Good!" Geoff said, standing up. "I could eat the saddle off a donkey!"

"Eat the whole donkey," George told him. "The one who's going to wake you up with his racket at six-thirty tomorrow morning."

"You don't know Geoff," said Gwen. "He'd sleep through a Rolling Stones concert."

"And *you* don't know Achladi donkeys!" said Petula.

In the kitchen, the huge, bearded proprietor was busy, fussing over his harassed-looking cooks. As Geoff entered he came over. "Good evenings, sir. You are new in Achladi?"

"Just today," Geoff smiled. "We came here for lunch but missed you."

"Ah!" Dimitrios gasped, shrugged apologetically "I was sleeps! Every day, for two hours, I sleeps. Where you stay, eh?"

"The Villa Eleni."

"Eleni? Is me!" Dimitrios beamed. "*I* am Villa Eleni. I mean, I owns it. Eleni is thee name my wifes."

"It's a beautiful name," said Geoff, beginning to feel trapped in the conversation. "Er, we're with George and Petula."

"You are eating? Good, good. I show you." Geoff was given a guided tour of the ovens and the sweets trolley. He ordered, keeping it light for Gwen.

"And here," said Dimitrios. "For your lady!" He produced a filigreed silver-metal brooch in the shape of a butterfly, with 'Dimi's' worked into the metal of the body. Gwen wouldn't like it especially, but politic to accept it. Geoff had noticed several female patrons wearing them, Petula included.

"That's very kind of you," he said.

Making his way back to their table, he saw Spiros was there before him. Now where the Hell had he sprung from? And what the Hell was he playing at?

Spiros wore tight blue jeans, (his image, obviously), and a white T-shirt stained down the front. He was standing over the corner table, one hand on the wall where it overlooked the sea, the other on the table itself. Propped up, still he swayed. He was leaning over Gwen. George and Petula had frozen smiles on their faces, looked frankly astonished. Geoff couldn't quite see all of Gwen, for Spiros's bulk was in the way.

What he could see, of the entire mini-tableau, printed itself on his eyes as he drew closer. Adrenalin surged in him and he began to breathe faster. He barely noticed George standing up and sliding out of view. Then as the bouzouki tape came to an end and the taverna's low babble of sound seemed to grow that much louder, Gwen's outraged voice suddenly rose over everything else:

"Get...your...filthy...paws...*off* me!" she cried.

Geoff was there. Petula had drawn as far back as possible; no longer smiling, her hand was at her throat, her eyes staring in disbelief. Spiros's left hand had caught up the V of Gwen's dress. His fingers were inside the dress and his thumb outside. In his right hand he clutched a pin like the one Dimitrios had given to Geoff. He was protesting:

"But I giving it! I putting it on your dress! Is nice, this one. We friends. Why you shout? You no like Spiros?" His throaty, gurgling voice was slurred: waves of ouzo fumes literally wafted off him like the stench of a dead fish. Geoff moved in, knocked Spiros's elbow away where it leaned on the wall. Spiros must release Gwen to maintain his balance. He did so, but still crashed half-over the wall. For a moment Geoff thought he would go completely over, into the sea. But he just lolled there, shaking his head, and finally turned it to look back at Geoff. There was a look on his face which Geoff couldn't quite describe. Drunken stupidity slowly turning to rage, maybe. Then he pushed himself upright, stood swaying against the wall, his fists knotting and the muscles in his arms bunching.

Hit him now, Geoff's inner man told him. *Do it, and he'll go clean over into the sea. It's not high, seven or eight feet, that's all. It'll sober the bastard up, and after that he won't trouble you again.*

But what if he couldn't swim? *You know he swims like a fish—like a bloody shark!*

"You think you better than Spiros, eh?" The Greek wobbled dangerously, steadied up and took a step in Geoff's direction.

"No!" the voice of the bearded Dimitrios was shattering in Geoff's ear. Massive, he stepped between them, grabbed Spiros by the hair, half-dragged, half-pushed him toward the exit. "No, *everybody* thinks he's better!" he cried. "Because everybody *is* better! Out—" he heaved Spiros yelping into the harbour's shadows. "I tell you before, Spiros: drink all the ouzo in Achladi. Is your business. But not let it ruin *my* business. Then comes thee *real* troubles!"

Gwen was naturally upset. It spoiled something of the evening for her. But by the time they had finished eating, things were about back to normal. No one else in the place, other than George and Petula, had seemed especially interested in the incident anyway.

At around eleven, when the taverna had cleared a little, the girl from Skymed came in. She came over.

"Hello, Julie!" said George, finding her a chair. And, flatterer born, he added: "How lovely you're looking tonight—but of course you look lovely all the time."

Petula tut-tutted. "George, if you hadn't met me you'd be a gigolo by now, I'm sure!"

"Mr Hammond," Julie said. "I'm terribly sorry. I should have explained to Spiros that he'd recover the fare for your ride from me. Actually, I believed he understood that but apparently he didn't. I've just seen him in one of the bars and asked him how much I owed him. He was a little upset, wouldn't accept the money, told me I should see you."

"Was he sober yet?" Geoff asked, sourly.

"Er, not very, I'm afraid. Has he been a nuisance?"

Geoff coughed. "Only a *bit* of a one."

"It was a thousand drachmas" said Gwen.

The courier looked a little taken aback. "Well it should only have been seven hundred."

"He did carry our bags, though," said Geoff.

"Ah! Maybe that explains it. Anyway, I'm authorized to pay you seven hundred."

"All donations are welcome," Gwen said, opening her purse and accepting the money. "But if I were you, in future I'd use someone else. This Spiros isn't a particularly pleasant fellow."

"Well he does seem to have a problem with the ouzo," Julie answered. "On the other hand—"

"He has *several* problems!" Geoff was sharper than he meant to be. After all, it wasn't her fault.

"—He also has the best beach," Julie finished.

"Beach?" Geoff raised an eyebrow. "He has a beach?"

"Didn't we tell you?" Petula spoke up. "Two or three of the locals have small boats in the harbour. For a few hundred drachmas they'll take you to one of a handful of private beaches along the coast. They're private because no one lives there, and there's no way in except by boat. The boatmen have their favourite places, which they guard jealously and call 'their' beaches, so that the others don't poach on them. They take you in the morning or whenever, collect you in the evening. Absolutely private...ideal for picnics...romance!" She sighed.

"What a lovely idea," said Gwen. "To have a beach of your own for the day!"

"Well, as far as I'm concerned," Geoff told her, "Spiros can keep his beach."

"Oh-oh!" said George. "Speak of the devil..."

Spiros had returned. He averted his face and made straight for the kitchens in the back. He was noticeably steadier on his feet now. Dimitrios came bowling out to meet him and a few low-muttered words passed between them. Their conversation quickly grew more heated, becoming rapid-fire Greek in moments, and Spiros appeared to be pleading his case. Finally Dimitrios shrugged, came lumbering toward the corner table with Spiros in tow.

"Spiros, he sorry," Dimitrios said. "For tonight. Too much ouzo. He just want be friendly."

"Is right," said Spiros, lifting his head. He shrugged helplessly. "Thee ouzo."

Geoff nodded. "OK, forget it," he said, but coldly.

"Is...OK?" Spiros lifted his head a little more. He looked at Gwen.

Gwen forced herself to nod. "It's OK."

Now Spiros beamed, or as close as he was likely to get to it. But still Geoff had this feeling that there was something cold and calculating in his manner.

"I make it good!" Spiros declared, nodding. "One day, I take you thee best beach! For thee picnic. Very private. Two peoples, no more. I no take thee money, nothing. Is good?"

"Fine," said Geoff. "That'll be fine."

"OK," Spiros smiled his unsmile, nodded, turned away. Going out, he looked back. "I sorry," he said again; and again his shrug. "Thee ouzo..."

"Hardly eloquent," said Petula, when he'd disappeared.

"But better than nothing," said George.

"Things are looking up!" Gwen was happier now.

Geoff was still unsure how he felt. He said nothing...

✤ ✤ ✤

"Breakfast is on us," George announced the next morning. He smiled down on Geoff and Gwen where they drank coffee and tested the early morning sunlight at a garden table on the patio. They were still in their dressing-gowns, eyes bleary, hair tousled.

Geoff looked up, squinting his eyes against the hurtful blue of the sky, and said: "I see what you mean about that donkey! What the Hell time is it, anyway?"

"Eight-fifteen," said George. "You're lucky. Normally he's at it, oh, an hour earlier than this!" From somewhere down in the maze of alleys, as if summoned by their conversation, the hideous braying echoed yet again as the village gradually came awake.

Just before nine they set out, George and Petula guiding them to a little place bearing the paint-daubed legend: "Brekfas Bar." They climbed steps to a pine-railed patio set with pine tables and chairs, under a varnished pine frame supporting a canopy of split bamboo. Service was good; the 'English' food hot, tasty, and very cheap; the coffee dreadful!

"*Yechh!*" Gwen commented, understanding now why George and Petula had ordered tea. "Take a note, Mr Hammond," she said. "Tomorrow, no coffee. Just fruit juice."

"We thought maybe it was us being fussy," said Petula. "Else we'd have warned you."

"Anyway," George sighed. "Here's where we have to leave you. For tomorrow we fly—literally. So today we're shopping, picking up our duty-frees, gifts, the postcards we never sent, some Greek cigarettes."

"But we'll see you tonight, if you'd care to?" said Petula.

"Delighted!" Geoff answered. "What, Zorba's Dance, moussaka, and a couple or three of those giant Metaxas that Dimi serves? Who could refuse?"

"Not to mention the company," said Gwen.

"About eight-thirty, then," said Petula. And off they went.

"I shall miss them," said Gwen.

"But it will be nice to be on our own for once," Geoff leaned over to kiss her.

"Hallo!" came a now familiar, gurgling voice from below. Spiros stood in the street beyond the rail, looking up at them, the sun striking sparks from the lenses of his sunglasses. Their faces fell and he couldn't fail to notice it. "Is OK," he quickly held up a hand. "I no stay. I busy. Today I make thee taxi. Later, thee boat."

Gwen gave a little gasp of excitement, clutched Geoff's arm. "The private beach!" she said. "Now that's what I'd call being on our own!" And to Spiros: "If we're ready at one o'clock, will you take us to your beach?"

"Of course!" he answered. "At one o'clock, I near Dimi's. My boat, him called *Spiros* like me. You see him."

Gwen nodded. "We'll see you then."

"Good!" Spiros nodded. He looked up at them a moment longer, and Geoff wished he could fathom where the man's eyes were. Probably up Gwen's dress. But then he turned and went on his way.

"Now we shop!" Gwen said.

They shopped for picnic items. Nothing gigantic, mainly small things. Slices of salami, hard cheese, two fat tomatoes, fresh bread, a bottle of light white wine, some feta, eggs for boiling, and a liter of crystal-clear bottled water. And as an afterthought: half-a-dozen small pats of butter, a small jar of honey, a sharp knife and a packet of doilies. No wicker basket; their little plastic coolbox would have to do. And one of their pieces of shoulder luggage for the blanket, towels, and swim-things. Geoff was no good for details; Gwen's head, to the contrary, was only happy buzzing with them. He let her get on with it, acted as beast of burden. In fact there was no burden to mention. After all, she was shopping for just the two of them, and it was as good a way as any to explore the village stores and see what was on offer. While she examined this and that, Geoff spent the time comparing the prices of various spirits with those already noted in the booze shop. So the morning passed.

At eleven-thirty they went back to the Villa Eleni for you know and a shower, and afterwards Gwen prepared the foodstuffs while Geoff lazed under the awning. No sign of George and Petula; eighty-four degrees of heat as they idled their way down to the harbour; the village had closed itself down through the hottest part of the day, and they saw no one they knew. Spiros's boat lolled like a mirrored blot on the stirless ocean, and Geoff thought: *even the fish will be finding this a bit much!* Also: *I hope there's some shade on this blasted beach!*

Spiros appeared from behind a tangle of nets. He stood up, yawned, adjusted his straw hat like a sunshade on his head. "Thee boat," he said, in his entirely unnecessary fashion, as he helped them climb aboard. *Spiros* "thee boat" was hardly a hundred percent seaworthy, Geoff saw that immediately. In fact, in any other ocean in the world she'd be condemned. But this was the Mediterranean in July.

Barely big enough for three adults, the boat rocked a little as Spiros yanked futilely on the starter. Water seeped through boards, rotten and long since sprung, black with constant damp and badly caulked. Spiros saw Geoff's expression where he sat with his sandals in half an inch of water. He shrugged. "Is nothings," he said.

Finally the engine coughed into life, began to purr, and they were off. Spiros had the tiller; Geoff and Gwen faced him from the prow, which now lifted up a little as they left the harbour and cut straight out to sea. It was then, for the first time, that Geoff noticed Spiros's furtiveness: the way he kept glancing back toward Achladi, as if anxious not to be observed. Unlikely that they would be, for the village seemed fast asleep. Or perhaps he was just checking land marks, avoiding rocks or reefs or what have you. Geoff looked overboard. The water seemed deep enough to him. Indeed, it seemed much *too* deep! But at least there were no sharks...

Well out to sea, Spiros swung the boat south and followed the coastline for maybe two and a half to three miles. The highest of Achladi's houses and apartments had slipped entirely from view by the time he turned in towards land again and sought a bight in the seemingly unbroken march of cliffs. The place was landmarked: a fang of rock had weathered free, shaping a stack that reared up from the water to form a narrow, deep channel between itself and the cliffs proper. In former times a second, greater stack had crashed oceanward and now lay like a reef just under the water across the entire frontage. In effect, this made the place a lagoon: a sandy beach to the rear, safe water, and the reef of shattered, softly matted rocks where the small waves broke.

There was only one way in. Spiros gentled his boat through the deep water between the crooked outcrop and the overhanging cliff. Clear of the channel, he nosed her into the beach and cut the motor; as the keel grated on grit he stepped nimbly between his passengers and jumped ashore, dragging the boat a few inches up onto the sand. Geoff passed him the picnic things, then steadied the boat while Gwen took off her sandals and made to step down where the water met the sand. But Spiros was quick off the mark.

He stepped forward, caught her up, carried her two paces up the beach and set her down. His left arm had been under her thighs, his right under her back, cradling her. But when he set her upon her own feet his right hand had momentarily cupped her breast, which he'd quite deliberately squeezed.

Gwen opened her mouth, stood gasping her outrage, unable to give it words. Geoff had got out of the boat and was picking up their things to bring them higher up the sand. Spiros, slapping him on the back, stepped round him and shoved the boat off, splashed in shallow water a moment before leaping nimbly aboard. Gwen controlled herself, said nothing. She could feel the blood in her cheeks but hoped Geoff wouldn't notice. Not here, miles from anywhere. Not in this lonely place. No, there must be no trouble here.

For suddenly it had dawned on her just how very lonely it was. Beautiful, unspoiled, a lovers' idyll—but oh so very lonely...

"You alright, love?" said Geoff, taking her elbow. She was looking at Spiros standing silent in his boat. Their eyes seemed locked, it was as if she didn't see him but the mind behind the sunglasses, behind those disparate, dispassionate eyes. A message had passed between them. Geoff sensed it but couldn't fathom it. He had almost seemed to hear Spiros say "yes", and Gwen answer "no".

"Gwen?" he said again.

"I see you," Spiros called, grinning. It broke the spell. Gwen looked away, and Geoff called out:

"Six-thirty, right?"

Spiros waggled a hand this way and that palm-down, as if undecided. "Six, six-thirty—something," he said, shrugging. He started his motor, waved once, chugged out of the bay between the jutting sentinel rock and the cliffs. As he passed out of sight the boat's engine roared with life, its throaty growl rapidly fading into the distance...

Gwen said nothing about the incident; she felt sure that if she did, then Geoff would make something of it. Their entire holiday could so easily be spoiled. It was bad enough that for her the day had already been ruined. So she kept quiet, and perhaps a little too quiet. When Geoff asked her again if anything was wrong she told him she had a headache. Then, feeling a little unclean, she stripped herself quite naked and swam while he explored the beach.

Not that there was a great deal to explore. He walked the damp sand at the water's rim to the southern extreme and came up against the cliffs where they curved out into the sea. They were quite unscalable, towering maybe eighty or ninety feet to their jagged rim. Walking the hundred or so yards back the other way, the thought came to Geoff that if Spiros didn't come back for them—that is, if anything untoward should happen to him—they'd just have to sit it out until they were found. Which, since Spiros was the only one who knew they were here, might well be a long time. Having thought it, Geoff tried to shake the idea off but it wouldn't go away. The place was quite literally a trap. Even a decent swimmer would have to have at least a couple of miles in him before considering swimming out of here.

Once lodged in Geoff's brain, the concept rapidly expanded itself. Before…he had looked at the faded yellow and bone-white facade of the cliffs against the incredible blue of the sky with admiration; the beach had been every man's dream of tranquility, privacy, Eden with its own Eve; the softly lapping ocean had seemed like a warm, soothing bath reaching from horizon to horizon. But now…the place was so like Cape Greco. Except at Greco there had always been a way down to the sea—and up from it…

The northern end of the beach was much like the southern, the only difference being the great fang of rock protruding from the sea. Geoff stripped, swam out to it, was aware that the water here was a great deal deeper than back along the beach. But the distance was only thirty feet or so, nothing to worry about. And there were hand and footholds galore around the base of the pillar of upthrusting rock. He hauled himself up onto a tiny ledge, climbed higher (not too high), sat on a projecting fist of rock with his feet dangling and called to Gwen. His voice surprised him, for it seemed strangely small and panting. The cliffs took it up, however, amplified and passed it on. His shout reached Gwen where she splashed; she spotted him, stopped swimming and stood up. She waved, and he marvelled at her body, her tip-tilted breasts displayed where she stood like some lovely Mediterranean nymph, all unashamed. *Venus rising from the waves*. Except that here the waves were little more than ripples.

He glanced down at the water and was at once dizzy: the way it lapped at the rock and flowed so gently in the worn hollows of the stone, all fluid and glinting motion; and Geoff's stomach following the same routine, seeming to slosh loosely inside him. *Damn* this terror of his! What was he but eight, nine feet above the sea? God, he might as well feel sick standing on a thick carpet!

He stood up, shouted, jumped outward, toward Gwen.

Down he plunged into cool, liquid blue, and fought his way to the surface, and swam furiously to the beach. There he lay, half-in, half-out of the water, his heart and lungs hammering, blood coursing through his body. It had been such a little thing—something any ten-year-old child could have done—but to him it had been such an effort. And an achievement!

Elated, he stood up, sprinted down the beach, threw himself into the warm, shallow water just as Gwen was emerging. Carried back by him she laughed, splashed him, finally submitted to his hug. They rolled in twelve inches of water and her legs went round him; and there where the water met the sand they grew gentle, then fierce, and when it was done the sea laved their heat and rocked them gently, slowly dispersing their passion…

About four o'clock they ate, but very little. They weren't hungry; the sun was too hot; the silence, at first enchanting, had turned to a droning, sun-scorched monotony that beat on the ears worse than a city's roar. And there was a smell. When the light breeze off the sea swung in a certain direction, it brought something unpleasant with it.

To provide shade, Geoff had rigged up his shirt, slacks, and a large beach towel on a frame of drifted bamboo between the brittle, sandpapered branches of an old tree washed half-way up the sand. There in this tatty, makeshift teepee they'd spread their blanket, retreated from the pounding sun. But as the smell came again Geoff crept out of the cramped shade, stood up and shielded his eyes to look along the wall of the cliffs. "It comes…from over there," he said, pointing.

Gwen joined him. "I thought you'd explored?" she said.

"Along the tideline," he answered, nodding slowly. "Not along the base of the cliffs. Actually, they don't look too safe, and they overhang a fair bit in places. But if you'll look where I'm pointing—there, where the cliffs are cut back—is that water glinting?"

"A spring?" she looked at him. "A waterfall?"

"Hardly a waterfall," he said. "More a dribble. But what is it that's dribbling? I mean, springs don't stink, do they?"

Gwen wrinkled her nose. "Sewage, do you think?"

"*Yecchh!*" he said. "But at least it would explain why there's no one else here. I'm going to have a look."

She followed him to the place where the cliffs were notched in a V. Out of the sunlight, they both shivered a little. They'd put on swimwear for simple decency's sake, in case a boat should pass by, but now they hugged themselves as the chill of damp stone drew off their stored heat and brought goose-pimples to flesh which sun and sea had already roughened. And there, beneath the overhanging cliff, they found in the shingle a pool formed of a steady flow from on high. Without a shadow of a doubt, the pool was the source of the carrion stench; but here in the shade its water was dark, muddied, rippled, quite opaque. If there was anything in it, then it couldn't be seen.

As for the waterfall: it forked high up in the cliff, fell in twin streams, one of which was a trickle. Leaning out over the pool at its narrowest, shallowest point, Geoff cupped his hand to catch a few droplets. He held them to his nose, shook his head. "Just water," he said. "It's the pool itself that stinks."

"Or something back there?" Gwen looked beyond the pool, into the darkness of the cave formed of the V and the overhang.

Geoff took up a stone, hurled it into the darkness and silence. Clattering echoes sounded, and a moment later—

Flies! A swarm of them, disturbed where they'd been sitting on cool, damp ledges. They came in a cloud out of the cave, sent Geoff and Gwen yelping, fleeing for the sea. Geoff was stung twice, Gwen escaped injury; the ocean was their refuge, shielding them while the flies dispersed or returned to their vile-smelling breeding ground.

After the murky, poisonous pool the sea felt cool and refreshing. Muttering curses, Geoff stood in the shallows while Gwen squeezed the craters of the stings in his right shoulder and bathed them with salt water. When she was done he said, bitterly: "I've *had* it with this place! The sooner the Greek gets back the better."

His words were like an invocation. Towelling themselves dry, they heard the roar of Spiros's motor, heard it throttle back, and a moment later his boat came nosing in through the gap between the rock and the cliffs. But instead of landing he stood off in the shallow water. "Hallo," he called, in his totally unnecessary fashion.

"You're early," Geoff called back. And under his breath: *Thank God!*

"Early, yes," Spiros answered. "But I have thee troubles." He shrugged.

Gwen had pulled her dress on, packed the last of their things away. She walked down to the water's edge with Geoff. "Troubles?" she said, her voice a shade unsteady.

"Thee boat," he said, and pointed into the open, lolling belly of the craft, where they couldn't see. "I hitting thee rock when I leave Achladi. Is OK, but—" And he made his fifty-fifty sign, waggling his hand with the fingers open and the palm down. His face remained impassive, however.

Geoff looked at Gwen, then back to Spiros. "You mean it's unsafe?"

"For three peoples, unsafe—maybe." Again the Greek's shrug. "I thinks, I take thee lady first. Is OK, I come back. Is bad, I find other boat."

"You can't take both of us?" Geoff's face fell.

Spiros shook his head. "Maybe big problems," he said.

Geoff nodded. "OK," he said to Gwen. "Go just as you are. Leave all this stuff here and keep the boat light." And to Spiros: "Can you come in a bit more?"

The Greek made a clicking sound with his tongue, shrugged apologetically. "Thee boat is broked. I not want thee more breakings. You swim?" He looked at Gwen, leaned over the side and held out his hand. Keeping her dress on, she waded into the water, made her way to the side of the boat. The water only came up to her breasts, but it turned her dress to a transparent, clinging film. She grasped the upper strake with one hand and made to drag herself aboard. Spiros, leaning backwards, took her free hand.

Watching, Geoff saw her come half out of the water—then saw her freeze. She gasped loudly and twisted her wet hand in Spiros's grasp, tugged free of his grip, flopped back down into the water. And while the Greek regained his balance, she quickly swam back ashore. Geoff helped her from the sea. "Gwen?" he said.

Spiros worked his starter, got the motor going. He commenced a slow, deliberate circling of the small bay.

"Gwen?" Geoff said again. "What is it? What's wrong?" She was pale, shivering.

"He..." she finally started to speak. "He...had an erection! Geoff, I could see it bulging in his shorts, throbbing. My God—and I know it was for me! And the boat..."

"What about the boat?" Anger was building in Geoff's heart and head, starting to run cold in his blood.

"There was no damage—none that I could see, anyway. He...he just wanted to get me into that boat, on my own!"

Spiros could see them talking together. He came angling close into the beach, called out: "I bring thee better boat. Half an hour. Is safer. I see you." He headed for the channel between the rock and the cliff and in another moment passed from sight...

"Geoff, we're in trouble," Gwen said, as soon as Spiros had left. "We're in serious trouble."

"I know it," he said. "I think I've known it ever since we got here. That bloke's as sinister as they come."

"And it's not just his eye, it's his mind," said Gwen. "He's sick." Finally, she told her husband about the incident when Spiros had carried her ashore from the boat.

"So that's what that was all about," he growled. "Well, something has to be done about him. We'll have to report him."

She clutched his arm. "We have to get back to Achladi before we can do that," she said quietly. "Geoff, I don't think he intends to let us get back!"

That thought had been in his mind, too, but he hadn't wanted her to know it. He felt suddenly helpless. The trap seemed sprung and they were in it. But what did Spiros intend, and how could he possibly hope to get away with it—whatever 'it' was? Gwen broke into his thoughts:

"No one knows we're here, just Spiros."

"I know," said Geoff. "And what about that couple who..." He let it tail off. It had just slipped from his tongue. It was the last thing he'd wanted to say.

"Do you think I haven't thought of that?" Gwen hissed, gripping his arm more tightly yet. "He was the last one to see them—getting on a ferry, he said. But did they?" She stripped off her dress.

"What are you doing?" he asked, breathlessly.

"We came in from the north," she answered, wading out again into the water. "There were no beaches between here and Achladi. What about to the south? There are other beaches than this one, we know that. Maybe there's one just half a mile away. Maybe even less. If I can find one where there's a path up the cliffs..."

"Gwen," he said. "Gwen!" Panic was rising in him to match his impotence, his rage and terror.

She turned and looked at him, looked helpless in her skimpy bikini— and yet determined, too. And to think he'd considered her naïve! Well, maybe she had been. But no more. She managed a small smile, said, "I love you."

"What if you exhaust yourself?" He could think of nothing else to say.

"I'll know when to turn back," she said. Even in the hot sunlight he felt cold, and knew she must, too. He started towards her, but she was already into a controlled crawl, heading south, out across the submerged rocks. He watched her out of sight round the southern extreme of the jutting cliffs, stood knotting and unknotting his fists at the edge of the sea…

For long moments Geoff stood there, cold inside and hot out. And at the same time cold all over. Then the sense of time fleeting by overcame him. He ground his teeth, felt his frustration overflow. He wanted to shout but feared Gwen would hear him and turn back. But there must be something he could do. With his bare hands? Like what? A weapon—he needed a weapon.

There was the knife they'd bought just for their picnic. He went to their things and found it. Only a three-inch blade, but sharp! Hand to hand it must give him something of an advantage. But what if Spiros had a bigger knife? He seemed to have a bigger or better everything else.

One of the drifted tree's branches was long, straight, slender. It pointed like a mocking, sandpapered wooden finger at the unscalable cliffs. Geoff applied his weight close to the main branch. As he lifted his feet from the ground the branch broke, sending him to his knees in the sand. Now he needed some binding material. Taking his unfinished spear with him, he ran to the base of the cliffs. Various odds and ends had been driven back there by past storms. Plastic Coke bottles, fragments of driftwood, pieces of cork…a nylon fishing net tangled round a broken barrel!

Geoff cut lengths of tough nylon line from the net, bound the knife in position at the end of his spear. Now he felt he had a *real* advantage. He looked around. The sun was sinking leisurely towards the sea, casting his long shadow on the sand. How long since Spiros left? How much time left till he got back? Geoff glanced at the frowning needle of the sentinel rock. A sentinel, yes. A watcher. Or a watchtower!

He put down his spear, ran to the northern point and sprang into the sea. Moments later he was clawing at the rock, dragging himself from the water, climbing. And scarcely a thought of danger, not from the sea or the climb, not from the deep water or the height. At thirty feet the rock narrowed down; he could lean to left or right and scan the sea to the north, in the direction of Achladi. Way out on the blue, sails gleamed white in the brilliant sunlight. On the far horizon, a smudge of smoke. Nothing else.

For a moment—the merest moment—Geoff's old nausea returned. He closed his eyes and flattened himself to the rock, gripped tightly where his fingers were bedded in cracks in the weathered stone. A mass of stone shifted slightly under the pressure of his right hand, almost causing him to lose his balance. He teetered for a second, remembered Gwen…the nausea passed, and with it all fear. He stepped a little lower, examined the great slab of rock which his hand had tugged loose. And suddenly an idea burned bright in his brain.

Which was when he heard Gwen's cry, thin as a keening wind, shrilling into his bones from along the beach. He jerked his head round, saw her there in the water inside the reef, wearily striking for the shore. She looked all in. His heart leaped into his mouth, and without pause he launched himself from the rock, striking the water feet first and sinking deep. No fear or effort to it this time; no time for any of that; surfacing, he struck for the shore. Then back along the beach, panting his heart out, flinging himself down in the small waves where she knelt, sobbing, her face covered by her hands.

"Gwen, are you all right? What is it, love? What's happened? I *knew* you'd exhaust yourself!"

She tried to stand up, collapsed into his arms and shivered there; he cradled her where earlier they'd made love. And at last she could tell it.

"I…I stayed close to the shore," she gasped, gradually getting her breath. "Or rather, close to the cliffs. I was looking…looking for a way up. I'd gone about a third of a mile, I think. Then there was a spot where the water was very deep and the cliffs sheer. Something touched my legs and it was like an electric shock—I mean, it was so unexpected there in that deep water. To feel something slimy touching my legs like that. *Ugh!*" She drew a deep breath.

"I thought: *God, sharks!* But then I remembered: there are no sharks in the Med. Still, I wanted to be sure. So…so I turned, made a shallow dive and looked to see what…what…" She broke down into sobbing again.

Geoff could do nothing but warm her, hug her tighter yet.

"Oh, but there *are* sharks in the Med, Geoff," she finally went on. "One shark, anyway. His name is Spiros! A spider? No, he's a shark! Under the

185

sea there, I saw…a girl, naked, tethered to the bottom with a rope round her ankle. And down in the deeps, a stone holding her there."

"My God!" Geoff breathed.

"Her thighs, belly, were covered in those little green swimming crabs. She was all bloated, puffy, floating upright on her own internal gasses. Fish nibbled at her. Her nipples were gone…"

"The fish!" Geoff gasped. But Gwen shook her head.

"Not the fish," she rasped. "Her arms and breasts were black with bruises. Her nipples had been bitten through—*right* through! Oh, Geoff, Geoff!" She hugged him harder than ever, shivering hard enough to shake him. "I *know* what happened to her. It was him, Spiros." She paused, tried to control her shivering, which wasn't only the after-effect of the water.

And finally she continued: "After that I had no strength. But somehow I made it back."

"Get dressed," he told her then, his voice colder than she'd ever heard it. "Quickly! No, not your dress—my trousers, shirt. The slacks will be too long for you. Roll up the bottoms. But get dressed, get warm."

She did as he said. The sun, sinking, was still hot. Soon she was warm again, and calmer. Then Geoff gave her the spear he'd made and told her what he was going to do…

There were two of them, as like as peas in a pod. Geoff saw them, and the pieces fell into place. Spiros and his brother. The island's codes were tight. These two looked for loose women; loose in their narrow eyes, anyway. And from the passports of the honeymooners it had been plain that they weren't married. Which had made Gwen a whore, in their eyes. Like the Swedish girl, who'd met a man and gone to bed with him. As easy as that. So Spiros had tried it on, the easy way at first. By making it plain that he was on offer. Now that that hadn't worked, now it was time for the hard way.

Geoff saw them coming in the boat and stopped gouging at the rock. His fingernails were cracked and starting to bleed, but the job was as complete as he could wish. He ducked back out of sight, hugged the sentinel rock and thought only of Gwen. He had one chance and mustn't miss it.

He glanced back, over his shoulder. Gwen had heard the boat's engine. She stood half-way between the sea and the waterfall with its foul pool. Her spear was grasped tightly in her hands. *Like a young Amazon,*

Geoff thought. But then he heard the boat's motor cut back and concentrated on what he was doing.

The put-put-put of the boat's exhaust came closer. Geoff took a chance, glanced round the rim of the rock. Here they came, gentling into the channel between the rock and the cliffs. Spiros's brother wore slacks; both men were naked from the waist up; Spiros had the tiller. And his brother had a shotgun!

One chance. *Only one chance.*

The boat's nose came inching forward, began to pass directly below. Geoff gave a mad yell, heaved at the loose wedge of rock. For a moment he thought it would stick and put all his weight into it. But then it shifted, toppled.

Below, the two Greeks had looked up, eyes huge in tanned, startled faces. The one with the shotgun was on his feet. He saw the falling rock in the instant before it smashed down on him and drove him through the bottom of the boat. His gun went off, both barrels, and the shimmering air near Geoff's head buzzed like a nest of wasps. Then, while all below was still in a turmoil, he aimed himself at Spiros and jumped.

Thrown about in the stern of his sinking boat, Spiros was making ready to dive overboard when Geoff's feet hit him. He was hurled into the water, Geoff narrowly missing the swamped boat as he, too, crashed down into the sea. And then a mad flurry of water as they both struck out for the shore.

Spiros was there first. Crying out, wild, outraged, frightened, he dragged himself from the sea. He looked round and saw Geoff coming through the water—saw his boat disappear with only ripples to mark its passing, and no sign of his brother—and started at a lop-sided run up the beach. Towards Gwen. Geoff swam for all he was worth, flew from the sea up onto the land.

Gwen was running, heading for the V in the cliff under the waterfall. Spiros was right behind her, arms reaching. Geoff came last, the air rasping in his lungs, Hell's fires blazing in his heart. He'd drawn blood and found it to his liking. But he stumbled, fell, and when he was up again he saw Spiros closing on his quarry. Gwen was backed up against the cliff, her feet in the water at the shallow end of the vile pool. The Greek made a low, apish lunge at her and she struck at him with her spear.

She gashed his face even as he grabbed her. His hand caught in the loose material of Geoff's shirt, tearing it from her so that her breasts lolled free. Then she stabbed at him again, slicing him across the neck. His hands flew to his face and neck; he staggered back from her, tripped, and sat down in chest-deep water; Geoff arrived panting at the pool and Gwen flew into his arms. He took the spear from her, turned it towards Spiros.

But the Greek was finished. He shrieked and splashed in the pool like the madman he was, seemed incapable of getting to his feet. His wounds weren't bad, but the blood was everywhere. That wasn't the worst of it: the thing he'd tripped on had floated to the surface. It was beginning to rot, but it was—or had been—a young man. Rubbery arms and legs tangled with Spiros's limbs; a ghastly, gaping face tossed with his frantic threshing; a great black hole showed where the bloated corpse had taken a shotgun blast to the chest, the shot that had killed him.

For a little while longer Spiros fought to be rid of the thing—screamed aloud as its gaping, accusing mouth screamed horribly, silently at him— then gave up and flopped back half-in, half-out of the water. One of the corpse's arms was draped across his heaving, shuddering chest. He lay there with his hands over his face and cried, and the flies came swarming like a black, hostile cloud from the cave to settle on him.

Geoff held Gwen close, guided her away from the horror down the beach to a sea which was a deeper blue now. "It's OK," he kept saying, as much for himself as for her. "It's OK. They'll come looking for us, sooner or later."

As it happened, it was sooner…

THE PIT-YAKKER

When I was sixteen, my father used to say to me: "Watch what you're doing with the girls; you're an idiot to smoke, for it's expensive and unhealthy; stay away from Raymond Maddison!" My mother had died two years earlier, so he'd taken over her share of the nagging, too.

The girls? Watch what I was doing? At sixteen, I barely *knew* what I was doing! I knew what I wanted to do, but the how of it was a different matter entirely. Cigarettes? I enjoyed them; at the five-a-day stage, they still gave me that occasionally sweet taste and made my head spin. Raymond Maddison? I had gone to school with him, and because he lived so close to us we'd used to walk home together. But his mother was a little weakminded, his older brother had been put away for molesting or something, and Raymond himself was thick as two short planks, hulking and unlovely, and a very shadowy character in general. Or at least he gave that impression.

Girls didn't like him: he smelled of bread and dripping and didn't clean his teeth too well, and for two years now he'd been wearing the same jacket and trousers, which had grown pretty tight on him. His short hair and little piggy eyes made him look bristly, and there was that looseness about his lips that you find in certain idiots. If you were told that ladies' underwear was disappearing from washing lines, you'd perhaps think of Raymond. If someone was jumping out on small girls at dusk and shouting *boo!*, he was the one who'd spring to mind. If the little-boy-up-the-road's kitten got strangled…

Not that that sort of thing happened a lot in Harden, for it didn't. Up there on the northeast coast in those days, the Bobbies on the beat were still

189

Bobbies, unhampered by modern "ethics" and other humane restrictions. Catch a kid drawing red, hairy, diamond-shaped designs on the school wall, and *wallop!*, he'd get a clout round the ear hole, dragged off home to his parents, and doubtless another wallop. Also, in the schools, the cane was still in force. Young people were still being "brought up", were made or at least encouraged to grow up straight and strong, and not allowed to bolt and run wild. Most of them, anyway. But it wasn't easy, not in that environment.

Harden lay well outside the fringes of "Geordie-land"—Newcastle and environs—but real outsiders termed us all Geordies anyway. It was the way we spoke; our near-Geordie accents leapt between soft and harsh as readily as the Welsh tongue soars up and down the scales; a dialect that at once identified us as "pit-yakkers," grimy-black shambling colliers, coal miners. The fact that my father was a Harden greengrocer made no difference: I came from the colliery and so was a pit-yakker. I was an apprentice wood-cutting machinist in Hartlepool?—so what? My collar was grimy, wasn't it? With coal dust? And no matter how much I tried to disguise it, I had that accent, didn't I? Pit-yakker!

But at sixteen I *was* escaping from the image. One must, or sex remain forever a mystery. The girls—the better girls, anyway—in the big towns, even in Harden, Easington, Blackhill and the other colliery villages, weren't much impressed by or interested in pit-yakkers. Which must have left Raymond Maddison in an entirely hopeless position. Everything about him literally shrieked of his origin, made worse by the fact that his father, a miner, was already grooming Raymond for the mine, too. You think I have a down on them, the colliers? No, for they were the salt of the earth. They still are. I merely give you the background.

As for my own opinion of Raymond: I thought I knew him and didn't for a moment consider him a bad sort. He loved John Wayne like I did, and liked to think of himself as a tough egg, as I did. But nature and the world in general hadn't been so kind to him, and being a bit of a dunce didn't help much either. He was like a big scruffy dog who sits at the corner of the street grinning at everyone going by and wagging his tail, whom nobody ever pats for fear of fleas or mange or whatever, and who you're sure pees on the front wheel of your car everytime you park it there. He probably doesn't, but somebody has to take the blame. That was how I saw Raymond.

So I was sixteen and some months, and Raymond Maddison about the same, and it was a Saturday in July. Normally when we met we'd pass the time of day. Just a few words: what was on at the cinema (in Harden there were two of them, the Ritz and the Empress—for this was before Bingo closed most of them down), when was the next dance at the Old Victoria Hall, how many pints we'd downed last Friday at the British Legion. Dancing, drinking, smoking, girls: it was a time of experimentation. Life had so many flavors other than those that wafted out from the pit and the coke ovens. On this Saturday, however, he was the last person I wanted to see, and the very last I wanted to be seen with.

I was waiting for Moira, sitting on the recreation-ground wall where the stumps of the old iron railings showed through, which they'd taken away thirteen years earlier for the war effort and never replaced. I had been a baby then but it was one of the memories I had: of the men in the helmets with the glass faceplates cutting down all the iron things to melt for the war. It had left only the low wall, which was ideal to sit on. In the summer the flat-capped miners would sit there to watch the kids flying kites in the recreation ground or playing on the swings, or just to sit and talk. There was a group of old-timers there that Saturday, too, all looking out across the dark, fuming colliery toward the sea; so when I saw Raymond hunching my way with his hands in his pockets, I turned and looked in the same direction, hoping he wouldn't notice me. But he already had.

"Hi, Joshua!" he said in his mumbling fashion, touching my arm. I don't know why I was christened "Joshua": I wasn't Jewish or a Catholic or anything. I *do* know why; my father told me *his* father had been called Joshua, so that was it. Usually they called me Josh, which I liked because it sounded like a wild-western name. I could imagine John Wayne being called Josh. But Raymond occasionally forgot and called me "Joshua."

"Hello, Ray*mond*!" I said. I usually called him "Ray," but if he noticed the difference he didn't say anything.

"Game of snooker?" It was an invitation.

"No." I shook my head. "I'm, er, waiting for someone."

"Who?"

"Mind your own business."

"Girl?" he said. "Moira? Saw you with her at the Ritz. Back row."

"Look, Ray, I—"

"It's OK," he said, sitting down beside me on the wall. "We're jus' talking. I can go any time."

I groaned inside. He was bound to follow us. He did stupid things like that. I decided to make the best of it, glanced at him. "So, what are you doing? Have you found a job yet?"

He pulled a face. "Naw."

"Are you going to?"

"Pit. Next spring. My dad says."

"Uh-huh." I nodded. "Plenty of work there." I looked along the wall past the groundkeeper's house. That's the way Moira would come.

"Hey, look!" said Raymond. He took out a brand new Swiss Army penknife and handed it over for my inspection. As my eyes widened he beamed. "Beauty, eh?"

And it was. "Where'd you get it?" I asked him, opening it up. It was fitted with every sort of blade and attachment you could imagine. Three or four years earlier I would have loved a knife like that. But right now I couldn't see why I'd need it. OK for wood carving or the Boy Scouts, or even the Boys' Brigade, but I'd left all that stuff behind. And anyway, the machines I was learning to use in my trade paled this thing to insignificance and made it look like a very primitive toy. Like a rasp beside a circular saw. I couldn't see why Raymond would want it either.

"Saved up for it," he said. "See, a saw. Two saws! One for metal, one for wood. Knives—*careful!*—sharp. Gouge—"

"That's an auger," I said, "not a gouge. But...this one's a gouge, right enough. Look," and I eased the tool from its housing to show him.

"Corkscrew," he went on. "Scissors, file, hook..."

"Hook?"

"For hooking things. Magnetic. You can pick up screws."

"It's a good knife," I told him, giving it back. "How do you use it?"

"I haven't," he said, "—yet."

I was getting desperate. "Ray, do me a favor. Look, I have to stay here and wait for her. And I'm short of cigs." I forked out a florin. "Bring me a packet, will you? Twenty? And I'll give you a few."

He took the coin. "You'll be here?"

I nodded, lying without saying anything. I had an unopened packet of twenty in my pocket. He said no more but loped off across the road, disappearing into one of the back streets leading to Harden's main road and shopping area. I let him get out of sight, then set off briskly past the groundkeeper's house, heading north.

Now, I know I've stated that in my opinion he was OK; but even so, still I knew he wasn't to be trusted. He just *might* follow us, if he could—out of curiosity, perversity, don't ask me. You just couldn't be sure what he was thinking, that's all. And I didn't want him peeping on us.

It dawns on me now that in his "innocence" Raymond was anything but innocent. There are two sides to each of us, and in someone like him, a little lacking in basic understanding…well, who is to say that the dark side shouldn't on occasion be just a shade darker? For illustration, there'd been that time when we were, oh, nine or ten years old? I had two white mice who lived in their box in the garden shed. They had their own swimming pool, too, made out of an old baking tray just two and a half inches deep. I'd trained them to swim to a floating tin lid for bits of bacon rind.

One day, playing with Raymond and the mice in the garden, I'd been called indoors about something or other. I was only inside a moment or two, but when I came back out he'd gone. Looking over the garden wall and down the street, I'd seen him *tip-toeing* off into the distance! A great hulk like him, slinking off like a cartoon cat!

Then I'd shrugged and returned to my game—and just in time. The tin-lid raft was upside down, with Peter and Pan trapped underneath, paddling for all they were worth to keep their snouts up in the air trapped under there with them. It was only a small thing, I suppose, but it had given me bad dreams for a long time. So…instead of the hard nut I considered myself, maybe I was just a big softy after all. In some things.

But…did Raymond do it deliberately or was it an accident? And if the latter, then why was he slinking off like that? If he had tried to drown them, why? Jealousy? Something I had that he didn't have? Or sheer, downright nastiness? When I'd later tackled him about it, he'd just said: "Eh? Eh?" and looked dumb. That's the way it was with him. I could never figure out what went on in there.

Moira lived down by the high colliery wall, beyond which stood vast cones of coal, piled there, waiting to fuel the coke ovens. And as a back-drop to these black foothills, the wheelhouse towers rising like sooty sentinels, coming into view as I hurried through the grimy sunlit streets; a colliery in the summer seems strangely opposed to itself. In one of the towers a massive spoked wheel was spinning even now, raising or lowering a cage in its claustrophobic shaft. Miners, some still in their "pit black", even wearing their helmets and lamps, drew deep on cigarettes as they came away from the place. My father would have said: "As if their lungs aren't suffering enough already!"

I knew the exact route Moira would take from her gritty colliery-street house to the recreation ground, but at each junction in its turn I scanned the streets this way and that, making sure I didn't miss her. By now Raymond would have bought the cigarettes and be on his way back to the wall.

"Hello, Josh!" she said, breathlessly surprised—almost as if she hadn't expected to see me today—appearing like a ray of extra bright sunlight from behind the freshly creosoted fencing of garden allotments. She stood back and looked me up and down. "So, you're all impatient to see me, eh? Or...maybe I was late?" She looked at me anxiously.

I had been hurrying and so was breathing heavily. I smiled, wiped my forehead, said: "It's...just that there was someone I knew back there, at the recreation ground, and—"

"You didn't want to be seen with me?" She frowned. She was mocking me, but I didn't know it.

"No, not that," I hurriedly denied it, "but—"

And then she laughed and I knew she'd been teasing. "It's all right, Josh," she said. "I understand." She linked my arm. "Where are we going?"

"Walking," I said, turning her into the maze of allotments, trying to control my breathing, my heartbeat.

"I know *that*!" she said. "But where?"

"Down to the beach, and up again in Blackhill?"

"The beach is very dirty. Not very kind to good clothes." She was wearing a short blue skirt, white blouse, a smart white jacket across her arm.

"The beach banks, then," I gulped. "And along the cliff paths to Easington."

"You only want to get me where it's lonely," she said, but with a smile. "All right, then." And a moment later: "May I have a cigarette?"

I brought out my fresh pack and started to open it, but looking nervously around she said: "Not just yet. When we're farther into the allotments." She was six months my junior and lived close by; if someone saw her smoking it was likely to be reported to her father. But a few minutes later we shared a cigarette and she kissed me, blowing smoke into my mouth. I wondered where she'd learned to do that. Also, it took me by surprise—the kiss, I mean. She was impulsive like that.

In retrospect, I suppose Moira was my first love. And they say you never forget the first one. Well, they mean you never forget the first *time*— but I think your first love is the same, even if there's nothing physical. But she was the first one who'd kept me awake at night thinking of her, the first one who made me ache.

She was maybe five feet six or seven, had a heart-shaped face, huge dark come-to-bed eyes that I suspected and hoped hadn't yet kept their promise, a mouth maybe a fraction too wide, so that her face seemed to break open when she laughed, and hair that bounced on her shoulders entirely of its own accord. They didn't have stuff to make it bounce in those days.

Her figure was fully formed and she looked wonderful in a bathing costume, and her legs were long and tapering. Also, I had a thing about teeth, and Moira's were perfect and very, very white. Since meeting her the first time I'd scrubbed the inside of my mouth and my gums raw trying to match the whiteness of her teeth.

Since meeting her...

That had been, oh, maybe three months ago. I mean, I'd always known her, or known of her. You can't live all your life in a small colliery village and not know everyone, at least by sight. But when she'd left school and got her first job at a salon in Hartlepool, and we'd started catching the same bus in the morning, that had opened it up for us.

After that there'd been a lot of talk, then the cinema, eventually the beach at Seaton that the debris from the pits hadn't ruined yet, and now we were "going together". It hadn't meant much to me before, that phrase, "going together", but now I understood it. We went places together, and we went well together. I thought so, anyway.

The garden allotments started properly at the end of the colliery wall and sprawled over many acres along the coast road on the northern extreme of the village. The access paths that divided them were dusty, mazy, meandering. But behind the fences people were at work, and they came to and fro along the paths, so that it wasn't really private there. I had returned Moira's kiss, and in several quieter places had tried to draw her closer once or twice.

Invariably she held me at arm's length, saying: "Not here!" And her nervousness made me nervous, too, so that I'd look here and there all about, to make sure we were unobserved. And it was at such a time, glancing back the way we'd come, that I thought I saw a face hastily snatched back around the corner of a fence. The thought didn't occur to me that it might be Raymond. By now I'd quite forgotten about him.

Where the allotments ended the open fields began, gradually declining to a dene and a stream that ran down to the sea. A second cigarette had been smoked down to its tip and discarded by the time we crossed the fields along a hedgerow, and we'd fallen silent where we strolled through the long summer grass. But I was aware of my arm, linked with hers, hugged close against her right breast. And that was a thought that made me dizzy, for through a heady half hour I had actually held that breast in my hand, had known how warm it was, with its hard little tip that felt rough against the parent softness.

Oh, the back row love seats in the local cinema were worthy of an award; whoever designed them deserves an accolade from all the world's lovers. Two people on a single, softly upholstered seat, thigh to thigh and hip to hip, with no ghastly armrest divider, no obstruction to the slow, breathless, tender, and timid first invasion.

In the dark with only the cinema's wall behind us, and the smoky beam from the projector turning all else to pitch, I was *sure* she wasn't aware of my progress with the top button of her blouse, and I considered myself incredibly fortunate to be able to disguise my fumblings with the second of those small obstacles. But after a while, when for all my efforts it appeared I'd get no farther and my frustration was mounting as the tingling seconds ticked by, then she'd gently taken my hand away and effortlessly completed the job for me. She *had* known—which, while it took something of the edge off my triumph, nevertheless increased the frisson to new and previously unexplored heights.

Was I innocent? I don't know. Others, younger by a year, had said they knew everything there was to know. Everything! There was a thought.

But in opening that button and making way for my hand, Moira had invited me in, as it were; cuddled up together there in the back row, my hand had moulded itself to the shape of her breast and learned every contour better than any actor ever memorized his lines. Even now, a week later, I could form my hand into a cup and feel her flesh filling it again. And *desired* to feel her filling it again.

Where the hedgerow met a fence at right angles, we crossed a stile; I was across first and helped Moira down. While I held one hand to steady her, she hitched her short skirt a little to step down from the stile's high platform. It was funny, but I found Moira's legs more fascinating in that skirt than in her bathing costume. And I'd started to notice the heat of my ears—that they were quite hot apart from the heat of the sun, with a sort of internal burning—as we more nearly approached our destination. My destination, anyway, where if her feelings matched mine she'd succumb a little more to my seductions.

As we left the stile to take the path down into the dene and toward the sea cliffs, I glanced back the way we'd come. I don't know why. It was just that I had a feeling. And back there, across the fields, but hurrying, I thought…a figure. Raymond? If it was, and if he were to bother us today of all days…I promised myself he'd pay for it with a bloody nose. But on the other hand it could be anybody. Saying nothing of it to Moira, I hurried her through the dene. Cool under the trees, where the sunlight dappled the rough cobbled path, she said:

"What on earth's the hurry, Josh? Are you *that* eager?"

The way I took her up in my arms and kissed her till I reeled must have answered her question for me; but there were voices here and there along the path, and the place echoed like a tunnel. No, I knew where I wanted to take her.

Toward the bottom of the dene, where it narrowed to a bottleneck of woods and water scooped through the beach banks and funneled toward the sea, we turned north across an old wooden bridge over the scummy stream and began climbing toward the cliff paths, open fields, and sand holes that lay between us and Easington Colliery. Up there, in the long grasses of those summer fields, we could be quite alone and Moira would let me make love to her, I hoped. She'd hinted as much, anyway, the last time I walked her home.

Toiling steeply up an earth track, where white sand spilled down from sand holes up ahead, we looked down on the beach—or what had been a beach before the pit-yakkers came—and remembered a time when it was almost completely white from the banks and cliffs to the sea. On a palmy summer day like this the sea should be blue, but it was grey. Its waves broke in a grey froth of scum on a black shore that looked ravaged by cancer—the cancer of the pits.

The landscape down there could be that of an alien planet: the black beach scarred by streamlets of dully glinting slurry gurgling seaward; concentric tidemarks of congealed froth, with the sick, wallowing sea seeming eager to escape from its own vomit; a dozen sea-coal lorries scattered here and there like ticks on a carcass, their crews shoveling pebble-sized nuggets of the wet, filthy black gold in through open tailgates, while other vehicles trundled like lice over the rotting black corpse of a moonscape. Sucked up by the sun, grey mists wreathed the whole scene.

"It's worse than I remembered it," I said. "And you were right: we couldn't have walked down there, not even along the foot of the banks. It's just too filthy! And to think: all of that was pure white sand just, oh—"

"Ten years ago?" she said. "Well, maybe not *pure* white, but it was still a nice beach then, anyway. Yes, I remember. I've seen that beach full of people, the sea bobbing with their heads. My father used to swim there, with me on his chest! I can remember things from all the way back to when I was a baby. It's a shame they've done this to it."

"It's actually unsafe," I told her. "There are places they've flagged, where they've put up warning notices. Quicksands of slag and slop and slurry—gritty black sludge from the pits. And just look at that skyline!"

South lay the colliery at Harden, the perimeter of its works coming close to the banks where they rolled down to the sea, with half a dozen of its black spider legs straddling out farther yet. These were the aerial trip dumpers: conveyor belts or ski lifts of slag, endlessly swaying to the rim and tripped there, to tip the refuse of the coke ovens down onto the smoking wasteland of foreshore; and these were, directly, the culprits of all this desolation. Twenty-four hours a day for fifty years they'd crawled on their high cables, between their spindly towers, great buckets of muck depositing the pus of the earth to corrode a coast. And behind this lower intestine of the works lay the greater pulsating mass of the spider itself: the pit, with its wheel towers and soaring black chimneys, its mastaba cooling towers and mausoleum coke ovens. Yellow smoke, grey and black smoke, belching continuously into the blue sky—or into a sky that looked blue but was in fact polluted, as any rainy day would testify, when white washing on garden lines would turn a streaky grey with the first patter of raindrops.

On the southern horizon, Blackhill was a spiky smudge under a grey haze; north, but closer, Easington was the same. Viewed from this same position at night, the glow of the coke ovens, the flare-up and gouting orange steam when white hot coke was hosed down, would turn the entire region into a scene straight from hell! Satanic mills? They have nothing on a nest of well-established coal mines by the sea…

We reached the top of the banks and passed warning notices telling how from here on they rolled down to sheer cliffs. When I'd been a child, miners used to clamber down the banks to the cliff edge, hammer stakes into the earth and lower themselves on ropes with baskets to collect gull eggs. Inland, however, the land was flat, where deep grass pasture roved wild all the way from here to the coast road. There were a few farms, but that was all.

We walked half a mile along the cliff path until the fields began to be fenced; where the first true field was split by a hedgerow inside the fence, there I paused and turned to Moira. We hadn't seen anyone, hadn't spoken for some time but I suppose her heart, like mine, had been speeding up a little. Not from our efforts, for walking here was easy.

"We can climb the fence, cut along the hedgerow," I suggested, a little breathlessly.

"Why?" Her eyes were wide, naïve, and yet questioning.

I shrugged. "A...shortcut to the main road?" But I'd made it a question, and I knew I shouldn't leave the initiative to her. Gathering my courage, I added: "Also, we'll—"

"Find a bit of privacy?" Her face was flushed.

I climbed the rough three-bar fence; she followed my example and I helped her down, and knew she'd seen where I could hardly help looking. But she didn't seem to mind. We stayed close to the hedgerow, which was punctuated every twenty-five paces or so with great oaks, and struck inland. It was only when we were away from the fence that I remembered, just before jumping down, that I'd paused a second to scan the land about—and how for a moment I thought I'd seen someone back along the path. Raymond, I wondered? But in any case, he should lose our trail now.

After some two hundred yards there was a lone elder tree growing in the field a little way apart from the hedge, its branches shading the lush grass underneath. I led Moira away from the hedge and into the shade of the elder, and she came unresisting. And there I spread my jacket for her to sit on, and for a minute or two we just sprawled. The grass hid us almost completely in our first private place. Seated, we could just see the topmost twigs of the hedgerow, and of course the bole and spreading canopy of the nearest oak.

Now, I don't intend to go into details. Anyone who was ever young, alone with his girl, will know the details anyway. Let it suffice to say that there were things I wanted, some of which she was willing to give. And some she wasn't. "No," she said. And more positively: "No!" when I persisted. But she panted and moaned a little all the same, and her voice was almost desperate, suggesting: "But I can do it for you this way, if you like." Ah, but her hands set me on fire! I burned for her, and she felt the strength of the flame rising in me. "Josh, no!" she said again. "What if...if..."

She looked away from me, froze for a moment—and her mouth fell open. She drew air hissingly and expelled it in a gasp. "Josh!" And without pause she was doing up buttons, scrambling to her feet, brushing away wisps of grass from her skirt and blouse.

"Eh?" I said, astonished. "What is it?"

"He saw us!" she gasped. "He saw you—me—like that!" Her voice shook with a mixture of outrage and fear.

"Who?" I said, mouth dry, looking this way and that and seeing no one. "Where?"

"By the oak tree," she said. "Halfway up it. A face, peering out from behind. Someone was watching us."

Someone? Only one someone it could possibly be! But be sure that when I was done with him he'd never peep on anyone again! Flushed and furious I sprinted through the grass for the oak tree. The hedge hid a rotting fence; I went over, through it, came to a panting halt in fragments of brown, broken timber. No sign of anyone. You could hide an army in that long grass. But the fence where it was nailed to the oak bore the scuff marks of booted feet, and the tree's bark was freshly bruised some six feet up the bole.

"You...*dog!*" I growled to myself. "God, but I'll *get* you, Raymond Maddison!"

"Josh!" I heard Moira on the other side of the hedge. "Josh, I'm so—ashamed!"

"What?" I called out. "Of what? He won't dare say anything—whoever he is. There are laws against—"

But she was no longer there. Forcing myself through soft wooden jaws and freeing myself from the tangle of the hedge, I saw her hurrying back the way we'd come. "Moira!" I called, but she was already halfway to the three-bar fence. "Moira!" I called again, and then ran after her. By the time I reached the fence she'd climbed it and was starting back along the path.

I finally caught up with her, took her arm. "Moira, we can find some other place. I mean, just because—"

She shook me off, turned on me. "Is that all you want, Josh Peters?" Her face was angry now, eyes flashing. "Well if it is, there are plenty of other girls in Harden who'll be more than happy to...to..."

"Moira, I—" I shook my head. It wasn't like that. We were going together.

"I thought you liked *me!*" she snapped. "The real me!"

My jaw fell open. Why was she talking to me like this? She knew I liked—more than liked—the real Moira. She *was* the real Moira! It was a tiff, brought on by excitement, fear, frustration; we'd never before had to deal with anything like this, and we didn't know how. My emotions were heightened by hers, and now my pride took over. I thrust my jaw out, turned on my heel, and strode rapidly away from her.

"If that's what you think of me," I called back, "—if that's as *much* as you think of me—then maybe this is for the best..."

"Josh?" I heard her small voice behind me. But I didn't answer, didn't look back.

Furious, I hurried, almost trotted back the way we'd come: along the cliff path, scrambling steeply down through the grass-rimmed, crumbling sand pits to the dene. But at the bottom I deliberately turned left and headed for the beach. Dirty? Oh the beach would be dirty—sufficiently dirty so that she surely wouldn't follow me. I didn't want her to. I wanted nothing of her. *Oh, I did, I did!*—but I wouldn't admit it, not even to myself, not then. But if she did try to follow me, it would mean...it would mean...

Moira, Moira! Did I love her? Possibly, but I couldn't handle the emotion. So many emotions; and inside I was still on fire from what had nearly been, still aching from the retention of fluids my young body had so desired to be rid of. Raymond? Raymond Maddison? By *God*, but I'd bloody *him*! I'd let some of *his* damned fluids out!

"Josh!" I seemed to hear Moira's voice from a long way back, but I could have been mistaken. In any case it didn't slow me down. Time and space flashed by in a blur; I was down onto the beach; I walked south under the cliffs on sand that was still sand, however blackened; I trekked grimy sand dunes up and down, kicking at withered tufts of crabgrass that reminded me of the grey and yellow hairs sprouting from the blemishes of old men. Until finally I had burned something of the anger and frustration out of myself.

Then I turned toward the sea, cut a path between the sickly dunes down to the no-man's-land of black slag and stinking slurry, and found a place to sit on a rock etched by chemical reaction into an anomalous hump. It was one of a line of rocks I remembered from my childhood, reaching out half a mile to the sea, from which the men had crabbed and cast their lines. But none of that now. Beyond where I sat, only the tips of the lifeless, once limpet- and mussel-festooned rocks stuck up above the slurry; a leaning, blackened signpost warned:

DANGER! QUICKSAND!

DO NOT PROCEED

BEYOND THIS POINT.

Quicksand? Quag, certainly, but not sand...

I don't know how long I sat there. The sea was advancing and grey gulls wheeled on high, crying on a rising breeze that blew their plaintive voices inland. Scummy waves broke in feathers of grey froth less than one hundred yards down the beach. Down what had been a beach before the invasion of the pit-yakkers. It was summer but down here there were no seasons. Steam curled up from the slag and misted a pitted, alien landscape.

I became lulled by the sound of the birds, the hissing throb of foamy waters, and, strangely, from some little distance away, the periodic clatter of an aerial dumper tilting its buckets and hurling more mineral debris down from on high, creating a mound that the advancing ocean would spread out in a new layer to coat and further contaminate the beach.

I sat there glumly, with my chin like lead in my hands and all of these sounds dull on the periphery of my consciousness, and thought nothing in particular and certainly nothing of any importance. From time to time a gull's cry would sound like Moira's voice, but too shrill, high, frightened, or desperate. She wasn't coming, wouldn't come, and I had lost her. We had lost each other.

I became aware of time trickling by, but again I state: I don't know how long I sat there. An hour? Maybe.

Then something broke through to me. Something other than the voices of the gulls, the waves, the near-distant rain of stony rubble. A new sound? A presence? I looked up, turned my head to scan north along the dead and rotting beach. And I saw him—though as yet he had not seen me.

My eyes narrowed and I felt my brows come together in a frown. Raymond Maddison. The pit-yakker himself. And this was probably as good a place as any, maybe better than most, to teach him a well-deserved lesson. I stood up, and keeping as low a profile as possible made my way round the back of the tarry dunes to where he was standing. In less than two minutes I was there, behind him, creeping up on him where he stood windblown and almost forlorn seeming, staring out to sea. And there I paused.

It seemed his large, rounded shoulders were heaving. Was he crying? Catching his breath? Gulping at the warm, reeking air? Had he been running? Searching for me? Following me as earlier he'd followed us? My feelings hardened against him. It was because he wasn't entirely all there that people tolerated him. But I more than suspected he *was* all there. Not really a dummy, more a scummy.

And I had him trapped. In front of him the rocks receding into pits of black filth, where a second warning notice leaned like a scarecrow on a battlefield, and behind him...only myself behind him. Me and my tightly clenched fists.

Then, as I watched, he took something out of his pocket. His new knife, as I saw now. He stared down at it for a moment, then drew back his arm as if to hurl it away from him, out into the black wilderness of quag. But he froze like that, with the knife still in his hand, and I saw that his shoulders had stopped shuddering. He became alert; I guessed that he'd sensed I was there, watching him.

He turned his head and saw me, and his eyes opened wide in a pale, slack face. I'd never seen him so pale. Then he fell to one knee, dipped his knife into the slurry at his feet, commenced wiping at it with a rag of a handkerchief. Caught unawares he was childlike, tending to do meaningless things.

"Raymond," I said, my voice grimmer than I'd intended. "Raymond, I want a word with you!" And he looked for somewhere to run as I advanced on him. But there was nowhere.

"I didn't—" he suddenly blurted. "I didn't—"

"But you did!" I was only a few paces away.

"I...I..."

"You followed us, peeped on us, messed it all up."

And again he seemed to freeze, while his brain turned over what I'd said to him. Lines creased his brow, vanishing as quickly as they'd come. "What?"

"*What?!*" I shouted, stepping closer still. "You bloody well *know* what! No Moira and me, we're finished. And it's your fault."

He backed off into the black mire, which at once covered his boots and the cuffs of his too-short trousers. And there he stood, lifting and lowering his feet, which went *glop, glop* with each up-and-down movement. He reminded me of nothing so much as a fly caught on the sticky paper they used at that time. And his mouth kept opening and closing, stupidly, because he had nothing to say and nowhere to run, and he knew I was angry.

Finally he said: "I didn't mean to...follow you. But I—" And he reached into a pocket and brought out a packet of cigarettes. "Your cigarettes."

I had known that would be his excuse. "Throw them to me, Ray," I said. For I wasn't about to go stepping in there after him. He tossed me the packet but stayed right where he was. "You may as well come on out," I told him, lighting up, "for you know I'm going to settle with you."

"Josh," he said, still mouthing like a fish. "Josh…"

"Yes, Josh, Josh," I told him, nodding. "But you've really done it this time, and we have to have it out."

He still had his knife. He showed it to me, opened the main blade. He took a pace forward out of the slurry and I took a pace back. There was a sick grin on his face. Except…he wasn't threatening me. "For you," he said, snapping the blade shut. "I don't…I don't want it no more." He stepped from the quag onto a flat rock and stood there facing me, not quite within arm's reach. He tossed the knife and I automatically caught it. It weighed heavy in my hand where I clenched my knuckles round it.

"A bribe?" I said. "So that I won't tell what you did? How many friends do you have, Ray? And how many left if I tell what a dirty, sneaky, spying—"

But he was still grinning his sick, nervous grin. "You won't tell." He shook his head. "Not what I seen."

I made a lunging grab for him and the grin slipped from his face. He hopped to a second rock farther out in the liquid slag, teetered there for a moment before finding his balance. And he looked anxiously all about for more stepping-stones, in case I should follow. There were two or three more rocks, all of them deeper into the coal-dust quicksand, but beyond them only a bubbly, oozy black surface streaked with oil and yellow mineral swirls.

Raymond's predicament was a bad one. Not because of me. I would only hit him. Once or twice, depending how long it took to bloody him. But this stuff would murder him. If he fell in. And the black slime was dripping from the bottoms of his trousers, making the surface of his rock slippery. Raymond's balance wasn't much, neither mentally nor physically. He began to slither this way and that, windmilled his arms in an effort to stay put.

"Ray!" I was alarmed. "Come out of there!"

He leapt, desperately, tried to find purchase on the next rock, slipped! His feet shot up in the air and he came down on his back in the quag. The stuff quivered like thick black porridge and put out slow-motion ripples. He flailed his arms, yelping like a dog, as the lower part of his body started to sink. His trousers ballooned with the air in them, but the stuff's suck was strong. Raymond was going down.

Before I could even start to think straight he was in chest deep, the filth inching higher every second. But he'd stopped yelping and had started thinking. Thinking desperate thoughts. "Josh…Josh!" he gasped.

I stepped forward ankle deep, got up onto the first rock. I made to jump to the second rock but he stopped me. "No, Josh," he whispered. "Or we'll both go."

"You're sinking," I said, for once as stupid as him.

"Listen," he answered with a gasp. "Up between the dunes, some cable, half-buried. I saw it on my way down here. Tough, 'lectric wire, in the muck. You can pull me out with that."

I remembered. I had seen it, too. Several lengths of discarded cable, buried in the scummy dunes. All my limbs were trembling as I got back to solid ground, setting out up the beach between the dunes. "Josh!" his voice reached out harshly after me. "*Hurry!*" And a moment later: "The first bit of wire you see, that'll do it..."

I hurried, ran, raced. But my heart was pounding, the air rasping like sandpaper in my lungs. Fear. But...I couldn't find the cable. Then—

There was a tall dune, a great heap of black-streaked, slag-crusted sand. A lookout place! I went up it, my feet breaking through the crust, letting rivulets of sand cascade, thrusting myself to the top. Now I could get directions, scan the area all about. Over there, between low humps of diseased sand, I could see what might be a cable: a thin, frozen black snake of the stuff.

But beyond the cable I could see something else: colors, anomalous, strewn in a clump of dead crabgrass.

I tumbled down the side of the great dune, ran for the cable, tore a length free of the sand and muck. I had maybe fifteen, twenty feet of the stuff. Coiling it, I looked back. Raymond was there in the quag, going down black and sticky. But in the other direction—just over there, no more than a dozen loping paces away, hidden in the crabgrass and low humps of sand—something blue and white and...and red.

Something about it made my skin prickle. Quickly, I went to see. And I saw...

After a while I heard Raymond's voice over the crying of the gulls. "Josh! *Josh!*"

I walked back, the cable looped in my lifeless hands, made my way to where he hung crucified in the quag; his arms formed the cross, palms pressing down on the belching surface, his head thrown back and the slop ringing his throat. And I stood looking at him. He saw me, saw the cable in my limp hands, looked into my eyes. And he knew. He knew I wasn't going to let him have the cable.

Instead I gave him back his terrible knife with all its terrible attachments—which he'd been waiting to use, and which I'd seen no use for—tossing it so that it landed in front of him and splashed a blob of slime into his right eye.

He pleaded with me for a little while then, but there was no excuse. I sat and smoked, without even remembering lighting my fresh cigarette, until he began to gurgle. The black filth flooded his mouth, nostrils, the circles of his eyes. He went down, his sputtering mouth forming a ring in the muck that slowly filled in when he was gone. Big shiny bubbles came bursting to the surface...

When my cigarette went out I began to cry, and crying staggered back up to the beach between the dunes. To Moira.

Moira. Something I'd had—almost—that he didn't have. That he could never have, except like this. Jealousy, or just sheer evil? And was I any better than him, now? I didn't know then, and I don't know to this day. He was just a pit-yakker, born for the pit. Him and me both, I suppose, but I had been lucky enough to escape it.

And he hadn't...

THE PLACE OF WAITING

I sit here by our swimming pool with one eye on my son in the water and the other on the seagulls lazily drifting, circling on high. Actually they're not just drifting; they're climbing on thermals off the nearby fields, spiralling up to a certain height from which they know they can set off south across the bay on their long evening glide to Brixham, to meet the fishing boats coming in to harbour. And never once having beaten a wing across all those miles, just gliding, they'll be there in plenty of time to beg for sprats as the fish are unloaded.

It's instinct with those birds; they've been doing it for so long that now they don't even think about it, they just do it. It's like at ant-flying time, or flying-ant time, if you prefer: those two or three of the hottest days of summer when all of a sudden the ant queens make up their minds to fly and establish new hives or whatever ant nesting sites are called. Yes, for the gulls know all about that, too.

The crying of gulls: plaintive, sometimes painful, often annoying, especially when they're flight-training their young. But this time of year, well you can always tell when it's ant-flying time. Because that's just about the *only* time when the seagulls are silent. And you won't see a one in the sky until the queen ants stream up in their thousands from all the Devon gardens, all at the same time—like spawning corals under the full moon—as if some telepathic message had gone out into an ant aether, telling them, "It's time! It's time!"

Time for the seagulls, too. For suddenly, out of nowhere, the sky is full of them. And their silence is because they're eating. Eating ants, yes. And I amuse myself by imagining that the gulls have learned how to interpret

207

ant telepathy, when in all probability it's only a matter of timing and temperature: Ma Nature as opposed to insect (or avian) ESP.

And yet...there are stranger things in heaven and earth—and between the two—and I no longer rule out anything...

My son cries out, gasps, gurgles, and shrieks...but only with joy, thank God, as I spring from my deck chair! Only with joy—the sheer enjoyment of the shallow end of the pool. Not that it's shallow enough, (it's well out of his depth in fact, for he's only two and a half) but he's wearing his water-wings and his splashing and chortling alone should have told me that all was well.

Except I wasn't doing my duty as I should have been; I was paying too much attention to the seagulls. And well—

—Well, call it paranoia if you like. But I watch little Jimmy like a hawk when he is in the water, and I've considered having the pool filled in. But his mother says no, that's just silly, and whatever it was that I *think* happened to me out on the moors that time, I shouldn't let it interfere with living our lives to the full. And anyway she loves our pool, and so does little Jimmy, and so would I, except...

Only three weeks ago a small child drowned in just such a pool right here in Torquay, less than a mile away. And to me—especially to me—that was a lot more than a tragic if simple accident. It was a beginning, not an end. The beginning of something that can *never* end, not until there are no more swimming pools. And even then it won't be the end for some poor, unfortunate little mite.

But you don't understand, right? And you never will until you know the full story. So first let me get little Jimmy out of the pool, dried and into the house, into his mother's care, and then I'll tell you all about it...

Have you ever wondered about haunted houses? Usually very old houses, perhaps victorian or older still? Well, probably not, because in this modern technological society of ours we're not much given to considering such unscientific things. And first, of course, you would have to believe in ghosts: the departed, or not quite departed, revenants of folks dead and long since buried. But if so, if you have wondered, then you might also have begun to wonder why it's these *old* houses which are most haunted, and only very rarely new ones.

And, on the same subject, how many so-called "old wives' tales" have you heard, ghost stories, literally, about misted country crossroads where spectral figures are suddenly caught in a vehicle's headlights, lurching from the hedgerows at midnight, screaming their silent screams with their ragged hands held out before them? Well, let me tell you: such stories are legion! And now I know why.

But me, I didn't believe in ghosts. Not then, anyway...

My mother died in hospital here in Torbay some four and a half years ago. And incidentally, I'm glad about that; not about her dying, no of course not, but that she did it in hospital. These days lots of people die in hospital, which is natural enough.

Anyway, it hit me really badly, moreso because I had only recently lost someone else: my wife, when we'd divorced simply because we no longer belonged together. It had taken us eleven years to find that out: the fact that right from the start, we hadn't really belonged together. But while our parting was mutually acceptable and even expedient, still it was painful. And I would like to think it hurt both of us, for I certainly felt it: a wrenching inside, like some small but improbably necessary organ was no longer in there, that it was missing, torn or fallen out. And at the time I'd thought that was the end of it; what was missing was gone forever; I wouldn't find anyone else and there would be no family, no son to look up to me as I had looked up to my father. A feeling of...I don't know, discontinuity?

But I had still had my mother—for a little while, anyway. My poor dear Ma.

Now, with all this talk of ghosts and death and what-not, don't anyone take it that I was some kind of odd, sickly mother's-boy sort of fellow like Norman Bates, the motel keeper in that *Hitchcock* film. No, for that couldn't be further from the truth. But after my father had died (also in hospital, for they had both been heavy smokers) it had been my Ma who had sort of clung to me...quite the other way round, you see? Living not too far away, she had quickly come to rely on me. And no, that didn't play a part in our divorce. In fact by then it had made no difference at all; our minds were already made up, Patsy's and mine.

Anyway, Patsy got our house—we'd agreed on that, too—for it had made perfectly good sense that I should go and live with Ma. Then, when it was her time (oh my Good Lord, as if we had been anticipating it!) her house would come to me. And so Patsy's and my needs both would be catered for, at least insofar as we wouldn't suffer for a roof over our heads...

Ma painted, and I like to think I inherited something of her not inconsiderable talent. In fact, that was how I made a living: my work was on show in a studio in Exeter where I was one of a small but mainly respected coterie of local artists, with a somewhat smaller, widespread band of dedicated, affluent collectors. I thank my lucky stars for affluent collectors! And so, with the addition of the interest on monies willed to me by my father, I had always managed to eke out a living of sorts.

Ma painted, yes, and always she looked for the inspiration of drama. The more dramatic her subject, the finer the finished canvas. Seascapes on the Devon coast, landscapes on the rolling South Hams, the frowning ocean-hewn cliffs of Cornwall; and of course those great solemn tors on the moor... which is to say Dartmoor: the location for Sherlock Holmes'—or rather Arthur Conan Doyle's—famous (or infamous) *Hound of the Baskervilles*.

Ah, that faded old film! My mother used to say, "It's not like that, you know. Well, it *is* in some places, and misty too. But not *all* the time! Not like in that film. And I've certainly never seen the like of that fearsome old tramp that Basil Rathbone made of himself! Not on Dartmoor, God forbid! Yes, I know it was only Sherlock Holmes in one of his disguises, but still, I mean... Why, if the moors were really like *that* I swear I'd never want to paint there again!"

I remember that quite clearly, the way she said: "It's not *like* that, you know," before correcting herself. For in fact it is like that—and too much like that—in certain places...

After she'd gone I found myself revisiting the locations where we had painted together: the coastlines of Cornwall and our own Devon, the rolling, open countryside, and eventually Dartmoor's great tors, which my dictionary somewhat inadequately describes as hills or rocky heights. But it was the Celts who called them tors or torrs, from which we've derived tower, and some of them do indeed "tower" on high. Or it's possible the name comes from the Latin: the Roman *turris*. Whichever, I'll get to the tors in a moment. But first something of Dartmoor itself:

All right, so it's not like that faded old Basil Rathbone *Hound of the Baskervilles* film. Not entirely like that, anyway; not *all* the time. In fact in the summer it's glorious, and that was mainly when I would go there; for I was still attempting to paint there despite that it had become a far more lonely business...often utterly lonely, on my own out there on the moors.

But glorious? Beautiful? Yes it certainly was, and for all that I don't go there any more, I'm sure it still is. Beautiful in a fashion all its own. Or perhaps the word I'm searching for is unique. Uniquely dramatic...gloriously wild...positively neolithic, in its outcrops and standing stones, and prehistoric in the isolation and sometimes desolation of its secret, if not sacred, places.

As for outcrops, standing stones and such: well, now we're back to the tors.

On Eastern Dartmoor my mother and I had painted that amazing jumble of rocks, one of the largest outcrops in the National Park, known as Hound Tor (no connection to Doyle's hound, at least not to my knowledge). But along with a host of other gigantic stacks, such as the awesome Haytor Rock or Vixen Tor, the Hound hadn't been one of Ma's favourites. Many a lesser pile or tranquil river location had been easier to translate to canvas, board, or art paper. It wasn't that we were idle, or lacking in skill or patience—certainly not my mother, whose true-to-life pictures were full of the most intricate detail—but that the necessities of life and the endless hours required to trap such monsters simply didn't match up to our limited time. One single significant feature of any given rock could take Ma a whole day to satisfactorily transcribe in oils! And because I only rarely got things right at the first pass, they sometimes took me even longer. Which is why we were satisfied to paint less awesome or awkward subjects, and closer to home whenever possible.

Ah, but when I say "closer to home"...surely Dartmoor is *only* a moor? What's a few miles between friends? Let me correct you:

Dartmoor is three hundred and fifty square miles of mists, mires, woodlands, rushing rivers, tors carved in an age of ice, small villages, lonely farmsteads and mazy paths; all of which forms the largest tract of unenclosed land in southern England. The landscape may range in just a few miles from barren, naked summits—several over five hundred metres in height—through heather-clad moorland, to marsh and sucking bog. There, in four national nature reserves and numerous protected sites, Dartmoor preserves an astonishing variety of plants and wildlife; all of this a mere twenty miles from Plymouth to the south, and a like distance from Exeter to the east.

Parts of the moor's exposed heath contain the remains of Bronze and Iron Age settlements, now home to the hardy Dartmoor ponies; but the river Dart's lush valley—cut through tens of thousands of years of planetary evolution—displays the softer side of rural Devon, where thatched cottages, tiny villages and ancient inns seem almost hidden away in the shady lee of knolls or protective hollows.

Dartmoor is, in short, a fascinating fantasy region, where several of the tors have their own ghosts—which is only to be expected in such a place—but I fancy their ectoplasm is only a matter of mist, myth, and legend. Most of them. Some of them, certainly...

I won't say where I went that first time—which is to say the first time anything peculiar happened—for reasons which will become amply apparent, but it was close to one of our favourite places. Close to, but not the precise spot, for that would have meant feeling my mother's presence. Her memory, or my memory *of* her, in that place, might have interfered with my concentration. And I'm not talking about ghosts here, just memories, nostalgia if you like: a sentimental longing for times spent with someone who had loved me all of her life, now gone forever. And if that makes me seem weak, then explain to me how even strong men find themselves still crying over a pet dog dead for months and even years, let alone a beloved parent.

And there is no paradox here, in my remembering yet needing to hold the memories to some degree at bay. I missed my Ma, yes, but I knew that I couldn't go on mourning her for the rest of my life.

Anyway, it was in the late summer—in fact August, this time of year—when less than an hour's drive had taken me onto the moor and along a certain second-class road, to a spot where I parked my car in a lay-by near a crossroads track leading off across the heather. Maybe a quarter-mile away there was a small domed hill, which faced across a shaded, shallow depression one of Dartmoor's more accessible tors: an oddly unbalanced outcrop that looked for all the world as if it had been built of enormous, worn and rounded dominoes by some erratic Titan infant and was now trying hard not to topple over. An illusion, naturally, because it was entirely possible that this was just one massive rock, grooved by time and the elements into a semblance of many separate horizontal layers.

And here I think I had better give the stack a name—even one of my own coining—rather than simply call it a tor. Let's call it Tumble Tor, if only because it looked as if at any moment it just might!

My mother and I had tried to paint Tumble Tor on a number of occasions, never with any great success. So maybe I could do it now and at least finish a job that we had frequently started and just as often left unresolved. That was the idea, my reason for being there, but as stated I would not be painting from any previously occupied vantage point. Indeed, since the moors seem to change from day to day and (obviously) more radically season to season, it would be almost impossible to say precisely where those vantage points had been. My best bet was to simply plunk myself down in a spot which felt totally strange, and that way be sure that I'd never been there before.

As for painting: I wouldn't actually be doing any, not on this my first unaccompanied visit to Tumble Tor. Instead I intended to prepare a detailed pencil sketch, and in that way get as well acquainted as possible with the monolith before attempting the greater familiarity of oils and colour. In my opinion, one has to respect one's subjects.

It had been a long hot summer and the ground was very hard underfoot, the soil crumbling as I climbed perhaps one third of the way up the knoll to a stone-strewn landing where the ground levelled off in a wide ledge. The sun was still rising in a mid-morning sky, but there in the shade of the summit rising behind me I seated myself on a flat stone and faced Tumble Tor with my board and paper resting comfortably on my knees. And using various grades of graphite I began to transpose my oddly staggered subject onto paper.

Time passed quickly…

Mid-afternoon, I broke for a ham sandwich with mayonnaise, washed down with a half thermos of bitter coffee. I had brought my binoculars with me; now and then I trained them on my car to ensure that it remained safe and hadn't attracted the attention of any overly curious strangers. The glasses were also handy as a means of bringing Tumble Tor into greater resolution, making it easy to study its myriad bulges and folds before committing them to paper.

As I looked again at that much wrinkled rock, a lone puff of cloud eased itself in front of the sun. Tumble Tor fell into shade, however temporarily, and suddenly I saw a figure high in one of the outcrop's precipitous shoulders: the figure of a man leaning against the rock there, peering in a furtive fashion—or so it seemed to me—around the shoulder and across the moor in the general direction of the road. Towards my car? Perhaps.

The puff of cloud persisted, slowly moving, barely drifting, across what was recently an empty, achingly blue sky, and I was aware of the first few wisps of a ground mist in the depression between my knoll and Tumble

Tor. I glanced again at the sky and saw that the cloud was the first of a string of cotton-wool puffs reaching out toward Exeter in a ruler-straight line. Following this procession to its source, I was able to pick out the shining silver speck that had fashioned the aerial trail: a jet aircraft, descending toward Exeter airport. Its long vapour trail—even as it broke up into these small "clouds"—seemed determined to track across the face of the sun.

I looked again at Tumble Tor, and adjusted the focus of my binoculars to bring the lone climber—the furtive observer of some near-distant event?—into sharper perspective. He hadn't moved except to turn his head in my direction, and I had little doubt but that he was now looking at me. At a distance of something less than four hundred and fifty yards, I must be visible to him as he was to me. But of course I had the advantage of my glasses...or so I thought.

He was thin and angular, a stick of a man, with wild hair blowing in a wind I couldn't feel, some current of air circulating around his precarious position. He wore dark clothing, and as I once again refocussed I saw that indeed he carried binoculars around his neck. Though he wasn't using them, still I felt he gazed upon me. I tried to get a clearer view of his face but the image was blurred, trembling with the movement of my hands. However, when finally I did manage to get a good look...it was his narrow eyes that left a lasting impression.

They seemed to glow in the shade of the rock with that so-called "red-eye" complication of amateur photography: an illusion—a trick of the light—obviously. But the way they were fixed upon me, those eyes, was somehow disconcerting. It was as if he was spying on me, and not the other way around.

But spying? Feeling like some kind of voyeur, I lowered my glasses and looked away.

Meanwhile, having swung across the sky, the sun had found me; soon my hollow in the side of the hill, rather than providing shade, was going to become a sun-trap. And so I reckoned it was time to call it a day and head for home. Before I could put my art things aside, however, a tall shadow fell across me and a deep voice said, "Aye, and ye've picked the perfect spot for it. What a grand picture the auld tor makes frae here, eh?"

Momentarily startled, I jerked myself around to look up at the speaker. He was a dark silhouette, blocking out the sun.

"Oh dear!" he said, himself startled. "Did I make ye jump just then? Well, I'm sorry if I've disturbed ye, and moreso if I've broken ye're mood.

But man, ye must hae been concentratin' verra hard not tae hear me comin' down on ye."

"Concentrating?" I answered. "Actually I was watching that fellow on the tor there. He must be a bit of a climber. Myself, I don't have much of a head for heights."

"On the tor, ye say?" Shading his eyes and standing tall, he peered at Tumble Tor, now bright once more in full sunlight. "Well then, he must hae moved on, gone round the back. I cannae see anyone on the rock right now, no frae here." Then, stepping down level with me, he crouched to examine my drawing close up. And in my turn—now that the sun was out of my eyes—I could look more closely at him.

A big, powerful man, I judged him to be in his mid-fifties. Dressed in well worn tweeds, good walking boots, and carrying a knobbed and ferruled stick, he could well have been a gamekeeper—and perhaps he was.

"I...I do hope I'm not trespassing here," I finally mumbled. "I mean, I hope this isn't private ground."

"Eh?" he cocked his head a little, then smiled. "What? Do ye take me for a gillie or somethin'? No, no, I'm no that. And as far as I ken this ground's free for us all. But a trespasser? Well, if ye are then so am I, and hae been for some twenty years!" He nodded at the unfinished drawing in my lap. "That's a bonny piece of work. Will ye no finish it? Ye'll excuse that I'm pokin' my nose in, but I sense ye were about tae leave."

"Was and am," I answered, getting to my feet and dusting myself off. "The sun's to blame...the shadows on the tor are falling all wrong now. Also, the back of my neck was getting a bit warm." I stooped, gathered up my art things, and looked at the drawing. "But I thank you for your comment because this is just—"

"—A preliminary sketch?"

"Oh?" I said. "And how did you know that?"

Again he smiled, but most engagingly. "Why, there's paint under ye're fingernails. And ye've cross-hatched all the areas that are the selfsame colour as seen frae here...stone grey, that is. Ye'll be plannin' a painting—am I no right?"

I studied him more closely. He had tousled brown hair—a lot of it for a man his years, —a long weathered face, brown, friendly eyes over a bulbous nose, and a firm mouth over a jut of a chin. His accent revealed his nationality, and he made no attempt to disguise it. The Scots are proud of themselves, and they have every right to be. This one looked as much a part of the moors as…well, as Tumble Tor itself.

Impulsively, I stuck my hand out. "You're right, I'm planning a painting. I'm Paul Stanard, from Torquay. I'm pleased to meet you."

"Andrew Quarry," he came back at once, grasping my hand. "Frae a mile or two back there." A jerk of his head indicated the knoll behind us. "My house is just off the Yelverton road, set back a wee in a copse. But—did ye say Stanard?"

"Paul Stanard, yes," I nodded.

"Hmm," he mused. "Well, it's probably a coincidence, but there's a picture in my house painted by one Mary May Stanard: it's a moors scene that I bought in Exeter."

"My mother," I told him, again nodding. "She sold her work through various art shops in Exeter and elsewhere. And so do I. But she…she died some nine months ago. Lung cancer."

"Oh? Well, I'm sorry for ye," he answered. "What, a smoker was she? Aye, it's a verra bad business. Myself, I gave my auld pipe up years ago. But her picture—it's a bonny thing."

I smiled, however sadly. "Oh, she knew how to paint! But I doubt if it will ever be worth any more than you paid for it."

"Ah, laddie," he said, shaking his head. "But I didnae buy it for what others might reckon it's value. I bought it because I thought it might look right hangin' in my livin'-room. And so it does."

Andrew Quarry: he was obviously a gentleman, and so open—so down-to-earth—that I couldn't help but like him. "Are you by chance going my way?" I enquired. "That's my car down on the road there. Maybe we can walk together?"

"Most certainly!" he answered at once. "But only if I can prevail upon ye tae make a little detour and drop me off on the Yelverton road. It'll be a circular route for ye but no too far out of ye're way, I promise ye."

As I hesitated he quickly added, "But if ye're in a hurry, then dinnae fret. The walkin's good for a man. And me: I must hae tramped a thousand miles over these moors, so a half-dozen more willnae harm me."

"Not at all," I answered. "I was just working out a route, that's all. For while I've crossed Dartmoor often enough, still I sometimes find myself confused. Maybe I don't pay enough attention to maps and road signs, and anyway my sense of direction isn't up to much. You might have to show me the way."

"Oh, I can do that easily enough," Quarry answered. "And I know what ye mean. I walk these moors freely in three out of four seasons, but in the fourth I go verra carefully. When the snow is on the ground, oh it's beautiful beyond a doubt—ah, but it hides all the landmarks! A man can get lost in a blink, and then the cold sets in." As we set off down the steep slope he asked: "So then, how did ye come here?"

"I'm sorry?"

"Ye're route, frae the car tae here."

"Oh. I followed the path—barely a track, really—but I walked where many feet have gone before: around that clump of standing stones there, and so on to the foot of this hill where I left the track, climbed through the heather, and finally arrived at this grassy ledge."

"I see." He nodded. "Ye avoided the more direct line frae ye're vehicle tae the base of the tor, and frae the tor tae the knoll. Verra sensible."

"Oh?"

"Aye. Ye see those rushes?" He pointed. "Between the knoll and yon rock? And those patches of red and green, huggin' close tae the ground? Well those colours hint of what lies underfoot, and it's marshy ground just there. Mud like that'll suck ye're shoes off! It would make a more direct route as the crow flies, true enough, but crows dinnae hae tae walk!"

"You can tell all that from the colour of the vegetation? The state of the ground, that is?" He obviously knew his Dartmoor, this man.

He shrugged. "Did I no say how I've lived here for twenty years? A man comes tae understand an awfy lot in twenty years." Then he laughed. "Oh, it's no great trick. Those colours: they indicate mosses, sphagnum mosses. And together with the rushes, that means boggy ground."

We had reached the foot of the knoll and set off following the rough track, making a detour wide of the tor and the allegedly swampy ground; which is to say we reversed and retraced my incoming route. And Quarry continued talking as we walked:

"Those sphagnums..." he said, pausing to catch his breath. "...That's peat in the makin'. A thousand years from now, it'll be good burnin' stuff, buried under a couple of feet of softish earth. Well, that's if the moor doesnae dry out—as it's done more than its share of this last verra hot summer. Aye, climatic change and all that."

I was impressed. "You seem to be a very knowledgeable man. So then, what are you, Mr. Quarry? Something in moors conservation? Do you work for the National Park Authority? A botanist, perhaps?"

"Botany?" He raised a shaggy eyebrow. "My profession? No laddie, hardly that. I *was* a veterinary surgeon up in Scotland a good long spell ago—but I dinnae hae a profession, not any more. Ye see, my hands got a wee bit wobbly. Botany's my hobby now, that's all. All the green things...I enjoy tae identify them, and the moor has an awfy lot tae identify."

"A Scotsman in Devon," I said. "I should have thought the highlands would be just as varied...just as suitable to your needs."

"Aye, but my wife was a Devon lass, so we compromised."

"Compromised?"

He grinned. "She said she'd marry me, if I said I'd come live in Devon. I've no regretted it." And then, more quietly, "She's gone now, though, the auld girl. Gone before her time. Her heart gave out. It was most unexpected."

"I'm sorry to hear it," I said. "And so you live alone?"

"For quite some time, aye. Until my Jennie came home frae America. So now's a nice time for me. Jennie was studyin' architectural design; she got her credentials—top of the class, too—and now works in Exeter."

We were passing the group of tall stones, their smoothed and rounded sides all grooved with the same horizontal striations. I nodded to indicate them. "They look like the same hand was at work carving them."

"And so it was," said Quarry. "The hand of time—of the ice age—of the elements. But all the one hand when ye think it through. This could well be the tip of some buried tor, like an iceberg of stone in a sea of earth."

"There's something of the poet in you," I observed.

He smiled. "Oh, I'm an auld lad of nature, for a fact!"

And, once again on impulse, I said, "Andrew, if I may call you that, I'd very much like you to have that drawing—that's if you'd care to accept it. It's unfinished, I know, but—"

"—But I would be delighted!" he cut in. "Now tell me: how much would ye accept for it?"

"No," I said. "I meant as a gift."

"A gift!" He sounded astonished. "But why on earth would a body be givin' all those hours of work away?"

"I really don't know." I shook my head, and shrugged. "And anyway, I haven't worked on it all that long. Maybe I'd like to think of it on your wall, beside my mother's painting."

"And so it shall be—if ye're sure...?"

"I am sure."

"Then I thank ye kindly."

Following which we were quiet, until eventually we arrived at the car. There, as I let Quarry into the passenger's seat, I looked back at the sky and Tumble Tor. The puffs of cloud were still there, but dispersing now, drifting, breaking up. And on that strange high rock, nothing to be seen but the naked stone. Yet for some reason that thin, pale face with its burning eyes continued to linger in my own mind's eye...

Dartmoor is criss-crossed by many paths, tracks, roads...none of which are "major" in the sense of motorways, though many are modern, metalled, and with sound surfaces. Andrew Quarry directed me expertly by the shortest route possible, through various crossroads and turns, until we'd driven through Two Bridges and Princetown. Shortly after that, he bade me stop at a stile in a hazel hedge. Beyond the stile a second hedge, running at right-angles to the road, sheltered a narrow footpath that paralleled a brook's meandering contours. And some twenty-five yards along this footpath, in a fenced copse of oaks and birch trees, there stood Quarry's house.

It was a good sized two-storied place, probably Victorian, with oak-timbered walls of typical red Devon stone. In the high gables, under terra-cotta pantiles, wide windows had been thrown open; while on the ground floor, the varnished or polished oak frames of several more windows were barely visible, shining in the dapple of light falling through the trees. In one of these lower windows, I could only just make out the upper third of a raven-haired female figure busy with some task.

"That's Jennie," said Quarry, getting out of the car. "Ye cannae mistake that shinin' head of hair. She's in the kitchen there, preparin' this or that. I never ate so well since she's been back. Will ye no come in for a cup of tea, Paul, or a mug of coffee, perhaps?"

"Er, no," I said, "I don't think so. I've a few things to do at home, and it's time I was on my way. But thanks for offering. I do appreciate it."

"And I appreciate ye're gift," he said. "Perhaps I'll see ye some other time? Most definitely, if ye're out there paintin' on the knoll. In fact, I shall make it my business to walk that way now and then."

"And I'll be there—" I told him. "—Not every day, but on occasion, at least until my painting is finished. I'll look forward to talking to you again."

"Aye," he nodded, "and so we shall." With which he climbed the stile with my rolled-up drawing under his arm, looked back and waved, then disappeared around a curve in the hedge…

The forecast was rain for the next day or two. I accepted the weatherman's verdict, stayed at home and worked on other paintings while waiting for the skies to clear; which they did eventually. Then I returned to the knoll and Tumble Tor.

I got there early morning when there was some ground mist still lingering over from the night. Mists are a regular feature of Devon in August through December, and especially on the moors. As I left the car I saw four or five Dartmoor ponies at the gallop, their manes flying, kicking up their heels as they crossed the road. They must have known where they were headed, the nature of the uneven ground; either that or they were heedless of the danger, for with tendrils of mist swirling half-way up their gleaming legs they certainly couldn't see where their hooves were falling! They looked like the fabulous hippocampus, I thought—like sea-horses, braving the breakers—as they ran off across the moor and were soon lost in the poor visibility.

Poor visibility, yes…and I had come here to work on my painting! (Actually, to begin the second phase: this time using water-colours.) But the sun was well up, its rays already working on the mist to melt it away; Tumble Tor was mainly visible, for all that its foot was lost in the lapping swell; a further half-hour should set things to right, by which time I would be seated on my ledge in the lee of the knoll.

Oh really? But unfortunately there was something I hadn't taken into account: namely that I wasn't nearly as sure-footed or knowledgeable as those Dartmoor ponies! Only leave the road and less than ten paces onto the moor I'd be looking and feeling very foolish, tripping over the roots of gorse and heather as I tried to find and follow my previous route. So then, best to stay put for now and let the sun do its work.

Then, frustrated, leaning against the car and lighting one of my very infrequent cigarettes, I became aware of a male figure approaching up the road. His legs wreathed in mist, he came on, and soon I could see that he was a "gentleman of the road", in short a tramp, but by no means a threat. On the contrary, he seemed rather time- and care-worn: a shabby, elderly, somewhat pitiful member of the brotherhood of wayfarers.

Only a few paces away he stopped to catch his breath, then seated himself upon one of those knee-high white-painted stones that mark the country verges. Oddly, he didn't at first seem to have noticed me; but he'd seen my car and appeared to be frowning at it, or at least eyeing it disdainfully.

As I watched him, wondering if I should speak, he took out a tobacco pouch and a crumpled packet of cigarette papers, only to toss the latter aside when he discovered it empty. Which was when I stepped forward. And: "By all means, have one of these," I said, proffering my pack and shaking it to loosen up a cigarette.

"Eh?" And now he looked at me.

He could have been anything between fifty-five and seventy years of age, that old man. But his face was so lined and wrinkled, so lost in the hair of his head, his beard, and moustache—all matted together under a tattered, floppy hat—it would have been far too difficult if not impossible to attempt a more accurate assessment. I looked at his hunched, narrow shoulders, his spindly arms in a threadbare jacket, his dark gnarled hands with liver spots and purple veins, and simply had to feel sorry for him. Rheumy eyes gazed back at me, through curling wisps of shaggy eyebrow, and lips that had been fretted by harsh weather trembled when he spoke:

"That's kind of you. I rarely begged but they often gave." It was as if with that last rather odd sentence he was talking to himself.

"Take another," I told him, "for later."

"I didn't mean to take advantage of you," he answered, but he took a second cigarette anyway. Then, looking at the pair of small white tubes in his hand, he said, "But I think I'll smoke them later, if you don't mind. I've had this cough, you see?"

"Not at all," I said. "I don't usually smoke myself, until the evening. And then I sometimes fancy one with a glass of..." But there I paused. He probably hadn't tasted brandy in a long, long time—if ever.

He apparently hadn't noticed my almost gaffe. "It's one of my few pleasures," he said, placing the cigarettes carefully in his tobacco pouch, drawing its string tight, fumbling it into a leather-patched pocket. Then:

"But we haven't been properly introduced!" he said, making an effort to stand, only to slump back down again. "Or could it be—I mean, is it possible—that I once knew you?" He seemed unable to focus on me; it was as if he looked right through me. "I'm sorry...it's these poor old eyes of mine. They can't see you at all clearly."

"We've never met," I told him. "I'm Paul."

"Or, it could be the car," he said, going off at a tangent again and beginning to ramble. "Your car, that is. But the very car...? No, I don't think so. Too new."

"Well, I have parked here before," I said, trying my best to straighten out the conversation. "But just the once. Still, if you passed this way a few days ago you might well have seen it here."

"Hmmm!" he mused, blinking as he peered hard, studying my face. Then his oh-so-pale eyes opened wider. "Ah! *Now* I understand! You must have been trying very hard to see someone, and you got me instead. I'm Joe. Old Joe, they called me."

And finally I understood, too. The deprivations of a life on the road—of years of wandering, foraging, sleeping rough, through filthy weather and hungry nights—had got to him. His body wasn't the only victim of his "lifestyle". His mind, too, had suffered. Or perhaps it was the other way around, and that was the cause, not the effect. Perhaps he had always been "not altogether there", as I've heard it said of such unfortunates.

And because I really didn't have very much to say—also because I no longer knew quite *what* to say, exactly—I simply shrugged and informed him, "I...I'm just waiting, that's all. And when this mist has cleared a bit, I'll be moving on."

"I'm waiting, too," he answered. "More or less obliged to wait. Here, I mean."

At which I simply had to ask: "Waiting? I didn't know this was a bus route? And if it is they're very infrequent. Or maybe you're waiting for a friend, some fellow, er, traveller? Or are you looking for a lift—in a car, I mean?" (Lord, I hoped not! Not that he smelled bad or anything, not that I'd noticed, anyway, but I should really hate to have to refuse him if he asked me.) And how stupid of me: that I should have mentioned a lift in the first place! For after all I was there to paint, not to go on mercy missions for demented old derelicts!

"Buses?" he said, cocking his head a little and frowning. "No, I can't say I've seen too many of those, not here. But a car, yes. That's a real possibility. Better yet, a motorcycle! Oh, it's a horrid, horrid thought—but it's my best bet by a long shot..."

And my best bet, I thought, would be to end a very pointless conversation and leave him sitting there on his own! Yes, and even as I thought it I saw that I could do just that, for the mist was lifting, or rather melting away as the sun sailed higher yet. And so:

"You'll excuse me," I said, with a glance across the moor at Tumble Tor, "but I'm afraid it's time..." And there I paused, snapping my head round to stare again at the ancient stack; at its grainy, grooved stone surfaces, all damply agleam, and its base still wreathed in a last few tendrils of mist. "...Afraid it's time to go."

And the reason I had frozen like that, albeit momentarily? Because he was there again: the climber on the tor. And despite that from this angle I could see only his head and shoulders, I knew at once that it was the same person I'd seen the last time I was here: the observer with the binoculars— perched so precariously on that same windy ledge—who once again seemed to be observing me! The sunlight reflected blindingly from the lenses of his glasses...

"I paid my way with readings," said the old tramp from his roadside stone, as if from a thousand miles away. "Give me your hand and I'll do one for you."

Distracted, I looked at him. "What? You'll do one?"

"A reading." He nodded. "I'll read your palm."

"I really don't—" I began, glancing again at Tumble Tor.

"—Oh, go on!" He cut me off. "Or you'll leave me feeling I'm in your debt."

But the man on the rock had disappeared, slipped away out of sight, so I turned again to Old Joe. He held out a trembling hand, and however reluctantly I gave him mine. Then:

"There," he said. "And look here, you have clearly defined lines! Why, it's just like reading a book!" He traced the lines in my palm with a slightly grimy forefinger, but so gently that I barely felt his touch. And in a moment:

"Ah!" He gasped. "An only son—that's you, I mean—and you were so very close to her. Now you're alone but she's still on your mind; every now and then you forget she's gone, and you look up expecting to see her. Yes, and those are the times when you're most likely to see what you ought *not* to be seeing!" Now he looked up at me, his old eyes the faded blue of the sky over a grey sea, and said, "She's moved on, your mother, Paul. She's safe and you can stop searching now."

Spiders with icy feet ran up and down my spine! I snatched my hand away, backed off, said, "W-w-what?"

"I'm sorry, so sorry!" he said, struggling to his feet. "I see too much, but so do you!" And as he went off, hobbling away in the same direction he'd come from, he paused to look back at me and called out, "You shouldn't look so hard, Paul." And once again after a short, sharp glance at Tumble Tor: "You shouldn't look so hard!"

Moments later a swell of mist like some slow-motion ocean rose up, deepening around him and obscuring him. His silhouette was quickly swallowed up in grey opacity, and having lost sight of him I once again turned my gaze on Tumble Tor. The moors can be very weird: mist in the one direction, clarity in the other! The huge outcrop continued to steam a little in the sun, but my route over the uneven ground was clearly visible. And of course the knoll was waiting.

Recovering from the shock Old Joe had supplied, determined to regain my composure, I collected my art things from my car's boot and set off on my semicircular route around Tumble Tor. Up there on the knoll twenty-five minutes later, I used my binoculars to scan the winding road to the north of the tor. Old Joe couldn't have got too far, now could he? But there was no mist, and there was no sign of Joe. Well then, he must have left the road and gone off across the moor along some track or other. Or perhaps someone had given him a lift after all. But neither had I seen any vehicles.

There was no sign of anyone on Tumble Tor either, but that didn't stop me from looking. And despite what Old Joe had said, I found myself looking pretty hard at that...

I couldn't concentrate on my work. It was the morning's strangeness, of course. It was Old Joe's rambling on the one hand, and his incredibly accurate reading on the other. I had always been aware that there were such people, certainly; I'd watched their performances on television, read of their extraordinary talents in various books and magazines, knew that they allegedly assisted the police in very serious investigations, and that seances were a regular feature in the lives of plenty of otherwise very sensible people. Personally, however, I'd always been sceptical of so-called psychic or occult phenomena, only rarely allowing that it was anything other than fake stage magic and "supernatural hocus-pocus".

Now? Well, what was I to think now? Or had I, like so many others (in my opinion) simply allowed myself to be sucked in by self-delusion, my own gullibility?

Perhaps the old tramp hadn't been so crazy after all. What if he'd merely used a few clever, well-chosen words and phrases and left me to fill in the blanks: a very subtle sort of hypnotism? And what if I had only imagined that he'd said the things he said? For of course my mother, comparatively recently passed on, was never far from my mind...anyone who ever lost someone will surely understand that the word "she"—just that single, simple word—would at once conjure her image, more especially now that there was no other "she" to squeeze her image aside.

Psychology? Was that Old Joe's special ability? Well, what or whichever, he'd certainly found my emotional triggers easily enough! Maybe I had worn a certain distinctive, tell-tale look; perhaps there had been some sort of forlorn air about me, as if I were lost, or as if I was looking for someone. But alone, out on the moors? Who could I possibly have been seeking out there? Someone who couldn't possibly be found, obviously. And Old Joe had simply extrapolated.

Stage magic, definitely...or maybe? I still couldn't make up my mind! And so couldn't concentrate. I managed to put a few soft pencilled guidelines onto the paper and a preliminary wash of background colour. But nothing looked right and my frustration was mounting. I couldn't seem to get Old Joe's words out of my head. And what of his warning, if that's what it was, that I shouldn't look so hard? I was looking "too hard", he'd said and I was "seeing too much"—seeing what I ought not to be seeing. Now what on earth had he been trying to convey, if anything, by that? One thing for sure: I'd had a very odd morning!

Too odd—and far too off-putting—so that when a mass of dark cloud began to spread across the horizon, driven my way by a rising wind out of the south-west, I decided to let it go and return to Torquay. Back at the car I saw something at the roadside, lying on the ground at the foot of the verge marker where Old Joe had seated himself. Two somethings in fact: cigarettes, my brand, apparently discarded, just lying there. But hadn't he said something about not wanting to be in my debt?

A peculiar old coot, to say the very least. And so, trying to put it all to the back of my mind, I drove home...

Then for the next three days I painted in my attic studio, listening to the sporadic patter of rain on my skylight while I worked on unfinished projects. And gradually I came to the conclusion that my chance encounter with Old Joe—more properly with his rambling, indirect choice of words and vague warnings—had been nothing more than a feeble, dazed old man's mumbo-jumbo, to which on a whim of coincidental, empathic emotions I had mistakenly attached far too much meaning.

And how, you might ask, is that possible? In the same way that if someone suddenly shouts, "Look out!" you jump…despite that nothing is coming! That's how. But now I ask myself: what if you *don't* jump? And what if something *is* coming?

Early in September, at the beginning of what promised to be an extended Indian summer, I ventured out onto Dartmoor yet again, this time fully determined to get to grips with Tumble Tor. It was a matter of pride by then: I wasn't about to let myself be defeated by a knob of rock, no matter how big it was!

That was my motive for returning to the moor, or so I tried to tell myself; but in all honesty, it was not the only reason. During the last ten days my sleep had been plagued by recurrent dreams: of a stick-thin, red-eyed man, gradually yet menacingly approaching me through a bank of dense swirling mist. Sometimes Tumble Tor's vague silhouette formed a backdrop to this relentless stalking; at other times there was only the crimson glare of Hallowe'en eyes, full of rabid animosity and a burning evil—such evil as to bring me starting awake in a cold sweat.

Determined to exorcise these nightmares, and since it was quite obvious that Tumble Tor was their source—or that they were the outcrop's evil *geniuses loci*, its spirits of place?—I supposed the best place to root them out must be on Dartmoor itself. So there I was once again, parking my car in the same spot, the place where a dirt track crossed the road, with the open moor and misshapen outcrop close at hand on my left, and in the near distance the steep-sided hill or knoll.

And despite that my imagination conjured up an otherwise intangible aura of—but of what? Of something lurking, waiting there?—still I insisted on carrying out my plans; come what may I was going to commence working! Whatever tricks the moor had up its sleeve, I would simply ignore or defy them.

To be absolutely sure that I would at least get something done, I had taken along my camera. If I experienced difficulty getting started, then I would take some pictures of Tumble Tor from which—in the comfort of my own home, at my leisure—I might work up some sketches, thus reacquainting myself with my subject.

As it turned out, it was as well that I'd planned it that way; for weather forecasts to the contrary, there was little or no sign of an Indian summer on

Dartmoor! Not yet, anyway. There was dew on the yellow gorse grasses, and a carpet of ground mist that the morning sun ha managed to shift; indeed the entire scene seemed drab and u1 and Tumble Tor looked as gaunt as a lop-sided skull, its dome sh wan sunlight reflected from its damp surface.

Staring at it, I found myself wondering why the hell I had wanted to paint it in the first place! But…

My usual route across the moorland's low-lying depression to the knoll was well known to me by now; and since the ankle-lapping mist wasn't so dense as to interfere with my vision at close range, I took up my camera and art things, made my way to the knoll, and climbed it to my previous vantage point. Fortunately, aware now of the moor's capriciousness, I had brought an old plastic raincoat with me to spread on the ground. And there I arranged the tools of my business as usual.

But when it came to actually starting to work…suddenly there was this weariness in me—not only a physical thing but also a numbing mental malaise—that had the effect of damping my spirits to such a degree that I could only sit there wondering what on earth was wrong with me. An uneasy expectancy? Some sort of foreboding or precognition? Well, perhaps…but rather than becoming aware, alert, on guard, I felt entirely fatigued, barely able to keep my eyes open.

A miasma then: some unwholesome exhalation spawned in the mist? Unlikely, but not impossible. And for a fact the mist was thicker now in the depression between the knoll and Tumble Tor, and around the base of the outcrop itself; while in the sky the sun had paled to a sickly yellow blob behind the grey overcast.

But once again—as twice before—as I looked at Tumble Tor I saw something other than wet stone and mist. Dull my mind and eyes might be, but I wasn't completely insensible or blind. And there he was where I had first seen him: the climber on the tor, the red-eyed observer on the rock.

And I remember thinking: "Well, so much for exorcism!" For this was surely the weird visitant of my dreams. Not that I saw him as a form of evil incarnate in himself, not then (for after all, what was he in fact but a man on an enormous boulder?) but that his activities—and his odd looks, of course—had made such an impression on me as to cause my nightmares in the first place.

These were the thoughts that crept through my numb mind as I strove to fight free of both my mental and physical lethargy. But the swirling of the mist seemed hypnotic, while the unknown force working on my body—even on my head, which was gradually nodding lower and lower—weighed me down like so much lead. Or rather, to more accurately describe my perceptions, I felt that I was being *sucked* down as in a quagmire.

I tried one last time to focus my attention on the figure on Tumble Tor. Indeed, and before succumbing to my inexplicable faint, I even managed to take up my oh-so-heavy camera and snap a few shaky pictures. And between each period of whirring—as the film wound slowly forward and I tried to refocus—I could see that the man was now climbing down from the rock...but so very *quickly*! Impossibly quickly! or perhaps it was simply that I was moving so slowly.

And now...now he had clambered down into the mist, and I somehow knew that my nightmare was about to become reality. For as in my dreams he was coming—he was now on his way to me—and the mental quagmire continued to suck at me.

Which was when everything went dark...

"What's this?" (At first, a voice from far, far away which some kind of mental red shift rapidly enhanced, making it louder and bringing it closer.) "Asleep on the job, are ye? Twitchin' like ye're havin' a fit!" And then, much more seriously: "Man, but I hope ye're *not* havin' a fit!"

"Eh?" I gave a start. "W-what?" And lifting my head, jerking awake, I straightened up so quickly that I came very close to toppling over sideways.

And there I was, still seated on my plastic mac, blinking up into the half-smiling, half-frowning, wholly uncertain features of Andrew Quarry. "G-*God*, I was dreaming!" I told him. "A nightmare. Just lately I...I've been plagued by them!"

"Then I'm glad I came along," he answered. "It was my hope tae find ye here, but when I saw ye sittin' there—jerkin' and moanin' and what all—I thought it was best I speak out."

"And just as well that you did," I got my breath, finding it hard to breathe properly, and even harder to get to my feet. Quarry took my elbow, assisted me as, by way of explanation, I continued: "I...haven't been sleeping too well."

"No sleepin'?" He looked me straight in the eye. "Aye, I can see that. Man, ye're lookin' exhausted, so ye are! And tae fall asleep here—this early in the mornin'—now, that's no normal."

I could only agree with him, as for the first time I actually felt exhausted. "Maybe it was the mist," I searched for a better explanation. "Something sickening in the mist? Some kind of—I don't know—some kind of miasma maybe?"

He looked surprised, glanced across the moorland this way, and that, in all directions. "The mist, ye say?"

I looked, too, across the low-lying ground to where Tumble Tor stood tall for all that it seemed to slump; tall, and oddly foreboding now, *and dry as a bone in the warm morning sunshine!*

At which I could only shake my head and insist: "But when I sat down there was a mist, and a thick mist at that! Wait..." And I looked at my watch—which was proof of nothing whatever, for I couldn't judge the time.

"Well?" Quarry studied my face, curiously I thought.

"So maybe I was asleep longer than I thought," I told him, lamely. "I must have been, for the mist to clear up like that."

His frown lifted. "Maybe not." He shrugged. "The moor's as changeable as a young girl's mind. I've known the mist tae come up in minutes and melt away just as fast. Anyway, ye're lookin' a wee bit steadier now. So will ye carry on, or what?"

"Carry on?"

"With ye're paintin'—or drawin'—or whatever."

"No, not now," I answered, shaking my head. "I've had more than enough of this place for now."

As he helped me to gather up my things, he said, "Then may I make a wee suggestion?"

"A suggestion?" We started down the hillside.

"Aye. Paul, ye look like ye could use some exercise. Ye're way too pale, too jumpy, and too high strung. Now then, there's this beautiful wee walk—no so wee, actually—frae my place along the beck and back. Now I'm no just lookin' for a lift, ye ken, but we could drive there in ye're car, walk and talk, take in some verra nice autumn countryside while exercisin' our legs, and maybe finish off with a mug of coffee at my place before ye go on back tae Torquay. What do ye say?"

I almost turned him down, but...the fact was I was going short on company. Since the breakdown of my marriage (it seemed an awfully long time ago, but in fact had been less than eighteen months) all my friends had drifted away. Then again, since they had been mainly couples, maybe

229

I should have expected that I would soon be cast out, to become a loner and outsider.

So now I nodded. "We can do that if you like. But—"

"Aye, but?"

"Is your daughter home? Er, Jennie?" Which was a blunt and stupid question whichever way you look at it; but having recognized the apprehension in my voice, he took it as it was meant.

"Oh, so ye're no particularly interested in the company of the fairer sex, is that it?" He glanced sideways at me, but for my part I remained silent. "Oh well then, I'll assume there's a verra good reason," he went on. "And anyway, I wouldnae want to seem to be intrudin'."

"Don't get any wrong ideas about me, Andrew," I said then. "But my wife and I divorced quite recently, since when—"

"Say no more." He nodded. "Ye're no ready tae start thinkin' that way again, I can understand that. But in any case, my Jennie's gone off tae Exeter: a day out with a few friends. So ye'll no be bumpin' intae her accidentally like. And anyway, what do ye take me for: some sort of auld matchmaker? Well, let me assure ye, I'm no. As for my Jennie, ye can take it frae me: she's no the kind of lassie ye'd find amenable to that sort of interference in the first place. So now ye ken."

"I meant no offence," I told him.

"No, of course ye didn't." He chuckled. "Aye, and if ye'd seen my Jennie, ye'd ken she doesnae need a matchmaker! Pretty as a picture, that daughter of mine. Man, ye couldnae paint a prettier one, I guarantee it!"

Along the usual route back to the car, I couldn't resist the occasional troubled glance in the direction of Tumble Tor. Andrew Quarry must have noticed, for he nodded and said, "That auld tor: it's given ye nothin' but a load of grief, is it no so?"

"Grief?" I cast him a sharp look.

"With ye're art and what all, ye're paintin'. It's proved a poor subject."

A sentiment I agreed with more than Quarry could possibly know. "Yes," I answered him in his own words, "a whole load of grief." And then, perhaps a little angrily, revealing my frustration: "But I'm not done with that rock just yet. No, not by a long shot!"

Leaving the car on the road outside Quarry's place, we walked and talked. Or rather *he* talked, simultaneously and unselfconsciously displaying his expertise with regard to the incredible variety of Dartmoor's botanical species. And despite my current personal concerns—about my wellbeing, both physical and mental, following the latest unpleasant episode at Tumble Tor—I soon found myself genuinely fascinated by his monologue. But if Quarry had shown something of his specialized knowledge on our first meeting, now he excelled himself. So much so that later that day I could only remember a fraction of it.

Along the bank of the stream, he pointed out stag's horn and hair mosses; and when we passed a stand of birch trees just fifty yards beyond his house, he identified several lichens and a clump of birch-bracket fungi. Within a mile and a half, never straying from the path beside the stream, we passed oak, holly, hazel and sycamore, their leaves displaying the colours of the season and those colours alone enabling Quarry's instant recognition. On one occasion, where the way was fenced, he climbed a stile, crossed a field into a copse of oaks and dense conifers, and in less than five minutes filled a large white handkerchief with spongy, golden mushrooms which he called Goat's Lip. When I asked him about that, he said:

"Aye, that's what the locals call 'em. But listen tae me: 'locals', indeed! Man, I'm a local myself after all this time! Anyway, these beauties are commonly called downy boletus—or if ye're really, *really* interested *Xerocomus subtomentosus*. So I think ye'll agree, Paul, *Goat's* Lip falls a whole lot easier frae a *man's* lip, does it no?" At which I had to smile.

"And you'll eat them?" I may have seemed doubtful.

"Oh, be sure I will!" he answered. "My Jennie'll cook 'em up intae a fine soup, or maybe use 'em as stuffin' in a roasted chicken…"

And so it went, all along the way.

But in no time at all, or so it seemed, we'd covered more than two miles of country pathway and it was time to turn back. "Now see," Quarry commented, as we reversed our route, "there's a wee bit more colour in ye're cheeks; it's the fresh air ye've been breathin' deep intae ye're lungs, and the blood ye're legs hae been pumpin' up through ye're body. The walkin' is good for a man. Aye, and likewise the talkin' and the companionship. I'd be verra surprised if ye dinnae sleep well the nicht."

So that was it. Not so much the companionship and talking, but the fact that he'd been concerned for me. So of course when he invited me in I entered the old house with him, and shortly we were seated under a low, oak-beamed ceiling in a farmhouse-styled kitchen, drinking freshly ground coffee.

"The coffee's good," I told him.

"Aye," he answered. "None of ye're instant rubbish for my Jennie. If it's no frae the best beans it's rubbish...that's Jennie's opinion, and I go along with it. It's one of the good things she brought back frae America."

We finished our coffee.

"And now a wee dram," he said, as he guided me through the house to his spacious, comfortable living-room. "But just a wee one, for I ken ye'll need to be drivin' home."

Seated, and with a shot glass of good whisky in my hand, I looked across the room to a wall of pictures, paintings, framed photographs, diplomas and such. And the first thing to catch my eye was a painting I at once recognized. A seascape, it was one of my mother's canvases, and one of her best at that; my sketch of Tumble Tor—behind non-reflective glass in a frame that was far too good for it—occupied a space alongside.

I stood up, crossed to the wall to take a closer look, and said, "You were as good as your word. I'm glad my effort wasn't wasted."

"And ye're Ma's picture, too," he nodded, coming to stand beside me. "The pencils and the paint: I think they make a fine contrast."

I found myself frowning—or more properly scowling—at my drawing, and said, "Andrew, just you wait! I'm not done with painting on the moor just yet. I promise you this: I'll soon be giving you a far better picture of that damned rock...even if it kills me!"

He seemed startled, taken aback. "Aye, so ye've said," he answered, "—that ye're set on it, I mean. And I sense a struggle brewin' between the pair of ye—ye'resel and the auld tor. But I would much prefer ye as a livin' breathin' friend than a dead benefactor!"

At which I breathed deeply, relaxed a little, laughed and said, "Just a figure of speech, of course. But I really do have to get to grips with that boulder. In fact I don't believe I'll be able to work on anything else until I'm done with it. But as for right now—" I half-turned from the wall, "I *am* quite done with it. Time we changed the subject, I think, and talked about other things."

My words acted like an invocation, for before turning more fully from the wall my gaze lighted on something else: a framed colour photograph hung in a prominent position, where the stone wall had been buttressed to enclose the grate and blackened flue of an open fireplace. An immaculate studio photograph, it portrayed a young woman's face in profile.

"Your wife?" I approached the picture.

"My Jennie," Quarry replied. "I keep my wife's photographs in my study, where I can speak tae her any time I like. And she sometimes answers me, or so I like tae think. As for my Jennie: well now ye've seen her, ye've seen her Ma. Like peas in a pod. Aye, but it's fairly obvious she doesnae take after me!"

I knew what he meant. Jennie was an extraordinarily beautiful woman. Her lush hair was black as a raven's wing, so black it was almost blue, and her eyes were as big and as blue as the sky. She had a full mouth, high cheeks and forehead, a straight nose and small, delicate ears. Despite that Jennie's photograph was in profile, still she seemed to look at the camera from the corner of her eye, and wore a half-smile for the man taking her picture.

"And she's in Exeter, with her boyfriend?"

Quarry shook his head. "No boyfriend, just friends. She's no been home long enough tae develop any romantic interests. Ye should let me introduce ye some time. She was verra much taken with ye're drawing. Ye hae that in common at least—designs, I mean. For it's all art when ye break it down."

After that, in a little while, I took my leave of him...

Driving home, for some reason known only to my troubled subconscious mind, I took the long route across the moor and drove by Tumble Tor; or I would have driven by, except Old Joe was there where I'd last seen him. In fact, I *didn't* see him until almost the last moment, when he suddenly appeared through the break in the hedge, stepping out from the roadside track.

He looked at me—or more properly at my car—as it sped toward him, and for a moment he teetered there on the verge and appeared of two minds about crossing the road directly in front of me! If he'd done so I would have had a very hard time avoiding him. It would have meant applying my brakes full on, swinging my steering-wheel hard over, and in all likelihood skidding sideways across the narrow road. And there on the opposite side was this outcrop, a boulder jutting six feet out of the ground, which would surely have brought me to a violent halt; but such a halt as might easily have killed me!

As it was I had seen the old tramp in sufficient time—but only *just* in time—to apply my brakes safely and come to a halt alongside him.

Out of my window I said, "Old Joe, what on earth were you thinking about just then? I mean, I could so easily—"

"Yes," he cut me off, "and so could I. Oh so very easily!" And he stood there trembling, quivering, with his eyes sunk so deep that I could scarcely see them.

Then I noticed the mist. It was just as Andrew Quarry had stated—a freak of synchronicity, sprung into being almost in a single moment—as if the earth had suddenly breathed it out; this ground mist, swirling and eddying about Old Joe's feet and all across the low-lying ground beyond the narrow grass verge.

Distracted, alienated, and somehow feeling the dampness of that mist deep in my bones, I turned again to the old man, who was still babbling on. "But I couldn't do it," he said, "and I shall *never* do it! I'll simply wait—forever, if needs be!"

As he began to back unsteadily away from the car, I said, "Old Joe, are you ill? What's the trouble? Can I help you? Can I offer you a lift, take you somewhere?"

"A lift?" he answered. "No, no. This is my waiting place. It's where I must wait. And I'm sorry—so very sorry—that I almost forgot myself."

"What?" I said, frowning and perplexed. "What do you mean? How did you forget yourself? What are you talking about?"

"It's here," he replied. "Here's where I must wait for it to happen... again! But I can't—I mustn't, and won't ever—try to *make* it happen! No, for I'm not like that one..."

Old Joe gave a nod and his gaze shifted; he looked beyond me, beyond the car, out across the moors at Tumble Tor. And of course, as cold as I suddenly felt, I turned my head to follow his lead. All I saw was naked stone, and without quite knowing why I breathed a sigh of relief.

Then, turning back to the old tramp, I said, "But there's no one there, Joe!" And again, in a whisper: "Old Joe...?" For he wasn't there either—just a curl of mist in the hedgerow, where he might have passed through.

And a few minutes later, by the time I had driven no more than a mile farther along the road toward Torquay, already the mist had given way to a wan, inadequate sun that was doing its best to shine...

I had been right to worry about my state of mind. Or at least, that was how I felt at the time: that my depression under this atmosphere of impending doom which I felt hovering over me was some kind of mild mental disorder. (For after all, that's what depression is, isn't it?) Even now, as I look back on it in the light of new understanding, perhaps it really was some sort of psychosis—but nothing that I'd brought on myself. I realize that now because at the time I *acknowledged* the problem, while psychiatry insists that the psychotic isn't aware of his condition.

In any case, I *had* been right to worry about it. For despite Andrew Quarry's insistence that I'd sleep well that night, my dreams were as bad and even worse than before. The mist, the semi-opaque silhouette of monolithic Tumble Tor, and those eyes—those crimson-burning eyes—drawing closer, closer, and ever closer. Half-a-dozen times I woke up in a cold sweat...little wonder I was feeling so drained...

In the morning I drove into town to see my doctor. He gave me a check-up and heard me out; not the entire story, only what I felt obliged to tell him about my "insomnia". He prescribed a course of sleeping pills and I set off home...such was my intention.

But almost before I knew it I was out on the country roads again. Taken in thrall by some morbid fascination or obsession, I was once more heading for Tumble Tor!

My tank was almost empty...I stopped at a garage, filled her up...the forecourt attendant was concerned, asked me if I was feeling okay...which really should have told me that something was very wrong, but it didn't stop me.

Oh, I agreed with him that I didn't feel well: I was dizzy, confused, distracted, but none of these symptoms served to stop me. And through all of this I could feel the lure, the inexplicable attraction of the moors, to which I must succumb!

And I did succumb, driving all the way to Tumble Tor where I parked in my usual spot and levered myself out of my car. Old Joe was there, waving his arms and silently gibbering...warning me about something which I couldn't take in...my mind was clogged with cotton-wool mist...everything seemed to be happening in slow-motion...those eyes, those blazing *evil* eyes!

I felt a *whoosh* of wind, heard a vehicle's tyres screaming on the road's rough surface, saw through the billowing mist the blurred motion of something passing close—much too close—in front of me.

This combination of sensations got through to me—almost. I was aware of a red faced, angry man in a denim jacket leaning out of his truck's window, yelling, "You *bloody* idiot! What the bloody hell...are you drunk? Staggering about in the road like that!" Then his tyres screeched again, spinning and smoking, as he rammed his vehicle into gear and pulled away.

But the mist was still swirling, my head still reeling—*and Old Joe was having a silent, gesticulating argument with a stick-thin, red-eyed man!*

Then the silence was broken as the old man looked my way, sobbing, "That wouldn't have been my fault! Not this time, and not ever. It would have been yours…or *his*! But it wouldn't have done him any good, and God knows I didn't want it!" As he spoke the word "his", so he'd flung out an arm to point at the thin man who was now floating toward me, his eyes like warning signal lamps as his shape took on form and emerged more surely from the mist.

And that was when I "woke up" to the danger. For yes, it was like coming out of a nightmare—indeed it could only have been a nightmare—but I came out of it so slowly that even as the mist cleared and the old man and the red-eyed phantom thinned to figures as insubstantial as the mist itself, still something of it lingered over: Old Joe's voice.

As I staggered there on the road, blinking and shaking my head to clear it, trying to focus on reality and forcing myself to stop shuddering, so that old man's voice—as thin as a cry from the dark side of the moon—got through to me:

"Get out of here!" he cried. "Go, hurry! He knows you now, and he won't wait. He'll follow you—in your head and in your dreams—until it's done!"

"Until what's done?" I managed to croak my question. But I was talking to nobody, to thin air.

Following which I almost fell into my car, reversed dangerously onto the crossover track and clipped the hedge, and drove away in a sweat as cold and damp as that non-existent mist. And all the way home I could feel those eyes burning on my neck; so much so that on more than one occasion I caught myself glancing in my rearview mirror, making sure there was no one in the back seat.

But for all that I saw no one there, still I wasn't absolutely sure…

Taking sleeping pills that night wasn't a good idea. But I felt I had to. If I suffered another disturbed night, goodness knows what I would feel like—what my overburdened mind would conjure into being—the next day. But of course, the trouble with sleeping pills is they not only send you to sleep, they'll *keep* you that way! And when once again I was visited by evil dreams, struggle against them as I might and as I did, still I couldn't wake up!

It started with Old Joe again, the old tramp, a gentleman of the road. Speaking oh-so-earnestly, he made a sort of sense at first, which as quickly lapsed into the usual nonsense.

"Now listen to me," he said, just a voice in the darkness of my dream, the silence of the night. "I risked everything to leave my waiting place and come here with you. And I may never return, find my way back again, *except* with you. So it's a big chance I'm taking, but I had to. It's my redemption for what I have thought to do—and what I have almost done—more times than I care to admit. And so, because of what *he* is and what I know *he* will do, I've come to warn you this one last time. Now you must guard yourself against him, for you can expect him at any moment."

"Him?" I said, speaking to the unseen owner of the voice, which I knew as well as I knew my own. "The man on the tor?"

While I waited for an answer a mist crept into being and the darkness turned grey. In the mist I saw Old Joe's outline: a crumpled shape under a floppy hat. "It's his waiting place," he at last replied. "Either there or close by. But he's grown tired of waiting and now takes it upon himself. He risks hell, but since he's already half-way there, it's a risk he'll take. If he wins it's the future—whatever that may be—and if he fails then it's the flames. He knows that, and of course he'll try to win...which would mean that you lose!"

"I don't understand," I answered, dimly aware that it was only a dream and I was lying in my bed as still and heavy as a statue. "What does he want with me? How can he harm me?"

And then the rambling:

"But you've *seen* him!" Old Joe barked. "You looked beyond, looked where you shouldn't and too hard. You saw me, so I knew you must see him, too. Indeed he *wanted* you to see him! Oh, you weren't looking for him but someone else—a loved one, who has long moved on—but you did it in *his place of waiting*! And as surely as your searching brought me up, it brought him up, too. Ah, but where I only wait, *he* is active! He'll wait no longer!"

Suddenly I knew that this was the very crux of everything that was happening to me, and so I asked: "But what is it that you're waiting for? And where is this...this waiting place?"

"But you've *seen* him!" the old tramp cried again. "How is it you see so much yet understand so little? I may not explain. It's a thing beyond your time and place. But just as there were times before, so there are times after. Men wait to be born and then—without ever seeming to realize it—they wait again, to die. But it's when and it's how! And after that, what then? The waiting, that's what."

"Gibberish!" I answered, shaking my head; and I managed an uncertain laugh, if only at myself.

"No, don't!" The other's alarm was clear in his voice. "If you deny me I can't stay. If you refute me, then I must go. Now listen: you know me— you've seen me—so continue to see me, but *only* me."

"You're a dream, a nightmare," I told him. "You're nothing but a phantom, come to ruin my sleep."

"No, no, *no!*" But his voice was fading, along with Old Joe himself.

But if only he hadn't sounded so desperate, so fearful, as he dwindled away: fearful for me! And if only the echoes of his cries hadn't lasted so long…

Old Joe was gone, but the mist stayed. And taking shape in its writhing tendrils I saw a very different presence—one that I knew as surely as I had known the old tramp. It was the watcher on the tor.

Thin as a rake, eyes burning like coals in a fire, he came closer and said, "My friend, you really shouldn't concern yourself with that old fool." His voice was the gurgle and slurp of gas bubbles bursting on a swamp, and a morbid smell—the smell of death—attended him. The way his black jacket hung loose on sloping shoulders, it could well have been that there were only bones beneath the cloth. And yet there was this strength in him, this feverish, hypnotic fascination.

"I…I don't want to know you," I told him then. "I want nothing to do with you."

"But you have everything to do with me," he answered, and his eyes glowed redder yet. "The old fool told you to avoid me, didn't he?"

"He said you were waiting for something," I answered. "For me, I suppose. But he didn't say why, or to what end."

"Then let me tell you." He drifted closer, his lank black hair floating on his shoulders, his thin face invisible behind the flaring of his eyes, those burning eyes that were fixed on mine. "I have a mystery to unfold, a story to tell, and I can't rest until I've told it. You are sympathetic, receptive, aware. And you came to my place of waiting. I didn't seek you out, you sought me. Or at least, you *found* me. And I think you will like my story."

"Then tell it and leave me be," I replied.

"You find me offensive," he said, his voice deeper and yet more dark, but at the same time sibilant as a snake's hiss. "So did she. But what she did, that was *truly* offensive! Yessss."

"You're making as much sense as Old Joe!" I told him. "But at least he kept his distance, and didn't smell of...of—"

"—Of the damp, the mould, and the rot?"

"Go away!" I shuddered, and felt that I was shrinking down smaller in my bed.

"Not until you've heard my story, and then I'll be glad to leave you... in peace?" With which he laughed an ugly laugh at the undefined question in his words.

"So get on with it," I answered. "Tell me your story and be done with it. For if that's all it takes to get rid of you, I'll gladly hear you out."

"Good!" he said, and moved closer yet. "Very good. But not here. I can't reveal it here. I want to show you how it wassss, where it wassss, and what happened there. I want you to see why I am what I am, why I did what I did, and why I'll do what I've yet to do. But not here."

"Where then?" I asked, but I'd already guessed the answer. "At your waiting place? Your place on the moor, the old tor?"

"In my place of waiting, yesss," he answered. "Not the old tor, but close, close." And then, changing the subject (perhaps because he thought he'd said too much?) "What is your name?"

I wanted to refuse, defy him, but his ghastly eyes dragged it out of me. "I'm Paul," I replied. "Paul Stanard." And then—as if this were some casual meeting of strangers in a street!—"And you?"

"Simon Carlisle," he answered at once, and continued: "But it's so very, *very* good to meet you, Mr Stanard." And again, as if savouring my name, drawing it out: "Paul Stanaaard, yessss!"

From somewhere in the back of my sub-subconscious mind, I remembered something. Something Old Joe had said to me: "If you deny me I can't stay. If you refute me, I must go." Would it be the same with Simon Carlisle, I wondered? And so:

"You are only a dream, a nightmare," I said. "You're nothing but a phantom, come to ruin my sleep."

But it didn't work! He moved closer—so close I felt the heat of his blazing eyes—and his jaw fell open in a gurgling, phlegmy laugh.

Abruptly then he stopped laughing, and his breath was foul in my face. "You would work your wiles on me? On that old fool, perhapsss. But on me? Old Joe came with goodness in his heart, yessss. Ah, but which is the stronger: compassion, or ambition? The old tramp is content to wait, and so may be put aside—but not me! I shall wait no longer. You came to my place, and now I have come to yours. But I can't tell my story here, for I want you to see, and to know, and...and to feel."

"I won't come!" I shrank deeper into my bed and closed my eyes, which were already closed.

"You will!" *His* eyes floated down on me, into me. "Say it. Say that you will come to my place of waiting."

"I...I won't."

His eyes burned on mine, then passed through them, to burn inside my head. "Say you'll come."

I could resist him no longer. "I'll come," I mumbled.

"Say you *will* come. Say it again, and again, and again."

"I *will* come," I said. "I will come...I'll come...I'll come, come, come, come, come!" Until:

"Yessss," he sighed at last. "I know you will."

"I *will* come," I was still mumbling, when my bedside telephone woke me up. "I will most definitely...what?"

Then, like a run-down automaton, blinking and fumbling, I reached for the 'phone and held it to my ear. "Yes?"

It was Andrew Quarry. "I just thought I'd give ye a call," he said. "See how ye slept, and ask if ye'd be out at the auld tor again. But...did I wake ye or somethin'?"

"Wake me? Yes, you woke me. Tumble Tor? Oh, yes—I *will* come—come, come, come."

And after a pause: "Paul, are ye all right? Ye sound verra odd, as if ye're only half there."

God help me, I *was* only half there! And the half that was there was in pretty bad shape. "Old Joe warned me off," I mumbled then. "But he's just an old tramp, an old fool. And anyway, Simon wants to tell me his story and show me something."

"Simon?" Quarry's voice was full of anxiety now. "And did I hear ye say Old Joe? But...Old Joe the tramp?"

"Old Joe," I nodded, at no one in particular. "And anyway, he says that I'm to take him back to his place of waiting. He's really not a bad old chap, so I don't want to let him down. And Andrew, I'm...I'm not at all well."

Another pause, longer, and when Quarry finally spoke again there was something more than concern in his voice. "Paul, will ye tell me where and when ye spoke to Old Joe? I mean, he's not there with ye this verra minute, is he?"

"He was last night," I nodded again. "And now I must go."

"Ontae the moor?"

"I *will* come," I said, putting the 'phone down and getting out of bed...

There was a mist in the house, in the car, on the roads, and in my mind. Not a really heavy mist, just some kind of atmospheric—and mental?—fogginess that had me squinting and blinking, but without completely obscuring my vision, during my drive out to Tumble Tor.

I had to go, of course, and all the way I kept telling myself: "I *will* come. I will, I will, I will..." While yet I knew that I didn't want to.

Old Joe went with me; he kept silent, but I knew he was in the car, relieved to be returning to his place of waiting. Perhaps he was reluctant to speak in the presence of my other less welcome passenger: the one with his cold fingers in my head. As for that one...it wasn't just that I could sense the corruption in him, I could smell it!

And in as little time as it takes to tell, or so it seemed to me, there we were where the dirt track crossed the road; and Tumble Tor standing off with its base wreathed in mist, and the knoll farther yet, a gaunt grey hump in the autumnal haze.

I, or rather we, got out of the car, and as Simon Carlisle led me unerringly out across the moor toward Tumble Tor, I knew that Old Joe fretted for me where we left him by the gap in the hedge. Knowing I was too far gone, beyond any sort of help that he could offer, the old tramp said nothing. For after all, what could he do to break this spell? He'd already done his best, to no avail. Half turning to look back, I thought I saw him by the white-painted marker stone which he'd used as a seat that time. Like a figure carved from smoke, he stood wringing his hands as he watched me go.

But Simon Carlisle said, "Pay him no heed. This is none of his businessss. His situation—in a waiting place such as his—was always better than mine. He has had a great many chances, yessss. How long he is willing to wait is for him to determine. Myself, I am done with waiting."

"Where are you taking me?" I asked him.

"To the tor," he answered, "where else? I want to see just one more time. I want to fuel my passion, as once before it was fuelled. And I want *you* to see and understand. Do you have your glasssses?"

I did. Like him, I wore my binoculars round my neck. And I knew why. "We're going to climb?"

He nodded and said, "Oh yessss! For as you'll soon see for yourself, this vast misshapen rock makes a superb vantage point. It is the tower from which I spied on *them*!"

My soul trembled, but my feet didn't stop. They were numb; I couldn't feel them; it was as if I floated through the swirling ground mist impelled by some energy other than my own. But all I could think of was this: "I...I'm not a good climber."

"Oh?" he said without looking back, his clothing flapping like a scarecrow's in the wind, while his magnetism drew me on. "Well I am. So don't worry, Paul Stanaaard, for I won't let you fall. The old tor is a place, yessss, but it isn't the place of waiting. That comes later..."

We drifted across the moorland, and despite the shadows in my mind and the mist on the earth I found myself scanning ahead for rushes and sphagnum mosses, evidence of boggy ground. Why I worried about that when there was so much more to concern me, I didn't rightly know. But in any case I saw nothing, and soon we approached the foot of the tor.

Simon Carlisle knew exactly where he was going and what he was doing, and all I could do was follow in his footsteps...if he had had any. But we continued to float, and it was only when we began to climb that gravity returned and our progress slowed a little.

We climbed the knoll side of Tumble Tor, where I had first witnessed Carlisle scanning the land beyond. And as we ascended above the misty moor, so he instructed me to place my feet just so, making opportune use of this or that toe-hold, or to secure myself by gripping this or the other jutting knob of stone, and so on; and even a blind man could have seen that he knew Tumble Tor intimately and had gone this route many times before.

We passed carefully along narrow ledges with rounded rims, through stepped, vertical slots or chimneys where the going was easier, from level to striated level, always ascending from one fearful vertiginous position to the next. But Carlisle's advice—his sibilant instructions—were so clear, timely, and faultlessly delivered that I never once slipped or faltered. And at last we came to that high ledge behind its shoulder of rounded stone, where I'd seen and even tried to photograph Carlisle as he scoured the moorland around through his binoculars.

"Now then," he said, and his voice had changed; no longer sibilant, it grated as if uttered through clenched teeth. "Now we shall see what we shall see. Look over there, a quarter-mile or so, that hollow in the ground where it rises like the first in a series of small waves; that very private place surrounded by gorse and ferns. Do you see?"

At first I saw nothing, despite that the mist appeared to have lifted. But then, as if Carlisle had willed it into being, the tableau took shape, becoming clearer by the moment. In the spot he had described, I saw a couple... and indeed they were coupling! Their clothing was their bed where they lay together in each other's arms, naked. Their movements, at first languid, rapidly became more frenzied. I thought I heard their panting, but it wasn't them—it was Carlisle!

And then the climax—their shuddering bodies, the falling apart, gentle caresses, kisses, and whispered conversation—the passion quenched, for the moment at least. *Their* passion, yes...but not Carlisle's. His panting was that of a beast!

Finally he grew calm, and his voice was as before. "If we were to stay, to continue watching, you'd see them do it again and again, yessss. But my heart was herssss! And as for him...I thought he was my friend! I was betrayed, not once but often, frequently. She gave me back the ring which was my promise and told me her love could not be, not with me. Ah, but it *could* be with him! And as you've seen, it wasssss!"

I didn't understand, not entirely. "She was your wife? But you said—"

"—I said she gave me back my ring—the *engagement* ring I bought for her. She broke her promise!"

"She found someone she loved better or more than you."

"*What?*" He turned to me in a rage. "No, she was a slut and would have had anyone before me! She betrayed me—deserted me—gave him what she could never give me. She sent me my ring in a letter, said that she was sssorry! Well, I made them *sssorry*! Or so I thought. But now, in their place of waiting, still they have each other while I have nothing. And if they must wait for ever what does it matter to them? They don't wait in misery and solitude like meeeee! Even now they make love, and I am the one who sufferssss!"

"*Blind hatred! Insane jealousy!*" Now, I can't be sure that I said those words; it could be that I merely thought them. But in any case he "heard" my accusation. And:

243

"Be very careful, Mr. Stanaaard!" Carlisle snarled. "What, do you think to test me? In a place such as this? In this dangerous place?" His red lamp eyes drew me from the stone shoulder until I leaned out over a gulf of air. For a moment I was sure I would fall, until he said, "But no. Though I would doubtless take great pleasure in it, that would be a dreadful waste. For this is not my waiting place, and there's that which you still must see. So come." As easily as that, he drew me back...

We descended from Tumble Tor, but so terribly *quickly* that it was almost as if we slid or slithered down from the heights. As before I was guided by Carlisle's evil voice, until at last I stood on what should have been solid ground—except it felt as if I was still afloat, towed along in the wake of my dreadful host to the far side of the outcrop. But I made no inquiry with regard to our destination. This time I knew where we were going.

And off across the moor he strode or floated, myself close behind, moving in tandem, as if invisibly attached to him. Part of my mind acknowledged and accepted the ancient, mist-wreathed landscape: a real yet unreal place, as in a dream; that was the part in the grip of Simon Carlisle's influence. But the rest of me knew I should be fighting this thing, struggling against the mental miasma. Also, for the first time, I felt I knew for sure the evil I'd come up against, even though I couldn't yet fathom its interest in me.

"Ghosts," I heard myself say. "You're not real. Or you are—or you were—when you lived!"

Half turning, he looked back at me. "So finally you know," he said. "And I ask myself: how is it possible that such a mind—as dull and unimaginative as yours—lives on corporeal and quick when one as sharp and as clear as mine is trapped in this place?"

"This place? Your place of waiting?"

"No, Mr. Stanaaard." He pointed ahead. "Theirs! Mine lies on the other side of the tor, half way to the bald knoll where first I saw you and you saw me. You'll know it when you see it: the mossesss, reedsss, and rushesss. But this place here: it's theirsss! It's where I killed them—where I've killed them a hundred times; ah, if only they could *feel* it! But no, they're satisfied with their lot and no longer fear me. We are on different levels, you see. Me riding my loathing, and them lost in their lust."

"Their love." I contradicted him.

He turned on me and a knife was in his hand; its blade was long and glittering sharp. "That word is *poison* to meeee! Maybe I should have let you fall. How I wish I could have!"

Logic, so long absent from my mind, my being, returned however briefly. "You can't hurt me. Not with a ghost knife."

"Fool!" He answered. "The knife is not for you. And as for your invulnerability: we shall see. But look, we are there."

Before us the place I had seen from Tumble Tor, the secret love nest surrounded by gorse and tall ferns; the lovers joined on their bed of layered clothing; Carlisle leaping ahead of me, his coat flapping, knife raised on high. The young man's broad back was his target; the young woman's half-shuttered eyes saw the madman as he fell upon them; the young man turned his head to look at his attacker—and amazingly, *he only smiled*!

The knife struck home, again and again. No blood, nothing. And Carlisle's crazed howling like a distant storm in my ears. Done with his rival, he turned his knife on the girl. Deep into her right eye went the blade, into her left eye, her throat and bare breasts. But she only shook her head and sadly smiled. And her eyes and throat and breasts were mist; likewise her lover's naked unmarked body: a drift of mist on the coarse empty grass.

"Ghosts!" I said again. "And this is their waiting place."

Carlisle's howling faded away, and panting like a mad dog he drifted to his feet and turned to me. "Did you see? And am I to be pitied? They pity me—for what they have and I haven't! And I can't *stand* to be here any longer. And you, Mr. Stanaaard—you are my elevation, and perhaps my salvation. For whatever place it is that lies beyond, it *must* be better than this place. Now come, and I shall show you *my* place of waiting."

Danger! That part of me which knew how wrong this was also recognized the danger. Oh, I had known the precariousness of my position all along, but now the terror was tangible: this awful sensation of my soul shrinking inside me. I felt that I was now beyond hope. But before my fear could completely unman me, make me incapable of speech, there was something I must know. And so I asked the ghost, ghoul, creature who was leading me on, "What is...what *is* a place of waiting?"

"Ah, but that's a secret!" he answered, as we drew closer to Tumble Tor. "Secret from the living, that is, but something that is known to all the dead. They wouldn't tell you, not one of them, but since you will soon *be* one of them..."

"You intend to kill me?"

"Mr. Stanaaard, you are as good as dead! And then I shall move on."

It began to make sense. "You...you're stuck in your so-called waiting place until someone else dies there."

"Ah, and so you're awake at last! The waiting places are the places where we died. And there we must wait until someone else dies in the same place, *in the same way!* To that treacherous dog and his bitch back there, it makes no difference. They have all they want. But to me...I was only able to do what I do, to watch as I did in life, to hate with a hatred that will never die, and to *wait*, of course. Then you came along, trying to look beyond life, searching for someone who had moved on—and finding me."

"I called you up," I said, faintly.

"And I was waiting, and I was ready. Yessss!"

"But how shall you kill me? I won't die of fright, not now that I know."

"Oh, you won't die by my insubstantial hand. But you will die of my doing, most definitely. Do you know that old saying, that you can lead a horse to water—"

"But you can't make him drink?"

"That's the one. Ah, but water is water and mire is mire."

"I don't understand," I said, though I was beginning to.

"You will understand," he promised me. "Ah, you will..."

Passing Tumble Tor, we started out across the low-lying ground toward the knoll. And in that region of my conscious mind which knew what was happening (while yet lacking even a small measure of control) I remembered something that Carlisle had said about his place of waiting:

"You'll know it when you see it: the mossesss, reedsss and rushesss."

"We're very nearly there, aren't we?" I said, more a statement of fact than a question. "The sphagnums and the rushes—"

"—And the mire, yessss!" he answered.

"The quagmire where you killed yourself, putting an end to your miserable life: that's your place of waiting."

"Killed myself?" He paused for a moment, stared at me with his blazing eyes. "Suicide? No, no—not I! Never! But after I killed *them* I was seen on the moor; a chance encounter, damn it to hell! And so I fled. I admit it: I fled the scene in a blind panic. But a mist came up—the selfsame mist you see now—and as surely as Satan had guided me to my deed, my revenge, so God or Fate led me astray, brought me shivering and stumbling here. Here where I sank in the mire and died, and here where I've had to wait...but no longer."

We were halfway to the knoll and the mist was waist deep. But still I knew the place. Andrew Quarry had pointed it out on the occasion of our first meeting: the sphagnums and the reeds, pointers to mud that would suck my shoes off. But it now seemed he'd been wrong about that last. Right to avoid it but wrong in his estimation, for it was much deeper than that and would do a lot more than just suck my shoes off.

And it was there, lured on in the ghostly wake of Carlisle—as I stumbled and flailed my arms in a futile attempt to keep my balance, managing one more floundering step forward and wondering why I was in trouble while he drifted upright and secure—it was there that what little remained of my logical, sensible self took flight, leaving me wholly mazed and mired in the misted, sucking quag.

Carlisle, this powerful ghost of a man, as solid to me now as any man of flesh and blood, stood and watched as it began to happen. His gaunt jaws agape, and his eyes burning red as coals in the heart of a fire, he laughed like a hound of hell. And as I threw myself flat on the mud to slow my sinking: "Murder!" he said, his voice as glutinous as the muck that quaked and sucked beneath me. "But what is that to me? You are my third, yes, but they can only hang a man once—and they can't hang me at all! So down you go, Paul Stanaaard, into the damp and the dark. And with your passing I, too, shall pass into whatever waits beyond…while you lie here."

It appeared I had retained at least a semblance of common-sense. Drawing my legs up and together against the downward tug of viscous filth, I threw my arms wide and my head back, making a crucifix of my body and limbs in order to further increase my buoyancy. Even so, the quag was already lapping the lobes of my ears, surging cold and slimy against my Adam's apple, and smelling in my nostrils of drowned creatures and rotting foliage; in which position desperation loaned voice to what little of logic remained:

"But where are you bound?" I asked him, aware of the creeping mud. "Do you know? Do any of you know? What if your waiting places are a test? What if someone—God, if you like—what if *He* is also waiting, to see what you'll do, or won't do? What if this was your last chance to redeem yourself, and you're throwing it away?"

"Do you think I haven't—we haven't—asked ourselves the very same questionsss?" he answered. "I have, a thousand times. But think on thisss: if the next place doesn't suit me, I shall move on again by whatever means available. And again, and again…alwaysss."

"Not if the next place is hell!" I told him. "Which I very much hope it is!"

"Wrong!" he said, and burst out laughing. "For my hell was here. And now it's yoursss!"

I strained against the suction of the mud. I tried to will myself to stay afloat, but the filthy stuff was lapping my chin and surging in my ears, and I could feel my feet sinking, going down slowly but surely into the mire. Weeds tangled my hair and slime crept at the corners of my mouth; immobilized by mud, all I could do was gaze petrified at Carlisle where he stood like a demon god on the surface of the quag, howling his crazed laughter from jaws that gaped in a red-glowing Hallowe'en skull, his lank limbs wreathed in mist and rotten cloth.

Muddy water was in my nostrils, trickling into my mouth. I felt the hideous suction and was unable to fight it. I was done for and I knew it. But I also knew of another world, more real than Simon Carlisle's place of waiting. The world of the quick, of the living, of hope that springs eternal. And at the last—even as I gagged at the ooze that was slopping into my mouth—I called for help, cried out until all I could do was choke and splutter.

And my cries were answered!

"Paul!" came a shout, a familiar voice, which in my terror I barely recognized. "Paul Stanard, is that ye down there? Man, what in the name of all that's—?"

"Help! Help!" I coughed and gurgled.

And Carlisle cried, "No! No! I won't be cheated! It can't end like this. Drink, drown, die, you bloody obstinate man! You are my one, my last chance. So die, *die*!"

He drifted toward me, got down beside me, tried to push at my face and drive my head down into the mud. But his hands were mist, his furious, burning face, too, and his cries were fading as he himself melted away, his fury turning to terror. "No, no, *noooo*!" And he was gone.

Gone, too, the mist, and where Carlisle's claw-like hands had sloughed into nothingness, stronger hands were reaching to fasten on my jacket, to lift my face from the slop, to draw my head and shoulders to safety out of—

—*Out of just six inches of muddy water!*

And Andrew Quarry was standing ankle deep in it, standing there with his Jennie, her raven hair shining in the corona of the sun that silhouetted her head. And nothing of that phantom mist to be seen, no sign of Carlisle, and no bog but this shallow pond of muddied rain-water lying on mainly solid ground...

"Did you...did you see him, or it?" I gasped, putting a shaking hand down into the water to push myself up and take the strain off Quarry's arms. But the bottom just there was soft as muck; my hand skidded, and again I floundered.

"Him? It?" Quarry shook his head, his eyes like saucers in his weathered face. "We saw nothin'. But what the hell *happened* to ye, man?" And again he tugged at me, holding me steady.

Still trembling, cold and soaking wet—scarcely daring to believe I had lived through it—I said. "It was him, Carlisle. He tried to kill me." As I spoke, so my fumbling hand found and grasped something solid in the muddy shallows: a rounded stone, it could only be.

But my thumb sank into a hole, and as I got to my knees I brought the "stone" with me. Stone? No, *a grinning skull*, and I knew it was him! All that it lacked was his maniac laughter and a red-burning glare in its empty black socket eyes...

At Quarry's place, while Jennie telephoned the police—to tell them of my "discovery" on Dartmoor—her father sat outside the bathroom door while I showered. By then the fog had lifted from my mind and I was as nearly normal as I had felt in what seemed like several ages. Normal in my mind, but tired, indeed exhausted in my body.

Andrew Quarry knew that, also knew why and what my problem had been. But he'd already cautioned me against saying too much in front of Jennie. "She would'nae understand, and I cannae say I'm that sure myself. But when ye told me ye'd been warned off, and by Old Joe..."

"Yes, I know." Nodding to myself, I turned off the shower, stepped out and began to towel myself dry. "But he's not real—I mean, no longer real—is he?"

"But he was until four years ago." Quarry's voice was full of awe. "He used tae call in here on his rounds—just the once a year—for a drink and a bite. And he would tell me where he had been, up and down the country. I liked him. But just there, where ye parked ye're car, that was where Old Joe's number came up. He must hae been like a wee rabbit, trapped in the beam of the headlights, in the frozen moments before that other car hit him. A tragic accident, aye." Then his voice darkened. "Ah, but as for that *other*..."

"Simon Carlisle?" Warm and almost dry, still I shivered.

"That one, aye," Quarry growled, from behind the bathroom door where it stood ajar. "I recognized his name as soon as ye mentioned it. It was eighteen years ago and all the newspapers were full of it. It was thought Carlisle had fled the country, for he was the chief suspect in a double moors murder. And—"

"I know all about it," I cut him off. "Carlisle, he...he told me, even *showed* me! And if you hadn't come along—if you hadn't been curious about my...my condition, my state of mind after what I'd said to you on the 'phone—he would have killed me, too. The only thing I don't, can't understand: how could he have drowned in just six inches of water?"

"Oh, I can tell ye that!" Quarry answered at once. "Eighteen years ago was a verra bad winter, followed by a bad spring. Folks had seen nothin' like it. Dartmoor was a swamp in parts, and *that* part was one of them. The rain, it was like a monsoon, erodin' many of the small hillocks intae landslides. Did ye no notice the steepness of that wee knoll, where all the soil had been washed down intae the depression? Six inches, ye say? Why, that low-lyin' ground was a veritable lake of mud...a marsh, a quag!"

Dressed in some of Quarry's old clothes, nodding my understanding, I went out and faced him. "So that's how it was."

"That's right. But what *I* dinnae understand: why would the damned creature—that dreadful man, ghost, thing—why would it want tae kill ye? What, even now? Still murderous, even as a revenant? But how could he hope tae benefit frae such a thing?"

At that, I very nearly told him a secret known only to the dead...and now to me. But, since we weren't supposed to know, I simply shook my head and said nothing...

As for those pictures I'd snapped, of Simon Carlisle on Tumble Tor: when the film was developed there was only the bare rock, out of focus and all lopsided. None of which came as any great surprise to me.

And as for my lovely Jennie: well, I've never told her the whole thing. Andrew asked me not to, said there was a danger in people knowing such things. He's probably right. We should remember our departed loved ones, of course we should, but however painful the parting we should also let them go. That is, if and when they *can* go, and if they're in the right place of waiting.

Myself: well, I don't go out on the moor any more, because for one thing I know Old Joe is out there patiently waiting for an accident to set him free. That old tramp, yes, and lord only knows how many others, waiting in the hedgerows at misted crossroads on dark nights, and in remote, derelict houses where they died in their beds before there were telephones, ambulances and hospitals...

❖ ❖ ❖

So then, now I sit in my garden, and as the setting sun begins to turn a few drifting clouds red, I rotate these things in my mind while watching the last handful of seagulls heading south for Brixham harbour. And I think at them: *Ah, but you've missed out on a grand fish supper, you somewhat less than early birds. Your friends set out well over an hour ago!*

Then I smile to myself as I think: *Well, maybe they heard me. Who knows, maybe that flying-ant telepathy of theirs works just as well with people!*

And I watch a jet airplane making clouds as it loses altitude, heading for Exeter Airport. Those ruler-straight trails, sometimes disappearing and sometimes blossoming, fluffing themselves out or pulling themselves apart, drifting on the aerial tides...and waiting?

Small fluffs of cloud: revenant vapour trails waiting for the next jet airplane, perhaps, so that they too can evaporate? I no longer rule out anything.

But I'm very glad my mother died in hospital, not at home. And I *will* have the pool filled in. Either that or we're moving to a house without a pool, and one that's located a lot closer to the hospital.

And when I think of disasters like Pompeii, or Titanic—

—Ah, but I mustn't, I simply mustn't...

THE MAN WHO KILLED
KEW GARDENS

The banks of makeshift air filters were whirring away, working overtime in the concrete ceiling of the great Operations Room, once the basement of the biggest shoe store in central London's Oxford Street. At first the monotony of their massed, whistling hiss was an aggravation—not unlike the subdued howling of an airplane's jet engines coming through the fuselage walls, which if you're subjected to it long enough will eventually turn into white noise—and I had been listening to the air filters for quite some time.

I was there early; I liked to have time to myself, to sit and think before my audience arrived. My audience: the flamers, slashers, poisoners, mulchers, and acid sprayers. An army actually, made up of sections, squads, platoons. I was here in the role of a Commander: to direct and inspire them, warn and forearm them; to issue their orders for the day or, where some of them were headed, for the endless night of underground London.

Why me? Probably because I'd seen the start of it, issued the very first warnings, understood—as best possible—what had happened and was still happening...which made me as good a choice as any, apparently. As a

253

conventional general there's no doubt I would be a dismal failure, but until recently I had been the assistant director at Kew Gardens. Enough said.

Rills of dust, dislodged by the vibration of distant jackhammers, trickled down from the ceiling, were stirred a little by the draft from the air filters. Somewhere up above they were digging out the Green, spraying acid, preparing to lay concrete and gradually turning London grey. *And the sooner the better,* I thought, *but never quickly enough.*

The sound of muted footsteps and the scrape of steel-framed chairs on the gritty floor brought me upright in my seat behind my desk on the podium. Two young men, yawning, gaunt-faced, had seated themselves side by side in the third row of four hundred as yet empty chairs. Early birds, new to the game, they awaited their instructions. Well, let them wait. The hundreds were still to come trickling in.

And not only here but all over England, all over the world. For each city had its volunteer army, and each morning the war started all over again. Indeed, it never stopped, couldn't ever stop, daren't stop. Not if we were to survive. The night shifts were coming off now, and the day shifts—the morning forays—were soon to begin. But never a stranger war than this.

The cities: they were our redoubts, concrete islands floating in an enemy ocean. As for the enemy: there were millions of square miles of him…

My notes were before me; updated every three or four hours during the night as reports from the battle areas came in, they were as current as could be. My job was simply to read them out loud to the army and then send the men out to their battle locations. But not until the troops were gathered here en masse.

Even as I thought that thought, more scraping sounded from the back of the marching ranks of empty chairs as another bunch of early birds adjusted their seats. And more dust came smoking down as the distant jackhammers started up again.

I tapped my microphone's grid and was reassured by its pop and crackle, then sat back. And with time to spare I let myself slump down in my seat a little, let my mind wander, remembering how it all began…

It was the meteorite, for sure. But it was probably more than just that. It may also have been—just *may* have been—what they were doing with the crops: genetically modified food. The scientists, botanists, geneticists, had engineered it so that the green things could fight back; fight disease, weeds, bugs, too much sun, hard rains, and yet still prosper in est soil, growing stronger and giving a better yield. We'd made i them to conquer all of their worst enemies, without taking int that *we* were their worst enemy. We were the ones—men, and th we bred—who *ate* them for God's sake! And now they're eating us.

Genetic modification, yes, and also the meteorite. In fact, mainly the meteorite.

It was a small thing, three and a half inches long, two and a half wide, like a big egg. A lump of pockmarked rock, seared black at the fat end, convoluted like a morel or a brain coral at the thin end. Not a meteorite shower, like in *The Day of the Triffids*, just one small rock. And no one woke up blind, and no one was in any way affected. Not at first, anyway.

But that first year: well, we might as well have *been* blind for all the attention we paid. I remembered it like it was yesterday...

Three years ago; just three years, my God! Two-thirty on an early June morning; a clear starry sky outside my window; something had started me awake. A pistol shot? The echoes of a drum roll quickly fading on the still, small-hours air? Thunder? No, not thunder. No way. So what, then?

I got up, went to the window and opened it wide, looked out and up and away. A vapour trail, curving down out of the stars, was already dispersing, blown on the soft night breeze. A trace of cordite or sulphur stink drifted in the air, also dispersing. And fifty or so yards away, in my next-door neighbour's garden, a thin column of smoke was spiralling up from the rose beds.

Had something crashed? Well obviously, but not an airplane, or it would be visible and there'd be an inferno. Had something fallen off an airplane, perhaps? Or a fragment of space debris, a bit broken off from one of the myriad satellites up there? Or...could it perhaps have been a meteorite?

It had taken me one or two minutes to come fully awake, so that by the time I'd thought all these things through the smoke from my neighbour's garden had thinned to nothing, likewise the vapour trail in the sky and the gunpowder plot smell. And everything seemed back to normal.

Except, of course, it wasn't...

He was called Gordon Sellick, a retired army colonel whose wife had died several years ago, and he lived next door or mainly in his garden...in fact he lived *for* his garden, because that was his life now. But when I say "next door" don't misunderstand me. We were neighbours, but ours were fairly large detached houses, each set in a quarter acre, with long gardens that ran parallel down to the river. A solitary type myself, I enjoyed living in the country a few short miles from my work. Commuting was easy and I didn't have to spend too much time in the cluttered noisy world between gardens, mine and the more extensive, more exotic ones at Kew.

I could see Gordon Sellick at a distance in his garden just about any old time, or close up to talk to on a Friday night in the Olde Horse and Carriage, our village pub at the bend in the river. But this thing from the sky had landed on a Saturday and I wasn't about to wait the week out. Up at eight, I breakfasted and then went round to his place.

He was in the garden, as I'd suspected he would be. And he had found the meteorite.

"So you heard it," he said, beckoning me closer.

"I'd have had to be deaf not to!" I answered. "Is that it?"

Sellick was leaning on his spade in the middle of a bed of beautiful roses, a few in full bloom but many just now budding. At his feet, a small crater was plainly visible, with good dark earth thrown out in typical ray fashion. "Went in about a foot, maybe an inch or so more," he said. And he handed it over, this rock as I've described it, which he'd only just this minute dug out.

"A meteorite," I nodded, brushing dust and dirt off it. "A good job it didn't hit the house. Would have come right through the tiles!"

"Would have been hot, too," he answered. "Gave me a hell of a fright! Rattled the windows like billy-o, but it doesn't seem to have damaged my roses. I'd have been pretty mad about that."

Gordon Sellick was all army. A six-footer in his youth, but beginning to bend a bit now, he still had his curling handlebar moustache and bristling brows—far more hair on his face than above it—and his shiny dome was brown as can be as a result of his interminable gardening. Out in all weathers, ex-Colonel Sellick.

I examined the rock, which was heavy. "This rounded end...fried off and blackened by atmospheric friction." I offered my opinion. "And the pointed end...hmmm! Looks odd." I frowned. "Might be crystalline. Some metallic ore forged in an exploding star, then pitted and patterned in the frozen deeps of space."

One of Sellick's ample white eyebrows went up, in something of surprise I supposed. "So then, you're a bit of a poet—eh, what? Well, can't complain about that, what with my garden and my roses and what all. Roses? Bloody flowers? Why, they'd have laughed me out of the bloody officers mess! Funny the things a man can get up to, when he's on his own and there's bugger all else to do."

He was a lonely one, the old colonel.

"What'll you do with it?" I handed the meteorite back.

He shrugged. "Oh, I'll make a few enquiries. Offer it to a museum. Might even try to sell it. See if they can find any of those Martian bugs in it—eh, what? *Hah!* And if none of that works, I'll sit it in a pot indoors with some of my cactuses."

In fact it went to a museum, into a case behind good thick glass. Best place for it. Better still if it had never arrived here at all...

Shooting stars, comets, meteorites. The way they've shaped this world of ours...it's incredible. And I wonder how many people have thought about it. I look back at all the mass extinctions, at what happened to the dinosaurs, and I wonder.

But for that BIG rock all those millions of years ago, it's even possible that some kind of dinosaur might be lording it in the world right now, living in dinosaur cities, and facing this new unthinkable threat instead of us. Unthinkable in that none of us would ever have thought of it.

But in fact the big rock landed, the dinosaurs were killed off, men evolved, and before you knew it these three kings were following a different kind of shooting star, one that didn't so much shoot as creep across the sky. And didn't *that* turn things around—"eh, what?" I'm told that some eighty per cent of all the world's wars were caused by religion, but not this current conflict, though it's a safe bet there's a babble of religious lunatics out there right now blaming it all on God...

Chairs were scraping again, and had been for some little time. Looking up, I met the massed weary gaze of maybe a fifth of my command— eighty men and youths—drooping where they'd fallen into their chairs. Barely recovered from yesterday's exertions, they slumped there, their legs stretched out before them, their arms hanging limp. But in little more than half an hour's time, ready or not, they'd be joining battle again, trying to avenge the comrades they'd lost yesterday.

Lost comrades, yes.

My mind returned to its wanderings...

I thought of old Sellick and his garden, the day he called me over, maybe six weeks after the meteorite incident, to show me the ivy growing up the bole of a fifty-year-old magnolia.

"What do you make of that?" he said.

But of what? So-called "expert" that I was, that I am, I couldn't see what he was on about, not at first. "The ivy?" I said. "It's a decorative variety, probably an Asian strain of *Hedera helix*, a five-lobed climber that's essentially fragile, and—"

"Six-lobed," he cut in. "Down near the bottom there, last year's growth: five-lobed. But up here, this new growth: each leaf has six lobes. And that's not all. The outer lobes on each leaf have tiny hooks to fasten to the tree. It can grow a damn sight faster if it doesn't have to root itself first. And it's not so bloody fragile, either! This is a mutant strain, or I'm not an ex-Guards colonel. Eh, what?"

I almost laughed, half-laughed, but managed to hold it back while making a mental note to consult the ledgers at Kew. There would be notes on this one, for sure. But still—and perhaps a little flippantly—I couldn't resist saying, "Colonel, you'll be telling me next there are four-leaved clovers on your lawn!"

"Yes." He nodded, deadly serious. "And quite a few with six leaves, too. Eh, what? I've been preserving them for posterity, pressing them under 'flora' in my old gardening dictionary, for at least a fortnight now!" Then he showed me his right forearm: a fresh red scratch deep enough to leave a scar. "See this? Got it from my 'thornless' roses—by God!" He scowled at the sore red gouge. "And what do you think of that? Eh, what?"

I scratched my head. "Something in the pollen? GM rapeseed maybe? I remember they were experimenting with it last year in a field not a quarter of a mile away. Some people from Friends of the Earth and a slew of other so-called eco-friendly groups were down there, ripping it out as quickly as they could plant it. But they didn't get it all. The police were there dragging them away, putting a stop to it. And then, just lately, there's been this problem with the bees."

"Eh, bees?" the colonel queried, somewhat absentmindedly. "Never bother with the little buggers. Eh, what? Got enough on my hands with the greenfly, sod 'em all! I did get stung once, though." Frowning, he sat down in one of his favourite places: a rustic oak bench where it circled the magnolia. And resting his back against the bole, he squinted up at me and asked, "So what's that you were saying? Something about the bees? Come to think of it, I haven't seen a bee in quite a while."

"That would be about right," I told him. "It seems there's something of a scarcity. The local beekeepers are complaining that the workers haven't been making it back to their hives."

Sellick clenched a military jaw, narrowed his eyes, gloomed out over his quarter acreage. "It's not right," he growled. "It doesn't feel the same. This year—I don't know—it's like it isn't my garden at all! Ever since that bloody meteorite! Well, bollocks to it! One way or the other, I'll get my garden back." And starting to his feet: "It's Friday. Do you fancy a pint?"

And I did, so we took the river path and made our way down to the Olde Horse and Carriage...

The following Monday I spent an hour looking for Sellick's ivy in the manuals at Kew Gardens. I never did find it, though. And I never will. It simply isn't there, never will be unless I name it and register it myself; name it after old Sellick, perhaps?

If ever I get the chance.

If we win this war with the rest of the damned foliage: the ivies, roses, and clovers—and the fungi, mosses, and ferns—these and every other botanical order and species that was ever catalogued, all of them changed now and forever changing. Every damned one of them. Hundreds, thousands of seething, continuously mutating species; most of them hostile to animal life, just as animal life was once inimical to them...

My mind went sideways again. Meteorites and shooting stars.

Those previously "crazy" people who believed that life came to Earth on meteorites or in the tails of comets. I mean, that was something I'd *never* been able to take on board! Here we had a world of soft oceans and rocks worn down into soils that were simply screaming to be inhabited; an oxygen rich atmosphere and free running rivers of fresh water; black smokers pouring their chemicals into the depths of soupy seas, and lifebuilding ribonucleic acids galore. Was it any wonder life happened here?

And then on the other hand we had this "ridiculous" theory of maggots from Mars and other places: space-rocks falling out of the skies to seed the predawn Earth with life. That was what I couldn't get my head around: rocks, without air, water, any-damned-thing at all, cruising the universe's most deadly environment, outer space, with these dormant seeds clinging to them. How in hell did those seeds get stuck on the meteorites, or in the comet's tail, in the first place? Where did they come from?

And that's not the end of it. For then this chunk of interstellar debris comes hurtling down at tens of thousands of mph, gets burned black from atmospheric friction—without damaging the seeds, of course—and slams down with sledgehammer force, releasing, but not hurting, its passenger/s. For me, that just wasn't logical. Not then, anyway.

No, for then I'd believed in Gaia, Mother Earth, Ma Nature, the planet perceived as a living entity. And that was where I'd made my mistake, me and thousands of others. We'd been thinking on a less than cosmic scale—indeed a microscopic scale—that was typical of human egocentricity; thinking in terms of a tiny little mudball Earth-nature, and almost completely ignoring the fact of the great big universe out there. Much like the Inquisition, we'd considered our world as the "Center of Everything", when the center of everything was an entire Big Bang away back at the beginning. What we should have been thinking wasn't Gaia but Galactica, or at the very least Megagaia: not Earth-mother but Galaxy- or Universe-mother.

A nature through all space and time that's just waiting for the right conditions. Planets form around a star; they cool; Ma Nature—Universal Nature—is waiting. She tried before, but her babies got burned up. No problem; she has plenty more; it's just a matter of hitting the right place at the right time. For after all, how many dandelion seeds land on rocks or in deserts or oceans? A very hit-and-miss process, true: trial and error, but they get there in the end. And time is on Megagaia's side.

So eventually the time is right; another rock falls out of the sky, slams down on the surface of this entirely conjectural planet. There are the makings of life on the new world, perhaps even the first amoebic stirrings on the fringes of soupy oceans, and that's what Universal Ma Nature is looking for. That's what she does. She assists. She releases the meteorite's gasses, or whatever it is that those bloody things contain: the catalysts that form chains in the RNA, that bring about life or—where it already exists—accelerate its evolution!

It was guesswork, of course, science fiction, but…just suppose I was right? And now I'm not thinking some conjectural world but Earth again. If I was on the right track, then maybe this wasn't the first time this had happened. Back then, after the big lizards and their killer rock, maybe there was another space pebble, something that balanced things up again, brought about mutations, caused life to continue. The dinosaur survivors became birds, and a certain branch of scared little mammal creatures became monkeys and then men.

And why not? I mean, they're still looking for the missing link. And maybe I can tell them where to find it: behind glass in a museum in a town not far out of London...

Two and a half years ago, that might have been when I poisoned Kew—but accidentally, of course. Anyway, Kew wasn't the only thing that was dying. Lots of things died.

I remember a certain story, a piece of fiction. (I used to read scads of macabre stuff, anything from E. A. Poe to Stephen King.) This one was by an American author whose name I've since forgotten. But he was very good. Coincidentally, it concerned a colour out of space, something that crashed out of the sky on a meteorite. It seems especially relevant now...though nowadays I can't think why I chuckled at the idea of malevolent, shining mutant skunk cabbages! Or I can...but it no longer strikes me as funny...

It was the last Saturday of summer. I had been down to the Olde Horse and Carriage last night, but old man Sellick hadn't shown up. That was peculiar; the colonel liked his Friday night pint. Something else that was rather odd: the pub's usually excellent menu wasn't nearly up to scratch. Meat, but no fresh vegetables...only frozen ones. Fish, but no homemade chips. And then, on overhearing a few snatches of conversation from a group of disappointed, would-be diners, I couldn't help but feel troubled:

"Salad days? Forget it! Tried buying tomatoes or a lettuce just lately? Rotten soil, no rain, no spuds...not that *taste* like spuds, anyway!" And: "My apples are blistered to hell and full of yellow shit. Taste like it, too. I caught some village kids scrumping in the orchard. Next thing, they're curled up in the grass crying and puking their guts out. Poor little buggers, I didn't have the heart to give them a hard time. But I'll give you odds they were shitting their pants all the way home!" And: "Don't talk to me about apples. Last year, mine were eaten rotten from the inside out by wasps. This year I'd be pleased just to see a bloody wasp!"

Trouble with the veg, yes, but all very local. The restaurants were shipping veg in! Blame it on the weather or something...or something.

So then it was Saturday morning and I gave old man Sellick a call. His phone rang but the colonel didn't answer. Yet from my upstairs balcony I could plainly make out something of him—the odd patch of suntanned skin, tatty jeans, and stained white shirt—stirring under the foliage in his garden. Not fifteen feet from his open door, he must surely hear the phone ringing—I could just about hear it myself—but he wasn't making any attempt to answer it.

Something had to be wrong, so I went round to his place and into his garden to enquire personally.

I couldn't believe how quiet the garden was as I approached down the crazy-paved path. No birds—not a one—and I truly missed the buzzing of bees. As to why I hadn't noticed anything before, I mean in my own garden: that's hard to say. I had been busier than usual, putting in a lot of overtime at Kew. There'd been a great many queries from the public about odd hybrid species; many specimens had arrived, been isolated, were being studied by various botanical specialists. Maybe that's the answer: I'd had too much on my plate to notice what was going on in my own or Sellick's garden, the weirdness that was happening.

But the old boy had noticed it, certainly; and right there and then on that garden path, suddenly I could feel it, too…I felt the strangeness, like an alien cloud hanging over everything. Oh, it was very obvious. And the colonel had had it dead to rights the day he'd told me, "It's not right—doesn't feel the same—not like *my* garden at all!" Dead to rights, yes.

But where was Sellick? I jumped twelve inches when a hedge cutter burst into clattering mechanical life. And there he was, the colonel: under a small mountain of *Clematis vitalba*, traveller's joy, where his garden shed had used to be. Hell no, where it was now—a considerable wooden structure—but buried deep in the clematis! What in the name of…? Why had he let it get so rank, so out of hand?

Anyway, as a great swath of it was sliced through and toppled to the ground, he saw me framed in the gap and switched off his machine. Then, stumbling over a heap of cut growth as dense as box hedge, finally he confronted me. Grimy, dishevelled, and with sweat rivering his dusty face, he panted a hoarse, resentful greeting and continued, "Meteorite? No, that was more than just any old meteorite. It was the green hand of God, advising us to go easy on the GM stuff! And for the last fortnight I've been fighting this…this green jungle that you bloody scientists…and *botanists*," (he literally spat that last word in my face,) "have conspired to make of my garden!"

"Colonel, I—" I began.

But waving his hedge cutter at me until I fell back a little, the old boy almost literally cut me off. "My roses are far bigger, and more beautiful than ever before," he snarled, "but their thorns are inches long, and for all that I keep trying I can't dead-head 'em. You know how you're supposed to nip their withered heads off to encourage new growth? Well, these things are like bloody rubber: they stretch but they won't break. And as for encouragement—I swear they don't need any! What? They don't even like being touched!" He showed me his arms, his new wounds criss-crossing a great many old ones.

"Gordon—"

"And look at this!" He hurled a bloodied arm to point at his shed where it leaned under the weight of rampant clematis. "Would you believe—*could* you believe—I cut this lot back just three days ago? You're lucky with your garden, which I'll admit I've long despised: all those flagged paths between segregated beds, more like a piece of fancy tatting than a garden proper! Lucky? Oh, yes: because you don't have half the damned greenery that I've got! Eh, what? Why, right now you haven't a tenth of it! And as for the grass...now tell me, what do you make of the bloody grass?"

"Gordon," I tried yet again. "I mean, am I to be allowed to speak, or what?"

He didn't answer, just stood there glaring at me, or if not at me at the world in general; stood there with his chest heaving and the sweat of his uneven fight running down his neck and staining his shirt.

But now that I was able to answer him I could find nothing immediate to say, except: "Grass? What on earth are you talking about?" Where we were standing there was a little grass—a few tufts coming up between the chinks in a small paved patio area—but apart from the fact that it was coarse and needed tending it looked normal enough to me.

"You haven't noticed?" He stared hard at me, then relaxed a little. "Ah, no, but then you wouldn't, would you? You've not got enough of the bloody stuff, not in your pallid little horticulturist's paradise!"

Now I was annoyed and told him so. "You're taking all your anger out on me," I said, "insulting me. But I didn't cause any of this and I don't much care for your accusations. Oh, I agree something is wrong with the vegetation—but the problem isn't special to you and your '*bloody*' precious garden! Weird looking plants, seeds, and fungi are arriving at Kew daily, and there's been some strange stuff happening in gardens all over the southeast. It seems we're right in the middle of this…this *infestation*, whatever it is. And it could well turn out that you're right and our extraterrestrial visitor was its source. I can't guarantee that, mind you. But I do care about what's happening; while on the other hand I *don't* much care for this tongue-lashing from a cranky old soldier! God, I only came round to see if you were okay! I missed you at the pub last night."

At that, whatever sort of fury—or funk?—he was in, the colonel snapped out of it at once. "Good Lord!" he said. "Oh my good God! Eh, what? But that wasn't like me at all! No, not one little bit. Not to a friend. And you've been a very good friend. But…" He gave a helpless, frustrated shrug. "It's the garden. I mean, it's really getting me down. I'm sorry. What more can I say or do?"

"Well, for a start, you might want to flush it out of your system!" I told him. "And first off: what's all this about the grass? Yes, as I've already allowed, there seem to be some serious problems with all sorts of greenery, but to the best of my knowledge no one's so far mentioned anything about grass!"

"Come," he beckoned. And as we walked, skirting the sprawling undergrowth—the rose tangles, and the overgrown brambles that not too long ago were cultivated blackberries—he inquired, "You don't have a lawn as such, do you?"

"No," I told him. "At the front I have a wide gravel drive, ornamental pools and fountains, two chestnut trees over clover, and floral borders—all of it walled. At the back: well, it's pretty much as you described it, except it too is walled, protected. As for grass: grass means work, and it isn't especially interesting…er, from my point of view, that is." (I didn't want to start him off ranting again.)

"But I *do* have a lawn," he said, "or I used to."

"Used to?"

"Just here," he nodded, grimly, "to the side of the house."

But as I went to turn the corner he caught my arm. And: "Go careful, my friend," he told me, very quietly, and in that same moment I thought I felt a shudder running through his hand into my arm. "I think we should go very carefully!"

I frowned at him, glanced around the corner of the house, and saw little or nothing that might be considered extraordinary or dangerous. A square, flagged path surrounded a lawn some ten by ten yards; and central in the lawn a white plastic table supported a floral parasol and was flanked by a pair of folding chairs. After a moment, I looked at the colonel enquiringly.

He gave an impatient nod of his head and said: "The grass—look at the grass."

The grass...was green, even, and looked in good health. I couldn't understand why he'd let it grow so long—a good eight or nine inches—but other than that...

"I cropped it last Thursday," he told me then. "Just a few days ago; cropped it as short as a bloody billiard table! *Nothing* normal grows that fast or that even. Every single blade is the same length. No meadow, no golf course or bowling green was ever so uniform. And there's something else. Something really—I don't know—macabre?"

He stepped round the corner of the house onto the path, and I followed in his footsteps, urging him: "Well, go on—what is it?"

"You see that mound," he said. "Near the far corner there?"

The ground had a small but definite hump where he was pointing. We followed the path to the corner in question, and as the colonel halted, crouched, and stared hard at the mound, I said, "Yes, I see it. What of it?"

"Look closer."

I did, and saw something of what he was getting at. Deep in the grass, the last six inches and scraggy tuft of a cat's tail stuck up out of the ground. And a few inches away, a furry paw, claws extended, was also visible.

"You buried a dead cat there," I said. "But not nearly deep enough."

"I did no such thing." He shook his head. "I buried nothing there—but the grass did! Let me tell you about it:

"Yesterday, I was battling with the garden, as usual. Hell, it's *my* bloody garden, after all! But working late, I was just too tired to bother going down to the pub. As the shadows lengthened I went upstairs; I would have an early night, and get an early start this morning. But looking from the window up there, I saw this manky old moggy come out of the shrubbery. I really hate cats because they piss on every-damn-thing in the garden! Anyway, this one appeared to be on his last legs: he was stiff and scraggy; his eyes bulged; he could hardly walk. But he made it this far before collapsing. I thought: 'Well, in the morning he'll either have moved on or he'll be dead—eh, what? And if the latter, then I'll bury him.'

"But this morning...I didn't have to bury him. The grass had done it for me." He nodded at the mound. "I found him like that, which was when I began attacking the foliage again. Damn it all, I refuse to be intimidated by bloody greenery!"

I shook my head. "Gordon—" (I rarely called him by his forename, though he'd years ago invited its use) "—the grass couldn't possibly have 'buried' this cat. He's actually *under* the soil—most of him, anyway."

"Under the soil, yes," he answered, "but very shallow, as you've already pointed out." The colonel's voice had fallen to a mere murmur, as if he were talking to himself rather than to me. "And there's a reason for that, why it's so shallow."

"A reason?" Truth to tell, I was beginning to wonder about the old boy's reason. He probably sensed it or heard something in my voice and frowned at me.

"Eh, what? You think I'm losing it, do you? Well, just you step back a few paces and yank some of that grass there. Go on, pull a few blades up by their roots."

I did as he suggested. The grass came out easily enough in my hand, and the roots were white.

The old boy nodded and stepped onto the grass close to the mound. And he too pulled grass...from directly over the spot where the cat was buried. Then, again nodding his head—knowingly now—he held the tuft out for my inspection. At which I drew back from him, wrinkling my nose in disgust.

The roots of the grass in his hand were red! And:

"You're the botanist," he said, very quietly. "Now tell me, what kind of weird morphology is it that uses blood as chlorophyll? What kind of bloody vampire is this—eh, what? I mean, how does it photosynthesize *that*, for God's sake?"

I could only shake my head...but I glanced hastily down, to make sure that I was still on the path.

"And look," he went on. "Look at my feet."

He was wearing tough wellington boots and had been standing up to his lower calves in the grass by the burial mound for two or three minutes, no more. But already the grass had curled inward, over his boots, and as he moved his feet the grass broke, so that his feet carried some of the severed blades back to the path with him.

Where he had been standing, the earth was almost bare, the grass *visibly* drawing down into the soil. It was like trying to watch the movement of the minute hand on the clock in the village clock tower—the motion was barely discernible—but the grass *was* moving!

I backed away down the path and tried to say, "Gordon," but all that came out was a gurgle. At my second try I managed, and said, "Gordon, it's time I made a few phone calls. In fact it's long since past the time! So if you'll excuse me now..."

He nodded and said, "And me, I must get back to killing all of this damned stuff. I'll turn it all to compost, start again. That's what I'll do— eh, what?"

"Whatever," I told him. And then I got out of there...

The near-distant jackhammers, silent for a while, resumed their clamour, their vibrations stronger than previously. Jarred back to the present—as the generators coughed and electric lights flickered, and rills of dust jitterbugged down from the ceiling—I gave a small start, blinked once or twice, let my audience, my troops, float back into focus.

There, seated in groups, I saw about half of them: some two hundred men, and as many still to come. They'd been arriving in a steady trickle, quietly thinking their private thoughts, automatically assembling with other members of their sections and platoons. Clad in grey coveralls and carrying grey, protective gloves, they were grey as can be and gaunt-faced to a man.

I recognized one of them sitting central in the front row. Yesterday he'd been squad leader of a spore patrol out towards Watford. The fern forest had been making big inroads, mutating as it came. Ignoring the season and propagating like crazy, it was hurling its spores before it, "galloping" over the fields, making exploratory forays up roadside verges and central reservations, and taking root wherever there was soil. Yesterday the winds had been fanning north-west out of London: ideal for the flamers. Whoever could have foreseen or imagined the day would arrive when we'd be burning our fields, our woodlands? And not only the Green but whatever doomed, terrified species of wildlife remained in it.

So there he sat, this squad leader: his hair crisped, hands gnarled and blistered from the heat of the flamethrowers, weary arms a-dangle. Now and then his thin frame would shudder, prelude to wracking fits of coughing. All of that burning must have leached the air from his lungs and seared them to so much blackened leather. So I thought—

—Until, once again, my thoughts went elsewhere...

Intelligence. We believed it was the province—the exclusive province— of the vertebrate mammalia. Well, okay, the cephalopods had the octopus, and two or three other orders had their individual geniuses, but on the whole it was the mammalia, and especially Man. But how does one measure intelligence in species other than or alien to the human variety? And when, at what point, does it take the next step up and *become* intelligence as opposes to mere instinct?

Consider the Venus fly trap. By what extremes of evolutionary process did this plant develop spiked, spring-loaded leaves to capture its victims? Or take for instance the squirting cucumber, a Mediterranean plant that squirts a weak acid at you if you brush against it. Actually, it's simply ejecting its seeds; but still we have to assume that a dose of acid in the eyes is a warning to wild animals or livestock, to stop them trampling on the plant. To me it's simply another example of weird vegetable instinct. And what if evolution was to take the next step up?

Well, thanks to the meteorite—and to a degree to genetic modification—plant evolution has taken and is taking the next step up. And the next, and the next...

After that episode with Sellick's grass, back in my own garden—my walled, almost entirely work-free, neatly laid out "horticulturist's paradise", as he had called it—I went from plot to plot, suspicious as a caged budgie in a house with cats. It seemed the walls might have saved me from any immediate influx. Well they probably had, from most of it. But not entirely.

I found several magnolia corms (I believe that's the word: those green pods that carry the tree's seeds) scattered in the flower beds parallel with the colonel's garden. This had never happened before; the magnolia's seed pods are fairly heavy and usually fall straight to the ground. Moreover, the old fellow's tree was well away from my wall, much deeper into his garden.

So then, had there been a storm which I hadn't especially noticed? I didn't think so. Or (laughingly) had the tree found a way to propel its would-be progeny abroad? Outrageous! And I gave that last thought only momentary consideration. But nevertheless, it was very late in the season to be discovering such as these in my garden, or any garden for that matter. Likewise the dandelions.

I had always been scrupulous with weeds however pretty some may be, and while admittedly I hadn't had much time for gardening recently,

I'd never failed to pull dandelions whenever they attempted another insidious invasion. But it appeared obvious I must have missed some, and the ones I'd missed were beauties!

Tall, thick-stemmed, with flowers twice their regular size and as golden as the sun, there were specimens in almost every plot. Some of them were into the seed phase of their existence, once again very late in the season... didn't these things know when to stop growing? Even as I stood frowning at them a breeze came up, snatched a puff of parasols into the air, carried them higher and higher, until they whirled away to the south-east. I found myself wondering where they'd land and try to take root:

Kent? East Sussex? The English Channel? (No luck there!)

Or perhaps some place much farther afield, such as France? Belgium? Germany? And for some reason that galvanized me, sent me hurrying indoors to do my telephoning...

I called Kew, David Johnson, who I knew was on duty that weekend. He was an old acquaintance of mine, an expert on Mediterranean flora who had studied with me twenty years previously.

"Hi," he said, a friendly voice coming over the wires; and yet there was an excited or nervous edge to it. "What can I do for you on this beautiful Saturday morning, when you should be out on the river—or in the pub, or your garden, or anywhere except where I am?"

"In my garden?" I said. "No, I don't think so. In fact I'd rather be any-where *but* there! I was already there this morning—and in the garden next door—and I didn't much like either one of them!"

"Ah, you've been neglecting things, right?"

"No, I've been noticing things."

"Oh yes? Well, me too. In fact I've just noticed something—or rather experienced something—that gave me quite a shock! Funny, really...and yet not."

There it was once again: that edge in David's voice, more properly an unfamiliar quavering that was quite out of character. And despite that there were things I must tell him, I was suddenly interested in what he patently wanted to tell me. For which reason:

"What's been going on?" I asked him. "What have you been up to?"

"Well, I'm on my own today," he began. "Gloria Hamilton is supposed to be in, too, but she's come down with something, so there's only me and the security guards; and of course they're doing their rounds."

"Sounds lonely," I said. "In fact you make it sound positively spooky! So what's this: a haunted greenhouse story?"

"Or something," he answered. And after a moment's silence: "Tell me, do you remember that old myth about mandrakes—how they scream when you pull them out of the ground?"

I felt my blood cooling as I answered, "I know the legend, yes." And I was almost afraid to ask, "What of it?"

"Well, I was in the Mediterranean section—my domain, the hothouse, as I call it—and you know something? That old myth is true! I yanked what I thought was a diseased mandrake—"

"And it screamed?" I beat him to it. And: "David, listen," I continued, in all earnestness. "No, I'm not a bit surprised. I suspect we haven't been nearly as careful or attentive as we should have been, and not only at Kew. By now that entire place is probably contaminated, not to mention the rest of the south-east!"

"What on earth are you...?" he began to ask, but yet again I cut him short:

"No, be quiet, I want you to listen: is Director Hawkworth still in America? I thought so. Which means I'm in charge, the man responsible. So: do you have a staff list there? Telephone numbers, addresses? Good, because I want you to start calling them, *all* of them, and get them in for an O-Group first thing Monday morning."

"An O-Group?" I could almost see the puzzled expression I knew he must be wearing. "Don't you mean a general meeting?"

"No," I told him. "I mean an Orders Group, as in military terminology. You thought a screaming mandrake was odd, David? Well yes, I have to agree. But I suspect that's just one small example of this thing, one small part. As for the whole of it: it's war, David. I do believe it's war!"

Then I had tried to get on to the Ministry of Agriculture and Fisheries. Pointless! Ridiculous! A complete waste of time and effort! At almost midday on a Saturday, no one was there. When I did reach them on Monday morning...they already knew about it.

As for the woman I spoke to, not the Minister himself (no, of course not!) but an underling: I sensed she was stalling me, hoping I would go away, just like her bureaucratic superior and a handful of lesser bean-counters in his office must have been hoping "the problem" would go away.

And you know, I might have expected it? For of course they were the ones who'd sanctioned all those GM experiments in the first place! And they probably believed the experiments were at the "root" of it—

—Which I have to admit was what I myself still believed, at least at that moment in time. It was my Earth Mother faith, etcetera, which, despite Sellick's meteorite, kept obstructing any positive acceptance of a then inchoate, at best unresolved Galactica or Universe Mother theory.

But the evidence was mounting, and the mountain was like a Welsh coal mine's slag tip in the rain: ready to slip and slide and bury us all...

And again the jackhammers, reminding me of where I was. Me and my audience, my army; our eyes turning up almost as one to look at the concrete ceiling, narrowing to avoid the last few trickles of loose dust.

Up there in Oxford Street or nearby, and all over London, men were clearing the vegetation—the remaining green areas, traffic islands, verges, decorative plots—right down to their raw concrete foundations. Then they'd spray sulphuric acid into the gaping holes to kill any roots, fill them with debris, finally level everything and seal their work with fresh concrete.

And as for the parks: God-only-knows how they were dealing with the parks!

While down here in this briefing room the small army of men waiting for me to speak must be thinking much the same thing as I was: that the city we'd known—the whole world we'd known—was no more and might even be gone forever...

Two or three rows of chairs remained almost empty. I looked at my watch—fifteen, maybe twenty minutes to go. How long had I been here? Some thirty or so minutes? Was that all? I supposed it must be. But then, memory is like that: past events, especially unpleasant ones, hurry across your mind like ripples over a pond on a windy day, eager to get done. Or rather, *you* are eager to get done with them.

I spoke into my microphone, but softly:

"You're on duty in about twenty minutes, after the briefing—for what that's worth—which I promise I'll keep brief. So we're able to give the latecomers a few minutes grace. That being so, I'll ask you to curb your impatience. I mean, I appreciate how *eager* you must be to get on with things, but we'll wait awhile longer anyway..."

That last was my idea of black humour, if only to calm the nerves and alleviate the tension, but no one laughed. Who could blame them? Not a single man-jack of them was "eager" to get on with any-damned-thing. This wasn't a conventional war, and they weren't conventional warriors. Those of them who were beginning to fidget were doing so not out of eagerness but a perfectly natural fear of the unknown.

Somewhere at the back of the basement a door clanged open and a messenger, a crippled kid whose legs had been shrivelled to useless twigs by mutant nettles, came speeding down a central aisle in his wheelchair. Clamped between his teeth he bore a sheet of paper. Even as I stood up, went down on one knee on the podium to take the note from him, I knew what it would be: a list of those who wouldn't be joining us, those who'd failed to make it through the night, injured or murdered in their own homes while protecting themselves and their families.

As the kid spun his chair about face and went off back up the aisle, I glanced at the typed sheet, saw that I was right, bulldog-clipped the list to the notes I would be reading in a few minute's time.

But before that I let my mind drift again, a sort of guilty "if only I..." trip back in time. A futile exercise really, for even back then it had probably been far too late to do anything about anything...

I think I may have said something somewhere about killing Kew. Actually, I don't think I killed Kew at all. It's just part of this guilt thing I seem to have developed, which I think began after the police contacted me. Contacted me? Well, it was something more than a mere contact.

It was probably the Min. of Ag. & Fish who put the police on to me, to sideline, marginalize and shut me up, I imagine; me and the rest of the staff at Kew. And at first those estimable officers of the law were pretty stiff with us, with me in particular.

Was it possible, they had wanted to know, that I'd smuggled something foreign and illegal out of Kew to give to the colonel or to grow in my own garden? Surely I was aware that the casual introduction of exotic strains into our finely balanced ecology was a serious offence? Just twelve years ago we had had mad cow disease; hadn't that been enough of a warning not to go messing with nature? What was I attempting to do, sabotage the ecology? Destroy the vegetation and crops that our populace, animals and wildlife lived on?

But then I reminded them about the local GM problem they'd dealt with some eighteen months ago. I told them that if memory served me well it had been they, the police themselves, who had stopped those Friends of the Earth people who had only been trying to avoid this sort of problem in the first place. And there was something else they should take into account: the meteorite that had landed next door. As for myself: I was merely a botanist, a scientist, a man with a conscience who respected the law and knew his responsibilities. Did they really think I would be smuggling forbidden botanical material out of Kew to ingratiate myself with a well known local eccentric? And if they did think so, then why didn't they question the colonel himself? And what items did they think I might have smuggled anyway? There was no more *Cannabis indica* at Kew Gardens than in any one of a thousand window boxes in Kensington! And anyway, wasn't it entirely legal now?

And so, eventually, I convinced them of my innocence.

At that time...well of course I played the meteorite card very carefully. For in light of my former belief—in a Gaia as opposed to a Universal Nature—I still wasn't one hundred per cent convinced of what I suspected *might* be going on here. And as for the police: I didn't for a moment think that these very down-to-earth law officers were ready to subscribe to a Galactica theory—

—Not just then, anyway...

Through the autumn and into winter, events seemed to slow down a little. Contra the initial suspicion and police enquiries, I had taken a six-lobed leaf *from* Sellick's Ivy (as I'd named it) *in* to Kew to have the real experts look it over. And three days later I was told that the leaf was as fresh as ever; it seemed it didn't want to die! But there was so much going on at Kew at that time—so many peculiar specimens had come in, mostly from within a twenty mile radius of my home in Surrey—and so much work was being done on them—that I simply lost track of the thing, stopped asking after it.

But guilty? For taking that single leaf in? No, the poison was already there in the guise of all those mutant species; my guilt lay in refusing to convert to Galactica! In that...and in the fact that I'm a botanist in name only.

There, I've admitted it. And therein lies my guilt: in not having been able to recognize and accept a seedling from space when I was shown one. Oh, I had my qualifications, achieved by sheer hard work and good fortune—by learning things one day and forgetting them the next, after the examinations—but my leanings led elsewhere. My forte was seen to be administration, hence my "exalted" position. And in that position I should have pushed and fought and done more. But as I've already stated, I believe the war was lost before we even started to fight back, lost on the morning that damned thing crashed down in old Colonel Sellick's garden.

So where was I? Ah, yes: the winter, two years ago. And the months passing by, and season following season…

But if the winter had slowed things down, the spring accelerated them almost beyond belief! So that this time when the police called me in it was to act as their local expert!

At last the government had surrendered to increasing public concern and pressure. MAF and their GM experiments had been accused, found guilty without trial, and thrown to the wolves; and as possible saviours of the situation, the botanists had become the new elite. Even then it had been only a "situation", not a full-blown disaster, and despite that I and a handful of others at Kew and similar institutes had been given a free hand, still we were seen by many as nothing more than scaremongers.

In May a resurgent MAF issued a statement: their "experts" were certain that given time, perhaps a year, the alien effects would be "diluted by absorption", or some such claptrap. To the best of my knowledge no one believed them, and rightly so. And all GM experiments were banned worldwide, irrevocably, now and forever.

Well, and it might have had something to do with GM—might *just* have—but mainly it was Sellick's meteorite. By then they had cut it open; it could be seen that it was most definitely a thing of "alien" or universal nature, spawn of Megagaia.

There were chambers inside: a honeycomb of minute chambers, connected by microscopic tubes to the outer surface. Heat, friction with Earth's atmosphere, would have caused any materials—liquids, gases—that were inside to expand, would have driven the living plasma along the tubules under pressure. And moments before impact the pressure would have shattered a brittle heat-shield sheath, releasing—

—All hell on Earth, as it turns out...

A cold breeze blew on my mind, sending the ripples on my mental pond fleeing ever faster. Memories that in the main didn't want to be remembered surfaced, fragmented like confetti shapes in a kaleidoscope, reformed into new, even less acceptable pictures.

In June something macabre. I was called to a local cemetery where the police had roped off a twenty foot perimeter around a family plot: mother, father, and small girl child, victims of a bad traffic accident. They had been buried just five days ago, but already the three graves had sprouted huge fungi, covering them with a canopy of thick fleshy parasols. Mushrooms were my department; I knew more about fungi than anything else in the botanical world. These were boletus, but mutated of course.

Boletus satanus, yes: "Satan's mushroom...poisonous when raw." Or in this case just pure poison.

Whereas the more common variety—the original variety—was rarely more than eight or nine inches across the cap, these *un*common growths were up to two or three feet across and leaned outwards from clumps so tightly packed that it was difficult to see the borders of the plot they were shading...in which their fat, barrel-shaped stipes were rooted. And they issued a sickly sweet stench promoting dizziness and nausea in anyone standing too close to them. Several relatives of the deceased were present, stretched out moaning on a gravel path, being looked after by a doctor in a gas mask. The police were wearing masks, too.

The doctor, a good distance from this abnormality, offered me his mask; I put it on and was approaching the graves when a man, probably another relative, came staggering down the lanes between plots. He was green, looked ill, had vomit on his shirt and carried an axe. "Bloody bastard *things*!" he gasped, breaching the cordon.

Then the smell, the alien scent, got to him. He went to his knees, choking, and the axe fell from his hand, the flat of its blade thumping against an outer stipe, one of the fat pink mushroom stems. Then the horror:

The skin of the cap less than twelve inches from the fallen man's face peeled back; a sphincter appeared, opened, hosed out a jet of some vile ichor.

The man screamed, shot upright, stumbled away hissing and frothing. His face was melting! He crashed to the ground, stone dead!

The stench must have increased tenfold...anyone not wearing a gas mask was driven almost physically back...the doctor cried, "My God! Oh God! *Oh God!* Cadaverine, it can only be!"

I dragged him away, helped him to sit, said, "Cadaverine?"

"That's...what...it...*smelt* like!" he said, shudderingly, looking at me with streaming eyes, his mouth sucking at air that was at least a little cleaner. "Cadaverine: *the loathsome juices that ferment in corpses!*"

We called in a spray truck, turned everything to slush with twenty gallons of fungicide, then sprayed the whole area with a fine sulphuric acid mist.

And while all that was going on—thinking of the boletus, of what they must be feeding on—I found myself a place to be sick behind someone's mausoleum. Even back there I had no lack of company; before I was done the doctor and one of the policemen had joined me...

In July the French closed the Channel Tunnel and banned all imports from the United Kingdom...well, what else was new? Remembering my dandelion seeds, however—not to mention an entire year's contact of one sort or another—it was too little, too late. In August the Germans embargoed France, and a week later, right across Europe, everyone else was forbidding contact with everyone else.

Until then America had been just a little complacent, distant, casual; then, suddenly, she was hit! The wheat, barley and maize—all the cereal crops—infected, poisoned by the same disease or "condition". And worse to come: a three-hundred-mile wide cloud of lethal, choking pollen and granular dust drifting east and south-east from the vast cereal "prairies", taking out entire towns and cities in its darkening path. Quincy, Chicago, Logansport, Lafayette and Bloomington...all gone. While fifty per cent of the population in the trapesium of Nashville, Pittsburgh, and the Appalachians was evacuated by presidential order into territory east of the Great Lakes. As for the other fifty per cent: they defied the order, stayed and faced death.

Once again the sleeping giant had been awakened, only this time there was no one to hit out at.

By mid-October millions of sheep were dead in New Zealand, the paddy fields were smoking alkaline swamps across China and the Far East, the

Australian Aborigines had wisely chosen to go walkabout, but no longer in the bush...now they did it in the desert, the only safe place. For now, at least...

Then it was winter again, but you would hardly know it. The weather was mutating along with the flora! Climatic change accelerated by what was happening to the green stuff, by weird new greenhouse gases. But at least the winter gave us a much-needed break, enabling our retreat into the towns and cities, allowing us to regroup, try to sort out some kind of defence. These mass evacuations were like scenes from one of the Great Wars, except there were no tanks in the streets, just tanks of herbicide and acid, and no distant rumbles of man-made thunder. (No, allow me to correct myself...we did in fact bomb several forests, which only served to spread it that much faster.)

And finally it was "spring"—last spring, perhaps *the* last spring—by which time all Mankind was under siege.

But enough, my mind was almost numb, memories merging, the ripples blurring into a froth on my mental pond. And yet a last few scenes continued to surface, despite that they were things I really didn't want to remember...

In April of this last year, months after the evacuations, old man Sellick called me at Kew. Most of the land-lines were down (the rampant vines and ivies) but he had retained my cellphone number from the old days. Even so he was lucky to get through; the atmospherics were that bad.

"You're still at home?" I could scarcely credit it. Just a day or two before what was to have been his forced evacuation, he'd told me he was heading north to his sister in Edinburgh.

"Yes," came his reply, almost drowned in static. "I fooled 'em, stayed on. Surrender? Me? No, *no*! Out of the question! Eh, what? But I've had it now. I'm tired. Can't win. So then...I know it's a tall order, but is there any chance you can get me out of here?"

"I'll do what I can," I said. "But I can't promise. You're deep in the heart of it—the *very* heart of it—and to tell the truth I don't know how you've survived."

"Well I have—until now," he told me, "but now it's fighting back—deliberately! Roots come up in the night, from under the floorboards. Searching, I suppose. I hear them groping. And the garden: I've taken it out, burned most of it to the ground. It'll make for a fine big black helipad for the chopper, that's if you have one. I know I'm asking a lot, but—"

"I'll see what can be done," I told him, before the static overwhelmed us.

I got on to Surveillance and was told that a chopper would be going out that way in a few days time. They picked me up; we sped out over the Green; at Sellick's place they put me down in a flurry of ashes in what had once been his garden. I was in my protective gear: the man from Mars in an NBC suit, gas mask and all. Next door, my old house was invisible under a green mound, sagging under the weight of foliage. Sellick's place, too.

But the colonel's big magnolia was still standing—God, it was still in leaf!—there in the one last patch of what looked like normal garden. I went down the old scorched path at a run, then skidded to a halt under the tree's now ominous canopy.

I just *couldn't* believe what I saw sitting there. Or rather I could for I'd seen its like before; it was just that I didn't *want* to believe. And in that grim grey-and-green wasteland deserted by all animal life, devoid of creature sounds, I stood on rubbery legs, gazing through eyes round as pennies, and reached out a trembling rubber-gloved hand to touch Sellick's mutilated, transfigured face.

Why did I do that? I don't know. Probably to confirm with a second sense the evidence I'd almost refused to accept from the first. But no, I wasn't nightmaring. It was all too real.

Old Sellick. Sometime in the last day or two he must have gone out into what was left of his garden, and as was his wont nodded off to sleep on the bench with his back against the magnolia. Then the attack...probably *not* of the green stuff; more likely the old boy's heart, because he was sitting there clutching his left arm, his head back and mouth wide open. I think it *must* have been that way—a heart attack—because he wouldn't have just sat there and let all...all of *this* happen.

The ivy: growing up his trousers and bulging out his shirt; entering him somewhere—I hate to think where!—and issuing forth from his dislodged eyes, from his ears, his gaping mouth. And the old colonel all dried up, wrinkled like a walnut—like a kernel!—with all the good sucked out of him, and the veins in the ivy's six-lobed leaves tinted pink with his liquids!

There was no point in staying. I used avgas to set fire to Sellick and the magnolia, returned to the chopper still hovering there, and went back with the patrol to London...

✤ ✤ ✤

Intelligence. It's a crazy idea...or is it? I mean, how does this thing, or these things, propagate? With no more—or damn few—birds, bees, wasps, flies, how do they do it? Is the wind sufficient, or do they help each other?

I remember what Colonel Sellick told me: about roots coming up through his floorboards, searching through the house.

And then there's what happened to David Johnson. For just a few weeks ago, David got his.

He was the last man out of Kew, a rearguard left behind to ensure that everything we had once nurtured was destroyed. Last to go would be that area of his own special interest, of course, the Mediterranean section. But after he'd been left there—on his own, for three days—finally someone remembered that David hadn't called.

So we called him, and got no answer.

We found him in the hothouse, examined him and figured out how he had died. A squirting cucumber had got him in the eyes: the blackened sockets and the blisters on his face told us that much. Backing off, he must have staggered into a patch of previously inoffensive cactus…they'd shot poisonous spines into him, and his body was puffed up like a balloon. And finally the mandrakes had got to him…they were sprouting in his decaying flesh. I didn't attempt to pull one.

As we opened up with the flamethrowers, the whole place was thrashing and seething—"screaming" if you like—in all its silent fury…

I became aware of someone standing at the foot of the podium. A young man, recently arrived, probably a driver. The chairs were mostly filled now; the empty ones…would wait until we found replacements.

"Yes?" I said.

"The stores are open, sir," he said. "The toshers are waiting outside, and the transport is ready up top."

I nodded, said, "Good, thank you," and then got on with it. I had promised them I'd be brief, and now I kept my word; kept things even shorter by omitting to read the names of those men they'd no longer be seeing. Why should I drench, or even drown, these already dampened spirits? Instead, the names of our dead, brave former comrades-in-arms would be posted where they could be read privately, allowing the living to deal with their losses in their own way in their own time.

There were eight platoons; I assigned four of them to a continuation of yesterday's work, the other four to an invasion on a brand new front.

"It's the sewers," I told them. "Fungus and a black alga. I don't know how the latter survives without sunlight, but in any case it's your job to ensure it doesn't survive. The fungus is a mutant species of puff- or earth-ball that grows in enormous clumps; it's yellow, warty, and the fruiting bodies are full of black spores. There's evidence that these spores will take root in flesh and produce mycelia, fungus strands that will spread through your tissues like wildfire! We got that evidence from an abundance of dead rats; in fact you won't find any *live* rats down there! Which just about says it all.

"You'll have gas masks, of course, but with the various gas pockets you are liable to encounter it's obvious that you won't be able to use flamers. So I'm afraid it's algicides and fungicides, and that's your lot. So, if anyone has an even slightly suspicious gas mask, get it changed!

"As for the algae: it crawls, however slowly. So every hour or so you'll surface and get your suits hosed down. Now listen, I know all this is new and strange to you, but you won't be on your own. In the old days—I mean the really old days, back in the 19th century—there were workers called 'toshers' down in the sewers. Scavengers mainly, they searched for valuables that had been flushed away. Well, we've been recruiting toshers, reinforcing our modern-day 'flusher' gangs, the workers who keep the sewers clean and in good order. Now they're working in tandem, but they're not so much treasure-hunting or repairing the sewers as cleaning them out—searching for the Green so that you can destroy it! But I'm not going to understate the danger: there's a lot of this stuff down there, and it's deadly. If we let it get up into our homes and buildings..." I tailed it off, let it go at that. And finally:

"Okay, that's it. But always remember: safety first! Suits, masks, equipment—check 'em all out. And tomorrow morning let me see all your ugly faces looking right back at me, just like today."

They began to leave, some faster, more eager, than others. The eager ones would be new to this...they wouldn't be quite so eager tomorrow. And I knew I wouldn't be seeing *all* of their ugly faces.

That thought was like an invocation.

The man in the front row, the squad leader—the man with the crisped hair and gnarly hands, whose coughing had made me think his lungs were suffering from the blown-back heat of the flame-throwers—had lurched to his feet. He coughed yet again, gurgling at me like a drain, and stumbled forward. I saw that his eyes were starting out, his hands clawing at thin air.

I jumped down off the podium, but too late to catch him as he fell over. He writhed on the floor, almost vibrating there, but only for a moment or two. And then he lay still.

Some of his men had come forward, staring transfixed, babbling half-formed questions. Waving them back, I got down on my knees beside the fallen man. He wasn't breathing. I put my ear to his chest. Nothing.

Then something:

A hooked green tendril with a bud at its tip uncurled from his right nostril! It elongated vertically to about six inches in length, swaying there. Then the bud turned in my direction where I lay frozen, with my head on the dead man's chest. And the damned thing opened and *hissed* at me!

Someone cried out, stepped forward with clippers, snipped the bud off so that it fell on the floor. As it writhed there, other men came forward and dragged me away. More tendrils were emerging from his ears, his mouth; there was nothing for it but to hose him down with sulphuric acid spray, reducing everything to slop…

There may be survivors. Maybe the Green won't go into the cold places, maybe it won't invade the deserts. Who can say but that an oasis pool, or perhaps the pack ice, or a black smoker down on the sea-bed, may well be the last refuge of animal life?

Or there again, maybe sixty million years from now another space rock will come hurtling from the sky, and this time it'll kick-start, revitalize the vertebrates…though it's possible it could just as easily announce the rise of the insects!

Who can say?

But I have remembered the name of that American author who wrote about a terrible colour out of space: he was called H. P. Lovecraft, and tonight when I go out and look at the sky, I may have a word with him. I may say, "Well, Mr. Lovecraft, wherever you are now, I just want you to know that the stars don't leer. But on the other hand, looking at them and wondering what else is out there, I'm pretty sure I know what you meant…"

MY THING FRIDAY

Voice Journal of Greg Griffiths,
3rd Engineer on the *Albert Einstein*
out of the Greater Mars Orbital Station.

Day One:

Probably the 24th Feb 2198 Earth Standard, but I can't be sure. The ship's chronometer is bust—like everything else except me—and I don't know how long I've been out of it. Judging by the hair on my face, my hunger, the bump on the back of my head and the thick blood scab that's covering it, it could have been two or three days. Anyway and as far as I can tell it's now morning on whichever day, which I'm going to call Day One…

What I remember:

We passed through the fringes of an old nebula; a cloud of gas that looked dead enough, but it seems there was some energy left in it after all: weird energy that didn't register on instrumentation. Then the drive started acting up and quit entirely maybe four or five light-years later. When we dropped back into normal space I put on a suit, went out and for'ard to check the fuel ingestors. They were clogged with this gas that was almost liquid, and dust that stuck like glue; it couldn't be converted into fuel and had hardened to a solid in the scoops…weird as hell, like I said. Ship's Science Officer, Scot Gentry, said it could well be "proto-plan-etary slag"—whatever the hell that's supposed to be!—and a total pain in the backside. And down in engineering we scratched our heads and tried to figure out some way to shift this shit.

Then the sub-light engines blew up and we saw that the dust was into everything. The anti-gravs were on the fritz but still working, however sporadically, and by some miracle of chance we were just a cough and a spit off a planet with water and an atmosphere: a couple trillion to one chance, according to Gentry. But by then, too, we knew we were way off course—light-years off course—because this proto-crap had got into the astronavigator, too.

As for the planet: it had continents, oceans, but there was no radio coming up at us, no sign of cities or intelligent life-forms. Well, if there had been, it would have been a first. The universe has been looking like a pretty lonely place for a long time now. And to me, *right* now, it looks lonelier than ever.

Coming in to make landfall the anti-gravs gave up the ghost...so much for a soft landing. Six thousand tons of metal with nothing holding us up, we fell from maybe a hundred feet in the air. Higher than that and I probably wouldn't be recording this. I was in a sling in a gravity tube, trying to burn slag off the gyros, when this uncharted planet grabbed us; the sling's shock absorbers bounced me around but saved my life.

As for the other crew members, all fifteen of my shipmates, they weren't so lucky—

—Or maybe they were. It all depends on what this place has in store for me. But right now I have to fix my head, eat, give myself shots, then get all the bodies off the ship or the place won't ever be liveable...

❖ ❖ ❖

Day Two: (morning.)

Yesterday was a very strange day...and by the way, I think the days here are just an hour or two longer than Earth standard. I reckon I was right about coming to fairly early in the morning, because it seemed like one hell of a long strange day; but then again—considering what I was doing—it would.

I had started to move the bodies out of the ship.

No easy task, that. And not only for the obvious reasons. I cried a lot, for the obvious reasons. But with the old *Albert E.* lying at thirty degrees, and her (or his) once round hull split at all the major seams, buckled and now oblate, and leaking all kinds of corrosives, lubricants and like that...

no, it was no easy task. Don't know why I bothered, really, because I see now there's no way I can live in the *Albert E.* Ship's a death trap! Perhaps I should have left the bodies as they were, sealed them in as best I could right there where they died; the entire ship with all these bodies—my buddies—in it, like some kind of big metal memorial. Rust in peace...

But it's way too late now, and anyway there's lots of stuff I have to get out of there. Medicines and such; ship's rations; a big old self-inflating habitat module from the emergency survival store; tools; stuff like that. A regular Robinson Crusoe, I be—or maybe a marooned Ben Gunn, eh, Jim lad? Oh, *Ha-harr*! But at least there's no sign of pirates.

I thank God for my sense of humour. Just a few days ago on board the *Albert E.*, why, I would crack them up so hard—they would laugh so hard—they'd tell me I'd be the death of them! Well, boys, it wasn't me. Just a fucking big cloud of weird gas and dust, that's all. But it cracked us up good and proper...

Later:

I managed to get more than half of them out of there before the sun went down, and I'll get the rest tomorrow. But tonight will be the *last* night I'll spend on board ship. It's nightmarish on the *Albert E.* now. Tomorrow I'll fix up the habitat I unloaded, get a generator working, power some batteries, set up a defensive perimeter like the book says. And whatever those things are I hear moving around out there in the dark—probably the same guys who were watching me from the forest while I worked—fuck 'em! I do have a reliable sidearm. Shouldn't need to use it too much though; once they've had a taste of the electric perimeter—that's assuming they're the overly curious kind—they won't be in too much of a hurry to come back for more.

As for tonight, I have to hope they're not much interested in carrion, that's all...

Day Three: (midday.)

I feel a lot better in myself, not so knocked about, no longer down. Well, *down*, naturally, but not all the way. I mean, hell, I'm alive! And just looking at the old *Albert E.* I really don't know how. But the air is very good here; you can really suck it in. It's fresh, sweet...unfiltered? Maybe it's just that the air on the ship, always stale, is already starting to stink.

I got a generator working; got my habitat set up, electric perimeter and all. Now I'll bring out all the ship's rations I can find, and while I'm at it I may come across the two bodies I haven't found yet. One of them is a dear pal of mine, Daniel Geisler. That will hit me hard. It's all hitting hard, but I'm alive and that's what matters. Where there's life there's hope, and all that shit...

I've been finding out something about the locals who I was listening to last night. I was in a makeshift hammock that I'd fixed up in an airlock; left the airlock open a crack, letting some of this good air in. Part way into the night I could hear movement out in the darkness. After an hour or so it got quiet, so it seems they sleep, too. Could be that night and sleep are universally synonymous. That would make sense...I think.

But how best to describe them? Now me, I'm not what you'd call an exo-biologist, Jim, lad, just a grease monkey; but I'll give it a try. From what I've seen so far, there appears to be three kinds of what is basically one and the same species. See what I mean about not being an exobiologist? Obviously they're *not* the same species; and yet there's this peculiar similarity about them that...well, they're very *odd*, that's all...

Anyway, let me get on.

There's the flying kind: eight foot wing span, round-bodied and skinny-legged; like big, beakless, stupid-looking pale-pink robbins. They hang out in the topmost branches of the trees and eat what look like fist-sized yellow berries. Paradoxically and for all their size they appear to be pretty flimsy critters; no feathers, they're more like bats or maybe flying squirrels than birds, and they leap and soar rather than fly. And when they're floating between the sun and me I see right through their wings. But they're not the only flying things. There are others of approximately the same size and design but more properly birdlike. And this other species—very definitely a separate, different species—they stay high in the sky, circling like buzzards. I kept an eye on these high-flyers because of what I was doing. I mean, I was laying out my dead shipmates, and buzzards and vultures are carnivores. On Earth they are, anyway...

Then there's the landlubbers or earth-bound variety. These are bipedal, anthropoid, perhaps even mammalian or this world's equivalent, though as yet I've seen no sign of tits or marriage tackle. Whatever, I reckon it's probably these man-like things—this world's intelligentsia?—that I heard bumping around in the darkness. But since they're the most interesting of the bunch I'll leave them till last, get back to them in a minute.

And finally there's the other land variety, the hogs. Well, I'll call them hogs for now, if only for want of a better name. They're some four or five feet long, pale-pink like the soaring things and the bipeds, and they rustle about in the undergrowth at the fringes of the forest eating the golfball-sized seeds of the big yellow berries. But they, too, have their counterparts. Deeper in the woods, there are critters more properly like big, hairy black hogs that snort and keep well back in the shadows.

And there you have it. But the "Pinks"—as I've started to call all three varieties of these pale-pink creatures: the quadrupeds, bipeds, and flyers— it's as if they were all cut from the same cloth. Despite the diversity of their design there's a vague similarity about them; their drab, unappealing colour for one thing, and the same insubstantial sort of flimsiness or— I don't know, wobbliness? Jellyness?—for another.

Fascinating really...*if* I was an exobiologist. But since I'm not they're just something I'll need to watch out for until I know for sure what's what. Actually, I don't feel intimidated by any of these critters. Not so far. Not by the Pinks, anyway.

More about the man-likes:

When I opened up the airlock this morning there was a bunch of them, maybe thirteen or fourteen, sitting in a circle around the remains of my shipmates. I've been laying my ex-friends out in their own little groups, their three main shipboard cliques, but all of them pretty close together with their feet in toward a common centre. Ended up forming a sort of three-leafed clover shape with four or five bodies to a leaf.

The aliens (yeah, it's a cliche, I know, but what are these things if not aliens? They're alien to me, anyway—though it's true that on this world I'm the only real alien—but anyway:) the *locals* were sitting there nestling the heads of the dead in their laps. And I thought what the hell, maybe they'd spent the whole night like that! Well, whatever, that's how it struck me.

So then, what were they doing? Wondering if these dead creatures were edible, maybe? Or were they simply trying to figure out what these things who fell from the sky were; these vaguely familiar beings, whose like they'd never known before? They did seem briefly, particularly, almost childishly interested in the difference between the *Albert E.*'s lone female crew member's genitalia and the rest of the gang's tackle, but that didn't last. Which was fine because she—a disillusioned crew-cut exobiologist dike called Emma Schneider—wouldn't have much liked it.

Anyway, there they were, these guys, like a bunch of solemn mourners with my old shipmates...

After I tossed down a spade and lowered a rope ladder, however, they stood up, backed off, and watched me from a distance as I came down and began to dig graves in this loamy soil. With so many holes to dig, even shallow ones, I knew to pace myself, take breaks, get things done in easy stages: a little preparatory digging, then search for usables in the ship, more digging, fix up my habitat, make another attempt at finding my two missing buddies, dig, set up my generator—and so on. And that's pretty much how it's been working out...

But as yet I haven't actually described the man-likes.

Well, Jim, lad, here's me recording this under my habitat's awning, and while I speak I'm watching the locals do their peculiar thing. Or perhaps it's not so peculiar and they're not so very alien. Well, not as alien as I thought. Because it appears they understand death and revere the dead—even my dead—or so it would seem. But how can it be otherwise? I mean, how else to explain this?

They've brought these instruments from somewhere—"musical" instruments, if you can call them that—from wherever they dwell, I suppose. And if this isn't some kind of lament they're singing, some kind of dirge I'm hearing from their drums, bang-stones, rattle-pods and bamboo flutes, then I really don't know what it is. And I think that the only thing that's keeping them at a respectable distance from my dead ones...is me.

I'm looking at them through binoculars. Can't tell the male of the species from the female; hell, I don't even know if they *have* sexes as such! Amoeboid? I shouldn't think so; *that* wobbly they're not! But human-*like*? They are. Emphasis on "like". They have two each of the things we have two of, er, with the exception of testicles, *if* they have males and if their balls aren't on the inside. Oh, and also with the exception of breasts—*if* and et cetera, as previously conjectured.

Their eyes are watery-looking; not fishy, no, but uninspiringly pale, limpid and uniformly grey, large in their faces and forming triangles with their noses. As for those noses: they're just paired black dots in approximately the right places. Their mouths are thin-lipped; their dull white teeth look fairly normal; their ears, are ears; and their shining black hair falls on their thin shoulders. Their hair is the most attractive—maybe even the only attractive—thing about them. They're about five foot five inches tall, with slender, roughly pear-shaped bodies thick end down. They've got three fingers to a hand, three toes to a foot. But while their legs seem strong, giving them a flowing, gliding, maybe even graceful mobility, their arms are much too thin and look sort of boneless.

So then, that's them, and I'm guessing they're the dominant species. Certainly they're head and shoulders above the rest of the fauna. And while I'm on about the rest of them:

Today I've seen several pink hogs doing their thing in the shrubbery at the forest's edge. Totally harmless, I'd say, and I'm not at all worried by them. From back in the deeper undergrowth, however, I've heard the occasional snuffling, grunting and growling of the pink hogs' cousins; their big, hairy black shapes trundling to and fro, but yet keeping a safe distance. Well good! And likewise the flying pinks in the treetops: I've seen them looking down at me but it doesn't bother me much. On the other hand *their* cousins, the actual high-flying buzzards—if that's what they are—well, there's something really ominous about their unending circling. But so far, since I haven't seen a one of them come down and land, I'm not too concerned.

Enough for now. I've had my break, eaten, brewed and drank a pot of coffee; now I'll go back into the *Albert E.*, see if I can find poor Daniel...

Later: (late afternoon, early evening.)

This is really amazing! It's so hard to believe I'm not sure if even seeing is believing! It started when I was in the ship.

I'd found Scot Gentry's body in his lab, crushed flat under everything that wasn't tied down. Then, while I was digging him out, I thought to hear movement elsewhere in the vessel. I told myself it was just loose wreckage shifting, settling down. When it happened a second time, however, the short hairs on the back of my neck stood up straight! What the...? After all this time, three days or more, could it be that I wasn't the only survivor after all, that someone else had lived through the wreck of the *Albert E.*? But there was only one someone else: my buddy Daniel Geisler! What would Dan's condition be?

Hell, he could be dying even now!

The way I went scrambling then, I could have broken my neck a dozen and more times on those sloping, often buckled, crazily-angled decks; skidding and sliding, shouting myself hoarse, and pausing every now and then to hold my breath and listen, see if I was being answered. Finally I did hear something, coming from the direction of the airlock that I was using.

It was four of the man-like pinks. They must have followed me up the ladder I'd left dangling, and...and they'd found my good buddy Daniel. But he wasn't alive, not with his head stove in and his back bent all the wrong way. And there they were, in the airlock, these four guys, easing Daniel into the sling that I'd fixed up and preparing to lower him to the ground.

Oh, really? And after they got him down, what else did they have planned for him? Advancing on them, I glared at them where they stood blinking back at me, with their skinny arms dangling and, as far as I could tell, no expressions whatsoever on their pink faces.

"All right, you weird fucks!" I yelled, lunging at them and waving my sidearm. "I don't know what you're up to, but—"

But one of them was pointing one of three skinny fingers at his own eyes, then at mine, finally out the airlock and down at the ground. It was like he was saying, "See for yourself." They backed off as I came forward and looked out. And down there...well, even now it's difficult to believe. Or maybe not. I mean, alien they may be—hell, they *are*—but that doesn't mean they don't have human-like emotions, routines, rituals, ceremonials. Like their cradling the dead, their dirges, and now this.

But now what—eh, Jim lad? *Now the shallow graves that the other pinks were digging down there*, that's now what! The whole group, using my spade, scoops made from half-gourds, even their bare three-digit hands, to dig as neat a set of graves as you'd never wish to see right there in that soft, loose loam!

Well, what could I say or do after that? Nothing that they'd understand, for sure. So letting the four pinks get on with it, I went back for Gentry's body. By the time I returned the sling was back in position and the four volunteers were out of there. They'd gone below and were working with the rest of the tribe, digging for all they were worth.

I might have liked to find a way to express my gratitude—to this quartet at least—but couldn't see how to do it. These creatures looked so much of a muchness to me, there was no sure way to tell my four apart from the rest of them. Ah, well...

✧ ✧ ✧

Day Four: (midday.)

I slept well last night; I suppose I was sort of exhausted. But I was also easier in my mind after letting the man-likes finish off burying the dead...

well, except for Scot and Daniel. They wouldn't bury those last two until they'd sat with them through the night, their heads in their laps. A kind of ritual—a wake of sorts, a vigil—that they go through with their dead. Also with mine, apparently. It isn't a job I would have cared to do. After four or more days dead, Scot and Dan weren't looking very pretty. They weren't smelling too good either. Could be the man-like pinks do it to keep the buzzards and hogs from scavenging, which is something else I don't much care to think about.

This morning, their yelping, rattling and piping woke me up just as they were finishing with filling in the last two graves. As I put up my awning I saw—just outside my habitat, outside the electric perimeter—one of the pinks sitting there watching me. Now I know I've said they don't have much in the way of facial expressions, but this one was cocking its head first one way and then the other, and if anything looked curious as hell. I mean curious about me. He, she, or it kept watching me while I boiled water, shaved, made and drank coffee and ate a ship's-rations facsimile homeworld breakfast.

I tossed the pink a sweet biscuit which it sniffed at, then carefully bit into, then got up, went unsteadily to the side of the clearing, leaned on a tree and threw up. Credit where credit's due for perseverance, though, if for nothing else, because when it was done throwing up it came right on back and sat down again, watching me like before but just a shade less pink. Then when I set out to have a look around, explore the place, damned if he, she, it didn't come gliding after, albeit at a discreet, respectful distance.

As for why I wanted to go walkabout: long before we discovered that the galaxy was a pretty empty place, someone wrote in the survival handbook that if you get stuck on a world and want to know if there are any higher civilizations, just take a walk along a coastline. Because if there *is* intelligent life, that's where you'll find its flotsam and jetsam. Doesn't say a hell of a lot for intelligence, now does it? Anyway, ever since I clambered from the wreckage of the *Albert E.* I've been hearing this near-distant murmur. And no matter where you are, the sound of small waves breaking on a beach is unmistakeable.

I followed a man-like track through the woods until I came across a fresh-water stream, then followed the stream and track both for maybe a quarter mile...and there it was, this beautiful ocean: blue under an azure sky, turning turquoise where it lapped the white, sandy beach; gentle as a pond and smelling of salt and seaweed. All that was missing was the cry of seagulls. Well, no, that's not all that was missing; there was no flotsam and jetsam, either. No ships on the horizon, no smoke rising in any direction, and no footprints in the sand except my own. But I did have my Man, Woman, Thing Friday, following dutifully behind me.

Sitting on a rock looking at all the emptiness, I told him, her, it: "You know something, you're sort of indecent? Well you *would* be, if you had a dick or tits or something!" There was no answer, just those huge limpid eyes watching me, and that small pink head cocked on one side, displaying—or so I thought—a certain willingness to at least try to understand what I'd said… maybe. And because of that, on impulse, I took off my shirt and put it on Friday, who just stood there and let me. The pink being small, that big shirt would have covered its naughty bits easily—if there had been any to cover! Anyway, it made Friday look just that little bit more acceptable.

We walked perhaps half a mile along the beach, then turned and walked back. But as we approached the stream and the forest track, that was when I discovered that there was a fourth variety of pinks. And as if to complement the others—the bipeds, the quadruped grubbers in the woods, and the soaring aerials in the treetops—this time it was the swimmers, where else but in the sea?

These two dolphin-like pinks were hauling a third animal—for all the world a real dolphin, or this world's equivalent—up from the deeper water into the shallows. The "real" dolphin was in a bad way, in fact on its way out; something big and, I have to assume, highly unpleasant had taken a very large chunk out of it. Almost cut in half, its plump body was gaping open, leaving a long string of guts trailing in the water behind it. I suppose that no matter where you are, if you have oceans you have sharks or things much like them. It did away with an idea I'd been tossing around that maybe later I would go for a swim. Reality was closing in on me again, and it was all pretty sick-making.

I moved closer, and Friday, oddly excited, came with me.

The ocean-going pinks didn't seem concerned about our nearness; preoccupied with pushing the "real" dolphin up out of the water, they more or less ignored us and I was able to get close up and take a good look at them. First the fishy dolphin:

Even as I watched it the poor thing expired. It just lifted its bottle nose out of the water once, gave a choked little cry and flopped over on its side. It was mammalian, a female, slate-grey on its back, white on what was left of its belly. If I had seen it in a Sea-World on homeworld I would have thought to myself: dolphin, probably of a rare species.

As for the sea-pinks: if I had seen *them* in a Sea-World I'd have thought to myself, weird! From the waist up they were much the same as the bipeds, even to the extent of having their thin rubbery arms. Maybe in their upper bodies they were more streamlined than the land-dwelling variety, but that seemed to be the only difference. Oh, wait; they also had blowholes, in the back of their necks. From their middles down, however, they were all dolphin, the pink merging into grey. And I could see just looking at them that they weren't stupid.

Meanwhile Friday had taken out a bamboo flute from a little bag on a string round his (let's for the moment say his) waist, and had begun tootling away in a high-pitched register that was almost painful. And before I knew it a half-dozen man-likes had come down the track to join us on the beach. Keeping their distance from me—almost ignoring me—they hurried to the water's edge and very carefully began to drag the dead dolphin creature up the beach into the shade at the rim of the forest. And while one of them sat cradling the dead thing's head the rest of them set to work scooping out a grave. Astonishing! But—

—Well, I thought, don't people have this special affinity with dolphins back on Earth? Sure they do. And as Friday and me headed back along the forest track toward the *Albert E.* and the clearing, already I could hear the mournful singing, the rattling and banging of the pink burial party on the beach. What was more, back at the wreck, I saw that they'd even been decorating the graves of my shipmates, putting little markers on them with various identifying squiggles.

Damn, but these guys revere the dead!

Later:

This afternoon I went back into the ship searching for anything that might make my life here just that little bit more comfortable, more familiar, and—what the hell—homeworldly? I took a small stack of Daniel's girlie magazines that I'd been coveting for God knows how many light-years, a photograph album with pictures of some ex-girlfriends of mine, some busted radio components I might try tinkering with, and various bits and pieces like that. Friday climbed up there with me, then went exploring on his own...

✥ ✥ ✥

Later:

It's evening now and raining. Even though the stream looks pure enough, I'm using my awning to collect the rain. Friday appears pretty fixated with me. He's taken to me like a stray dog. So I switched off the perimeter and let him in out of the rain. He's sitting there in one corner, not doing much of anything. When I ate I didn't offer him any; as we've seen, ship's rations don't much agree with him.

Speaking of rations, what I didn't realize till now is that most of the stuff I took from the *Albert E.*'s galley was damaged in the crash. I've preserved what I could but at least seventy-five per cent of it is wasted. I'll burn it tomorrow.

Which means, of course, that some time in the not too distant future I'll have to start eating local. Maybe I should keep an eye on the pinks, see what they eat. Or maybe not. If Friday can't eat my stuff, it seems unlikely that I can eat his.

It's all very worrying…

✥ ✥ ✥

Day Five: (mid-morning.)

When I woke up this morning I caught Friday going through Dan's soft porn mags. My old photograph album was lying open, too, so it looks like Friday's curiosity knows no bounds! Alas, he also appears to be disrespectful of my personal property. Thoroughly PO'd with him, without really knowing why (I suppose I was in a bad mood,) I switched off the perimeter and shooed him the hell out of here, then went walkabout on my own. The last time I saw him he looked sort of down in the mouth—about as far down as a pink is able to look, from what I've seen of them so far—as he went drifting off in the general direction of the *Albert E.*

Something entirely different:

I've discovered that the man-likes go hunting, with spears. I saw a bunch keeping very low and quiet, sneaking off into the thick of the forest. There was a second bunch, too, with half a dozen members who were watching me just a little too closely as I moved around the clearing. It seemed to me they were interested in *my* interest in these graves I've been discovering. I can tell that these mounds in the forest's fringing undergrowth are graves because of the markers on them. But not all of them have markers, only the more recent ones, which are easily identified by the freshly turned earth. I don't know if that's of any real significance.

Anyway, this second party of hunters kept looking at me, at each other, and at their spears, as if wondering if they should—or if they dare—have a go at me! Maybe they didn't like me looking at the graves because I wasn't showing sufficient reverence or something; I don't know, can't say. But it was as I was examining the more recent graves that these hunter pinks became especially disturbed. Then, as I knelt to examine a thick-stemmed cactus or succulent that was sprouting in a marked mound—a fleshy, sickly-looking green thing with a pinkish head, something like a bulbous great asparagus spear—that was when the hunters displayed the most anxiety, even to the extent of looking more than a little hostile.

However, whatever *might* have happened next was averted when the first party of hunters came bursting from the forest in hot pursuit of a hairy black hog who was also in pursuit of a small pink grubber. The big black was rampant so I could only suppose that the small pink was on heat; but however that might be, the hunters were only interested in the black. And again I *supposed* they'd been using the little pink as bait. Well, right or wrong in that respect, at least I now knew what they had been hunting and could reasonably assume that this was what they ate—that it was one of their staples, anyway.

In the confusion, as the big horny hog tore round the clearing after the small scurrying pink, I tried to make it back to my habitat. Bad idea. In rapid succession the hog took three or four long thin spears in his back and flanks, lost all interest in the small pink grubber and went totally crazy! Squealing and trying to gore everything in sight, with both parties of hunter pinks now getting in their best shots as they glided after him, he turned, saw me, came slavering and snorting straight at me!

Of course I shot him; my bolt stopped him dead, exploded in his skull, sent blood and brains flying. He immediately bit the dust, twitched once or twice, and lay still...following which there was total, motionless silence; so that even with the hunters all over the place, they'd become so frozen into immobility that the clearing looked like nothing so much as an alien still-life!

And that's the way it stayed, with nobody moving so much as a muscle until I broke the spell, holstered my weapon, and made my way stiff-legged and head high right on back to my habitat.

Friday was already in there, sitting in his corner on a box of old clothes he'd rescued from the *Albert E.* Probably figured he was doing me a favour bringing stuff out of there. Anyway, I was glad to see he was still my pal, and maybe even my only pal in these parts now.

Looking out from under my awning, I watched the end of this business with the hog. Finding their mobility again, several of the hunters hoisted the dead tusker and carried their trophy in a circle round the clearing in an odd, paradoxically muted celebratory procession. At least I'm supposing that's what it was. But when they passed out of sight, that was the end of that and I haven't seen the hog since. But I imagine there'll be a merry old feast in the clearing tonight.

✤ ✤ ✤

Later:

Toward evening I ventured out again. There was no sign of festive preparations, no fires, nothing. Come to think of it, I've never yet seen a fire. Maybe they don't have fire. Me, I can't say I fancy raw hog!

Anyway, there was no sign of the spearsmen, and the handful of pinks who were out and about seemed as bland and harmless as ever; they paid little or no attention to me. But in any case I wasn't out too long before it started in to rain again, so that was the end of tonight's excursion.

Friday is already asleep (I think) on a layer of old clothing in his corner. Not a bad idea.

So it's goodnight from me, Jim lad…

✤ ✤ ✤

Day Six: (mid-morning.)

Didn't sleep too good and it's left me grumpy. Late last night the pinks were at it again, howling, thumping and rattling, and that includes Friday. I woke up (very briefly) to find him gone and my defensive perimeter switched off—the little pink nuisance! I got up long enough to switch it on again then went back to sleep. But I *must* find a way to get through to him, warn him against doing that. It's either that or simply ban him from the habitat altogether.

Everything tastes lousy this morning, even the coffee. Must be the water: it's *too* clean, *too* sweet! My poor old taste buds are far more accustomed to the recycled H_2O aboard the *Albert E.* Maybe I should climb up there one last time and drain off whatever's left in the system. Also, I should look for a remote for my defensive perimeter switch; the habitat didn't have one.

Actually, there are several items in the handbook that the habitat doesn't have: inexcusable deficiencies! Some dumb QM's assistant storeman on the Greater Mars Orbital should have his ass kicked out of an airlock!

As for last night's ceremonial rowdyism:

There's a new grave under the low vegetation at the rim of the clearing. I reckon it's the hog. Having eaten the thing—or at least the parts they wanted—the pinks must have buried whatever was left. So their rituals extend even to their prey. This is all conjecture, of course; but again, as with the dolphin, I can't find this practice altogether strange. I seem to remember reading somewhere that many primitive tribes of Earth had a similar attitude toward Ma Nature's creatures: an understanding, appreciation and respect for the animals they relied upon for food and clothing.

Later:

I've managed to fix up a remote from some of the electrical kit I took from the *Albert E.* Now I can switch on my defensive perimeter from outside. Not that the man-likes have been intrusive—well, except for my man Friday—but I like to think that my few personal possessions are secure, and that I'm retaining at least a semblance of privacy...

Today I went fishing with a bamboo pole and line I managed to fix up. Friday went with me, showed me the grubs in the sand that I could use as bait. I brought in an eight-inch crab-thing that Friday danced away from. It had an awful lot of legs and a nasty stinger, so I flipped it back into the sea. The fish that I caught were all small and eel-like, but they taste fine fried and make a welcome change from ship's rations. I offered one to Friday, which he didn't hesitate to accept and eat. So it seems these small fish are another pink staple.

Later: (evening.)

I had a sleep, woke up in the afternoon feeling much refreshed, and went walkabout with Friday. We chose to walk a forest trail I never used before; Friday seemed okay with it so I assumed it was safe enough. When we passed a group of pinks gathering root vegetables, I paused to point at a small pile of these purplish carrot-like things and raise a questioning eyebrow. Friday must have understood the look; he pointed to his mouth and made chewing motions. Going to the pile, he even helped himself to three of the carrots. None of the gatherers seemed to mind. So I have to assume that these tubers are yet another pink staple.

Then, because it was getting late, we headed for home. But, did I say home? I must be going native!

Back at the habitat as we were about to enter, I witnessed something new. Or if not exactly new, different. First off, as I went to use the remote to cancel the electrical perimeter, I noticed Friday looking up into the sky above the clearing. And Friday wasn't the only one. As if suddenly aware of some imminent occurrence, all the other man-likes were sneaking back into the shadows to hide under the fringing foliage. Several of them had taken up spears from somewhere or other, and they were all peering up into the sky.

I went into the habitat with Friday, and we both looked out from under the awning. At first I couldn't see anything of interest. But then, on a level with the highest of the treetops, I saw a small shape drifting aimlessly to and fro. It was a young aerial pink; (I immediately thought of it as a fledgling, which if it had any feathers I suppose it would have been.) Whatever, it was a pink flyer getting nowhere fast, looking all confused and lost up there.

Then, much higher overhead, I spotted something else. Spiralling down from the dusky indigo sky there came a black speck, faint at first but rapidly increasing in size. Its wings—real wings this time—gradually folded back, becoming streamlined, until in the last moment the hawk-buzzard-vulture dropped like a stone and stooped on its prey...and itself *became* the prey!

In the instant before it could make deadly contact with the young floater, a great flock of adult aerials launched themselves from the high canopy, converged on the buzzard and slammed into it from all sides. Squawking its pain, winded and flapping a broken wing, the thing tumbled into the clearing. Even before it hit the ground there was a spear through its neck and it had stopped complaining. And up in the treetops, the aerial ambushers were already drifting back to their various roosts.

Now, if I hadn't witnessed this event with my own eyes, I'd *never* have believed that the adult flyers could move so fucking fast and with such deadly intent! Not only that, but to my mind the incident formed a perfect parallel with what had happened to the black hog: both had been examples of deliberate entrapment. And I wasn't in the least surprised as night came on once again to hear the mournful ceremonial wailing, rattling, thumping and piping of the man-likes...

Another staple? Possibly. Another grave in the morning? I'd bet my shirt on it—if I hadn't already given it to Friday...

✦ ✦ ✦

Day Nine: (midday.)

I'm getting a bit lax with this. But the less I have to do, the more I feel like doing nothing! The last two days I've spent my time on the beach fishing, dozing, getting myself a tan that my old shipmates would have killed for. It's alarming how pasty we used to get in space, keeping away from naked sun and starlight and all the gamma radiation. But this is a friendly sun and I'm protected by atmosphere. Friday's skin must be a lot more fragile than mine; he made himself a shelter from spiky palm fronds and spent most of his time in the shade.

Then again, he has been looking kind of droopy just lately, all shivery and sweaty. Since my human routines, activities and such aren't naturally his, I think it's possible that Friday's been spending too much time in my company and that it's beginning to tell on him. I find I can't just shoo him off, though, because now it seems I've grown accustomed to his face. (Ugh!)

✦ ✦ ✦

Day Twelve: (early to mid-morning.)

For breakfast I sliced and fried up some of the purple carrots that Friday has been bringing in for me. Wary at first, I took just a single small bite. Not at all bad, they taste something like a cross between chilli peppers and green onions; but like an Indian curry, they do cause internal heat and lots of sweating. Maybe Friday has been eating too many of them, because he gets sweatier day by day! Then again, I've seen quite a few of the man-likes with the same condition: their skin glistens and moisture drips from their long-nailed fingers, especially when they cradle the dead before burial.

And speaking of the dead:

Just an hour or so ago, a hunting party of five pinks went out into the forest. In a little while they were back, four of them carrying the fifth between them. He'd been torn up pretty badly—gutted in fact, I expect by a black hog—and he died right here in the clearing. His hunter buddies at once took up his body again, headed off down one of the tracks with it, and the regulation party of mourners and "musicians" went trooping after.

So they obviously have a special burial place for their own kind somewhere in the woodland...

❖ ❖ ❖

Later: (towards noon.)

Friday's veggies have given me bad indigestion. Maybe I should have left them alone, but I was trying to show my appreciation of his generosity. Anyway, since I know I'll have to start living on local stuff sooner or later, it probably makes sense to start eking out my dwindling stock of ship's rations right now with anything I can forage—or whatever Friday can forage for me.

❖ ❖ ❖

Later: (mid-afternoon.)

Midday, after Friday went off on his own somewhere, I took the opportunity to sneak into the forest along the same track taken by the man-like burial party. This was after they had returned, because I didn't want them to get the idea that I was spying on them, which I was. Maybe a mile along the track I chanced upon their village and discovered something weird and wonderful!

For some time I had been wondering about biped society: did they have a communal place—I mean other than the clearing—where they lived and brought up their kids?...stuff like that. Because until now I hadn't seen any man-like children. Only now I had found just such a place. But it wasn't only man-like kids that I saw.

The track ended at a limestone cliff that went up sheer for perhaps eighty, ninety feet. And there were ladders, ledges and even tottery-looking balconies fronting the hollowed-out caves. The cliff face was literally honeycombed with these troglodyte dwellings. And that was it; the biped pinks were cave-dwellers. But that wasn't what was weird and wonderful.

I've told how these pink species seem to parallel the various types you might more reasonably expect to find on a burgeoning world: feathered birds, wild forest tuskers, even dolphins. Now I saw that there was something more to it than that, though exactly what I couldn't say. But the extensive cleared space at the foot of the cliffs was like a pinks playground watched over by a handful of adults, and they weren't just looking after the man-like kids who were playing there. No, for there were little pink hogs running around, too, also being cared for. And on the lower ledges, and in the many creepers climbing the cliff face, that's where gatherings of infant pink floaters roosted. What's more, in a freshwater pool fed by a gentle waterfall, I thought I could even make out a young pink dolphin practicing "walking" on his tail! The whole place was a pinks kindergarten, but for *all* pink species, not just man-likes! And hiding behind a tree, suddenly I knew my being there wasn't in order and my presence wouldn't be appreciated.

Then, hurrying back toward the clearing, I glimpsed hunters heading my way and moved quickly, quietly aside into the forest shade. The hunting party passed me by; but back there under the trees I had found another pink graveyard—*the* pink graveyard, the graveyard of the man-likes! All of the graves had the weird asparagus plants growing out of them; some with as many as four spears, each as thick as my forearm and from eighteen inches to two feet tall, with bulbous tips as big as a clenched fist. But there were also some with collapsed stems and bulbs with empty, shattered husks. And once again I experienced that sensation of trespassing, of feeling that I really shouldn't be there.

How did I know this was the biped graveyard? Because every plot was well tended and marked with unmistakable, stylized *pictures* of man-likes drawn on papery bark, that's how. And one of the graves—a mound *without* the weird plants—was brand new and the soil still wet!

I would have left at once but the strangest thing happened. One of the fattest of several asparagus stems on an older grave had started quivering, and the leaves or petals on the big bulb at its tip were peeling back on themselves and leaking a gluey liquid. Not only that, but something was wriggling in there—something pink!

That was enough and I got the hell out of there.

Luck was with me; I got back to the clearing and my habitat without encountering any more pinks, and Friday was waiting for me with a big bunch of those purple carrots. This time, though, I haven't accepted them. Actually, I've only just realized that I've been feeling a little sick and dizzy ever since breakfast.

Day Fourteen: (I think...or maybe Fifteen?)

God, I'm not at all well. And what happened this morning hasn't much helped the way I feel.

I was dreaming. I was with this woman and it was just about to turn into a wetty. We were in bed and I was groping her: one hand on her backside, the other on her breasts, while the, er, best of me searched for the way in; but damned if I could find it! And even for a guy who has spent most of his time in space, that wasn't at all like me. I mean, it simply wasn't there! But anyway, as I went to kiss her she breathed on me, causing me to recoil from her strange, sweet breath—and likewise from the dream.

I woke up—came starting awake—and saw these big limpid, alien eyes staring straight into mine! It was Friday, under the sheet with me, and both of us were sweaty as hell!

What the screaming fuck? He (shit, maybe I should have been calling Friday "she" all this time!) was holding my face in *its* wet, three-fingered hands, its body trembling with some kind of weird passion. I jerked back, kicked it out of there and was on my feet before it could get up from the dirt floor. But finally it did, and there it stood in a padded bra, frilly knickers and a lacy chemise that could only have belonged to Emma Schneider. And I knew it was so because Friday's mouth was a ghastly crimson gash that was thickly layered with the *Albert E.'s* ex-exobiologist's fucking hideous lip gloss!

Jesus H. Christ!

And out he, she, *it* went; out of my habitat, out beyond the defensive security perimeter, and out of what's left of my life in this fucking place for good. And I hurled the February, 2196 issue of *Lewd Lustin' Lovers* it had left lying open on my folding card-table right out there into the clearing after it! But even after I'd washed myself top to toe, still I felt like I'd been dipped in dog dirt, and here it is noon and I still do…

Later: (mid-afternoon.)

I went down to where a stream joins the ocean to swim in a pool there. I'm still not a hundred percent, crapping like a volcano blowing off, and throwing up purple, but at least my skin feels clean again.

When I was in the water I thought I saw Friday lurking near the rocks where I left my pants, socks and shoes, but he wasn't there when I came out and dried off. Back in the habitat when I went to switch on the perimeter I couldn't find my remote…I could have sworn it was in my pants pocket. And that's not all; the perimeter's wiring had been yanked out of the generator's connection box. It's not impossible that Friday did it accidentally when I tossed him out of bed, but it's also possible he's been in here sabotaging stuff. When I'm feeling better I'll fix things up again, try to knock together a new remote.

But that's for when I'm feeling better. Right now I'm feeling lousy, so I'm going to have to get my head down...rest and recuperation, Jim lad.

Later: (early evening.)

Went back to the old *Albert E.* I was going to climb the ladder, go looking for tools, electrical gear, and like that. No way, I was too weak. Made four rungs and had to come down again before I fell.

Down there under the ship's crumpled hull, it suddenly occurred to me maybe I should pay my respects to the crew, which I haven't been doing for a while now. And what do you know, these slimy shoots were gradually uncoiling, standing up out of their graves.

Dizzy and staggering about like I was falling-down drunk, I went to kick the things flat, crush, destroy and...and murder them? But a bunch of bipeds got a hold of me, guiding and half-carrying me back to my habitat.

I thought I saw Friday standing there, just watching all of this—the little pink fairy! But hell, it could have been any one of them. No, I reckon it was him. And now I can't help wondering if maybe he's poisoned me— and if so, was it deliberate?

My temperature's way up...I'm sweaty and dizzy as all get out...puking all over the place but bringing nothing up. What the hell? Is this the end of it?

Don't know what day it is but it feels like morning.

They've carried me out into the clearing, and I think it's Friday who's cradling my head. He doesn't seem to mind me talking to my personal log. He's seen me do it often enough before; probably thinks it's some kind of ritual, which in a way it is or has become. Well, and we all have our rituals—right, Jim lad?

I'm no longer sweating; in fact I feel sort of dry, almost brittle. But my mind is very clear now and I think I've figured it out. Something of it, anyway. It's that thing called evolution. If I was an exobiologist like Emma Schneider I might have worked it out earlier; but no, I'm just a grease monkey.

Evolution, yes. We human beings became the Earth's dominant species by evolving. We walked upon the dirt—the earth under our feet, terra firma—but wanted a whole lot more. What about the winds above the earth, and the vast waters that flowed over it? So we made machines, vessels to sail on the seas and in the skies; finally we even built space-ships, to journey beyond the skies. So you might say that in a way we achieved our dominance mechanically: that old opposing thumb-theory-thing.

Well, the pinks are also becoming dominant, on their world as we did on Earth. Except so far, with them, it's all biological. For the time being they don't have much need for machines; they're conquering the skies, seas, and forests without mechanical devices, by utilizing and changing the DNA of the various species that live in those environments and then by inhabiting them themselves.

On Earth we took out the predators, who were our competitors, by killing them off. Well, the pinks are doing it, too—except they are doing it by *becoming* them! It explains why the vultures stay way high in the sky and why the black hogs stick mainly to the deeper woods—because having evolved alongside the pinks they're learning to keep their distance. As I should have kept mine...

I must have passed out but now I'm back. Probably for the last time, Jim lad.

Friday is still cradling my head, but his sweating has become something else. The pinks are unisexual, I'm pretty sure of that now. I can't any longer feel my body, my limbs...can only just speak or whisper, and I'm able to turn my head a few inches but that's all. My eyes are still working, however, and from time to time as Friday relaxes his efforts (fuck it, I've gone and made him a "he" again!) I can see it's his time. What time? Well see, he's not sweating any more, he's ovulating!

I see these silvery droplets with their tadpole cores issuing drip by drip from beneath the steeply arched nails on his central digits, his ovipositors. And now he sticks his fingers deeply into my neck. I can barely feel it, for which I'm truly, truly glad, Jim lad.

Who knows, maybe me and my old *Albert E.* shipmates—or I should say our pink descendants somewhere down the line—maybe they'll get back out into space again. Because it surely has to follow that whatever issues from us will be a lot more man-like than these man-likes.

And that, I think, is all for now, probably forever. Uh-oh! Maybe we should make that definitely forever, because here come the musicians...

THE DISAPPROVAL
OF JEREMY CLEAVE

My husband's eye," she said quite suddenly, peering over my shoulder in something of morbid fascination. "Watching us!" She was very calm about it, which ought to say quite a lot about her character. A very cool lady, Angela Cleave. But in view of the circumstances, a rather odd statement; for the fact was that I was making love to her at the time, and somewhat more alarming, her husband had been dead for six and a half weeks!

"*What!?*" I gasped, flopping over onto my back, my eyes following the direction of her pointing finger. She seemed to be aiming it at the dresser. But there was nothing to be seen, not anywhere in that huge, entirely extravagant bedroom. Or perhaps I anticipated too much, for while it's true that she had specified an 'eye', for some reason *I* was looking for a complete person. This is perhaps readily understandable—the shock, and what all. But no such one was there. Thank God!

Then there came a rolling sound, like a marble down a gentle slope, and again I looked where she was pointing. Atop the dresser, a shape wobbled into view from the back to the front, being brought up short by the fancy gilt beading around the dresser's top. And she was right, it was an eye—a glass eye—its deep green pupil staring at us somehow morosely.

"Arthur," she said, in the same breathless, colourless voice, "this really makes me feel very peculiar." And truth to tell it made me feel that way, too. Certainly it ruined my night.

But I got up, went to the dresser and brought the eye down. It was damp, or rather sticky, and several pieces of fluff had attached themselves to it. Also, I fancied it smelled rather, but in a bedroom perfumed as Angela Cleave's that was hard to say. And not something one *would* say, anyway.

"My dear, it's an eye," I said, "only a glass eye!" And I took it to the vanity basin and rinsed it thoroughly in cold water. "Jeremy's, of course. The… vibrations must have started it rolling."

She sat up in bed, covering herself modestly with the silk sheet (as if we weren't sufficiently acquainted) and brushed back a lock of damp, golden hair from her beautiful brow. And: "Arthur," she said. "Jeremy's eye was buried with him. He desired to be put to rest looking as perfectly natural as possible—*not* with a patch over that hideous hole in his face!"

"Then it's a spare," I reasoned, going back to the bed and handing it to her. She took it—an entirely unconscious act—and immediately snatched back her hand, so that the thing fell to the floor and rolled under the bed. And:

"*Ugh!*" she said. "But I didn't *want* it, Arthur! And anyway, I never knew he had a spare."

"Well, he obviously did," I sighed, trying to get back into bed with her. But she held the covers close and wouldn't have me.

"This has quite put me off," she said. "I'm afraid I shall have a headache." And suddenly, for all that she was a cool one, it dawned on me how badly this silly episode had jolted her. I sat on the bed and patted her hand, and said: "Why don't you tell me about it, my dear?"

"It?" she looked at me curiously, frowning.

"Well, it has to be something more than just a silly old glass eye, now doesn't it? I mean, I've never seen you so shaken." And so she told me.

"It's just something he said to me," she explained, "one night when I was late home after the opera. In fact, I believe I'd spent a little time with you that night? Anyway, in that perfectly *vulgar* way of his, he said: 'Angela, you must be more discreet. Discretion, my girl! I mean, I know we don't have it off as often as you'd possibly like—but you can't accuse me of holding too tight a rein, now can you? I mean—har! har!—I don't keep too close an eye on you—eh? Eh? Not *both* of 'em anyway, har! har!'

"So I asked him what on earth he meant? And he answered, 'Well, those damned *boyfriends*, my dear! Only right you should have an escort, me being incapacitated and all, but I've a position to maintain and scandal's something I won't hear of. So you just watch your step!'"

"Is that all?" I said, when it appeared she'd finished. "But I've always understood that Jeremy was perfectly reasonable about...well, your *affairs* in general." I shrugged. "It strikes me he was simply trying to protect his good name—and yours!"

"Sometimes, Arthur," she pouted then, "you sound just like him! I'd hate to think you were going to turn out just like *him*!"

"Not at all!" I answered at once. "Why, I'm not at all like him! I do... everything he didn't do, don't I? And I'm, well, entire? I just can't understand why a fairly civil warning should upset you so—especially now that he's dead. And I certainly can't see the connection between that and...and this," and I kicked the eye back under the bed, for at that moment it had chosen to trundle out again.

"A civil warning?" she looked at me, slowly nodded her agreement. "Well, I suppose it was, really." But then, with a degree more animation: "But he wasn't very civil the next time!"

"He caught you out again?"

"No," she lifted her chin and tossed back her hair, peevishly, I thought, "in fact it was you who caught me out!"

"Me?" I was astonished.

"Yes," she was pouting again, "because it was that night after the ball, when you drove me home and we stopped off at your place for a drink and...and slept late."

"Ah!" I said. "I suspected there might be trouble that time. But you never *told* me!"

"Because I didn't want to put you off; us being so good together, and you being his closest friend and all. Anyway, when I got in he was waiting up for me, stamping round the place on that pot leg of his, blinking his one good eye furiously at me. I mean he really was raging! 'Half past three in the morning?' he snorted. 'What? *What*? By God, but if the neighbours saw you coming in, I'll...I'll—'"

"Yes," I prompted her. "'I'll—?'"

"And then he threatened me," she said.

"Angela, darling, I'd already guessed that!" I told her. "But *how* did he threaten you—and what has it to do with this damned eye?"

"Arthur, you know how I dislike language," her tone was disapproving. But on the other hand she could see that I was getting a bit ruffled and impatient. "Well, he reminded me how much older he was than I, and how he probably only had a few years left, and that when he was gone everything would be mine. *But*, he also pointed out how it wouldn't be very difficult to change his will—which he would if there should be any sort of scandal. Well of course there wasn't a scandal and he didn't change his will. He didn't get the chance, for it was…all so very sudden!" And likewise, she was suddenly sniffling into the hankie she keeps under the pillow. "Poor Jeremy," she sobbed, "over the cliff like that." And just as quickly she dried up and put the hankie away again. It helps to have a little cry now and then.

"But there you go!" I said, triumphantly. "You've said it yourself: he *didn't* change the will! So…not much of a threat in that!"

"But that's not all," she said, looking at me straight in the eye now. "I mean, you know how Jeremy had spent all of that time with those *awful* people up those *awful* rivers? Well, and he told me he'd learned something of their jojo."

"Their juju," I felt obliged to correct her.

"Oh, jojo, juju!" She tossed her hair. "He said that they set spells when they're about to die, and that if their last wishes aren't carried out to the letter, then that they send, well, *parts* of themselves back to punish the ones they held to trust!"

"Parts of them—?" I began to repeat her, then tilted my head on one side and frowned at her very seriously. "Angela, I—"

But off she went, sobbing again, face down in the pillows. And this time doing it properly. Well, obviously the night was ruined. Getting dressed, I told her: "But of course that silly glass eye *isn't* one of Jeremy's parts; it's artificial, so I'm sure it wouldn't count—*if* we believed in such rubbish in the first place. Which we don't. But I do understand how you must have felt, my darling, when you saw it wobbling about up there on the dresser."

She looked up and brushed away her tears. "Will I see you tomorrow night?" And she was anxious, poor thing.

"Of course you will," I told her, "tomorrow and every night! But I've a busy day in the morning, and so it's best if I go home now. As for you: you're to take a sleeping draft and get a good night's sleep. And meanwhile—" I got down on my knees and fished about under the bed for the eye, "—did Jeremy have the box that this came in?"

"In that drawer over there," she pointed. "What on earth do you want with that?"

"I'm simply putting it away," I told her, "so that it won't bother us again." But as I placed the eye in its velvet lined box I glanced at the name of the suppliers—Brackett and Sanders, Jewellers, Brighton—and committed their telephone number to memory…

❖ ❖ ❖

The next day in the City, I gave Brackett and Sanders a ring and asked a question or two, and finished by saying: "Are you absolutely sure? No mistake? Just the one? I see. Well...thank you very much. And I'm sorry to have troubled you..." But that night I didn't tell Angela about it. I mean, so what? So he'd used two different jewellers. Well, nothing strange about that; he got about a fair bit in his time, old Jeremy Cleave.

I took her flowers and chocolates, as usual, and she was looking quite her old self again. We dined by candlelight, with a background of soft music and the moon coming up over the garden, and eventually it was time for bed.

Taking the open, somewhat depleted box of chocolates with us, we climbed the stairs and commenced a ritual which was ever fresh and exciting despite its growing familiarity. The romantic preliminaries, sweet prelude to boy and girl togetherness. These were broken only once when she said:

"Arthur, darling, just before I took my draft last night I tried to open the windows a little. It had got very hot and sticky in here. But that one—" and she pointed to one of a pair of large, pivot windows, "—wouldn't open. It's jammed or something. Do be a dear and do something with it, will you?"

I tried but couldn't; the thing was immovable. And fearing that it might very well become hot and sticky again, I then tried the other window which grudgingly pivoted. "We shall have them seen to," I promised.

Then I went to her where she lay; and in the next moment, as I held her in my arms and bent my head to kiss the very tip of a brown, delicious...

Bump!

It was perfectly audible—a dull thud from within the wardrobe—and both of us had heard it. Angela looked at me, her darling eyes startled, and mine no less; we both jerked bolt upright in the bed. And:

"What...?" she said, her mouth staying open a very little, breathing lightly and quickly.

"A garment, falling from its hanger," I told her.

"Nevertheless, go and see," she said, very breathlessly. "I'll not be at ease if I think there's something trapped in there."

Trapped in there? In a wardrobe in her bedroom? What could possibly be trapped in there? She kept no cats. But I got out of bed and went to see anyway.

The thing fell out into view as soon as I opened the door. Part of a mannequin? A limb from some window-dresser's storeroom? An anatomical specimen from some poor unfortunate's murdered, dismembered torso? At first glance it might have been any of these things. And indeed, with the latter in mind, I jumped a foot—before I saw that it was none of those things. By which time Angela was out of bed, into her dressing-gown and haring for the door—which wouldn't open. For she had seen it, too, and unlike me she'd known exactly what it was.

"His leg!" she cried, battering furiously at the door and fighting with its ornate, gold-plated handle. "His bloody *awful* leg!"

And of course it was: Jeremy Cleave's pot left leg, leather straps and hinged kneejoint and all. It had been standing in there on its foot, and a shoe carton had gradually tilted against it, and finally the force of gravity had won. But at such an inopportune moment. "Darling," I said, turning to her with the thing under my arm, "but it's only Jeremy's pot leg!"

"Oh, of *course* it is!" she sobbed, finally wrenching the door open and rushing out onto the landing. "But what's it doing there? It should be buried with him in the cemetery in Denholme!" And then she rushed downstairs.

Well, I scratched my head a little, then sat down on the bed with the limb in my hands. I worked its joint to and fro for a while, and peered down into its hollow interior. Pot, of one sort or another, but tough, quite heavy, and utterly inanimate. A bit smelly, though, but not unnaturally. I mean, it probably smelled of Jeremy's thigh. And there was a smear of mud in the arch of the foot and on the heel, too…

By the time I'd given it a thorough bath in the vanity basin Angela was back, swaying in the doorway, a glass of bubbly in her trembling little hands. And she looked like she'd consumed a fair old bit of the rest of the bottle, too. But at least she'd recovered something of her former control. "His leg," she said, not entering the room while I dried the thing with a fluffy towel.

"Certainly," I said, "Jeremy's *spare* pot leg." And seeing her mouth about to form words: "Now don't say it, Angela. Of *course* he had a spare, and this is it. I mean, can you imagine if he'd somehow broken one? What then? Do you have spare reading glasses? Do I have spare car keys? Naturally Jeremy had spare…things. It's just that he was sensitive enough not to let you see them, that's all."

"Jeremy, sensitive!" she laughed, albeit hysterically. "But very well—you must be right. And anyway, I've never been in that wardrobe in a donkey's years. Now do put it away—no, not there, but in the cupboard under the stairs—and come to bed and love me."

And so I did. Champagne has that effect on her.

But afterwards—sitting up in bed in the darkness, while she lay huddled close, asleep, breathing across my chest—I thought about him, the "Old Boy", Jeremy.

Adventurer, explorer, wanderer in distant lands. That was him. Jeremy Johnson Cleave, who might have been a Sir, a Lord, a Minister, but chose to be himself. Cantankerous old (old-*fashioned*) bugger! And yet in many ways quite modern, too. Naïve about certain things—the way he'd always trusted me, for instance, to push his chair along the airy heights of the cliff tops when he didn't much feel like hobbling—but in others shrewd as a fox, and nobody's fool. Never for very long, anyway.

He'd lost his eye to an N'haqui dart somewhere up the Orinoco or some such, and his leg to a croc in the Amazon. But he'd always made it back home, and healed himself up, and then let his wanderlust take him off again. As for juju: well, a man is liable to see and hear and touch upon some funny things in the far-flung places of the world, and almost certainly he's like to go a bit native, too…

The next day (today, in fact, or yesterday, since it's now past midnight) was Friday, and I had business which took me past Denholme. Now don't ask me why, but I bought a mixed posy from the florist's in the village and stopped off at the old graveyard, and made my way to Jeremy's simple grave. Perhaps the flowers were for his memory; there again they could have been an alibi, a reason for my being there. As if I needed one. I mean I had been his friend, after all! Everyone said so. But it's also a fact that murderers do, occasionally, visit their victims.

The marble headstone gave his name and dates, and a little of the Cleave history, then said:

> Distant lands ever called him;
> he ever ventured,
> and ever returned.
> Rest in Peace.

Or pieces? I couldn't resist a wry chuckle as I placed my flowers on his hollow plot.

But…hollow?

"Subsidence, sir," said a voice directly behind me as a hand fell on my arm. Lord, how I jumped!

"What?" I turned my head to see a gaunt, ragged man leaning on his shovel: the local gravedigger.

"Subsidence," he said again, his voice full of dialect and undisguised disgust, gravelly as the path he stood on. "Oh, they likes to blame me for it—saying as 'ow I don't pack 'em down tight enough, an' all—but the fact is it's the subsidence. One in every 'alf-dozen or so sinks a little, just like Old J.J.'s 'ere. This was 'is family seat, y'know: Denholme. Last of the line, 'e were—*and* a rum un'! But I suppose you knows all that."

"Er, yes," I said. "Quite." And, looking at the concave plot: "Er, a little more soil, d'you think? Before they start blaming it on you again?"

He winked and said, "I'll see to 'er right this minute, sir, so I will! Good day to you." And I left him scratching his head and frowning at the grave, and finally trundling his barrow away, doubtless to fetch a little soil.

And all of this was the second thing I wasn't going to report to Angela, but as it happens I don't suppose it would have made much difference anyway…

So tonight at fall of dark I arrived here at their (hers, now) country home. and from the moment I let myself in I knew that things weren't right. So would anyone have known, the way her shriek came knifing down the stairs:

"Arthur! *Arthur!*" her voice was piercing, penetrating, very nearly unhinged. "Is that you? Oh, for *God's sake* say it's you!"

"But of course it's me, darling, who else would it be?" I shouted up to her. "Now what on earth's the matter?"

"The matter? The matter?" She came flying down the stairs in a towelling robe, rushed straight into my arms. "I'll tell you what's the matter…" But out of breath, she couldn't. Her hair was wet and a mess, and her face wasn't done yet, and…well, she looked rather floppy all over.

So that after a moment or so, rather brusquely, I said: "So tell me!"

"It's *him!*" she gasped then, a shudder in her voice. "Oh, it's him!" And bursting into tears she collapsed against me, so that I had to drop my chocolates and flowers in order to hold her up.

"Him?" I repeated her, rather stupidly, for by then I believe I'd begun to suspect that it might indeed be 'him' after all—or at least something of his doing.

"Him!" she cried aloud, beating on my chest. "Him, you fool—*Jeremy!*"

Well, 'let reason prevail' has always been my family motto, and I think it's to my merit that I didn't break down and start gibbering right there and then, along with Angela...Or on the other hand, perhaps I'm simply stupid. Anyway I didn't, but picked up my flowers and chocolates—yes, and Angela, too—and carried them all upstairs. I put her down on the bed but she jumped up at once, and commenced striding to and fro, to and fro, wringing her hands.

"Now what *is* it?" I said, determined to be reasonable.

"*Not* in that tone of voice!" she snarled at me, coming to a halt in front of me with her hands clenched into tight little knots and her face all twisted up. "Not in that 'oh, Angela's being a silly again' voice! I said it's him, and I *mean* it's him!"

But now I was angry, too. "You mean he's here?" I scowled at her.

"I mean he's *near*, certainly!" she answered, wide-, wild-eyed. "His bloody bits, anyway!" But then, a moment later, she was sobbing again, those deep racking sobs I just can't put up with; and so once more I carried her to the bed.

"Darling," I said, "just tell me all about it and I'll sort it out from there. And that's a promise."

"Is it, Arthur? Is it? Oh, I do hope so!"

So I gave her a kiss and tried one last time, urging: "Now come on, do tell me about it."

"I...I was in the bath," she started, "making myself nice for you, hoping that for once we could have a lovely quiet evening and night together. So there I am soaping myself down, and all of a sudden I feel that someone is watching me. And he was, he was! Sitting there on the end of the bath! Jeremy!"

"Jeremy," I said, flatly, concentrating my frown on her. "Jeremy... the man?"

"No, you fool—*the bloody eye!*" And she ripped the wrapper from the chocolates (her favourite liqueurs, as it happens) and distractedly began stuffing her mouth full of them. Which was when the thought first struck me: *maybe she's cracked up!*

But: "Very well," I said, standing up, striding over to the chest of drawers and yanking open the one with the velvet-lined box, "in that case—"

The box lay there, open and quite empty, gaping at me. And at that very moment there came a well-remembered rolling sound, and I'll be damned if the hideous thing didn't come bowling out of the bathroom and onto the pile of the carpet, coming to a halt there with its malefic gaze directed right at me!

And: *Bump!—bump!* from the wardrobe, and *BUMP!* again; a final kick so hard that it slammed the door back on its hinges. And there was Jeremy's pot leg, jerking about on the carpet like a claw freshly wrenched from a live crab! I mean not just lying there but…active! Lashing about on its knee-hinge like a wild thing!

Disbelieving, jaw hanging slack. I backed away from it—backed right into the bed and sat down there, with all the wind flown right out of me. Angela had seen everything and her eyes were threatening to pop out of her head; she dribbled chocolate and juice from one corner of her twitching mouth, but still her hand automatically picked up another liqueur. Except it wasn't a liqueur.

I waved a fluttery hand, croaked something unintelligible, tried to warn her. But my tongue was stuck to the roof of my mouth and the words wouldn't come. "*Gurk!*" was the only thing I managed to get out. And that too late for already she'd popped the thing into her mouth. Jeremy's eye— but *not* his glass eye!

Oh, and what a horror and a madness and an asylum then as she bit into it! Her throat full of chocolate, face turning blue, eyes bulging as she clawed at the bedclothes going "Ak—ak—*ak!*" And me trying to massage her throat, and the damned pot leg kicking its way across the floor towards me, and that bloody nightmare glass eye wobbling there for all the world as if its owner were laughing!

Then…Angela clawed at me one last time and tore my shirt right down the front as she toppled off the bed. Her eyes were standing out like organ stops and her face was purple, and her dragging nails opened up the shallow skin of my chest in five long red bleeding lines, but I scarcely noticed. For Jeremy's leg was still crashing about on the floor and his eye was still laughing.

I started laughing, too, as I kicked the leg into the wardrobe and locked it, and chased the eye across the floor and under Angela's dressing-table. I laughed and I laughed—laughed until I cried—and perhaps wouldn't have sobered yet, except…

What was that?

That bumping, out there on the landing!

And it—he—Jeremy, is still out there, bumping about even now. He's jammed the windows again so that I can't get out, but I've barricaded the door so that *he* can't get in; and now we're both stuck. I've a slight advantage, though, for I can see, while he's quite blind! I mean, I *know* he's blind for his glass eye is in here with me and his real eye is in Angela! And his leg will come right through the panelling of the wardrobe eventually I suppose but when it does I'll jump on it and pound the thing to pieces.

And he's out there blind as a bat hopping around on the landing, going *gurgle, gurgle, gurgle* and stinking like all Hell! Well sod you Jeremy Johnson Cleave for I'm not coming out. I'm just going to stay here always. I won't come out for you or for the maid when she comes in the morning or for the cook or the police or anybody.

I'll just stay here with my pillows and my blankets and my thumb where it's nice and safe and warm. Here under the bed.

Do you hear me, Jeremy?

Do you hear me?

I'm—not—coming—out!